"But you know I can't sleep with you."

As she spoke, Willy tried to ignore the memory of his gentle touch and the tingling of her nerves.

"I understand," Hyde consoled. Then, as he tried to get her arms into her nightgown, he urged, "Come on, Willy." But she remained unresponsive, and he felt ridiculous.

Once she mumbled, "You don't really understand," but that was all.

He had tried to be all business as he'd undressed her and tucked the heavy quilt around her chin. Yet as he stood in her doorway before snapping off the lights, he couldn't forget that his hands had brushed along her silky thighs, had touched the soft flesh of her high breasts.

Hyde switched off the lights, closed the door, and swore softly into the cool darkness.

Also available from MIRA Books and
LYNN ERICKSON

ASPEN

LYNN ERICKSON

SNOWBIRD

ISBN 1-55166-058-X

SNOWBIRD

Printed in U.S.A.

This book is dedicated to Andy Mill,
Aspen's own downhiller.

ONE

It was a Tuesday, Willy would always remember, when the letter came.

"Dear Willy," it began—and Willy Patterson could hear Andrea's strange pronunciation of her name—"Vee-lee"—as clearly as if her friend was standing right in front of her. She read on.

> We start our training here in Chili early this year so I take this chance to send you a letter. Very hard to find a time alone but I find it. Pleese, Willy, have care with this matter.

Willy shook her honey-blond head, puzzled. This did not sound like her old friend at all. Fun-loving Andrea never took the time to write letters. Usually she phoned from someplace on the ski-racing circuit: Switzerland, Yugoslavia, Canada. Willy's blue-gray eyes scanned the quaint writing on the page. After all, Andrea Pavlevitch had learned to write in Cyrillic script, English was a second language to her.

> I can take no longer this life. Next year they make me big coach and I must see the team to win or it is my head. So I must do this thing, you see. And you must help me, my good friend.

What thing? wondered Willy as her wide mouth turned up in inadvertent amusement at Andrea's writing. Oh well, she thought, it was better than hers in Russian!

> I want to defect. Please do not think bad of me but my country is no longer tolerable.

My God, flashed through Willy Patterson's mind. *Andrea wants to* defect! *My God....* Her eyes raced on.

> And there is no one to ask but you, I am very afraid of American government and it must happen when I am in U.S. at a race. Willy, my friend, you must help me, but be very careful, I repeat. If I am found, if this letter is found, I will never leeve Russia again. They will not let me.
>
> Help me Willy. You are my one chance. I will try to be in tutch.
>
> All my love, Andrea

Willy looked blindly up toward Aspen Mountain, her heart beating madly, her wintry eyes unfocused in the bright cool September sun, while the letter dangled from her fingers.

Andrea Pavlevitch wanted to defect! The enormity of it struck Willy like a blow. Andrea wanted Willy to help her defect! Things like that only happened in spy thrillers or in the newspaper. To *other* people. Not to Wilhelmina Patterson, art gallery owner, ordinary law-abiding citizen of Aspen, Colorado.

Well, Willy had to admit ruefully, not exactly ordinary. No one was completely ordinary who was born and brought up in the small quaint mountain resort; the meeting ground of ranchers, ski bums made good, world-renowned intellectuals and movie stars. And of course, if she hadn't been born in Aspen and put on skis at two years of age, she wouldn't have been on the U.S. Ski Team—a pretty darned good downhiller. And if she hadn't been on the team she never would have met Andrea Pavlevitch, her alter ego on the Russian team, and if she hadn't met Andrea she would never have received the letter. . . .

Damn! she thought with a spurt of irritation toward Andrea. *Now* what should she do?

Willy had been leaning against the sun-warmed fender of her old yellow Jeep in front of the Aspen post office reading Andrea's letter. She straightened her long lean frame and climbed behind the wheel. Her hand reached for the ignition, but then she paused, snatched up Andrea's letter and read it again, her golden brows knotted in perplexity.

"Hey, lady!" yelled a dusty-headed stonemason leaning out the window of his truck. "You planning on moving or what?"

Willy's head snapped around. "Sorry," she called back. "Be out of your way in a minute."

Skillfully she backed up the old Jeep and pulled out of the parking place, shrugging apologetically to the irate mason. But her movements were automatic, her mind being wholly occupied with the letter. Andrea Pavlevitch—Russia's great hope for a gold medal in the World Cup downhill this winter. And Andrea was good enough to do it. She'd already won the gold twice before, but had been sidelined by a bad knee injury for two years. Last year Andrea had missed the gold by a few measly points. This year she'd take it for sure.

And—everyone knew—the World Cup finals would be held in Aspen in March.

Willy's eyes strayed toward the golden autumn face of Aspen Mountain right in front of her as she stopped for the light at the corner of Mill and Main streets. In her mind's eye she traced the course she knew so well: the start-up on Ruthie's Run, hidden by a fold in the hill now, then the flat road to Aztec, the mind-boggling sixty-mile-an-hour descent on the wall of Aztec, the horrendous corner at the bottom that tore at your thigh muscles like the torture rack, then Straw Pile and Fifth Avenue to the finish.

Oh yes, Willy knew that course all right. She'd been teethed on it, so to speak, taken up there by her father when she was six, carried up to watch the races, and filled with the lore and excitement of ski racing ever since she could remember.

As she let out the Jeep's stiff clutch when the light changed, she could feel a twinge of pain in her leg where it had been broken. Not that it bothered her much anymore; it was only an occasional faint reminder of her own fallibility.

Andrea.

It was mid-September. Andrea would be racing in Aspen in less than six months, barring injuries of course—always the ski racer's nemesis.

Shouldn't Willy contact the government? There were agencies that handled these things. But then she remembered Andrea's horrific tale of her father's disappearance and her mother's squelched physics-research projects. Willy knew Andrea could never, *never* trust any government. The KGB actually *accompanied* the Russian ski team on the circuit, watched their contacts with the other skiers, censored their mail and phone calls. Willy wondered how Andrea had even managed to get this particular letter to her at all.

She pulled the Jeep into her parking space in the alley behind her gallery and gathered up the day's lot of mail to carry inside.

"Hey, Willy," called Gayle. "I sold one of your sketches! Amazing in the off-season. A nice couple from Atlanta. Now what on earth were they doing here?"

Willy shrugged her shoulders and smiled. "Supporting the Cooper Street Gallery, I guess. I'm going to go through the mail, okay?"

"Sure. Can you come out front later though, while I have lunch with Beth?"

"Just give me a call when you're ready, Gayle."

Willy went into her tiny cubicle of an office, plunked down into the old captain's chair and tossed the mail down on the rolltop desk.

Andrea.

She pulled the letter out from the pile of scattered mail and read it again. Andrea seemed anxious, a bit harried. Not scared. Just . . . well, unhappy and on edge.

The thought of the millions of possible complications in a defection suddenly overwhelmed Willy. Where would Andrea live? What would she do? Did she have to apply for citizenship? What would she live on? Would the U.S. even accept her automatically?

She leaned back in her chair, thinking. She couldn't just spirit a Russian girl away from a race, then take her by the hand to the nearest government office and say, "Here she is, a nice Russian girl. She'll be a good American." It didn't work that way. Did Andrea realize what she was asking?

But of course Willy would manage *something*. She was, she knew, inherently incapable of both ignoring a challenge and not helping a friend. It just wasn't in her to let this thing go.

Logistics. It was all in logistics. How to get Andrea away—where? When?

She'd need help, of course. The government would have to be involved. Willy made a slight grimace and began biting her nails—an old bad habit. The government would surely make a mess of everything. They always did. Vietnam, the hostages in Iran, Central America. The Bay of Pigs, for Lord sakes! But they could be useful, Willy supposed, *after* she had figured out how to get Andrea away. *Then* the government could take over. Debriefing, she supposed, change of name? Change of appearance? But no, that ballet dancer Nureyev, and the tennis player, Martina Navratilova; they hadn't had to hide. And Andrea was as well-known as they were, if not more so. She could coach skiing at a college somewhere, even at the national level.

Willy sighed in exasperation. There she went again, planning ahead too fast, jumping to conclusions. First things first, her mother always said.

She'd need help. On the mountain. It had to happen on the mountain. During a practice run? During the race itself? A downhill racer was free, truly free, during a race, freed from all restraints of time and space. Outside the existence of mortal men in a way. Flying through space like a powerful bird. Andrea would be going thirty miles an hour on the slow parts, sixty or more on the steeper ones. She could disappear so fast no one would ever know....

But where to? And how to elude the KGB long enough to escape without leaving a trail?

Willy looked out of her tiny rectangular office window, trying to concentrate. She glanced at the mail scattered on her desk, and then looked at her watch. Twelve-fifteen. Lunchtime. Damn.

Well, Gayle could catch up on the mail later. Gayle was wonderfully dependable, a pretty, trim mother of two teenage sons. She loved working for Willy, did every chore willingly and watched the shop like a mother hen on a nest of eggs. She even had a good critical eye for line and color. Oh, Gayle was a gem all right, and thank God she was or Willy would never find time to paint—or ski those glorious powder mornings in the winter....

Gayle poked her head in the office. "I'm going now."

"All right. Have a good one."

"I will."

Willy went into the gallery, but she never saw the lovely watercolor of the Maroon Bells or the sketch of Mount Sopris or the black-and-white of Independence Pass. She roamed the shop, straightening a picture automatically, thinking, her mind whirling with her problem.

She stopped in front of the large plate-glass window and stared up at the face of the mountain that rose from the southern edge of Aspen, dominating the town and giving it boundary and definition. It seemed to loom over Aspen like a huge petrified tidal wave, stopped forever at its crowning. Andrea's defection would take place on Aspen Mountain. She knew that. But how and when and exactly where were yet to be decided.

Willy—Wilhelmina—Patterson lived in a tiny old cedar-sized Victorian house on West Hopkins Street. She had bought it with her father's help three years earlier and had paid him back every last cent within eighteen months. The house was her pride and joy. The bay windows were crowded with geraniums, a huge old blue spruce filled the front yard and a white picket fence surrounded the corner lot. Willy always paused at the gate and looked at the pretty picture it made. Besides being a good investment and a lovely place to live, Willy's house was a symbol of her own success as an artist and businesswoman.

Inside, the old house was what Willy's mother, Rachel, called "thrift-shop funky." It was cozy, with a potbelly stove, hanging plants, worn couch and a round oak table. There was a small studio off the kitchen and two bedrooms and a bathroom up the narrow stairs.

That Tuesday Willy did not notice her house's charm. She went straight to the phone and dialed a familiar number. Naturally, it being the middle of the afternoon, he wasn't home. There was only one thing to do then, Willy knew. Painting was out of the question. She was consumed with Andrea's letter, burning with nervous excitement and ready to rush into it one hundred percent, with no holding back. As she did everything.

"You're going to get yourself into some real trouble someday," warned her down-to-earth mother.

"You have to learn a little *control*, Willy," admonished Edward, her tall hearty father. "You can't go through life with the gas pedal to the floor all the time."

"If I was like that, dad, I wouldn't be any good as a downhiller. I only know one way—all stops out."

"She's still young," sighed Rachel.

"And she *is* a damn good downhiller," relented Edward.

That conversation had taken place seven years ago, when Willy was twenty and going to the University of Colorado in Boulder. In fact, she remembered, it was just before she had broken her leg in that race in Adelboden. The accident had taught her many things, such as patience and tolerance for pain and dogged determination, but mostly it had taught her about limits. Not fear, just limits.

She ran out to her Jeep again, pulling her baseball cap down over her eyes to keep her straight, honey-colored hair from flying in the open-topped vehicle, and pulled away from the curb.

She knew Reeves Baxter was working on a house up on fashionable Red Mountain. She also knew she should wait until he was off work so his fellow workers wouldn't snicker, but she couldn't. She'd learned about her own limits, all right, but impatience still overcame her. Everything had to be done *now.*

She steered easily through the quaint downtown section—a mere five blocks broken by the relatively new malls. But for Aspen's small area, it had a tremendous wealth of grace, good taste and character. It had actually been written up several times as one of the most cosmopolitan spots in the world.

Hard to believe that, Willy thought as she was forced to stay behind a young man in a green pickup who was chatting away with two dainty little bicyclists in the middle of Mill Street. She tugged on the brim of her hat and ground her teeth, waiting, but no one in Aspen would ever sit on a horn. It simply wasn't done.

Finally the guy noticed Willy behind him in her Jeep and he smiled, shrugged, and then talked to the girls for at least another minute before putting his pickup in gear and moving away.

Typical Aspen, Willy mused irritably.

But it hadn't always been that way. When she'd been a kid, before her parents had sold the ranch west of town and bought the condo, Aspen had been *really* tiny. Off-season in September had meant two cars on Main Street; today it meant two hundred.

Lord, it had grown. The skiers had come in droves, and then the jet-setters and finally the big-name celebrities. They walked around town every day. Ordinary folks. They drove their kids to school, ran errands, skied the mountains on powder days. Just plain regular people. And God forbid if anyone asked one of them for an autograph!

This was Aspen. It wasn't done....

The Jeep lumbered across the bridge over the Roaring Fork River, past the tidy Pitkin Green homes and began to climb Red Mountain, which sat facing Aspen Mountain across the sweeping valley floor.

Willy downshifted, moved over into a pothole to let a Mercedes pass, and then took up the whole steep path again.

There was a lot of "money" on Red Mountain. She shuddered to think of the cost of a building lot alone. A house on a lot? A million easy....

And how many of her paintings hung in these homes? Enough. It grated on her nerves to think that some purchased her work not because of her talent as an artist but because of the link with skiing and the name Willy Patterson. Silver medal—'74 Olympics.

She found the big, half-finished house near the top of Red Mountain. Yes, there was Reeves's old Datsun pickup. She stood up in her Jeep in the driveway, cupped her hands and called out his name.

"What the hell?" A dark handsome head poked out of an unfinished doorway.

"It's me!" She tried to ignore the leers from the other workers. "Can you come talk for a sec?"

"Willy, for God's sake. Sure, okay." Reeves, his carpenter belt around his waist, climbed down a ladder, hitching up his faded jeans. He wore a red-and-black wool shirt rolled up at the sleeves. Reeves was definitely Mr. Outdoors.

She jumped down from the Jeep and hurried to meet him. "Sorry to bother you, but something's come up."

Reeves's dark brown eyes, nearly on level with Willy's, met hers with good humor. "Something's always coming up with you, babe."

"Come here." She motioned to him to walk farther toward the end of the driveway. "I want to tell you something very important." She stopped and faced him, her expression serious, her blue-gray eyes searching his face. "I trust you, you know."

"Spill it, babe. I've got to get back to work."

"You remember I told you about Andrea Pavlevitch? My friend on the Russian ski team?"

"Yeah, I guess so."

"I just got a letter from her today." Willy paused for dramatic effect and folded her arms beneath her breasts. "She wants me to help her defect."

Reeves stared at her with a crooked grin pulling at his mouth. "Sure, and I'm the king of England."

"Reeves!" She sputtered impatiently.

He paused, studying the graceful face. "My God, you're serious."

"Yes."

"Defect? You can't write a friend a letter about *defecting*. 'Dear Willy,'" he said facetiously. "'How are you? I'm fine. Please help me defect.' Come on, babe."

"It's true. Will you help me?"

"Me?"

"Reeves, I need your help. It'll happen during the World Cup...."

"What on earth are you getting at?"

"It's perfect, don't you see? With you head of the ski patrol, it's a natural. Please, Reeves...."

"Look Willy, let me think a little. I've got to get back to work. I'll call you later, okay?"

"You won't back out?"

"Since when was I in?" He laughed wryly.

"Since I told you about it."

"Boy, you sure are one crazy chick," said Reeves, shaking his dark handsome head.

"Call me later. Promise?"

"Okay, I promise."

Willy stood in the driveway and watched Reeves walk back toward the half-finished house. He wasn't tall, but he had flashing dark eyes and was well-muscled, compact and as hard as a rock. A super athlete, a charmer, a fun person. She liked Reeves a lot. They'd been seeing each other for a year. He attracted her very much in a way, yet they weren't serious. She didn't love Reeves Baxter—not yet, but she'd bet that in time she just might.

When Reeves finally called her about five-thirty, she was bursting with impatience and ideas and plans. "Come over here right away," she breathed. "I'll fix you dinner."

"Mind if I shower?" came Reeves's lazy drawl over the phone.

"Yes. No. Just hurry."

"Okay. I'm down at the Cooper Street Pier. Let me finish my beer and run home for a shower. Forty-five minutes, babe."

Somehow Willy had to fill the forty-five minutes. She quickly took a shower herself and blow-dried her heavy straight honey-blond hair. A little mascara, a touch of gray-brown shadow, clean jeans and a turtleneck sweater in pale shell pink. That was dressy for Aspen—*clean* jeans. She loved the informal life-style, the carefully casual dress of Aspen, the refusal to ape big-city ways even though the mood of the resort town was terribly sophisticated.

She found some tomato sauce and some frozen ground beef and started the fixings for spaghetti. Reeves wasn't fussy, just hungry. Cucumber salad. A day-old loaf of French bread. It'd be all right warmed up with garlic butter.

Reeves didn't knock. His dark hair was still damp, slicked down from his shower, and his broad shoulders strained at the seams of his clean wool plaid shirt.

Willy, wordlessly handing him a can of Coors and Andrea's letter, pointed to the one big chair. Reeves flashed her a white smile, took the beer and the letter and sat down negligently.

She stalked the room impatiently while he read the letter, waiting until his dark eyes reached hers. "Look, we can do it," began Willy. "I've been thinking some more."

"So have I. It's totally insane, babe." Calmly, Reeves sipped at his Coors.

"But Andrea—"

"Tell your father. He'll know what to do."

"My father is a representative, a member of the House, not a foreign-relations expert! Besides, he'd never agree. You know dad. He's much too much of a politician. He wouldn't touch this with a ten-foot pole. I don't intend for him even to find out about it."

"Until it's all over," put in Reeves dryly.

"Right." Then Willy had to laugh. "You know me too well."

"Not nearly well enough," leered Reeves over his beer can.

Spontaneously Willy flushed. She just couldn't take those kind of remarks in stride as everyone else did. They just hit a touch too close to home for comfort. It was her little failing.

She sat on the faded sofa, her long, jean-clad legs stretched out. "Now, look. Andrea will race here in March. We can get her away. On the mountain somewhere. Probably during the race. It's so crazy up there. You know...."

"Yeah, I know. But Willy, it's not so simple. *If,* I say *if* we got her away, then what? Where do we take her? What do we do with her?"

Willy frowned. "I haven't figured that far yet. It'll come. First things first. The race."

"Fake an accident and put her in an ambulance?"

"They'd find her in the hospital in a jiffy," scoffed Willy.

"Don't take her to the hospital. . . ."

"Remember, the KGB will be here on their toes. Don't you think they'd have their star under close guard? They'd follow the ambulance."

Reeves stared at the top of his beer can. "Could she get lost, ski off the course into the trees?"

"Better, but they'd be onto her in a minute."

"Yeah. The problem is to get their attention off Andrea long enough to get her away somewhere safe." Reeves stood up, scrubbed a hand through his crisp dark hair and paced the small space in front of the potbelly stove. Then he stopped and faced Willy. "You're crazy. This is crazy. It'll never work. Call the—"

"Call who?"

"The CIA. The White House. The National Security Adviser. Somebody."

"Andrea wouldn't go along with that. Never." Willy shook her head. "I can't let her down."

"Damn it, babe, this is way over our heads."

"No it isn't. We can do it and you know it. There's nobody around who knows that mountain better than we do. We can hide her up there somewhere."

"Willy, you're going to have to call in somebody for afterward. Andrea can't go wandering around the good ol' U.S. of A. by herself. She's got to be official somehow."

"I know. But we'll get her away first. Then they can take her. Can you imagine a bunch of spies up there during World Cup week trying to get Andrea? They'd be like foxes in a chicken house. The whole world's going to be here that week."

"It would be kind of comical. Wonder if any of those spy types ski?" he asked with a grin.

"Reeves, think about it. We'll figure this out together. I know it. And I'll find out who to contact in Washington."

"How are you going to do that, babe?"

"I'll ask my mother, the most famous hostess on Capitol Hill. Who else?"

Reeves laughed. "You're a card. Ask your mother who handles defections of Russians but don't tell your father."

"It's logical, you know. Come on, let's eat. I'm starved."

They discussed the problem over spaghetti and garlic bread. The same dead end popped up every time: how to keep attention off Andrea for a sufficient time. Everyone in the world would be watching her, either on television or on the mountain itself. How do you draw attention from the star of the show?

"In the movies they always create a diversion," mused Willy.

"Sure. You stand in the middle of the racecourse and strip. Then Andrea can ski off into the trees and disappear and no one will notice. It's simple."

"Reeves, be serious."

"Never!"

After dinner he helped her clean up. He made small talk: the job he was working on, the budget problems he was going to have for the ski patrol the coming season, the threat of an early snow. And then, as it always did, a vague tension arose between them. Willy knew he wanted to stay and sleep with her; he always did. And she was unable to respond to that side of their attraction wholeheartedly. It hurt him; it hurt her; it ripped holes in the fabric of their relationship.

"Do you want me to stay?" he finally asked softly.

Willy took a deep breath. He was so sweet, so careful of her at times like this, even though he didn't understand. She turned her face up to his, her heart thudding painfully in her chest. "Do you mind if you don't?" she whispered. "I'm so damned keyed up over this thing with Andrea. It'd be no good at all. Do you mind awfully?" Her huge blue-gray eyes begged him.

"Look, Willy..." began Reeves. Then, "No, that's okay. I know you're into this thing."

"I'm better alone. I'll probably stay up late and paint. Sometimes it helps me think." Excuses, excuses. More original than "I've got a headache," but basically the same rejection. God, she felt rotten inside. But she couldn't. It was one of those times when she couldn't force herself to. She was unnatural, she knew, unlike other more normal women. But sometimes, too often, she couldn't bear Reeves touching her. And it would be far too humiliating to explain to him why.

"Okay, babe. Thanks for dinner. Take it easy. See you soon." Reeves gave her a kiss on the cheek, a squeeze of the hand. In her heart she was closer to him at that moment than ever, closer even than when they were physically together. She almost loved him.

"Bye." The door closed behind him with a final snick, and then Willy wanted to cry out to him to come back, to be with her. But she couldn't.

She didn't paint; she was much too distracted. She turned on the TV but there was an inane situation comedy on and she couldn't bear it. She went to her studio finally but nothing made any sense.

Andrea.

She curled up in bed with the new issue of *Powder* magazine, but that made no sense, either. Get the attention away from Andrea. That was virtually impossible. Then an idea flashed through her mind and was gone. What had it been? "Damn," whispered Willy to her bedroom walls. Attention on Andrea. Tricks with mirrors...it wasn't really Andrea.... *What if it wasn't Andrea skiing the race?*

Of course, it had to be she at the start. Of course. But a switch later? How? Everyone's eyes were riveted on that narrow icy rutted strip that snaked down the mountain like a roller coaster. Switch. How? Simple. Where else? In the trees.

Willy found that she was biting her nails again and snatched them out of her mouth. Could Andrea ski into the trees as if out of control? Or fall, slide into the trees? Where were there trees on the racecourse? Top of Aztec, off Ruthie's. Anywhere lower and Andrea would just end up back in town. The switch would have to be up high enough for her to get off the course and disappear over the back slope of Aspen Mountain.

Lord, it might work.

A smile touched Willy's wide mouth. She pulled her quilt up to her chin. It just might work.

Sure. But what then? Well, then the government could step in. Surely Andrea would understand that Willy couldn't handle all the red tape by herself.

That meant, she realized suddenly, a trip to visit her parents in Virginia. Her mother—who knew everything—would know whom to contact in the government.

It was off-season. She'd have to go soon. Maybe she'd even go in the next few days—start arranging things. There wasn't much going on in the early autumn anyway. Gayle could handle the shop; Reeves could water the plants and feed the cat....

Won't mother be surprised, Willy thought, *when I tell her that I'm coming?* Rachel Patterson would have a million questions.

"Oh," Willy would say, "I just flew to Washington to visit and help my friend defect...."

TWO

It was warm that morning on the veranda of the Pattersons' Alexandria, Virginia home—unusually warm, even for September.

Dressed in her navy blue-and-white jogging shorts, Willy sipped her orange juice, quietly observing her mother, Rachel, over the glass rim. It seemed a shame they couldn't just while away the soft southern morning chatting, reminiscing, putting their honey-blond heads together and gossiping like college girls. Lord, they hadn't had the leisure to do that for so long....

Somewhere a bee droned, insects buzzed and clicked in the perfectly cropped lawn, a bird hopped along cocking its head to listen. It was an idyllic morning in Virginia. So different from the clear chill September mornings in western Colorado where her breath would show white and a light frost often tipped the silvery aspens. Summer was still alive back East, alive and green and moist. After selling their ranch in Aspen and moving, Willy's parents had taken to the warm humid East quite easily; but Willy always found it a bit too close, too stifling.

Still, it *was* a lovely morning. It seemed a pity she was about to spoil it all.

"This is the first time in ages I can remember a September visit from you," Rachel was saying as she dabbed at her lips with a yellow patterned napkin. "And right out of the blue."

Willy put down her juice glass and pushed aside the half-eaten toast. "I know it's sudden and all, mother, but something's come up."

Rachel's pale brow arched. "You do sound a little uptight, Willy. Are you all right, dear?"

Willy smiled affectionately, pushing her sunglasses to the top of her head. "I'm fine. Fine, mother. It's just that I've . . . well, this is going to sound awfully ridiculous. . . ."

"Go on, dear."

"You've got to promise you won't tell dad." Willy folded her arms on the table, leaning closer.

"Now, Willy. . . ."

"Please. It's terribly important."

Curiosity finally bested Rachel. "All right, Willy. You have my word. Now, for heaven's sake, what *is* on your mind?"

Willy let out a breath she seemed to have been holding. "I got a letter from Andrea . . . Pavlevitch. You remember? The Russian ski racer."

"Oh yes! Terribly Slavic-looking, big girl. Her father was a dissident or something and her mother. . . . Let me see now, her mother was a physicist."

"Her mother died last year."

"Oh. I am sorry." Rachel paused, regarding her daughter quizzically. "But did you have to come two thousand miles to tell me that? I mean, Willy, the visit is wonderful, but—"

Willy laughed, beginning to feel all keyed up again. "No, mother, that's not quite why I've come." She looked at Rachel Patterson levelly, holding her gaze. "Andrea wants me to help her defect."

"She *what?*" gasped Rachel.

"You heard me," said Willy flatly. "She wants to defect."

"Good God. . . ." Suddenly Rachel's blue eyes widened. "You aren't considering. . . ."

Willy smiled defiantly. "But I am."

"Hey you two!" came Edward Patterson's gruff voice from the other end of the terrace. "I'm off to work now." He held his briefcase up for a moment as if to explain. "Good to have you here, Willy!" he called.

"I'm glad to be here, dad!"

"Now behave yourselves, girls. Bye!"

"Bye. . . ." Willy looked back at her mother. "You look as if you've seen a ghost," she said, giving Rachel's hand a squeeze. "It's not really all that shocking, mother."

"Oh no, it's commonplace. My daughter is going to help a Russian girl defect."

Willy could not stifle a grin. "It does sound insane."

"It's worse than insane, Willy. Please," she implored, "don't even consider it. You've always been too headstrong, a little too wild for your own good."

"This isn't wild," Willy hastened to explain. "It's to help a friend, mother, a person who's terrified to go to the proper authorities."

"But why, for heaven's sake?" Rachel Patterson pushed herself up from the wrought-iron table, shoved her smooth brown hands into her skirt pockets and began pacing the flagstones.

Willy watched her quietly, leaned back in her chair and crossed her long slim legs. "Try to understand," she began again. "Andrea's father went to the proper authorities time after time, trying to get his works published. Then finally he disappeared. To this day, mother," Willy said softly, "Andrea doesn't know if he's dead or alive. It's been fifteen years. You can see why she doesn't trust governments."

"So she's come to you," put in Rachel thoughtfully, coming to stand behind her daughter, placing her hands on Willy's shoulders.

"Yes. And I'm going to do everything in my power to help her." Willy smiled wistfully and squeezed her mother's hand. "If only I could do it all myself."

"Yes," mused Rachel. "If you had the power or the know-how. You realize that eventually Andrea is going to have to go through channels. The CIA, or is it the State Department?" She laughed ruefully. "You see? I'm not even sure under whose jurisdiction it would fall. It's all so complicated. Your father," she said, "might know."

"Oh no!" Willy sat up straight in her seat. "You know how dad is. And if he thinks the tiniest thing will upset his reelection hopes . . . well. . . ."

"Yes," sighed Rachel, "you're right." Then, "And what if some wild scheme you concoct *does* involve his reputation, somehow?"

"It won't." Willy smiled brightly. "How could it?"

Willy decided to try the CIA, figuring that if they couldn't help her friend then she could always go to the State Department next.

"You know," she called to her mother from the hallway, "you can look up the CIA right in the phone book! Isn't that amazing?"

"Amazing," agreed Rachel from the living-room door.

"Well—" Willy rose from the stool "—I'm going for a jog anyway. I think I'll just phone from a booth."

"You can call from here," said Rachel. "I mean, really Willy, this isn't a plot for a spy novel."

"You never know," put in Willy impishly. "Maybe dad's phone is tapped."

Rachel sighed, exasperated. "That's against the law, my dear. But if it makes you happy to phone from a booth, then by all means do so."

Willy dropped some change into the breast pocket of her white cotton shirt, put a twisted sweatband around her head and whistled for Linda.

"Come on, girl, let's go!" She patted her knee as Edward Patterson's prize golden retriever came loping across the front circular drive. "Wanna go for a run?" Linda's ears perked up, her burnished head cocked to one side, and her tail flailed madly in the air.

Normally Willy would have jogged west through the rolling green hills, but it made more sense to head toward a shopping district where she'd find a phone booth. Linda ran alongside dutifully, heeling like a champ. Edward used her to goose hunt on Chesapeake Bay in the late autumn, and five-year-old Linda loved to run.

Sweat began to bead Willy's face and neck. Then her arms and legs grew moist as she paced herself into mile two. She began, as she ran along the rural roadside, to form the words in her mind that she would say on the telephone.

No doubt whomever she first spoke with would have fits of laughter.

"My name is Wilhelmina Patterson," she began, "and my dear friend Andrea Pavlevitch wants to defect."

Ha ha.

Perhaps she shouldn't jog too far, Willy thought abruptly, or the oxygen would leave her brain completely and she'd really make a jackass of herself on the phone.

She was rounding a narrow curve when a delivery van was forced to stop as the driver tried to make the turn too hastily.

"Hey! Watch it!" He poked his head out the window. "You wanna get killed?"

Willy's head snapped up. When she ran she was oblivious to all else. She was forced to stop for a moment, running in place, as the laundry van blocked her path.

"Sorry," she breathed deeply.

The young man swept her body with a bold eye. It didn't take much to see that Willy had a great shape.

"You wanna ride, lady?" he asked, grinning widely.

She tried to ignore him but it was difficult with his van blocking her way. "No," she said, adding, "thank you anyway." It struck her that they were very much alone on that back road.

"Wouldn't be no trouble." He smiled again.

He's harmless, she told herself, *just a little too fresh.* Yet she admitted to herself that being on a less-than-populated road alone with a strange man made her nervous. She was fine in social situations; fine in a crowd. It was only at these awkward lonesome times that the old fears bubbled up from the well of the past to choke her. It always surprised her whenever it happened, too, for after all these years she was so sure she'd overcome most of her anxieties.

She made her way around the front of his vehicle and began to run again down the side of the road as she heard him put the van in gear. She ventured a look behind her; he was driving off in the opposite direction.

In spite of the fact that she was jogging, Willy breathed a little more easily.

She ran for another ten minutes until finally she could see a phone booth ahead near a bank and a service station. There was someone in the booth and the motor of his car was still running.

This *is* ridiculous, Willy thought as she slowed her pace. Calling the CIA from a phone booth, telling them a wild story, expecting them to believe her. My God, she was twenty-seven years old now, an upstanding citizen.

Still the whole crazy idea of Andrea's defection and Willy's role in it did appeal to that often suppressed madcap side of her. Of course she knew that to try to pull the whole thing off without some assistance would be utter madness, but she really only needed official help in getting Andrea settled once she'd defected. The rest she could set up herself. With Reeves's help, of course.

A man was using the phone. When Willy approached he closed the glass door and turned his back. She could hear snatches of his conversation: "I won't come home then . . . I told you, it was business. . . ." Finally he hung up, shot Willy a distasteful glance and got into his car.

I'm not your wife, she wanted to say, but wisely kept silent. *Men*, she shook her head. Thank goodness Reeves didn't behave like a child. At least he had the maturity to treat her like an adult, to give her the breathing space she needed. That was one of the reasons she suspected they might never marry—they both enjoyed their freedom too much.

Linda stood panting by the phone booth, her huge brown eyes reaching up to Willy's face, imploring her to go on running.

"In a minute." Willy fluffed Linda's soft ears. "Unless, of course," she said playfully, "the CIA rushes up and grabs us." Then she laughed with excitement. "Just don't tell them anything, old girl. Hear me?"

She reached into her pocket, pulled out the coins and gave Linda another look. "Well," Willy breathed, "here goes nothing. . . ."

Glancing up and down the street, she suddenly felt terribly melodramatic. How ridiculous! And what was she doing phoning them anyway? She hated "big government" and things like covert operations and worldwide spy brotherhoods. Good Lord. . . .

She dialed the number listed in the directory and heard the clicks of the exchange. This was really the most bizarre thing she'd ever—

"CIA." That was all. Not hello, nothing. Just a woman's voice and the initials.

Willy cleared her throat, and felt sweat bead her upper lip in the stuffy, close telephone booth. "Ah, yes," she began, "I need to speak with an agent." Silence. A burst of anxiety seized her. "Is that possible?"

"Of course."

My God . . . just like that!

"And what is this concerning?"

"A friend—" Willy took a deep breath "—a Russian friend who needs help." Good God.

"Please hold."

Willy could feel her knees wobbling slightly as she waited. This was too ridiculous. The CIA indeed!

"Extension 6464. Ted here," came a clear expressionless voice. "May I have your name please?"

Ted—no last name? Willy swallowed with difficulty.

"Wilhelmina Patterson."

"Your address, Mrs.—"

"Miss," she corrected quickly. "I'm in Virginia now but I live in Aspen, Colorado . . . on Hopkins Street." She gave a short laugh. "Is this necessary?"

"If you're not a crank caller it is." Flatly.

"All right."

"Now please give me your father's full name and your mother's maiden name."

Willy hesitated. "There may be a problem here, Mr., ah, Ted."

"Then I must end our conversation, Miss Patterson."

Oh hell, thought Willy frantically. Still, there was no reason they would involve her father in any way. Once they had his name, that would be all. This was Willy's problem, not Edward's. They already had her name and where she lived—they'd find out the rest anyway.

"Miss Patterson?"

"I'm here." Slowly, she told Ted a few brief details of her background. Once he stopped her when she mentioned the name Andrea.

"Let's keep this conversation casual," he said easily, as if they might have been discussing the weather. Then, "May I have a number where we may reach you concerning your friend in, say, fifteen minutes?"

Willy turned in the hot confining booth to read off the numbers on the telephone.

"All right then, Miss Patterson. You wait at the booth and you'll be contacted shortly. If you must leave for any reason whatsoever, then please do not contact this agency again from the same booth."

"All right," she breathed, hanging up the receiver. Then it struck her. An icy cold hand ran up her spine. She hadn't mentioned it—not even once—and he had known she was calling from a booth!

Willy sat on the curb, her head on her knees, her hand absently patting Linda's burnished belly. "You still love to have your tummy rubbed," she said smiling weakly at the dog.

God, what if they didn't call back? How long could she wait there? Then would she ever have the nerve to call again?

Willy glanced at her wristwatch. It had been seven minutes. It seemed like an hour. Two, maybe. She began to chew on her nails—at least she didn't smoke—then forced herself to stop as she lay back on the warm grass next to the curb.

Passersby must think she'd had a heart attack. Perhaps they thought the dog had attacked her and stood over the spoils, salivating with excitement.

Willy smiled to herself nervously. Well, she'd always loved a good adventure.... She took several long breaths, holding the air in her lungs and then letting it out slowly to relax herself.

Ted. Was he a preppy like so many of the CIA were reported to be? He'd probably graduated from Duke or Princeton or somewhere terribly chic and his present assignment was "Telephone calls—crazy." What was this Ted character doing right then? Was he trying to get a computer to spew forth information on her or at least on her father? Certainly he'd be trying to ascertain if she was a kook or for real.

Willy could not imagine, as she lay there on the grass with Linda licking her face, the CIA putting an experienced agent on the phone with her. Maybe later she would talk to a *real* agent, the one who would help Andrea and find a place for her in American society.

Ten minutes passed.

Willy sat up, pushing Linda away. "Stop licking me, for Pete's sake!" she complained. Then she noticed a woman with two small children eyeing her from across the street.

Why hadn't he called? How long could it take to find out if one Wilhelmina Patterson called the CIA on a daily basis? Damn....

At twenty-three minutes past eleven, when she could see through the foliage behind the booth the digital temperature on a bank sign switch to eighty-six, the telephone rang shrilly.

Her heart gave a great leap in her breast. Automatically her hand went to the spot.

Linda eyed the booth. She barked, and then lay down with a groan.

Again it rang.

Willy moved quickly back into the booth and grabbed the receiver, trying to shut the glass doors behind her. "Hello...." She was breathless.

"Miss Patterson?" came a cool authoritative male voice.

"Is this...Mr., I mean, Ted?" Perspiration suddenly rolled down between her breasts. The digital thermometer visible through the trees now read eighty-seven degrees.

"No. I prefer not to use names on the telephone. Is that clear?"

Notions crowded her mind. Whereas Ted had sounded mildly intimidating over the phone, he now seemed a poodle compared to this Doberman. There was something about this man, his deceptively calm voice, something....

Instantly Willy distrusted him.

"Concerning your friend," the deep male voice went on, "when and by what means were you first contacted?"

"Well Andrea and I—"

"No names please." Smoothly, easily.

"Well, yes, my friend and I go back a ways. We both ski...."

"We already know that."

Lord, Willy thought, feeling unnerved by the invasion of her privacy. The wonderful age of computers. "She wrote me."

"When?"

"Three days ago."

"You mean, I assume, that you received a letter from her three days ago, not that she wrote to you then."

"Yes, isn't that obvious?"

There was a slight pause over the phone. "Nothing is ever obvious," the voice stated so unemotionally that Willy wondered if she wasn't speaking to a machine. "There are reasons for all my questions," he added patiently.

Willy drew in a deep breath. "Look, Mr. . . . whoever you are, I need to know if you can help me."

"That determination has not yet been made as I'm sure you can fully understand. I suggest a meeting at three."

"*This* afternoon?"

"At the Lincoln Memorial. Are you familiar—"

"Of course, but how will I know you?"

"You won't. I'll know you."

There was a click and the line went dead. A chilling voice, a time, a place.

Willy pushed open the door to the telephone booth and drew in the fresh air while Linda stretched, watching her. Suddenly Willy looked down at her white cotton T-shirt and blue-and-white running shorts.

She was drenched in sweat.

THREE

Hyde Vandemeer glanced at his watch. Two forty-five. He shifted his weight easily in the BMW's cushy brown interior. He was early by fifteen minutes, perhaps twenty if the Patterson girl was late.

Idly he reached into the glove compartment and took out a partially crushed pack of Winstons. They'd been in there for two months. The pack was half-full. Why was he so damn reluctant to give the vile things up altogether?

Sandy, he couldn't help recalling, had smoked Winstons. In fact, she'd given him his first one back in—when was it?—'67. They'd been juniors then at Penn. State and he'd been the star of the football team, the almighty quarterback.

The Lincoln Memorial sat in stolid dignity before him now but Hyde could only see Sandy, her blond hair falling in her eyes so that she looked like a clone of Veronica Lake. Then there was the way Sandy's mouth parted expectantly, the soft sway of her hips, the ease with which she found fulfillment.

He'd choked like hell on that first cigarette. "God, Sandy! These things'll kill you!"

"Oh, you're just too groovy to smoke," she'd teased, that shimmering pale curtain of hair half hiding her face in the old Chevy's interior.

He'd stubbed the cigarette out and pulled her close to him. She hadn't given up her virginity that night, although they'd clung to one another in breathless panting agony. No. Sandy had waited. He tried to remember if the long-heralded event had happened the night after their big win over Ohio, but he wasn't exactly sure. Anyway, Hyde recalled with utter clarity the way Sandy had clung to him, dug her long pink nails into his back, wrapped her freshly shaved legs around his hips.

My God, how he had worshiped her. There wasn't a man at Penn. State who hadn't lusted after Sandy Waxman. Not a one. But she'd had eyes only for him—the intellectual, the athlete, the star quarterback. Oh, he'd certainly had it all going for him then.

"You've got the most divine green eyes, Hyde," Sandy used to purr as she'd press her rose-tipped breasts against the wall of his chest. "No one could ever hold a candle to you."

He'd been good-looking then. Tall, full of sparking energy, handsome, powerfully built, yet lean, the perfect quarterback.

They'd married, eloped actually, in the autumn of their last year at State. The Waxmans had been pleased. The Vandemeers were a well-to-do family from the Pittsburg steel community. Sandy's father was a mill foreman near the West Virginia border. Why shouldn't the Waxmans have been pleased?

Hyde had found Sandy naked in their bed with Jerry standing over her fully dressed just before graduation. He'd lost his head completely until Sandy and Jerry explained that Jerry had simply been looking for him and had accidentally awakened Sandy.

It was pretty stupid of Jerry but no harm had been done. And Hyde had all but forgotten the incident the moment Sandy had pulled the sheet away from her body, let that long sleek hair fall half-over a breast....

"But they can't draft you!" she'd wept that July. "They just can't!"

He'd only been out of school a month. But they *could* draft him. "I'm sorry, Sandy." He'd stroked her soft thigh. "But it won't be too bad."

"They'll send you to Vietnam!" Her full lips drew downward into a sensual frown.

"Oh, I don't think it'll come to that."

Of course, Hyde had known all along that he was destined for Nam. He just hadn't thought it would come so damn quickly. But back in '68 none of them had guessed their destiny. He'd taken his boot-camp training at Fort Dix; then they had shipped him off to the West Coast where he'd had the good sense to apply for OCS—Officer's Candidate School.

"First they draft you into the army, for God's sake," Sandy had complained bitterly over the phone, "then they send you two thousand miles from me and I can't even get hold of you on the telephone!"

He'd tried to comfort her with soft words, he paid for her to travel to the West Coast, spent every possible minute with her in the sack till his unit had shipped out. His fellow officers kept telling him how lucky he was to have a knockout like Sandy for a wife.

Nam not only lived up to but surpassed everything the newspapers said; it was steamy and hellish and brutal and half the guys were stoned all the time. Perhaps the insanity evolved because there was no support back home for the war. None. He remembered when the major had bought it. They'd been standing over his blown-up corpse. It was raining.

"No one gives a damn anyway," Private Moseley had stated, sucking on a pipe packed with grass. "We could all get our butts blown off and no one would care."

Moseley had summed it up neatly.

Sandy had seemed to love him when she'd come to Tokyo that spring of '69. They had spent four days rolling around on the hard tatami mats rediscovering each other's flesh, doing sexual things that had surprised even Hyde. And he'd thought he'd seen it all in Saigon....

"Intelligence," his colonel had said, "is the future of the military, Vandemeer. Get into intelligence."

And so the seasoned Hyde had. And he was good at it, too. He soon developed a flair for ferreting out information from villagers and would-be informants. He seemed to be able to pick out the truth from a passel of lies. He could follow a path of half-truths into the jungle from village to village, up uncharted rivers. He even, amazingly, liked it.

It was nearly three when Hyde reached for another cigarette but then checked himself. Why was Sandy's memory still so damn distracting? It had been years....

He glanced up and down the wide terrace spread before the gleaming white Lincoln Memorial. It was September and all the kids were back in school. Very few tourists wandered around. Anyway, it could have been jammed—he'd be able to spot the woman no matter what.

He'd stepped off the plane in southern California in January of '70. Hardened. A touch disillusioned by it all but nonetheless proud that he had served, proud to have the prettiest damn wife in the world waiting for him.

"But I'm not giving up my career," Sandy had pouted that night in the dingy Los Angeles hotel room. "I'm a damn good interior decorator and I refuse to sit home with a bunch of brats."

They'd made love. Actually, it had been pure sex, like a raw B movie. Whether it had been satisfying, Hyde really couldn't recall. Funny. It had been the last time they'd slept together; you'd think he'd remember it.

"His name is Vic," Sandy had said over breakfast, no doubt thinking that Hyde would not create a scene in a public dining room.

She'd been wrong.

The divorce was final by the autumn of '70 but Hyde had vowed to stay clear of emotional entanglements long before he had papers in his hand.

He guessed now that marriage and the CIA didn't quite mix, anyhow. An agent was like a cop: odd working hours, possible danger, too many new faces, too many new women. Yes, marriage and the CIA made poor bedfellows.

In the spring of '73 he had met Joseph Thine, another Vietnam vet, and was interviewed by Joe's boss at the CIA.

He'd never forget the first time he went to the CIA Langley headquarters with Joe. The building was secluded, surrounded by a twelve-foot fence topped with barbed wire, patrolled by armed guards and dogs. The security check system was thoroughly intimidating.

And then, on the marble wall of the main lobby, he'd read the plaque.

And ye shall know the truth,
And the truth shall make you free.
John 8:32

He'd grinned, shaken his head, glanced at Joe and rolled his eyes. Joe's face was impeccably sober; he did not respond.

Clandestine Services was the department seeking Hyde's expertise and it took him a while to get used to the department title. Some of the guys—to make matters worse—called it the Department of Dirty Tricks.

"No one on earth would believe 'Clandestine Services,'" he'd said to Joe.

"Then you'll never believe that we call our boss 'Uncle.'"

"You're right." Hyde had quirked a brow. "Is there a comedian in the group?"

And so Uncle did indeed become Hyde's boss and Clandestine Services his specialized department. All the departments at the CIA had specific titles. Hyde recalled one day as he was walking down corridor D at Langley that there was a new department sign nailed to an unobtrusive door. It read Sabotage. The next day, Hyde could have sworn the same door bore the title Terrorism. The following day it was a men's room.

The CIA was one place where no department really knew much about the others. It was called "security consciousness" in CIA jargon. How the U.S. expected to achieve peace and détente abroad when its own agencies were completely secretive and paranoid within their own frameworks eluded Hyde. But then, it had ceased to matter since he'd grown up. Well, since Nam....

He occasionally dated Myrna Carlson now. She'd come to the CIA from a small West Virginia town fresh out of college and slowly made her way from the steno pool to Uncle's private secretary to full-blown agent. She was an efficient coworker. They'd first shown interest in one another in the Sudan on a routine assignment. It had started in the bar at a hotel and ended in Myrna's bedroom beneath the mosquito netting. Once in a while they reenacted the scene. He liked the relationship. Simple. No strings. Mostly he liked Myrna because her hair was short and black and her eyes dark and she was only five feet four and tended to be a little heavy at times.

Myrna was very much the opposite of Sandy.

It was Myrna who had pulled up the information about Wilhelmina Dorothy Patterson from the computer at precisely 11:05 that morning.

"Umm," Myrna had commented. "She's quite pretty. And an up-and-coming artist, it seems."

Hyde, along with Ted Weston, had been standing looking over her shoulder, both hunched slightly. "Five feet seven, hundred and twenty-five pounds, blond hair, blue eyes," Hyde had read. "The daughter of Representative Edward Patterson, Democrat, Colorado. Not very earthshaking."

"The daughter appears to have led a more exciting life than her father." Myrna punched up more history onto the screen. "Ah ha! No wonder this Willy knows the Russian girl."

Hyde nodded pensively. "U.S. Ski Team member, circuit 1971-1977. Silver medal, '74. Impressive...."

"And in the downhill," put in Ted with a touch of awe.

"Yes. But look here." Hyde leaned closer to better read the green-lit print. "Broken leg. Retired."

"Obviously she's kept in touch with Andrea Pavlevitch," said Myrna.

"Seems so." Hyde straightened, putting a hand to the back of his neck.

"Well then—" Myrna turned around in her seat and crossed her shapely legs "—I'd say your little Miss Patterson is probably on the level, Ted."

"Maybe," Hyde said half under his breath.

"Well, she runs an art gallery now. Sells her own stuff. Owns her own house. She's not a kook."

"Probably not," commented Hyde.

"A touch wild, I'd guess."

"That was years ago, Myrna."

"Ah, but cats don't often change their stripes."

Hyde had glanced over at Ted Weston. "Look, I know you took this call but I'd rather leave you on your present job."

"Yeah," Ted drawled sarcastically, "monitoring an embassy is so much more fascinating than working on a Russian defection."

Hyde's green eyes held his steadily. "If this Andrea Pavlevitch is the 'Andrea' Miss Patterson mentioned, then it would be a nice feather in our cap—"

"Beat the State Department out of one," commented Ted Weston dryly.

Myrna frowned.

"That's not the object," Hyde said sternly. "We're not in competition here." But he knew it was a lie.

Myrna glanced at her watch. "Hyde, we're supposed to call her in two minutes. . . ."

"I'm sure she'll wait," Ted said.

"But what would be the object in that?" Hyde turned his back and strode out of the room.

He had dialed the telephone-booth number in private, but as always, he had taped the entire conversation.

He had imagined, as she spoke tensely on the phone, what she looked like. Of course there had been a computerized photo, but they often served to confuse.

Miss Patterson's voice was husky yet feminine; she seemed to want help yet he had detected a note of reluctance in her voice. Something told him, as he had played back the entire conversation earlier that afternoon, that Wilhelmina Patterson was going to prove to be contentious and headstrong.

In the field, a contact either faded into the woodwork or insisted on popping up at the most inopportune moments. Wilhelmina, he surmised, would be a veritable jack-in-the-box.

Uncle—Gary Gibbons—was back from his meeting with the director when Hyde had knocked on his boss's door.

"Sit down, Hyde," the pale, thin-faced man had directed. "Now what's on your mind?"

Hyde began his tale. "We've had a telephone contact from a House Representative's daughter. A Wilhelmina Patterson." He went on to tell Uncle about her Russian ski-team friend.

"And what about her father again?"

"Edward Patterson, sir. Democrat. Colorado."

"Ah yes." Gary steepled his fingers on the polished desk top. "Committee on Synthetic Fuel. Is there a connection, Hyde?"

Hyde was silent for a long moment. Then he answered soberly, "I seriously doubt it, sir, but I fully intend to pursue that possible aspect of this case."

"Good. Then I assume you're going to meet this Patterson girl."

"Yes, sir, at three today."

Gary Gibbons nodded. Then a slow smile gathered at the corners of his thin lips. "Andrea Pavlevitch," he said wistfully, selfishly. "Quite a big name in the skiing world. Yes, it wouldn't do us any harm at all to get that one."

"No, sir." Hyde's expression remained totally impassive. "It wouldn't hurt at all."

FOUR

Willy arrived back at her parents' house with only an hour to cool down, shower and dress before she'd have to leave for her appointment in front of the Lincoln Memorial. She took Linda around the back of the house, turned on the hose, filled the dog's bowl for her, and then drank from the hose herself.

It was scorching out!

"Willy," came a voice from a second-story window, "is that you?"

She glanced up. "Yes, mother. I'm just getting some water."

"Well, come on up here when you're done and tell me what happened."

Willy stood in her parents' bedroom, a damp towel around her shoulders, leaning her head against the doorframe. "I'm meeting this agent at three," she explained, "all very hush-hush. They really are paranoid at the CIA, mother. All this stuff about 'no names.' I'd like to be a fly on the wall in *those* offices."

"What did you expect, dear? An afternoon tea and swim?" Rachel Patterson turned on her dressing-table seat to face her daughter. "Willy... I... well, I *am* a little concerned."

She could see the tension in her mother's face. "Come on," she said softly, "it's all on the up and up, I'm sure. We'll just discuss Andrea's problem."

"The CIA." Rachel shook her blond head. "One hears so many awful things nowadays. It's all so dark and secret . . . frightening. . . ."

"Oh, mother," Willy sighed.

"You said it yourself, dear. They're very hush-hush—paranoid. You put it exactly right. And here you are going off to meet some agent, a perfect stranger."

"But he works for the government, mother. I'm sure he's all right . . . at least, *that* way. Why, he'll probably turn out to be some old fuddy-duddy with horn-rimmed glasses and false teeth."

Rachel looked at Willy impatiently. "You don't know that."

"Of course not. But everything will be fine, mother." Then Willy paused and thought a moment, phrasing her next words carefully. "I do appreciate your worrying about me, mother, but I'm all grown-up now. I'm twenty-seven, not fifteen."

Rachel expelled a weary breath. "Sometimes you can be too carefree. You're just too much of a spunky little girl to me."

A lukewarm shower revived Willy after the jog, and relaxed her. She really did feel good about the meeting and was certain that the CIA would help. But it was a shame that her mother still worried so. After all these years. . . .

Rachel Patterson was the only person in whom Willy had confided about that terrible night. She hadn't told her best friend; she hadn't been able to tell her mother about it until nearly a year afterward. For months she'd slept restlessly, been unable to attend school mixers, go to a friend's house for an impromptu party, or accept a blind date.

In retrospect, Willy had come to realize that her hesitancy to think or speak of it hadn't stemmed from shame alone. No. It had come from the fact that she had been flirting with those boys, "asking for it," as one of them had jeered afterward. And at the time and for a long, long time afterward she'd almost believed that it had been her fault. But now, of course, she knew better. No human being had the right to do that to another. No matter what.

Willy turned the cold water up, letting it stream down her back. Lord, it felt good! But she had better not stay in too long—this agent might not like waiting.

She towel dried her hair, powdered herself and shook out her icy-blue silk blouse and beige linen skirt. No hose. It was way too hot for them. Her hair dried naturally, falling into a shining curtain just past her shoulders and curling slightly under. She put on a touch of eye shadow, a little mascara and a pale red lipstick that enhanced her summer tan and white teeth.

She checked herself quickly in the mirror before phoning for a cab.

"What, no shorts or jeans? Now that's unusual. Where're you going?" asked Edward Patterson as he tossed his briefcase onto the hall sofa.

"Oh," Willy fumbled—he was home early. "I'm off to see . . . Liz."

"Liz?" He came over to where Willy was seated by the telephone. "Liz Anderson?"

"Yes. You remember, dad. Her family still lives in Falls Church."

"I suppose. Well dear, take the station wagon. We won't be using it today."

"Oh, that's all right, dad," said Willy quickly. "It's too hard to park there. I'll take a cab."

Edward quirked a gray bushy brow. "Hard to park in Falls Church?"

Willy shrugged, blushing. "Well, you know what I mean. . . ." Of course, he didn't. But how could she tell him that she was going to the Lincoln Memorial, not Falls Church?

"Well then," he said with a smile, "take a cab but let me give you some money."

"No, dad," she said quickly. "For pity sake, I'm twenty-seven years old. I can afford my own transportation."

"All right, dear," he said, patting her on the head.

Willy laughed. "Won't you ever let me grow up?"

"No," but Edward smiled agreeably.

Knowing the taxi would be a while getting to the Patterson's rural address, Willy decided she had time to make a couple of calls to Aspen. She walked up the steps to her room, carefully closing the door.

"Gayle? This is Willy."

"Oh Willy! I'm glad you called. You know that watercolor of the Maroon Bells you did last year?"

"Yes. . . ."

"Well, this man wants it but says three hundred is way too much."

"What did he offer?"

"Two hundred, and listen to this one. He said he'd throw in dinner with you at Andre's to make up the difference."

"He *what?*"

"You heard me. He remembers you from your silver-medal days and really, Willy, I don't think he knows the first thing about painting."

"You mean he just wants dinner?"

"You got it."

"Well, I should be flattered, I guess, but tell him the price is firm—three hundred. And *no* dinner."

"Okay."

Next, Willy dialed Reeves's number. She was ready to hang up when he finally answered.

"I didn't think I'd catch you in at—" she glanced at her watch and noted it was quarter past two "—twelve-fifteen."

"It's snowing. Had to quit work for the day."

"Snowing? Heavens, Reeves, it's nearly ninety here. Can you believe it?"

"No. How are you, Willy? I mean, have you talked to anyone yet?"

"Yes. And I'm meeting him in forty-five minutes."

"Him?"

"Yes, Reeves. Some old fish from the CIA I talked to on the phone this morning. I haven't met him yet."

"I hate the idea of your going through all this alone. I wish I was there, Willy."

She smiled to herself, smoothing the linen skirt absently with her hand. "You know you'd rather be in Aspen. Now tell the truth."

"Well, maybe. But I do worry about you, babe. With all your wild schemes, I wonder sometimes."

"Well, not to worry. I can handle things. Just don't fink out on me when the time comes. I'll only need you for a few minutes, Reeves, but I'd never make it without you. . . ."

"Ah, you're just flattering this guy."

"I miss you," she said, "but I've gotta run now."

"Take good care."

"I will."

They never said "love you." It simply wasn't a phrase in either one's vocabulary.

The taxi was late getting to the Pattersons', so late that Willy was ready to use the bulky station wagon—traffic or no traffic. And it didn't help matters to run into a traffic jam near the entrance to the Beltway. She sat in the back seat with her hands clutched at her sides, trying desperately not to raise the left one and start chewing on her nails.

The cabby swore several times, mopped his perspiring brow with an old handkerchief, complained bitterly about the heat.

"You from D.C., Miss?" he asked once.

Willy met his eyes in the rearview mirror. "No."

"Then this heat must be killin' you. Worst September I ever seen."

"Yes, it is hot." She could feel her hair growing damp at the back of her neck; the waistband of her linen skirt began to feel sticky. Unconsciously she let her brown leather sandal flop on her foot as she rolled the back window all the way down. Whatever happened to air-conditioned cabs?

It was stop-and-start traffic the nearer they got to northwest Washington. Why the Lincoln Memorial? Did the CIA enjoy traffic jams? And by the time this interview was over, she'd be stuck in rush-hour traffic. Stuck, that is, if she could even find a taxi.

White and pure and massive where it stood at the end of the Reflecting Pool, the domed Lincoln Memorial finally came into view. Her parents lived quite close to the Capitol Hill area, about ten miles away, yet it always seemed to take an eternity to get anywhere around Washington. Willy would take the Colorado mountains anytime.

The cab pulled up next to the curb behind a school bus picking up its passengers. They looked to Willy like high school seniors, but it was so hard to remember what a senior looked like. As she stepped out onto the curb and leaned over to pay the driver, two boys whistled at her and she shot them a hard look. Then she took several steps across the walkway, looked around surreptitiously, but saw no one suspicious or out of the ordinary. What, really, did an agent look like?

Behind her the taxi pulled away from the curb, blowing its horn for no apparent reason, and Willy suddenly felt terribly conspicuously alone. What a queer feeling, to seem alone in a crowd!

A hot wind off the Potomac River whipped long strands of light hair into her eyes. She held the stray hair away from her brow with one hand as she glanced around once more. Then a lone page of a newspaper blew across the pavement and she stepped out of its path feeling more and more ridiculous and self-conscious. Was he even there at all? Would he come to meet her or was it all a bad joke?

Damn you, Andrea, she swore silently. But she didn't mean it. In truth, she would have done anything in the world to help her old friend. Even meet a CIA agent—a total stranger—alone in the middle of a bustling metropolis.

She pulled her courage around her as if it were a heavy coat and began walking toward the memorial itself. Slow easy strides. If he was watching, she wasn't about to let him see her tension.

"I'll know you," the steely voice had said on the phone.

Was he watching her at that very moment, following her with shadowed eyes?

The temperature in the nation's capital was now ninety-four degrees, yet goose bumps rose on Willy's flesh.

All right, she thought, *you've made your point. You can come out now, wherever you are.*

FIVE

It was exactly 3:05 when the Patterson woman's taxi pulled up to the curb at the memorial. Hyde watched with detached interest as she stepped out onto the curb and paid the driver. Two boys from a school group gave her the once over, liked what they saw and whistled. She shot them a frigid yet somehow uncomfortable glance. Hyde was mildly intrigued by the somewhat unusual reaction on her part and tucked it away in his memory to be called up, perhaps, later.

He'd seen the photo printout of Wilhelmina Dorothy Patterson—the one where she and her ski team comrades had been standing on a slope somewhere, arms around each other's shoulders, laughing and silly. Wilhelmina looked very much like that photo, but now she was not laughing nor could he detect any of the clown in her.

Strange. There appeared to be no tension in her as she stood gazing up and down the wide terrace. Obviously she'd been in pressure situations before. And he noticed something else he hadn't detected from the photo: she moved like an athlete, each step a pose of confidence. Strong shapely legs beneath the beige linen skirt. Firm but modest breasts under the silky blouse. Tanned. She spent a lot of time outdoors. A woman like her would.

She turned sideways. A honey-blond curtain of hair blew into her eyes. Absently she held it aside with her hand and Hyde was reminded of another woman.

Strike one against Miss Patterson.

He stepped out of the BMW and moved toward her.

Her back was to him then. Nice shape from behind....

Quickly he corrected the isolated thought. This was business. Strictly business.

Automatically his hand went up to straighten his hair. He'd slicked it down some, changed the part. He reached into the breast pocket of his lightweight sport coat and pulled out a pair of dark-rimmed glasses, which lent him the look of a Georgetown intellectual rather than a "regular guy" from western Pennsylvania, a former athlete. The change of appearance, which had taken all of six seconds to accomplish, was just enough to confuse someone who might be trying to describe him later. Probably it was unnecessary in this instance but one never knew. And too, Wilhelmina Patterson—any woman—would feel more comfortable around the Clark Kent type.

He was two feet from her back. The fresh scent of a light cologne reached his nostrils.

"Miss Patterson." He stood still now, hands in his pockets casually.

She came around a little breathlessly, apparently startled for a moment. Then commendably she recovered. "I'm afraid you have the advantage, uh...."

"Call me Hyde."

"All right, Hyde." Her eyes, which caught the afternoon sun, were an unusual blue-gray hue. Very attractive. "Well," she began as she smiled tentatively, "my friend and I are going to have to ask you for a little help."

"A little help?" *Damn,* he thought, even as his facial expression remained unreadable, *another one of those liberated women who thought the CIA worked expressly for them.* "And how is that, Miss Patterson?"

The smile on Wilhelmina Patterson's lips faded. "It's going to take a few minutes to explain, Mr.... I mean, Hyde. Shall we walk?"

She didn't wait for his reply; apparently she didn't feel she needed his permission. He watched for a second as her easy stride moved her away from him, crossing the traffic circle and heading toward the Reflecting Pool. He shoved his hands back in his pockets, smiled cynically, shrugged his shoulders and began to follow.

She strode gracefully, her head up in the warm afternoon sun, her hair swinging with each movement of her long lithe legs. Hyde caught up with her easily and swung into step with her as they crossed the lawn. She glanced at him out of the corner of her eye. Curious, naturally.

"I don't have much, um, practice at this sort of thing," she said. Yet there was no apology in her voice. "But I'm supposed to ask you for some kind of identification, aren't I?"

Smart girl. He pulled out his wallet, flipped it open and watched her study the card. Her sea-blue eyes scanned his face, comparing it to the photo on the laminated plastic card.

"I guess it's you," she finally said.

"Terrible picture."

"It isn't great," she agreed.

"Do you want to tell me about your friend?" he asked guardedly.

"Yes, but where do I start?" She laughed with constraint.

"The initial contact."

"First things first, as my mother always says," she quipped.

"Yes."

They were approaching an empty bench by the side of the pool, under a cherry tree. He gestured for her to sit. She sank down onto it, crossed a shapely leg over her knee and swung one foot.

"Well—" she turned those wide unusual eyes onto him "—it's like this. I got this letter from my friend Andrea—Andrea Pavlevitch—from Chile where the Russian team is training, and she says she wants to defect and asks me to help her."

"Do you have the letter with you?" asked Hyde, absently pushing at his glasses with an index finger.

"Of course." She rummaged in her leather shoulder bag and handed him an international aerogram. He opened it and read the awkwardly written script carefully, folded the letter and handed it back to her silently.

"Well?" she asked anxiously.

"Sounds sincere."

"Sounds sincere! Of course she is. Do you think she's a double agent or something?" Her voice was filled with sudden humor.

"It does look a bit fishy. For instance, why didn't your friend just contact the American consulate in Chile? She could be a plant. It happens all the time," he said mildly.

She sighed in exasperation. "You don't know Andrea. I do. She would never go to any official or any government."

"Why not? If she wants to become an American." He shrugged.

"Andrea's father was a writer. He tried for years to get his poetry published but he had a black mark against him politically." She straightened fine shapely shoulders. "I don't know what he did. It was ages ago. They wouldn't print his work so he tried to get it printed underground. He disappeared fifteen years ago. Andrea and her mother never saw him again. She told me she used to have nightmares about him, where he was and so on. Then her mother, just because she had been married to him, was not allowed to pursue her research. She was a physicist. They made her work in a lab as a technician, instead. It was horrible. She died last year."

"I see." It was an all-too-familiar story, one repeated by dozens of defectors over the years. Perhaps this Andrea did have reason. "But why didn't she defect before? Why now?"

"Well, I guess because her mother is gone now. And she also wrote about them making her coach next year. I don't know exactly, but it must have been a last straw. You have to understand that Andrea is a free spirit. Ever since I met her she's been cheerful and optimistic. And now I suppose she sees an end to her happy life. She loves to ski so much."

"And she doesn't want to coach?"

"She doesn't want to be forced to do anything, I guess. You've got to remember that she's quite privileged. The year I took the silver she got the gold. And she's even better now."

"Isn't she a bit, well, old for racing?" he asked carefully.

Willy flashed him an impish smile and tossed her golden hair. "She's younger than I am. A couple of years, I think. And she's still very good, so of course they kept her on. What does age have to do with it?"

"Well, you quit, for instance. Seven years ago." His glance strayed unintentionally to her legs, her swinging foot; he caught himself and raised his eyes to meet her cool gaze.

"Why bother asking questions if you already know all the answers?"

"Not *all* the answers, Miss Patterson," he said dryly. "I'd like to hear your version."

"Well, you may know about my broken leg." She met his gaze levelly. "I had to quit for a year because of that and then I graduated and got more involved with my painting. And now I'm awfully busy with my gallery and all that."

"Do you still ski?"

She threw back her head and laughed. Her throat made a long graceful arc. "Do I ski?" Her white teeth flashed, her eyes sparkled with merriment. "*Of course* I ski! Whenever I can! Why else would I live in Aspen?" Then she studied him, amused. "Do *you* ski, Mr. . . . Hyde?"

Momentarily disconcerted, Hyde stared at her. "Some," he finally said. "I'm not Olympic material."

"Neither am I anymore, but I can still turn 'em."

"Yes, I'm sure you can."

"Can we get back to Andrea?"

"I can hardly give you any definite commitments right now. I have to discuss this with my superior. There are channels to go through."

"You *have* to accept her," Willy said intensely. "I mean, you wouldn't refuse her, would you?"

"It is not within my power to answer that question yet," he said tonelessly. Never give an answer where an evasion would suffice.

"Come on, give me a guess. You have an educated opinion, don't you?"

"I might hazard a guess that Miss Pavlevitch would be welcomed, but that is not official, Miss Patterson. There are always problems."

"If you're worried about how to get her out, there's no problem at all. I have it nearly all figured out." She spoke with supremely innocent confidence.

Hyde smothered a smile by raising a hand to readjust his glasses again. "Oh, you do. How interesting."

"Don't patronize me. I do have a plan, but I won't tell you until I know you'll help me with Andrea and that you'll take care of her after I get her away from the Russians."

He leaned back against the bench, tilted his head up and squinted into the sun. He took a few deep breaths. Silence usually succeeded in getting them off guard better than any number of words.

"Well?"

He turned to look at her, surprised once again by the faint hint of familiarity in her face and her gestures and by the utter newness too—the freshness and openness of her features, the warmth and clarity of her expression, the strength and pride of her carriage. "These matters are ultrasecret, very touchy. Amateurs can't be involved. It's dangerous." Somehow the thought of this confident honest young woman doing his kind of dirty work disturbed him. It was a curious sensation, as if he was somehow trying to protect her.

"Look," she was saying, "I would never have come to you at all if I could have done without your help, believe me. Frankly, I don't trust you—I mean your organization—and I'd much rather do it alone. This storybook spy stuff really turns me off."

"I'm disappointed in you, Miss Patterson," he said coolly. "The CIA is quite necessary to your very comfortable and prosperous existence." Pointedly, he swept her with his eyes, lingering on her expensive casual linen skirt, silk blouse and chic sandals. "And yet you say you distrust us. Would you prefer the secret police in Argentina, or how about the KGB?"

Her eyes shifted away from him then. She might not admit it but he suspected that she had accepted his point—if only grudgingly. He pressed his advantage. "Do you really think you can pull off a defection under the nose of the KGB and get off scot-free? Those are dangerous men you're talking about. Only someone naive or foolhardy would try to go up against the KGB unassisted, and I don't think you're either of those, Miss Patterson."

For a long moment she stared at him curiously, weighing his words. "All right. Maybe I can't do it entirely alone," she finally said. "But the part on the mountain—"

"Mountain?" he interrupted.

"Aspen Mountain. That's where we'll get Andrea," she said impatiently. "*That* part, I do alone. I know that mountain as well as you know—" she looked around, gesturing with an expressive hand "—Washington."

Her face was solemn, burning with an inward faith in her own ability. He almost believed that she *could* do it for a moment.

"I need to get back to my office to consult a few people," he said. "Then we'll need to talk some more."

"Okay. When? I'm here for a few days."

"Tonight." He was aware of the startled glance from her big smoky-blue eyes. "And I prefer privacy."

She watched him warily, a little uncomfortably, the way she'd looked at those schoolboys for a moment. He wondered then....

"Privacy," she was saying. "But where?"

Hyde studied her for a moment. Then for some reason he decided to push her a little, to test her mettle. "Why not my place?" Yes, she was a bit tense. "We can eat and talk at the same time," he pushed on.

She shook her blond head hesitantly. "I don't know...."

"Everything will be on the up-and-up, Miss Patterson. We need to talk. And it's got to be private." He waited and beneath the glasses his green eyes stared at her without expression. Once she glanced at him but her eyes slid away quickly. What would her decision be?

"You guys really are paranoid." She laughed uneasily, crossing her other leg.

"For good reason, Miss Patterson, but we prefer to call it security consciousness."

"You'd better call me Willy. I guess we have a date."

"Okay, Willy."

"I'm staying with my parents—" she began.

He cut her off. "I assumed so. I'll pick you up at eight. Alexandria."

She eyed him cynically, her long lashes half-lowered over her eyes. The sun glinted off them with golden lights. "Of course," she said sarcastically, "I shouldn't bother telling you anything, should I?"

Somehow he resented her words. Oh, he'd heard them all before in his line of work, but Miss Patterson... Willy...had a way of saying things so that they rang with undeniable truth. Everything she said was a challenge and he didn't always have a pat answer for her provocative remarks.

"That's not true." He grinned, deliberately defying her irritation. It was a game he played, manipulating people. It was his job. "I'm only human. I'll cook you dinner tonight and prove it."

"You cook?" She was obviously disbelieving. "Somehow—"

"I know, but I manage. Then we can relax and discuss your Russian friend. I may have some answers for you by then."

Willy stood, smoothing her skirt over lean hips and thighs. She was quite tall; her eyes seemed to be on level with his, but that was merely an illusion. "Tonight at eight, Hyde."

He paused. "By the way, could I have that letter? I'd like to take it to my office and verify the handwriting."

"Well, all right. I guess I don't need it anymore." Looking down, she reached into her bag. The sun gilded her hair as it swung across her cheek, its beauty both poignant and painful to Hyde.

"Here." She held out the letter; their fingers touched for a split second as he took it from her.

"See you tonight and, I might as well warn you, I'm always on time."

"Good," she said levelly. "So am I."

Hyde watched her walk away through the rows of trees toward Constitution Avenue. A lovely figure, strong, lean, chiseled like a Greek statue. *Too damn lovely,* he thought. Then he turned and began to walk toward the Memorial Circle where he had left his BMW. You meet all kinds, he reminded himself. But this girl was honest, he'd bet on that. Totally sincere in her desire to help her friend.

Andrea Pavlevitch. A good catch. Maybe Willy Patterson did have a lead on how to get her out. She might be useful. He needed to get her on his side, make her understand the dangers, the complications of a defection. It wasn't like playing with dolls.

He'd use his charm on her, the old college-boy charm dear Sandy had so adored, for a time, until it bored her. He could still charm a woman if he tried, and Willy Patterson, he already suspected, was quite a woman.

And yet he felt a twinge of distaste for his own unscrupulousness as he crossed the freshly mown grass toward his car. Why couldn't he have an ordinary job like an insurance adjuster, a salesman, an engineer? Was there some failing in his own character that made him so good at deception?

SIX

"Good Lord, Willy," whispered Rachel Patterson. "It's half past five! I've been dying of curiosity for over an hour!"

"It took longer than I thought," Willy started to explain as she closed the front door behind her. "Traffic."

"Home so soon?" Edward rounded the corner from the living room, the *Washington Post* clasped in one hand, his pipe in the other.

"Oh . . . yes, dad." Willy smiled brightly and shot her mother a bemused glance.

"And how is Liz?"

"Liz?"

"For Pete's sake, Willy," Edward grumbled, "has the mountain air in Aspen gotten thinner? I said, how is Liz?"

"Oh," Willy breathed. "She's fine, dad."

"Good." He began to turn back toward the living room. "Say, you look a little done in by the heat. How about a nice wine cooler? I'm buying."

"Okay, dad," said Willy. "I'll just kick off my shoes and be back down in a minute."

"I'll help Willy kick off her shoes." Rachel smiled. "We'll be down soon, dear."

Edward raised a brow and shook his head at his two best girls.

"So how did it go?" pressed Rachel conspiratorially as they mounted the steps to the second floor.

"Fine. At least, I think so."

"And what was the agent like?" Rachel sat on Willy's bed, watching her daughter slip out of her silk blouse.

"Cool as a cucumber, mother. He's terribly professional."

"Is he awfully officious?"

"Well...no. He's just...aloof." Willy's finely arched brows lowered into a frown. "Actually," she said half to herself, "he's the most unemotional person I think I've ever met."

"Maybe he's one of those women haters," suggested Rachel.

"No. It's not that exactly, mother. I'd say he's just hard. Impersonal, too. I imagine he treats everyone the same." Then she gave a short tense laugh. "He reminds me a little of Clint Eastwood in all those spaghetti westerns. You know, macho and detached and all that."

"Ugh," put in Rachel, feigning a shiver. "Sounds awful to me."

"Oh, he's not *that* bad, really, mother. In fact, if it was still the sixties, I'd say he was a total square. That wet-hair look and those glasses. It'll be dull if he's the one Andrea will have to see."

"Is he going to help, then? I mean, it is a bit wild. And then coming from a nice girl like you...."

Willy sat at her dresser, pulling a comb through her heavy hair. "It's not wild in the least, mother, especially for the CIA. It's right up their alley. In fact, I think they'll give me all the help I'll need."

"*You'll* need? Are you still planning—"

"You bet I am. Oh, Mr. Stiff-face thinks I'm some kind of a crackpot but I think he got the point."

"What's his name?" asked Rachel.

"Hyde. Just plain old Hyde." She rolled her eyes toward the ceiling.

"They're that secretive?"

"I guess so. He called it 'security consciousness.'"

"Oh, I see. Now tell me, do you have to meet with him again? I almost hope you do," Rachel mused with a smile, "because then we'll have you here even longer."

Willy laughed. "Some way to get me to visit! But yes, I do have to see him again." She caught her mother's gaze in the mirror. "In fact," Willy said slowly, "he's cooking dinner for me."

"No! He's not. . . ."

"Oh yes. And he was quite emphatic about it being at his place. He said he'd pick me up at eight."

"Good Lord, Willy! I wish you hadn't given him our address."

"I didn't."

"How—"

"He simply said he'd pick me up in Alexandria at eight."

Rachel let out a doleful sigh. "It's a little frightening, isn't it?"

"More than a little."

When Willy's father heard that she wouldn't be dining with them but was being picked up by a "friend" instead, he commented, "Maybe he'll marry you and your mother will quit complaining about no grandchildren."

To which Rachel Patterson pouted and replied, "That's not fair, Edward."

Willy adored her parents and wished more than anything that her own life was not so removed from theirs. Still, the Pattersons did come to Aspen to use their condominium at least three times a year. But the more years they put behind them, the more they preferred a vacation in the Bahamas or Mexico. Sometimes Willy managed to join them for a week; other times it was "on season" in Aspen and the gallery was far too busy to leave. Then there was skiing. . . .

Willy finished her wine cooler, checked the time and decided to head upstairs. The air conditioner was on full blast but it was still warm and close in her room. She ran a bath, borrowed some of Rachel's expensive bath oil and lazed in the silky water. She had plenty of time to relax before dressing.

He couldn't be married, she thought to herself, or surely he would not be taking her to his place. Of course, maybe he was wealthy and kept an apartment for just such occasions.

Suddenly her heart sank. Could he be one of those married men who kept a bachelor pad? Did Hyde have a side to him not apparent at first glance?

But no, Willy convinced herself, he couldn't. He was such a . . . a square. Yes, that was it. He was one of those perfectly harmless, bookish, dull men. She envisioned him in her mind's eye; the tweedy look, the too neat, almost wet hair, the ubiquitous glasses. Still, he was a CIA agent. How dull could an agent be, really?

Somehow she couldn't quite fit him into any category, but she did have a gut feeling that he was "safe."

Maybe, she thought, he was a machine after all.

There were only three dresses hanging in the closet; Willy kept them there just in case. And who needed dresses in Aspen anyway?

She slipped into a red-and-white Chinese print cut in a simple classic style—no frills, cap sleeves, a plain plunging vee neck. It flattered her golden tan and enhanced the rich honey color of her thick straight hair. But what she liked best about the dress was the fact that she needn't wear a bra. She could often get away without one, her breasts being neither too large nor too noticeably small. Around her neck she clasped a thin gold necklace—it too would serve any occasion. Then earrings. Studs of tiny golden aspen leaves. Elegant but simple. Hyde would find her dressed suitably for any setting, even though she would feel more comfortable in her well-broken-in jeans. She couldn't help wondering about his place, though. Was it contemporary, art deco, antique?

And why, really, had he asked her to dinner? Of course they needed to talk more and in private. But dinner at his place? And he had seemed a bit less icy toward her near the end of their meeting. Maybe the stone-faced man was merely following CIA rules; or maybe there wasn't anything at all behind the invitation except common courtesy.

And yet Willy felt small twinges of nervousness and apprehension shiver up and down her spine. Perhaps she should have refused or insisted they meet in a public place. It was just that she was so terribly sensitive on the subject. She always thought everyone would question her motives if she was prudish, and she had a horror of that. Living in a small community like Aspen protected her from much of that sort of pressure. In Washington she was vulnerable.

Willy's mother popped into her room just before eight. Rachel was dressed to the teeth in a mauve belted creation, which flattered her still-lovely figure.

"Where are you going?" asked Willy.

"Oh, your father asked me out on a date." She winked. "I'm sorry you can't join us."

"I am too," agreed Willy sincerely.

"Oh sweetie, please be careful. I mean, you hardly know this man and . . ."

"I'll be fine, mother." Willy took her mother's hands in her own. "I promise. He's such a proper old thing anyway." Was she trying to convince her mother or herself?

"Old?"

"Well, not *old*. But thirty-fivish."

"My. That *is* old," Rachel said, mocking breathlessness.

Car lights flashed past Willy's bedroom window. "That must be him." Rachel walked to the window and peered out. "Nice car."

"What kind?"

"Something foreign. How should I know?"

As Willy came down the front steps it struck her that her father might well ask the CIA agent an embarrassing question or even something about where he had met his daughter. As the front doorbell chimed, she prayed, just this once, that her father would let someone else do all the talking.

"I'll get it," called Edward as he came from the living room, placing his cocktail down on a hall table.

It was impossible, from where Willy stood on the bottom step, to reach the door first. Her heart beat just a little too rapidly.

Edward swung open the door.

At first Willy was certain that the tall, strikingly attractive man standing on the Patterson threshold was not her agent. Gone were the glasses, replaced by bold green eyes. And his hair—surely there was more of it tonight. It was lighter, too. Chestnut brown. Slightly curling. His carriage was all wrong, too. This man exuded an air of total self-assurance, an ease of bearing. Yet reason told her it could be no one else.

Willy never heard the beginning of the conversation between Hyde and her father. All she knew was that over her father's shoulder, the CIA man's eyes found hers and held her gaze for a frozen moment in time before his polite attention reverted once again to her father.

Reality washed back over her. How long had she been standing there, openmouthed?

She took a deep breath, a last step down and crossed to the two tall men.

"Just been chatting with Mr. Vandemeer here," Edward said, and she thought to herself, yes, Hyde Vandemeer—the name fit. Well, bookish dull Hyde had disappeared into a phone booth and reemerged as someone else entirely—Mr. Vandemeer. Someone much more intimidating.

"Got time for a drink?" Edward was asking him.

"Now, dear," came Rachel's voice from behind, "you know we'll never get into that Greek restaurant if we don't get going."

Edward shrugged, smiling apologetically at Hyde Vandemeer. "Next time then, young man." They shook hands firmly. "Take good care of my girl here."

Willy colored and protested hotly, "Dad...."

His pipe came up to his lips. "Sorry dear."

They all said good-night and Willy felt Hyde's hand under her elbow as they walked down the four steps to his deep-metallic-blue BMW.

It had been ages, she realized abruptly, since a man had shown her such courtesy. Reeves was always so casual.

Unaccountably breathless, Willy let him open the car door for her and close it safely before he walked around to the driver's side.

"You have very gracious parents," he commented offhandedly as he started the engine.

"Thank you," she said.

It was dusk in Virginia, nearly dark as they pulled out of the long drive. To the west the sky was a deep rich purple. Above, a few early stars shone weakly.

Willy turned slightly in the seat, allowing herself a glance of his profile. "You know the way back out to the highway?" she asked needlessly, noting the generous straight line of his nose and the almost arrogant curve of his nostrils. He had a strong chin, square and firmly set; a muscle worked in the flat plane of his cheek. Around his eyes were crinkle lines, although it was too dark to really judge his age now. Quietly, she returned her glance to the windshield.

"I do remember the way."

"Yes," Willy said, feeling a vague anxiety now that she was alone with this strange, dangerously attractive man. She obscured it with her usual flippancy. "I suppose you would." Then—even though she knew better—she couldn't resist asking. "Where're your glasses? Don't you need them to drive?" Her voice was cool, noncommittal, yet she'd been unable to keep the tinge of nervous sarcasm from sneaking through.

Hyde pinned her for a moment with his hard green gaze and a slight lift to one dark eyebrow. "I only need them during the day."

She pushed on just a little harder. "And I'd have sworn your hair was thinning...."

He met her statement with studious silence as he deftly steered the BMW through a series of low hills and curves. Finally he said, "Nice countryside out here. Always liked this part of Virginia."

"Yes," Willy replied, suppressing the sudden urge to nibble on just one nail. "It is pretty. Much greener than Colorado."

And so the conversation went. Light, meaningless, unemotional on his part, edgy on hers. Willy never bothered to ask him where he lived. It might have been Baltimore for all she knew. Still, they were heading into the city—northwest, Foggy Bottom area. Must be Georgetown.

She was correct on that score. Hyde's apartment house was in a tiny neighborhood off M Street. The building itself sat in the middle of the block, a little shabby, a little funky for Georgetown, with its elegantly tidy town houses. Hyde's three-story building needed paint; as she pushed open the wrought-iron gate, Willy could feel the black chipped enamel under her hand. The tiny lawn needed mowing; the bushes along the front needed a trim; the late summer flowers lay half on the ground.

"Watch the walk," came Hyde's voice from behind as his strong hand gripped her arm beneath the elbow. "Mrs. Rohrstad keeps promising to fix the old cement but sure as hell she's going to have a lawsuit before she gets around to it."

"Mrs. Rohrstad?" Willy did nearly trip over the cracked pavement.

"My landlady. Quite a character." Hyde unlocked the door and pushed it open for Willy. The spacious entrance hall that spread before her was nothing less than a Victorian nightmare: huge, dark furniture sat squatting against the walls, dusty prism lamps, sat on ornate mahogany end tables, dingy lace doilies hung from the sofa's arms, and an old ratty Persian carpet lay beneath Willy's feet. It was all a terrible conglomeration of lavender and burgundy and smelled faintly of mold and mothballs.

"My God," Willy whispered fervently, "it's ghastly!"

Then, for the first time, Hyde laughed. Willy turned toward him to catch the half smile on his thin lips and the way one corner of his mouth curved up more than the other. *My, my,* she thought, *perhaps he's human after all....*

"It does take a while to get used to it." Hyde shrugged, then closed the door behind them.

"But I love it," Willy explained. "It's absolutely charming!"

He quirked a dark brow. Then, "Ah yes, the artist's eye."

"How did you...?" But then she remembered. Hyde Vandemeer knew all. Thanks to her father's position in government and perhaps her own one-time fame on the skiing circuit, she no longer wondered. It discomfited her to think he knew so much about her.

"Oh, there you are," came an aged cracking voice from a dark doorway at the end of the entrance hall. "I need you to change this damn light bulb, Hyde." Standing before them was an adorable old woman—Mrs. Rohrstad, Willy assumed—an ankle-length, sequined black gown hanging off her bony shoulders, a cigarette dangling from her lips. "Is this Mrs. Vandemeer?" The old woman adjusted her wire-rimmed spectacles and studied Willy sharply.

"You know it isn't," Hyde chided gently. "This is Miss Patterson."

"Oh." Then she produced the light bulb from the drapes of her black skirt and shoved it into Hyde's hand. "It's over the kitchen sink," she said simply and turned, walking back toward her quarters.

"Look," Hyde began, "go on up. I'll just be a minute. Third floor. The door's open." He half smiled again. "And would you mind checking the oven?" Then he was gone, disappearing behind Mrs. Rohrstad.

Willy stood for a moment, completely bewildered. It seemed to her suddenly that she'd walked onto the wrong stage: all the lines were wrong, the characters were out of place, and the setting seemed like something out of *Arsenic and Old Lace*.

Well, there wasn't anything she could do about it. And besides, the characters did seem harmless enough, at least so far. She mounted the dimly lit staircase, stopped for a moment on the second-floor landing, and then climbed to the third floor. At the top of the steps was a small landing and a single door. So he had the entire third floor all to himself, she surmised, as she reminded herself that he was a respectable man, a government agent. Cautiously she opened his door.

What in heaven's name would she discover inside?

Her hand found the light switch and flicked it on. Before her was a warm, somewhat cluttered but quite enchanting living room done in soft earth tones and filled with wooden antique furniture. Baskets and plants were everywhere, cushions lay scattered on the long couch, too many magazines graced the scarred coffee table, and the white-painted walls were filled with pictures. It was a jammed room but welcoming and cozy. Was this Hyde Vandemeer?

Somewhere a cat meowed.

Willy tossed her purse on a sagging wing chair and walked toward the kitchen. On her right was a breakfast nook, loaded with plants and an old wooden dining table. The rear wall of the nook was all glass with a small narrow door leading out to a sun porch on the roof.

The kitchen to her left was a little too cluttered also. It seemed impossible to envision Hyde Vandemeer—CIA agent—standing in this narrow kitchen. Did he wear an apron? No way.

She peeked in the oven as he'd asked. It smelled delicious, whatever it was. She took a pot holder and pulled out the rack. "Umm," she sighed, recognizing a perfectly cooked eggplant-Parmesan casserole. How curious it was to be poking around in this man's apartment—alone—looking in his oven. It was as if he was an old friend; the apartment a familiar visiting place. It gave her a strange feeling to be experiencing this side of a stranger's life for the first time without his presence. It was uncomfortably intimate, much closer than she ever wanted to get to him.

"Hope you like it," came a voice from behind.

Willy jumped. "Lord! You scared me," she managed. Then, "I adore it and it seems to be fine in there."

"Not burnt?" He peeked over her shoulder.

"No," she replied, stiffening as she felt his warm breath brush her left shoulder.

"Do you like wine?" he asked.

"Yes. Red, if you have it."

He pulled two long-stemmed crystal wineglasses out of a cupboard above the old refrigerator. Willy could see immediately that they needed washing, or at least dusting, but he paid no attention as he popped the cork on a '77 Mouton Cadet and poured.

So much for his perfect domestic capabilities. It had seemed too much to expect anyway.

"Excellent wine," Willy commented, forcing herself to relax. Did he see the slight tremor in her lips? Was an agent trained to notice such things?

"Thank you," he said simply. "Let's sit in the living room."

"Can't we sit on the deck?" Willy nodded toward the glass door in the nook. Somehow, she'd feel better out in the open.

"I forgot," he smiled.

"Forgot what?"

"That you love the outdoors." He held open the door for her, nodding toward a rickety lounge chair. "You'll have to take your chances on that thing, but if you fall through, I'll help you up." Again he smiled.

She didn't fall through and surprisingly, the old lounge was quite comfortable. Hyde folded his lean frame onto a painted stool across from her.

She sat gingerly, on edge, the warm evening breeze caressing her skin. Overhead a plane droned somewhere; next to her the cat finally appeared, large and orange and scarred. She reached out her hand and patted it. "You smell Linda," she said to the cat.

"Who's Linda?" Hyde seemed sincerely curious.

"My father's dog."

"I didn't see a dog."

Suddenly Willy sat up. "I wish you'd stop that," she bit out irrationally.

"What?"

"Always having to know *everything!* Good Lord . . ." her voice trailed away.

"I'm sorry." But he didn't sound in the least sorry. "I guess it's just my job. Old habits, you know."

"Well, I don't appreciate it." She relented a little. "It makes me feel like I'm in the Twilight Zone all the time. It's eerie."

"Sorry. I'll try to do better." Again his tone was noncommittal. He *was* a cool customer.

Half under her breath Willy said, "Yes, but you'll still be thinking the same things."

She sipped slowly at her wine, trying to relax in the lounge chair while rubbing the large tomcat's neck. "What's his name?"

"I don't know," Hyde confessed.

"You mean to tell me there's something you don't know?"

"He's not mine. He just visits most of the time."

"Oh." Willy smiled. "A permanent houseguest."

"Something like that."

They sat in silence for a few minutes while Willy searched her mind desperately for something to say. The lull in the conversation seemed to have no effect on Hyde Vandemeer. Perhaps he had let the conversation drop for some purpose of his own—to unnerve her?

"Would you like more wine while we talk?" He rose finally and walked toward the door.

Willy shook her head. "No, but how is dinner?"

"Probably burnt," he said with no hint of humor. "Guess we ought to eat before that talk, right?"

Willy set the table in the nook. Hyde's silverware consisted of various pieces, unmatching, of stainless steel. Presumably he didn't entertain too often.

She watched as he pulled the casserole out of the oven, almost burning himself when he set it on the scarred table. Then he produced a salad from the refrigerator, tossed it with Italian dressing and placed it on the table. "Not very formal, Willy." He stood with his hands on his hips surveying the fare.

"It looks great. And I'll take that wine now." She seated herself and watched him as he went to get the wine bottle. He was six feet tall, at least. Maybe six one. And he was beautifully built. Like an athlete but certainly not a skier. His hips were too lean, the long thigh muscles too tapered. He was shaped more like a runner. He'd taken off his light jacket and his blue shirt-sleeves were rolled up to just below the elbows. His forearms were strong, tanned and furred with sunlightened hair. There was a powerful look to him as he strode back to the table. He moved, she noticed once again, like someone with a great deal of confidence in himself.

"You know," he said as he sat down, "this is the only dish I can make consistently without screwing it up." Then he smiled that lopsided smile and suddenly Willy felt heat rise to her cheeks.

"What would you have done if I'd said I didn't like eggplant Parmesan?"

"Sent out for pizza."

It was a well-prepared dish. It tasted as good as it smelled and his salad was perfect. But then, everyone's salad always tasted better than hers did.

Hyde seemed comfortable with almost any subject they touched on and she realized that no matter who was asking the questions, she was the only one really answering anything. How clever this agent was, she thought as she took a last bite of her dinner. He'd said they would need to talk that night and she'd kept waiting for him to ask her specific questions. He hadn't, and yet she'd been volunteering information all evening. Very clever indeed. And when was he going to pry out of her the details of her plan? Wouldn't he be surprised, she thought, when he found out that she had the perfect, foolproof plan to get Andrea away safely.

There was, Willy finally discovered, a way of getting information out of Mr. Hyde Vandemeer. Ask him directly.

"Mind if I make coffee?" she volunteered, half rising, wanting to be doing something.

"Go ahead." He helped himself to more casserole. "My coffee is lousy anyway."

Willy asked him a few questions as to where his pot and cups were located, and then began spooning the grounds into the coffee maker.

"Why did Mrs. Rohrstad ask if I was your wife?" she asked casually, keeping her gaze on the coffee scoop.

"I don't know exactly."

Some answer. "Were you . . . *are* you married?" There. He couldn't evade that!

"Yes and no."

"You're divorced, then."

"Correct."

"I'm sorry."

"I'm not." Just the steely cruel tone of his voice told her everything she'd wanted to know.

She dropped the subject like a tainted thing. "How did you come to work for the CIA, or aren't I allowed to ask?"

Between forkfuls of food, he replied, "Had a little experience in Vietnam."

"And?" She came back to sit down.

"And it seemed a logical move after my stint with military intelligence there."

"I see." She leaned her chin on her hands, elbows on the table. "Were you married when you were in Vietnam?"

Hyde raised his green eyes to meet her gaze. His look was calm, carefully removed. "Why do women always want to hear about a man's marriage?" he countered coolly.

Willy held her ground. "Maybe it tells us something about a person."

He stared at her carefully, making her quite uncomfortable, before he went back to finishing his casserole.

"Are you going to be able to help Andrea?" She finally broached the subject.

"I think the coffee's done." He nodded toward the kitchen.

Willy stood and walked into the kitchen. "Well, are you?"

"Of course."

She turned quickly to see the expressionless look on his face, the way his hard green eyes followed her, boring through her composure. For an endless moment she held his gaze in hers, aware of his strong, austerely modeled features sharply outlined in the lamp's light. Again, she noted his uncompromising jawline and his hard straight mouth. His stare was unflustered and she slowly became aware of the fact that she was glaring at him fiercely, with unaccountable anger.

"Of course," she repeated his curt reply slowly, suddenly seething inside. "And what does *that* mean?"

"Simply," he said easily as he rose from the chair, "that one way or another, Willy, we'll get Andrea Pavlevitch out."

Willy drew in her breath sharply. "I thought I'd made myself plain today," she said stiffly. "*I'm* the one who'll get my friend *out,* as you put it. Andrea, as I said before, hasn't any trust in governments and believe me, that means ours, too." Willy knew she was becoming more and more heated, yet some little imp deep within longed to get a reaction out of him.

"So you're going to outwit the KGB all on your own," he said mildly. But she detected a hint of sarcasm in his tone.

Good, thought Willy. "Yes. If I have to outwit the whole USSR, then I will. Andrea is my friend. . . ."

"And you love a good adventure."

"Yes." She put her hands on her hips, defiantly facing him. "I have it all planned out. During the World Cup races in Aspen, in March, when Andrea takes her run we'll pull a switch. *I'll* ski down instead of Andrea. Meanwhile she'll be going through the trees over the back side of the mountain to Castle Creek Road—"

"Whoa there. The layout of this thing may be in your head, but I need a map."

He went to his cluttered desk to find a pencil and paper. "Here, draw me a rough sketch."

She was aware of him watching her hands outline the map deftly. He'd probably forgotten she was an artist, as at home with pencil and paper as he was with a . . . well, a gun perhaps.

"See," she said, pointing, "here's the racecourse and Aspen Mountain drops away off to that side down into the Castle Creek Valley. Here. It's rough but she can get through. Then you meet her with a car there. It's simple. I've got a friend on the ski patrol. He'll take Andrea with him."

Hyde watched her with unblinking interest. "*You'll* ski down?"

"Well, if Andrea falls, of course she can't finish the race, but she—I mean I—will come out of the trees and ski down alongside the course to the finish line."

"Do you look enough like her to pass?"

"She's my height but a little heavier. Her hair is darker but with helmet and goggles and downhill suit no one will ever know." She had to convince him. "Don't you see? It's so simple. By the time they realize Andrea is gone she'll be safe. It's a cinch to work." She looked at him anxiously but there was no reaction in his expression, only the same hard unyielding detachment. Did nothing ever crack that cold facade?

"And once you pull off this master plot of yours, what do you plan on doing with Miss Pavlevitch then?" He was standing over her, his unrelenting green eyes pinioning her.

Willy sucked in a breath, feeling her knees go wobbly. "That's where you come in," she breathed.

A caustic smile uptilted one corner of his mouth. "Why, thank you, Willy. I'm sure the director will appreciate the little tidbit of action you're throwing our way."

Suddenly Willy knew she couldn't face him anymore. She was too unnerved by his close regard, and she'd lose too much ground. She began to turn away to put some distance between them.

"Wait." His hand reached out and took hold of her arm, a firm but careful grip, and she was acutely aware of what he held back rather than what he showed to the world. The very power and hue of ever-present danger in him caused her to stand still, waiting, her heart hammering with the old unrealistic fear.

With those steely unflinching eyes he searched her face. Then he smiled coolly and said, "You've got a great deal of courage, Willy."

"I only want to help my friend." Her eyes were locked with his, unable to tear away. She felt like a bird in a trap, someone's dinner-to-be. She tried to shake the feeling off, but it held on, just as his eyes held hers in their implacable grip.

There was a curious cold distrust sparking in his eyes and, paradoxically, a solemn interest.

What kind of man was he? Should she trust or fear him?

Silence hung between them, electric and crackling with nameless currents.

Then he seemed to deliberately interrupt the energy flow. "You're an interesting woman," he said.

"I'll take that as a compliment," she mumbled, feeling foolish, on the defensive. Hating the feeling, she turned her head away. But his hand seemed to come out of nowhere, turning her chin so that she faced him again.

Time stopped. The beating of her heart was so loud she knew Hyde must be able to hear it. And then his head was moving down to hers, closer, ever closer and her whole body froze as she realized what was happening, what she'd always been afraid would happen....

Her eyes met his for an eternal moment. She knew she must look shocked or scared; she hated that reaction in herself. He'd be laughing at her in a minute. And yet she swayed inadvertently toward him as if pulled by a magnet.

For an endless time they stood like that on the threshold of his kitchen, smoke-blue eyes locked with green. She could see a kind of wary puzzlement in his eyes. Then he drew back and it was as if she was released from a spell. Automatically she drew in a lungful of air, realizing she'd been holding her breath all that time.

She tried to control a vague panic that prickled up and down her spine. "I... would you take me home...?"

He thought at her calmly, studying her. "Of course, but I thought...." Then he caught himself and shrugged.

"All you men *just think* and you never ask," she lashed out at him.

He shot her a barely tolerant look.

"Well—" she went on as she grabbed her purse "—not all women enjoy that sort of thing, Mr. Vandemeer." Then his hands were on her shoulders and carefully he was turning her face to him.

"You're right," he said slowly, "I did assume too much. I apologize, Willy. Come on, sit down for a minute and catch your breath."

Willy sighed deeply, realizing that he really meant her no harm. Whatever strange currents had flowed between them were gone now, reduced to mere courtesy. It could have been her imagination....

She sat down on the couch, smiling weakly. "I'm sorry, too," she began. "I have someone in Aspen and I—"

"You don't have to explain," he countered coldly. "I'm afraid we men just assume that such devotion went out when you women started wearing the pants."

His bitter statement took several long moments to sink in. Then Willy laughed tightly, her back rigid. "You really got fried in your marriage, didn't you?" The words came tumbling out before she could stop them and the look with which he pinned her was scathing.

Finally, after an agonizing wait, he spoke. "You're really very observant, aren't you, Willy?"

"Yes," she breathed, trying to gather courage around her, "I am at times."

"And I must admit—" he smiled coldly "—that this little game of yours is new to me."

"Game?" she gasped. "You think I'm playing some sort of game because I choose to be loyal to someone? My God." Then, fixing him with stormy eyes she said, "Did it ever occur to you that there are some things in this world that you cannot possibly know about? Did you ever think that maybe, just maybe, people have valid reasons for behaving the way they do?"

He said nothing. His expression might have been mildly curious but she thought not.

"Well, Mr. Hyde Vandemeer," she said finally, "just take my word for it. There are some things even your almighty computers don't know."

And then he looked at her hard, with sharp-edged interest, and Willy smugly felt a wave of satisfaction sweep through her.

He insisted on driving her home and it turned into a scene at the corner of his street.

"I'll get a taxi," she kept saying as she strode purposefully toward M Street.

"For heaven's sake," Hyde protested as he walked helplessly alongside, "I can drive you home without an argument."

"No you can't," she retorted childishly. "And what's more, I want an answer tomorrow as to whether or not the CIA will help me with Andrea. And I mean *me!*"

Hyde ground his teeth. "Not so loud, please, Willy."

"I don't care!"

"Look—" he ran a hand through his dark hair as they stood spatting at the corner "—let me drive you home and we'll hash this out. . . ."

"There's nothing to hash out." Unaccountably, she was delighted with his angry reaction.

Finally a cab stopped, screeching to a halt at the curb so suddenly that Hyde was forced to jump back, swearing under his breath. "Look, Willy," he said as quietly as possible, "we've got to talk some more. You can't possibly understand the dangerous game you'd be playing."

"I've said all I'm going to say, Hyde." She opened the cab door and began to swing herself onto the rear seat. "There's no more talking to be done. Either you help me or I go it alone."

"Willy. . . ."

"Hey, mister," said the driver, "why don't you leave the little lady alone? Besides, I gotta get moving here."

Hyde's face twisted coldly as he shot the man a murderous glance. "I suggest you stay out of this."

"Ya wanna make something of it?"

Hyde leaned over, opened the driver's door as if to grab the driver, but then he shook his head, drew back and put his hand on Willy's door handle. "I'm going to drive you back."

"No you're not." She stared straight ahead, unmoving. Finally, he stood back, jammed his hands in his pockets and once again his expression went blank as if the whole ugly scene had never happened.

At least, Willy mused as the cab pulled away, she'd gotten a rise out of Agent Hyde Vandemeer, and somehow it made the whole nerve-racking evening seem worthwhile.

SEVEN

He'd let it get too personal. He'd never, in all his years of intelligence service, let it get that way before. Who'd ever believe he'd almost nailed a cab driver last night!

Well, it wouldn't happen again. There might be another time, or lots of times, he would work with Miss Wilhelmina Patterson, but from here on out it was strictly professional. Even if—for some remote reason—he took her to bed, it would be for the CIA, his country and God . . . in that order.

Hyde rubbed the shaving cream on his whiskers, tipped his chin back and began to stroke the sharp razor along his throat. Cold green eyes—Myrna had once called them cruel—stared back at him from the mirror. He had that look of a pro, easy, self-confident, dangerous if he wanted it that way. A look of being a chosen one to the detriment of others not so favored, it had been whispered behind his back.

He'd just zipped up his khaki trousers when Myrna appeared in his living room.

"You really ought to lock your door," she observed as she poked her head into his bedroom.

"True." Hyde put his arms into his shirt. "But I can hear footsteps all the way up from the first floor."

"You can?" She smiled, taking in his lightly furred, tanned chest as he began buttoning the shirt.

"Yeah." His eyes came up to meet hers. "You always stop for around five seconds on the second-floor landing."

"I do, do I?" She made a face. "Well maybe if I get this last five pounds off and quit smoking, I'll get it down to under a second."

"You do fine." When Hyde gave a compliment it was a rare occasion, and usually so flatly stated that it went sliding unnoticed past most recipients.

Myrna, however, did not miss that one. "Thought I'd stop in and see how that meeting went with your little skier." She walked back into the living room, glancing around casually. "Mind if I get a cup of coffee?"

"Go ahead," he called.

"Dinner for two," Myrna said under her breath when she saw the dishes stacked in the sink. She fixed her coffee and walked back toward the bedroom. "So?" she said mildly, her dark eyes resting on Hyde as he bent to tie his shoe. "What happened?"

He glanced up at her for a moment, registering somewhere in his subconscious that it was too early for so much makeup. Still, Myrna was a damned fine-looking woman. "Coffee smells good. Think I'll get some, too," he said, shouldering past her into the living room.

Myrna frowned as she sat down on his partially tattered wing chair. "You shouldn't let that stupid cat claw your furniture," she commented.

"I don't mind." Hyde sat opposite her on the sofa, coffee mug in one hand, leafing with the other through the *Post* lying on the table.

"So you think your skier is for real?" asked Myrna lightly.

Hyde uttered a noncommittal sound as he sipped from the mug. Then, "I'm sure she is," he finally responded.

"And she's really been contacted by Andrea Pavlevitch . . . *the* Andrea?"

"Oh yes, no doubt about it."

"Lord. . . . The Russians will be furious if she gets out of their hands."

Hyde glanced up from the paper. "So what?"

"Well—" Myrna smiled "—I mean, it's hard telling what they'll retaliate with."

"They rarely retaliate." He fixed her for a moment with his hard green gaze, and then began scanning the paper once again.

"You going to Uncle with this one?"

"Of course. I'll head out to Langley around ten."

"You know, Hyde," said Myrna softly, the faint trace of her West Virginia mountain accent playing in her voice, "Andrea Pavlevitch might be a plant."

"Umm." He rattled the paper.

"And if she is," went on Myrna, "then maybe all this trouble you're going through is a waste of time."

He didn't reply.

"I could do some checking for you, Hyde. See if Andrea is the type to defect. I'm almost done with my present case anyway...."

"I've already had someone on it, checked out the letter and all that, but thanks anyway."

Myrna watched him for a minute as he scanned the latest headlines on the Mideast, and then said, "Well, if you need help on anything.... How about a lift? I've got my car."

"No. I've got to drop off the BMW near the offices for an oil change anyway. But thanks."

"No problem." Then, "Well, there's an hour before you've got to leave and I'm not due in till eleven."

His head came up slowly again. Myrna sat with her well-modeled legs crossed, the coffee cup empty now and dangling from her fingers lazily. A slight smile sculpted itself on her red glossy lips.

"I just finished dressing," said Hyde lightly.

"I don't care." Her voice was a little husky. "I'll help you back into your clothes afterward...." She was already unbuttoning his shirt.

Myrna had come over to his place before. Once or twice was all, though. He had known, really, when he'd heard her footsteps on the second-floor landing, why she'd come. And even though he was still tired from the emotional turmoil of the previous evening, he would be a fool to turn Myrna down.

She disrobed slowly and languorously before him, aware that she had all the right equipment even if she did constantly battle five pounds. Hyde wondered this time, as he had before, if she always wore that expensive Fredericks-of-Hollywood-style underwear, or if she only put it on for "special" occasions. Anyway, in spite of a mild urge to doze off, he finished undressing and enjoyed the show, reclining on his pillow, his hands behind his head.

Myrna finally came to him, her red lips parted, her full breasts brushing his chest as she leaned over him to kiss his mouth. Her scent filled his head, heavy and feminine, like something he'd smelled in the jungle once in Nam. Jasmine? No....

He took her face in his hands, kissed those moist lips and felt himself grow hard as her heavy breasts pressed into his chest. She stretched out her full length on top of him then, and his hands found her buttocks as she moved sensually to a tune of her own. Her flesh was white and flawless. Myrna would never sun—she took far too much care of herself for that. Once she'd told him that she'd saved a fortune for the "old face-lift routine" when it became necessary, and that other than chocolate sodas, a few cigarettes and spending lots of money on clothes, she had very few vices.

He gently rolled her off him, pinned her to the covers with a leg and sought her mouth with a hard kiss. She liked it that way—a little rough.

Since that first night in the Sudan hotel—the name of which he'd forgotten—he'd slept with Myrna on and off. It had been going on for two years. Of course, he hadn't been the only one.

He recalled now, as his mouth moved along the ivory column of her throat, that he'd been furious when he had first found out that good old Myrna was also sleeping with Joe Thine—his old buddy who was now stationed in New York.

Oh yes, Myrna wasn't about to "be tied down with anyone," as she'd so aptly put it more than once. "Why can't I sleep with whoever I want?" He'd had no answer for that one. Maybe, he thought, as she took the initiative, pushing him onto his back, he ought to introduce her to Sandy. They'd get along fine.

She kissed the corded muscles along his neck and across his collarbone. Her fingers played an enchanting fanciful tune on his flesh. His mind wandered pleasantly—back to Nam, to ivory-skinned women with long satiny flowing hair; bones as delicate as porcelain. And then to Sandy: lovely, inventive Sandy, her face half-hidden by a curtain of straight golden hair.

He did, finally, slip away into that beckoning world of fantasy. And he dozed, probably for only a few seconds.

"Hyde. . . ."

"Umm. . . ."

"I don't believe this." She moved away, onto her back, gazing at the ceiling with its slightly chipped plaster.

Hyde's arm came up across his eyes. He groaned. "I guess I fell asleep." A tenuous laugh escaped him as he felt for her arm with his free hand. "Some lover, aren't I?"

"Oh, the best." She reached toward the bedside table for her ever-present pack of cigarettes. "You must be pretty tired. Up late?"

Quite late, for him. "Not really," he replied mildly, wondering how in hell a man could doze off with a woman equipped like Myrna lying naked by his side.

Myrna finally lit a cigarette and passed it to him.

"I'm trying to quit," he said lazily. "It's been two months and I've smoked maybe half a pack."

"Good for you." She stuck her tongue out. "Me, I like the damn things too much." Then she rolled over onto her side, her breasts pressed together looking like two flattened melons. For long moments the room was filled with only light and silence. "Did you have the Patterson girl for dinner?"

Hyde's head turned slowly on the pillow to face her. "That's right," he replied casually.

Myrna met his steady gaze. "Did she stay. . . long?"

"She didn't spend the night, Myrna, if that's what you're driving at." Although ordinarily Myrna was far too liberated to care what he did or whom he saw, he could hardly blame her for asking under the circumstances.

"I was just wondering," she said easily, her finger tracing a path down the light crisp hairs that ran down his chest in a thin line. "So I assume you two hashed everything out about Andrea Pavlevitch."

"Not exactly." He frowned, remembering.

"Oh? A problem?"

"I'm afraid there may be one."

"And what would that be?"

Hyde's lips curled upward into a teasing smile. "Inquisitive today, aren't we?"

"Well," she said a shade curtly, "I was only curious. After all, a big name like Pavlevitch. . . ."

By the time Hyde had cleaned up and dressed again he had just enough time left to make his ten o'clock appointment with Uncle.

They drove off down M Street in separate cars. Hyde shifted down, pulled the BMW easily into the outside lane and then accelerated through three green lights in a row. He wondered then, as he waited impatiently at the fourth traffic light, why he had really asked Willy to his place for dinner. Had it just been the easiest thing to do, the most private spot he knew to soften her, to win her trust? Or could there have been another reason?

Of course, he hadn't realized at the time he'd asked her that she had a boyfriend back in Aspen. He really should have known. A girl who looked like her would certainly have a number of men on her scent. And too, it was probably a damn good thing she had not reacted to his advance or he would have sacrificed his professionalism for a few minutes in the hay with her. Well, he could thank her, at least, for that. And it certainly wasn't going to happen again.

He was shown right into Uncle's office by his flaxen-haired secretary, the one who had replaced Myrna two years earlier.

"Sit down, Hyde." Uncle—Gary Gibbons, actually—was signing a few papers, his attention focused on the pages. "How did the meeting go?"

"A little differently than I expected, sir."

"Go on."

"The Patterson girl is genuine. I read the letter from her friend, Andrea, and I believe she's the X-Type." He referred to the personality traits of a defector.

"Good."

"I had the Russian girl's letter authenticated yesterday. It's valid, all right. And I got together with the guys at Strategic

Operations. They came up with some ideas, a little sketchy for now. But the Pavlevitch girl will be vulnerable on the circuit so there will be some good chances. One of those S.O. jokers has already tagged it Operation Snowbird."

"Sounds as if things are moving along. Has Miss Patterson been cleared?"

"They're working on it, sir."

"Well, I'm sure there won't be any problem—with her father and all."

"Yes, well, there is one problem. Willy—Miss Patterson—insists on being involved directly in the operation."

"She does?" Gary Gibbons raised a graying brow but continued scanning the pages nevertheless.

"It's going to be a bit tricky. She's a very strong-minded young woman. You know what an amateur can do to an operation."

"Well, why does she want to be in on it in the first place?" He shook his head.

"Number one, sir, Andrea Pavlevitch is terrified of any government. She even asked Miss Patterson in her letter to help her—alone. And secondly—" Hyde's lips turned up at one corner a touch "—Miss Patterson, for all her very feminine aspects, is something of a thrill seeker."

"Is that so . . . ?"

"Yes. You couple that with her friend's plea and the fact that she's got enough guts to run a downhill ski race on the Olympic level—"

"She *did* have enough guts."

"I suspect, sir, that this girl still does."

"Then—" finally Gary Gibbons looked up "—let's use her."

"No."

"Now, Hyde, I understand where you're coming from but for Pete's sake, this is too big a prize to miss out on. If the State Department got hold of Miss Patterson—"

"I know. But it's too dangerous. You should hear her idea of how to get the Pavlevitch girl away. It's what you call a C-Action, sir." To the more witty agents of the company, C stood for crazy.

"It is? Well, let's hear it, Hyde. Perhaps I might be a less-prejudiced judge."

Hyde had heard *that* one before. Oh yes—in South-east Asia—Cambodia. Three years ago. Uncle had wanted this "job" done on a CIA infiltrator and had gone to the limits to have his way.

"Hing Lu Sung is harmless," Uncle had said over the overseas scrambler phone, "so just let him think he's set you up and meet his friends up the river. Of course, they'll feel confident and you can get the drop on the lot of them, Hyde."

"Sung," Hyde had said firmly, "is a true Red. He's not just betraying us for a couple of chocolate bars and some nylons, sir. He and his boys will be waiting up the river to slit our throats."

"Look, Hyde. You've gone this far and we need the information that Sung possesses. Besides, he deserves to have a job done on him. Can't play both sides of the fence forever. Meet him. I'm telling you he's your typical Cambodian. One minute he's a democrat, the next a Red. He's harmless. Trust this less-prejudiced eye."

Well, Uncle had gotten his information and the "job" done on Sung, but Hyde and his partner had damn near bought the whole farm that time. Harmless. Easy enough to say when you're halfway around the world.

Still, what Gary Gibbons wanted, he generally got.

Cautiously Hyde explained to his boss the rough details of Willy's plan.

"Sounds feasible to me," Uncle said predictably.

"What about the danger to the Patterson girl? If one thing were to go wrong. . . ."

"But," said Uncle coolly, "you'll see that it doesn't."

Their eyes met and locked. "No, sir," Hyde said slowly, "it can't work. We'll need our own people."

Gary studied his top agent for a long thoughtful moment. Finally he rose from his seat and came around to the front of the desk, leaning against it with arms folded. "This is the one thing about you, Hyde, that will keep you from going to the top."

Here it comes, thought Hyde impatiently.

"You buck the system. Oh, not all the time, but often enough. You've got to learn to follow orders, Hyde." A thin smile upturned his lips. "We *all* have to follow orders."

Hyde did not reply nor did he nod. He'd heard *that* one before, too. In truth, Gary Gibbons was covering himself. If anything ever went wrong out in the field, Uncle could say to the director, "I was afraid something like this would happen. I've had to reprimand Agent Vandemeer before...." It was all a game they played and Uncle was a consummate player.

"Look," Hyde said finally, "I'm just not going to let this amateur run an operation of this magnitude. Not only is it dangerous, but if she slipped up just once, we'd be sitting in Aspen with egg on our faces, no Russian superstar and maybe even a dead civilian."

"I'll compromise," Uncle said mildly, holding Hyde's gaze. "Lead the Patterson girl on. Let her make contact and set up the arrangements with Pavlevitch. You'd be wise to go that route anyway. Then in the end, simply ace Miss Patterson out of the action if you want. Do whatever you feel comfortable with."

Hyde rubbed a flat-planed, freshly shaved jaw. "I don't know. She *is* a representative's daughter. It makes me nervous as hell to think of the consequences if anything went foul."

"Do you think I'd like to face Representative Patterson...?"

"So I let her contact Andrea with the details and let her think she'll be in on the whole operation...."

"That's right." Uncle smiled tentatively.

"Well, one thing's certain. She'll have to get some training at The Farm."

"The Farm is probably not advisable...."

"Then no compromise."

"But she's a civilian, Hyde."

"Plenty of one-time agents have gone through the program before. A kind of crash training. Just to be on the safe side."

"I never liked it, either."

"And Myrna can go with her. That way, if anyone at The Farm gets too nosy, Myrna can run interference." Good old CIA interdepartmental paranoia, Hyde thought, grimacing inwardly. God forbid if another department found out about the defection before the fact.

"The Farm," repeated Uncle to himself. "Myrna will have to make sure Miss Patterson doesn't see the wrong things out there."

"Myrna can handle it. And I'll be close by, too. We'll give her a few weeks there and then if she should get in a squeeze when she contacts the Russian, she'll be better able to handle herself."

They fell silent for a moment. Both men knew it might work although each felt the other's thinking was not quite on target. Nothing new there.

"You know," said Gary finally, "I could, one of these days, quit arguing with you and get one of the other agents instead. One that follows directives. . . ."

"But you can't on this one, sir," objected Hyde quietly.

"Oh?" A raised brow.

"Who else skis around this place?"

Willy was just bending over to tie the laces on her running shoes when the phone rang. "I'll get it," she called to her mother. "Hello?"

"Miss Wilhelmina Patterson?" came a deep indolent male voice.

"Yes. Who . . . ?" But she knew, of course.

"Hyde." Abrupt, as if he didn't want anyone on the line to know who he was. Paranoid.

"Oh! Agent Vandemeer," said Willy sweetly—and clearly. "I was just going out for a run before it gets too hot. Is this going to take long?" There, she thought, it was easy when he wasn't standing face-to-face with her.

"I have some details to discuss with you. When can we meet?" His tone was matter-of-fact, emotionless.

Her heart began to beat a little more rapidly; they'd decided to help her! Childishly, she felt as if she'd just won round number one. "Well, since you've exhausted your culinary talents, perhaps we might meet someplace more neutral this time?" suggested Willy, knowing she was being unnecessarily nasty but finding it difficult to stop now that she had a slight edge.

There was a moment of silence on the line then. "Can you drive up to Rock Creek Park and meet me? We can go for a run together and talk."

"Rock Creek's all the way across town . . ." began Willy. "Well, okay, but I'm doing five miles today. Think you can keep up?"

"I can certainly try, Willy," said Hyde, and she could have sworn there was a hint of ironic humor in his voice this time. Was he making fun of her? Was it because of the night before? What did he really think she'd been upset about? She wouldn't give him the satisfaction of reacting like that again. She had the upper hand now and she was going to keep it.

"Fine then. Say in an hour? At the main entrance, on the left. There's a parking lot there, right?"

"Yes. In an hour. Be on time."

"I'm *always* on time, Agent Vandemeer," Willy replied coldly and hung up.

Well, of all the arrogant, conceited . . . ! Ordering her around—go there, come here, meet me, be on time! Who did he think he was—her father? Her *husband*, for heaven's sake? It was too bad she'd have to work with Hyde Vandemeer and not some nice easy-going sort of guy. She did need his help and she was stupid to antagonize him. But she couldn't help it. He just made her grit her teeth with annoyance. That cool emotionless facade, as if there were no feelings behind that handsome face, those clear emerald-green eyes, that wide, thin-lipped mouth.

Willy wondered suddenly what Hyde Vandemeer really did feel. What went on behind that standoffish facade? She knew about his ex-wife. That must be part of it, but she wondered what really had created Hyde Vandemeer's icy severity. Curiosity swept her. He was so closed, like a carefully carved, lovingly polished door that was forever locked so that nobody would ever know what went on behind it.

"Can I use the station wagon, mother?" called Willy, running up the stairs two at a time, opening the door to her mother's bedroom. "I'll be back in a couple of hours."

"What for, dear? I have a hair appointment at three."

"Oh, I'll be back before then. I've got to meet Hyde Vandemeer at Rock Creek Park."

"Like *that?*" Rachel gestured to Willy's blue nylon running shorts and white T-shirt.

Willy looked down at herself. "Sure. We're going for a run."

"In *my* day, ladies dressed," said Rachel. "Girdles, dresses, gloves, stockings, hats."

"Yes, mother, but you didn't run, did you?"

"No, dear, I certainly did not."

"The keys?"

"Be back before three—" warned Rachel, rummaging through her purse for the keys "—and watch that agent of yours. He's too smooth for his own good."

"That much I've already figured out," Willy said over her shoulder as she left Rachel's room. "I'll take Linda, okay?"

She was standing outside of the car in the parking lot five minutes early, doing a quick stretching routine when the now-familiar blue BMW drove up.

"I was ready to start without you," she said dryly. "Figured you could catch up."

"Thanks for waiting." He stepped out of his car, wearing shorts and an old T-shirt, army or something, faded olive drab.

"Who's this?" he asked, motioning toward the tongue-lolling Linda.

"That's Linda, remember? She likes to run, too. Do you mind?"

"No, not at all."

Willy could not help but notice the lean tapered muscles in his arms, the broad shoulders pulling the faded fabric taut. She tried not to look, but it was all on display in front of her eyes and she felt slightly self-conscious. Hyde didn't seem to notice her bare legs, though, or her slim tanned arms, or her heavy blond hair up in a ponytail. He was all business.

"Which way do you want to go?" he asked politely as he straightened from checking his shoelaces.

"Oh, you know the place better than I do. Pick a trail."

He pointed, the sinews of his arm pulling and stretching under smooth firm skin. "That path is a good one. Goes by the old reservoir. It's about five miles around."

They started out, warming up slowly, getting the feel of each other's pace. Hyde ran along steadily to one side of her, his long, well-muscled legs catching the dappled sunlight through the trees. Linda trotted at Willy's heels, her collar chain rattling, her pink tongue dripping.

"Well-behaved dog," commented Hyde, and Willy caught herself glancing at Hyde's strong throat above the drab T-shirt.

"Linda is my dad's pet. He sent her to obedience school." They passed a few huge shade trees and a pond. Linda checked out the ducks on the pond, casting a beseeching glance at Willy. "Heel, Linda," Willy commanded sternly, patting her leg.

"Am I going too fast for you?" asked Hyde.

"Not at all," replied Willy coolly. Then, "I didn't expect the CIA to come to a decision so quickly."

"In this business," he said soberly, "too much red tape can be very costly." Then his glance met hers for a moment. "The letter was verified. The case is going to the interagency committee where it will be reviewed."

"Reviewed for what?"

"Your friend has no established bona fides yet." He caught Willy's puzzled look. "Is she really a defector or a double agent? I told you—"

"How long before she's proven okay?"

He shrugged and continued to run steadily alongside her for several minutes. He had a good strong stride; in fact, she had to push herself to keep up although she'd never let him suspect.

"Then what happens?" pressed Willy as they crested a hill. She could feel sweat beading between her breasts, on her forehead and above her upper lip. The humidity in the East!

"If she turns out to be okay, we start planning."

"I've got the plan already. . . ."

"There's more than just the snatch, if you will. There's a safe house, debriefing, a resettlement team, her case officer, identity papers, a job. It's quite complicated."

Linda darted after a squirrel, unable to contain herself.

"Heel!" yelled Willy as the squirrel scolded the dog from a safe branch.

Abruptly Hyde laughed. It was as if he had at last been let loose from a kind of captivity and was flying free. It was a complete laugh, as young as a school-boy's and just as infectious. It made him look younger, more carefree. His eyes crinkled; his teeth were even and strong and white. A dimple appeared in the flat plane of his cheek.

The metamorphosis gripped Willy with bewilderment. She thought she'd known what kind of man he was—cold, hard, and a viewer of everything from a safe discreet distance. He had turned into a human being who laughed, went for runs in the park, and was polite and pleasant to her own sharpness. Her determination to keep him at a distance, to dislike him, began to dissolve.

"You like dogs?" she asked finally.

"Sure. Love 'em. But it'd be cruel to keep one in my place. Old Tomcat will have to do." His voice was matter-of-fact, pleasant; he turned to look at her with a congenial smile on his thin-lipped mouth.

Willy found herself staring at that mouth as if memorizing the austere curves of it, the way his white teeth glistened in the sunlight. She caught his gaze on her, noncommittal, a touch curious, and she averted her eyes swiftly, staring straight ahead at the path, her heart pounding just a little too quickly for their pace.

They ran on two miles or so. Willy could feel the perspiration rolling down her temples. She raised an arm and brushed it away. From the corner of her eye she could see the sweat beading Hyde's forehead and dampening his shirt in a long line at the back.

"What happens next? I mean, where do I fit in?" breathed Willy. "My plan." She felt the need to discuss something neutral.

"You'll have to contact her, probably in Europe somewhere. We'll get the World Cup race schedule. It may be tricky. Everything will have to be relayed in that one, presumably brief, meeting."

Willy was silent, pushing up a slight grade, puffing a little. Hyde came up right behind her.

"Mind if I take my shirt off?" he asked. "I'm sweltering."

"So am I. Damn," said Willy. "Go ahead." Carefully, she kept her eyes straight ahead.

He dragged the T-shirt over his head in that funny way men have of pulling their shirts off inside out with both hands. Women never did it that way, Willy reflected idly. He tucked it in his waistband and kept running. Perspiration sliced his skin, making his smooth muscular chest shiny.

The hard ridges of his stomach continued to work, and his muscular arms pumped easily. He had a patch of curling hair on his chest that thinned in a vertical descent to his navel. Willy tried to keep her gaze off him but, still, she could see every bit of his body; the sinews in his neck straining, the bulge of shoulder muscles, the contraction of long lean thigh muscles. It was, she thought for a second, as if he was deliberately trying to disconcert her. But, no, he couldn't possibly suspect how she felt....

They were running by the reservoir now, a teardrop-shaped body of water, its shores lined with maple trees. It was very green, rolling and bursting with vegetation.

"I'm not used to all the green," said Willy. "Aspen is pretty dry. We're so close to the desert. And by mid-October it's all brown anyway."

"I've never been there. I skied at Sun Valley once when I was in college, but never went anywhere else out West."

"Aspen has wonderful skiing, that's for sure. Whatever they say about the old place, the skiing never changes."

Silence. They ran along side by side in cautious companionship. Willy could feel her heart pounding steadily, comfortably. Running always put her in a good mood. She could even stand Agent Vandemeer's presence; they could be two ordinary people, anywhere, out for a weekend run.

"You have an art gallery in Aspen," he said eventually, his green eyes turned on her.

"Yes. Well, you already know all that. Linda! Heel!" The dog came trotting back, wispy tail wagging, tongue hanging.

"Can you leave it for about a month?"

She turned to stare at him in confusion. "What for? The trip to Europe?"

"No. Not that. At least, not yet."

Willy frowned. "Don't be so damned secretive. What are you driving at?"

He shook his dark head, drops of moisture shooting off his hair like so many diamonds in the dappled sunlight. "I don't think you're going to like this," he said pensively.

"Like *what?*"

They were running down a long hill on the other side of the reservoir. Linda finally began lagging behind.

"You couldn't possibly do it anyway."

"*What?*" Irritation tinged her voice.

"Well, you see, Willy... anyone who works with us has to undergo some sort of training. Demolitions, self-defense, locks and picks, stuff like that. It's very physical, too. Hard stuff."

"So? Why can't I do it?"

"For one thing, it would take up an entire month of your very valuable time. Without reimbursement, I might add. And it's hard—long, tedious and hard."

Willy felt anger well up in her. Why was he discounting her abilities before she'd even tried? Damn, he was aggravating! "I certainly can take the time if I have to do it to help Andrea. I don't think you understand how determined I am to go through with this, Hyde."

"Oh, I can tell you're determined, but you haven't seen The Farm yet."

"The Farm?"

"Our training camp. Camp Peary, actually. All agents go through training there. Some go on to much more involved training. Yours would be a very abbreviated course, but still tough."

"Where is this place?"

"Virginia."

"Virginia is a big state. Can't you be more specific?"

"Sorry."

"When do I get to go?"

"I don't know that you do."

Willy stopped suddenly, faced him, hands on hips, chest heaving with anger and breathlessness. "I will go! I'm in good physical shape and I'm not stupid. What else do I need?"

He had stopped also, eyeing her with calm tolerant approval. His chest glistened with sweat, rising and falling easily with each breath. They stood terribly close together. She could see the tiny dots of whiskers on his cheeks, the way his green eyes held her gaze.

"I figured you'd laugh at it. Refuse to go."

She shrugged her shoulders, whistled to Linda and began jogging again. "I'll play along with your crazy routine if I have to. It's for Andrea. And it might even prove interesting."

"You'll be totally incommunicado there. No phone calls, no letters, no breaks except for an emergency. It'll be tough. Do you think you can take it?"

"Of course I can *take* it!" snapped Willy, turning to glare at him.

But he was looking straight ahead, his strong profile unreadable, his arms pumping rhythmically, as if he was totally unconcerned, as if they'd never even discussed the matter.

"When do I go?" she asked again.

"I'll be in touch," he said coolly. "Go home and get your things in order."

"How long do I have?"

"A week or two. Maybe three."

"Can you be a little more specific?"

"No."

They were coming back to the parking lot. Willy stopped, put her hands on her hips and drew in a few deep lungfuls of air to slow her breathing.

"Good run," remarked Hyde. "Thanks."

"Sure, anytime." She could not bury the tinge of sarcasm.

"You'll get a plane ticket in the mail, and a schedule, directions and all." He bent down to ruffle Linda's ears.

"Very mysterious," scoffed Willy.

"Very necessary, Miss Patterson," he said, suddenly cold and formal again. "This information goes no further than right here, you understand? And you'll need a cover story, so your friends and your parents won't ask questions."

"I understand perfectly," Willy said as she stood over him, watching as Linda nuzzled her runny nose onto his knees. "I don't think it's necessary though. I'm in awfully good shape."

Hyde turned his head up toward hers; his crystalline eyes squinted in the sun. "Oh, it's necessary all right. You never know when something can go wrong and you're in a tight spot."

"What on earth could happen to *me*?" asked Willy unconvinced.

"Well, for example, after your switch with Andrea. What happens if one of the KGB men waiting for Andrea panics when she doesn't show up, and pulls a gun? There are innocent bystanders all around, you're in the line of fire—"

"They'd never dare!"

"You want to bank your life on that?" he asked tolerantly. "Or, then again, they might hold you hostage. It's a ticklish situation. You'd be open to a lot of exposure; that is, if you decide to go through with it."

"I'm going through with it," she said tightly.

"I'm sure you intend to. We have to protect ourselves, too. What kind of press do you think we'd get if anything happened to you during the defection?"

For some inexplicable reason, his statement struck an overpowering chord in her. She longed to ask how *he* would feel, yet she failed to understand why the question would have formed in her mind.

"So you can understand why we want you to undergo a little training," he was saying.

"I suppose," she replied, still mulling over his words.

She stood holding on to Linda's collar, watching as Hyde climbed into his car. He'd pulled his old faded shirt over his head, hiding the splendid, gleaming chest and shoulders. He rested one hand on the steering wheel, gave her a casual wave with the other, pulled out and was gone. And the curious question still revolved in her mind, around and around, like a broken record: How would Agent Hyde Vandemeer feel if anything *did* happen to her?

EIGHT

Willy tapped her foot in time to the music, something raw and wildly sultry by Donna Summers. Reeves squeezed her hand and smiled as he tried to be heard over the music's loud din. Then he shrugged.

Willy laughed. "I can't hear you!" she half yelled in his ear before giving up.

Then they were dancing—Reeves was an excellent, well-coordinated partner—in the blinking strobe lights, and the upstairs disco at Andre's took on the atmosphere of a mad charade. Everything was distorted in stop-motion: the antique-brick walls pulsed, the stained glass seemed to swell and quake, ready to explode, the ferns hanging over the long polished bar grew as if in a time-lapse motion picture.

Willy breathed in the smoke-laden air, twisting and spinning to the lead of Reeves's singular dance style, which was something between late '40s jitterbug and the mashed potatoes of the '60s. Crazy!

Finally there was a break in the music. "Quick," teased Willy, holding Reeves's hand, "let's talk before it starts again!"

Reeves laughed, giving her a big kiss on the cheek as he led her off the dance floor. "You wanna go downstairs where we can talk?"

"Lord, yes! I thought you'd *never* ask!" She took her pigskin jacket off the back of the bar stool and left her half-finished drink.

On the main floor of Andre's, they found a quiet table next to the front window, which overlooked Galena Street and a corner of the mall. The town seemed packed for mid-October—off-season. Of course, it *was* Saturday night and it simply wouldn't do to stay home with a good book. Not in Aspen.

A heavy wet snow was tumbling out of the night sky, but it melted as soon as it settled on something. It was a beautiful autumn night in the quaint mountain town. The iridescent halos of the antique streetlamps reflected warmly on the passersby, the blue-and-white striped awnings across the street from Andre's gleamed wetly in the town's glow, and couples walked the streets arm in arm, laughing, turning their red-cheeked faces up to the sky and reveling in the season's first real snow—even though by noon Sunday it would be gone. Too early yet to stick except in the high country.

"I can't believe the ski season's almost here again," said Reeves as he sipped on his bottled beer. "We've got three more weeks at least before the roof's on that Red Mountain house."

"The owners must adore you guys," put in Willy.

"Oh yeah. Typical. It rained most of August and they expect us to finish ahead of time. Actually—" Reeves's dark eyes smiled "—I'll be glad to get back on the old skis this year."

"I'm looking forward to it, too." Willy took a drink of her rum and Coke. "I wish I didn't have to go away tomorrow...."

"So do I," said Reeves thoughtfully. "And for the life of me, I can't figure out how you got talked into it in the first place."

"Oh, that was easy." She sighed wistfully as she spun the ice around and around in her glass. "I think Hyde Vandemeer could talk anyone into anything."

"Yeah, but you're no pushover, Willy."

"I was for him." Quickly she looked up from her glass, realizing what she'd implied. "I didn't mean it *that* way, Reeves," she explained. "I meant about my going away and all...."

"You sure?" He held her gaze steadfastly.

"Of course I'm sure, Reeves. You think I don't know who I...well, you know..." Her voice dropped to a whisper. "I mean, it's not as if I fall into bed with every guy...."

Reeves put his hand over hers on the table top. "I know you don't. I'm sorry, Willy. Of all the girls I've known in my days you're the . . . strangest when it comes to . . . well, you know, sleeping arrangements."

Willy's gaze fell away to a spot over his shoulder. She could feel heat rising in her cheeks. "I know I'm not...into that sort of thing as much as some—"

"That's an understatement," Reeves threw out before he could stop himself.

Willy felt tears press behind her eyelids. "I'm sorry."

He let out a long sigh. "Nice guy, aren't I? Willy—" he squeezed her hand harder "—I didn't mean that. You're the sweetest girl I know."

"Thanks." Soulfully.

"You know what I mean, babe. You're worth ten of any of these other chicks around here and you know it."

"Sure I am."

"Well, you are. And if you must know, I'm mad as hell that you're leaving and you won't even tell me exactly where or how I can get in touch with you or anything. I think this guy has you wrapped around his little finger, babe!"

Willy pulled her hand away and took another long drink from her glass. Reeves was wrong, but not *that* far wrong. "I'm mad I have to to go, too. It's not only a bad time of year to be leaving the shop but I've had to double Gayle's salary to get her to watch the store, and even though I've painted my heart out these last few weeks I'll never be caught up for the season." She sighed. "I wish I could tell you everything, give you a phone number...."

"You can. Unless, of course," he said bitterly, "this Vandemeer guy means more to you that I do."

"That's not fair and you know it."

Silently he sat back in his wooden chair, folded his arms and watched her intently.

"Come on, Reeves," she tried again. "Lighten up on me. I can't stand the man."

"Oh sure."

"Well I can't!" Then quickly she looked around, embarrassed. "He's a cold SOB and has about as much charm as a king cobra."

"Yep."

"I'm not kidding. He's your typical male macho pig, if you'll pardon my saying so." She studied Reeves for a long moment but thought about Hyde's warnings and his hush-hush attitude. Big deal. Why should she stay silent about where she was headed? To hell with the CIA anyway! "The place I'm going is Camp Peary. It's called The Farm." She saw Reeves's dark brows lift in interest. "Silly, isn't it? But that's what they call it. It's somewhere in Virginia but I'm not sure where, and he made it real plain that communication with the outside world would be very censored and infrequent. I'm even supposed to give everyone a cover story about going to an art school in Virginia."

"I've heard of Camp Peary," Reeves reflected. "It's like the army's boot camp."

"A little, I guess."

"So why you, Willy?"

"Just in case. He's afraid that if I get into any trouble when I contact Andrea—"

"Trouble? So he's protecting you, is that it?"

"No. And quit sounding so jealous. What he's doing is protecting his precious operation. Not me, for Pete's sake."

"Sure."

She shrugged, ignoring his sarcasm. "He said that any number of things could go wrong when I see Andrea face-to-face."

"Like the KGB snatching you?"

"I don't know. But you needn't be so caustic, Reeves. If we're to help Andrea then it's just got to be this way."

Finally Reeves leaned forward over the table and took both her hands in his. "I don't want to lose you," he whispered fervently. "Don't go, Willy. This guy is after more than your friend."

Willy felt breathless, confused, torn. "Reeves, I—"

"Don't go!"

Willy shook her head. "I don't know what to do, Reeves. I have to help Andrea. . . ."

"We'll do it alone, babe, just you and me."

Again she shook her head. "No. We can't. Don't you see? Once we got Andrea where would we go with her? If we don't cooperate now then they'll simply turn her away."

"They'd never do that. Don't be naive. He's got you totally convinced."

She pulled her hands away. "No one, Reeves, *no one*, tells me what to do or how to think. I just know that the government is involved now and that's the way it's going to stay. *I'll* help Andrea escape. *I'll* make sure nothing goes wrong, and *I'll* be there when the good old CIA gets done grilling her afterward!" She took a deep breath. "And if they want me to play their little game at their top-secret farm and if they want to follow me around or tap my phone or anything at all, I'll go along with it because in the end, Reeves, it will be *me* skiing down off that hill because there's no one else who can imitate Andrea on that downhill course except me! *No one!*"

Reeves whistled through his teeth. "I get the message."

"All right, then. Tomorrow I get on that plane and do whatever I have to. If you can't wait—"

"Let's get out of here," Reeves said suddenly, standing. He threw a couple of bills on the table for the cocktail waitress, and then helped Willy on with her jacket. Several heads turned as they made their way through the tables and Willy knew she'd been talking too loudly and had caused a scene. People must think she was a crazy lady. Still, she honest-to-goodness didn't care.

It was raw outside. The wet heavy snow struck her face. She shoved her hands in her pockets and bowed her head against the huge wet flakes.

"You want my hat?" Reeves automatically took off his Coors baseball cap and plunked it on her head.

"Thanks," she mumbled.

"No problem. Where to?"

"My place."

"You sure? I mean. . . ."

She knew exactly what he meant. She'd been home for over three weeks and hadn't once slept with him. Well, she thought, all that would change tonight.

"Yes, I'm sure," she stated flatly.

They trudged down Galena Street, through the Hyman Street Mall and onto Hopkins. As they left the mall area, it grew darker. The streets were wet and slushy. Willy walked quickly, her long lean legs keeping pace with Reeves's stride. He took her arm in his.

"Are we fighting?" he asked.

"No. But I'm mad."

"At me?"

"Not really. I'm more angry at that jerk in Washington."

"Listen," Reeves said gently. "I'm sorry about what I said earlier. I know you wouldn't go to Washington for a week and... hop into bed with someone."

"You're right," said Willy coolly. "I wouldn't." And then she thought about how little men knew of women—how just plain stupid they could be sometimes. She'd been seeing Reeves Baxter for over a year now; had slept with him on occasion and he never even suspected her lack of fulfillment. He didn't even notice.

Lord, she recalled, even Mr. Know-it-all in D.C. had failed to recognize her for what she was and had tried to kiss her. Now, *he* was one guy a girl could never fool, one would think. Her practiced facade of normality must be good, then.

And suddenly Willy realized that she'd been damn lucky he'd tried no more than he had. She'd have been terrified. And he would have known, or at least suspected. And if anyone *ever* found out, other than her mother... well, she'd die of mortification.

Reeves pushed open her door and smiled. "Ladies first," he gestured with a hand.

The stream of light from the outdoor lamp fell on her face as Willy met his eyes. She could love Reeves. If she'd just let herself, she could love him. What did sexual fulfillment mean anyway? It was all in books. People made such a big deal out of it—too big a deal. Even Gayle had once complained about her ex-husband. Willy had been all ears.

"Jack was about as exciting in bed as a wet mop." Gayle had laughed. "And to think, Willy, he used to wonder why I never enjoyed it!"

So not all women fell panting into bed every minute of every day.

"Mind if I get a beer?" asked Reeves.

"Go ahead. And bring me one, too." She ignored his raised brow. "Should I stoke up the potbelly?"

"Yeah. Your flight doesn't leave until eight forty-five. We've got all night to freeze in this place."

"You know—" Willy laughed "—I've been meaning to have the furnace fixed since '82...."

"Yeah, well, not all of us are born-and-raised mountain goats, babe." He handed her a can of Coors and plunked himself down onto her couch. "I mean, some of us like indoor heat."

Willy made a silly face at him, tossed a split log into the stove and kicked closed the iron door with her boot. "Thar ya go, pardner," she mimicked. "Suit ya all right?"

"That's my gal." He patted the place next to him.

She tossed his baseball cap aside and stretched out on her back with her chin tilted upward in his lap. "Kiss me," she said, feeling her heart hammer several times in her chest.

As Reeves's head descended to hers she gripped the beer can whitely in her hand. Did she know what she was doing? Could she see it to its natural conclusion this time?

Willy's lips parted beneath his and she felt guilt sweep her, knowing he could sense her tension. She tried to relax, willing herself to lie there feeling his mouth on hers, searching softly. *It feels wonderful,* she told herself. *I love it when Reeves kisses me....*

Then his hand was on her turtleneck sweater just to the side of her breast. She felt herself go rigid but once again willed herself to relax. It worked.

It wasn't really unpleasant. And she trusted Reeves totally. If she said "no, I can't tonight," he'd stop.

She did not say no.

The wood in the potbelly stove hissed and crackled. The beer was forgotten, their cans placed on the floor next to the couch. Reeves reached over and turned out the lamp so that only the light spilling in from the kitchen illuminated them obscurely.

He helped her out of her sweater, then unfastened the beige bra and dropped it to the floor along with the boots and sweater. Her jeans came next, shrugged off to join the rest of her clothes in a careless heap. His work-roughened hands stroked the soft flesh of her sides and hips, and Willy forced herself to remain pliable beneath his caresses. He kissed her on the mouth, along the long sleek column of her neck, and lower, along the fine collarbone and the hollows beneath. And still lower, to the soft feminine swell of her breasts.

She always froze inside then. Always.

This time, however, she didn't, and she conjured up a silent prayer of thanks. She'd made it through this time....

She was mistaken. Later, alone in her bed that night, she guessed she should have had more to drink at Andre's and finished her beer downstairs.... The alcohol always helped her relax.

It had happened when Reeves had pulled off his own clothes and lain back down beside her. She just couldn't. Not that time.

He'd been sulky—she didn't blame him—as he'd tugged back on his jeans and buttoned his plaid shirt unevenly.

"You know," he'd said in a low husky voice, "we've got to talk this out sometime, Willy. I can't keep giving in like this."

And she'd been a little frightened. If he couldn't keep giving in, then what? Would he try to force her?

She'd never, ever, let a man do that to her. Not again.

She did not get much sleep that night, and when her alarm clock sounded at six she was already wide awake.

She packed her clothes—two sets, as weather could be very changeable back East in the autumn. What did one wear on The Farm anyway? She put in a few sketch pads and pencils, just in case.

At seven-thirty, fifteen minutes before Reeves was supposed to arrive, Gayle stopped by.

"You're up early on a Sunday," Willy said.

Gayle poured herself a coffee. "I know. The boys have football practice today and I had to get up anyway."

"Listen," said Willy sincerely, "I really appreciate everything you're doing."

"You're paying me, Willy," teased Gayle, "handsomely."

Willy smiled. She hated having to lie to Gayle but Hyde had told her to give everyone a cover story, so she had tried to. Not a very good one, she was afraid. She'd told Gayle she was going to an art seminar in Virginia—one that her mother had told her about. It was very intense, she explained, and "back to nature" so no one was supposed to receive calls or letters for a month. She'd told her mother a similar story and said that she'd check with her when the seminar was over. Rachel had questioned the veracity of this strange explanation, but didn't press the matter.

"You've got my mother's address and phone number to leave messages?"

"At the gallery. Can I water the plants? Feed the cat?"

"No, but thanks. Reeves and a neighbor are doing all that. Just don't forget the mail and don't be afraid to make decisions at the shop. Right or wrong, I'll back you up."

"Okay." Gayle put her coffee mug in the kitchen sink and shoved her hands into her down vest pockets. "Well. See you in a few weeks...."

Willy smiled. "Come here."

They hugged. Gayle's eyes grew moist. "I'm so silly. It's just that I'm going to miss you."

"Me too." Willy's heart swelled with warmth toward her very good friend.

"Well, whatever it is that you're doing, Willy, I know you'll get a lot out of it."

"Let's hope so!" Willy forced a laugh.

"Hi!" came Reeves's voice from the living room. "Where is everyone?"

"Just saying goodbye," called Willy from the kitchen.

"Take care." Gayle gave Willy's hand a last tight squeeze.

When she was gone, Reeves picked up Willy's suitcase, took it outside and put it into the back of his Datsun pickup. "You all ready?" He stood in her doorway, arms folded.

Willy glanced around. "Yes, I guess so." Then, "You might think I was going to the moon...." She gave a short tense laugh.

They drove to the Aspen airport, some four miles from town, in silence. Willy kept looking out the window as if she was seeing things for the last time.

Lord, I'm being melodramatic, she told herself.

Reeves parked right in front of Rocky Mountain Airways in spite of the tow-away signs. This was still Aspen, after all . . . a small town at heart.

She checked in, and then walked to the vending machines with Reeves so he could get a cup of coffee.

"Damn thing works!" he said as the paper cup popped out and coffee began to fill it in a dark stream.

They sat by the window facing the runway. The Snowmass ski area loomed behind the ridge to the south; they could just see the tip of the area, snow capped already.

"I feel as if I'm leaving forever," she mused aloud, picking at a piece of lint on her wool skirt.

"Now where's that Patterson spirit?" chided Reeves.

"Gone but not forgotten." She smiled faintly.

"I'll try to phone you, but I'm betting I'll never get through."

"You're right about that. Hyde said. . ." but her voice trailed away softly.

It was almost boarding time. Willy glanced at her watch nervously. "I feel as if I'm leaving for combat or something."

Reeves did not smile. He finished his coffee and made a basketball shot into a trash can with the squashed cup. "There's something I've got to tell you, babe," he began quietly.

Willy looked at him, puzzled. "You sound as if it's the end of the world. . . ."

He smiled tentatively. "Nothing so simple. Look—" he paused, taking a deep breath "—while you're gone I'd like to . . . well, maybe take someone out. . . ."

Willy went stiff all over. She was frozen in her seat. "Any 'someone' in particular?" With all the inner strength she possessed, she tried to smile.

Reeves did not meet her gaze. "Sue Lerner."

"Oh. . . ." Sue. Tall, dark complected, absolutely gorgeous. Lots of money. "Well then, see her, Reeves." What else could she say? After all, Willy thought darkly, she had no claim on Reeves. Never had one. Hadn't they, a hundred times, talked about giving one another space to breathe? "Listen—" she rose coolly "—I've got to go now. My plane. . . ."

"I know." He smiled weakly. "Look . . . I'm sorry. It's really stupid but she's been bugging me to take her up hunting and it's no big deal anyway. Can you understand?"

Oh sure, thought Willy. "Sure," she said, "I understand completely."

"You're not mad?"

"No. We've always said we could do what we wanted, haven't we?"

"Yeah."

Reeves kissed her at the door to the runway. Her lips were like ice beneath his. Her eyes burned painfully in their sockets.

"Take good care, Willy," he said, his hands still gripping her arms.

"I will." She began to turn away.

"Willy. . . ." He stopped her abruptly. "I *do* love you, babe. You know that. But. . . ."

One hot tear found its way over her bottom eyelid. "But what?"

"But you've got to get over this...this reluctance of yours, well, you know. . . ."

"Say it." Pain welled in her chest.

"About sleeping together. It's weird, babe."

"Goodbye, Reeves," she breathed. "I'll write."

He frowned, and then shrugged. "Have a safe trip. And Willy, I'm sorry."

"So am I." From the steps of the plane she turned to look at him one last time.

It wasn't fair. Maybe she didn't get butterflies in her stomach every time he touched her, but damn it all, she did love him in her own way.

She stepped onto the plane, pulled her sunglasses down over her eyes and let the tears come.

NINE

Camp Peary, Virginia—The Farm—consisted of four hundred eighty heavily wooded acres in the south-eastern part of the state. On its grounds were weapons ranges, jump towers, the simulated border of a mythical communist country and several heavily guarded off-limit areas, which Willy never even approached. There were barracks, offices, classrooms and an officers' club grouped around a central point—very tidy, very dull, very military.

Willy was given a room of her own—Spartan and neat and cold—and she wondered whether it was a privilege or whether they wanted her isolated. Then she was directed to an office where she was given a polygraph test. Luckily she wasn't expecting it or she would have been a nervous wreck; as it was, she answered the questions easily. She had, after all, no secrets. The only tough moment came when the poker-faced operator asked, "Do you sleep with someone on a regular basis?" She answered yes and prayed it was acceptable.

"Okay, you're done."

"Did I pass?"

"I have to analyze the test."

"Why did I have to take it? Am I suspected of something?"

"Every new agent has to take the test," replied the operator without inflection.

Agent? thought Willy, stunned for a moment. Was *that* what he thought she was? Good Lord!

The first evening she met the other trainees in the cafeteria. They were an odd lot, mostly college graduates, midwestern ones, predominantly male. A few foreigners were there but they seemed to stick together; they were mostly from Eastern bloc countries, although there were two young men from Cuba.

A couple of pretty young college girls showed up, very serious and self-important, and an older woman—short and dark and attractive, quite self-possessed. Willy guessed her age at thirty-five. Her clothes were completely wrong for The Farm: a lavender velour warm-up suit that was at the same time too casual and too dressy, besides which the color made her dark complexion sallow and faded.

The woman sat down next to Willy at the Formica-topped cafeteria table and smiled. "I'm Myrna Carlson. Glad to meet you." She held out a small dainty hand. A large diamond cocktail ring glinted on her right pinkie. A gold Rolex watch and two heavy gold necklaces completed her wardrobe.

Willy took her hand and shook it. "Willy Patterson."

"You're new," Myrna said. "I'm on a refresher course. Once a year."

"Oh," said Willy, picking at her mashed potatoes. "So you already work for the CIA?"

"Yes, I'm what's known as a field operative." Myrna had a faint but distinct accent. It was in her vowels or something. Willy tried to place it—not quite southern, not western. Hillbilly, that was it. Studiously disguised but still there. It did not at all fit with her clothes.

"Hyde told me to look you up."

"Hyde?" Willy turned a surprised face toward Myrna.

"Hyde and I go back a long way. We often work together. We may well work together on Operation Snowbird."

"Operation Snowbird?" Willy felt as if she had been left out of a very important decision or two.

"That's the name they've given it; the defection of your friend."

"Oh, I see. Operation Snowbird," Willy mused. "Very cute." Somehow she resented Myrna's polite but vaguely condescending attitude, as if Willy was to be kidded along. And she didn't like the way Myrna had smugly just happened to throw in that she and Hyde "went back a long way." What exactly did *that* mean?

"Look," Willy said, "if Hyde sent you up here to baby-sit me, please don't trouble yourself. I'm quite capable of taking care of myself."

"Of course he didn't," replied Myrna, acting as if she was surprised. "I told you—all operatives have to come here every year."

But Willy didn't believe her protestation of innocence. It was too coincidental. What was Hyde up to? Didn't he trust her? Or was this some new quirk: take good care of the representative's daughter and the House will vote higher appropriations for the CIA. It bothered Willy. She wanted to prove herself on her own. Challenge was always important to her, and she couldn't bear the idea of being mollycoddled.

After dinner there was a little welcoming speech by the head of the trainees, a heavy-browed sergeant type in an expensive suit—in itself an odd combination. Then schedules were passed out.

Sundays off.

The rest was work, from 7:00 a.m. to 7:00 p.m. Exercises, forced marches, classes, lectures, field practice, tests. There was training in light weapons, explosives and demolition, locks and picks. Hwarang-do and self-defense, foreign-intelligence systems, intelligence analysis, and Russian was offered on Sundays to those so desiring it.

"Hwarang-do," muttered Willy under her breath.

"It can always come in handy," whispered Myrna next to her.

"Good Lord," breathed Willy. It was all like one of those crazy Saturday-morning cartoons the kids watched. How had she ever let Hyde bulldoze her into this?

"It's for your own protection," he'd said calmly that day in Rock Creek Park, and the image of his hard lean body shining with sweat flashed into her mind's eye.

But really, she thought, explosives and demolition? Self-defense? She had the feeling everyone around her was insane and she was the only clearheaded one in the room.

They were given a lecture by the heavy-browed sergeant on security consciousness—secrecy. *Paranoia*, thought Willy.

She began looking at everyone around her suspiciously after that. Boy, the company's system really worked. She had to give them that!

She walked back with Myrna in the cool October evening. Their rooms were in the same barracks as the other women. "How nice," Willy had murmured at that information.

"Yes, isn't it?" replied Myrna brightly. "Although we'll be so tired it won't matter where we are. They could put me in the middle of the men's dorm and I'd still fall asleep."

What would Myrna do in the men's dorm if she wasn't tired? Willy wondered maliciously, catching the scent of the expensive perfume Myrna wore in the damp Virginia night.

The next morning, it was boot camp. Up at 5:00 a.m., breakfast, calisthenics, the obstacle course, and then a lecture by a former Green Beret weapons specialist who babbled on about a twenty-two caliber Colt Woodsman, which he flipped around in his hand as if it was a toy.

"This baby here," he boomed out, "is what we used in Nam when we needed a silencer. She's as quiet as a geisha whisperin' in your ear."

Willy's back bristled. Obviously there were women present. Did he have to be such a blatant chauvinist?

"And this here—" he was saying as he picked up another cold-looking weapon "—is the German-made Walther PPK. She'll put a good-sized hole in the best of 'em," he intoned, laughing. Willy's stomach flip-flopped.

Then there was the actual weapons range target practice, and finally a class in foreign intelligence systems: KGB stood for *Komitet Gosudarstvennoi Bezopasnosti;* in Italy it was SID, *Servizio Informazioni Difesa;* in England MI6; in France the *Sûreté Nationale.*

Before lunch they saw a film of Moscow and the Kremlin, and then learned the names of the top men in the politburo, as well as those of the French intelligence leaders, the English and Italian. She heard the stern-faced instructor in front of the class say, "Always secure an alternative escape route in any situation," and Willy had images of dark hallways, back stairs, guns, sneaking shadows. When would she ever need to *escape* anything?

Willy scribbled notes. Myrna sat in front of her, listening idly, playing with her diamond ring. She hadn't been on the obstacle course that morning. She wore a peach-colored sweat suit, her hair had been set and her makeup was perfect. Willy wore an old gray sweat suit and had her hair up in a ponytail; she still felt sticky from the early-morning workout. Refresher course, indeed! she thought scathingly.

Lunch was a blessed half hour, although Willy felt strong and alert. The two college girls were dog tired, but the men glanced at Willy with new respect.

"Tell me how you met Andrea Pavlevitch," urged Myrna at lunch. She stuck to Willy like a burr. "I've followed her career. I adore skiing myself."

Willy couldn't imagine Myrna getting any further than an expensive Bogner suit and the base lodge at Vail, but she didn't want Hyde getting bad reports about her own sarcastic tongue. "We raced on the same circuit for several years. Opponents, but friends. Andrea always had more potential than I did. We kept in touch. I saw her a few years ago at the World Cup in Aspen, but then she hurt her knee and was out for a couple of years."

"Do you trust her?"

"Implicitly," Willy said vehemently.

"I hear that her letter has been validated."

Willy hated the idea of Andrea's letter being common knowledge; still, she supposed it would have to be by now. "Yes, I know, but then I knew it was valid the moment I got it," Willy remarked shrugging.

"I do hope you enjoy the class after lunch," said Myrna, changing the subject.

Willy pulled out her schedule. "Locks and picks. Sounds amusing."

"I've been asked to teach it today," Myrna replied. "It's one of my specialties."

"I see." Now where had Myrna learned that sort of thing?

In Myrna's class they began with basics like the old credit-card trick, but then Myrna led them off into realms that Willy found truly fantastic. Glass cutting to get into a house, hair pins and paper clips to open a lock, *plastic* to blow a safe, a stethoscope to hear the tumblers fall into place in a combination lock. And so it went. Myrna knew her subject. She was cool and competent; a good lecturer. She had the trainees try some sample locked doors for practice.

"Willy—" no one was ever called by more than a first name at The Farm "—you try the padlock," suggested Myrna with a smile.

Willy struggled over the heavy padlock, trying wire, a small screwdriver, everything Myrna had told them to try. Then she tried prying the padlock itself apart; Myrna had said they were often cheaply made and easy to break. This one wasn't. Willy took the wire cutters and tried to cut the shackle of the padlock. No result.

She looked up to find Myrna staring at her with a tiny smile on her glossy red lips.

"That one is special," said Myrna finally. "No one's ever been able to open it. It's West-German made, high-tensile steel, fine craftsmanship."

Willy turned the padlock over in her hand; a German name was stamped on the back along with a serial number. It was heavy in her hand and barely scratched by all of her tampering.

"You've got to learn to recognize these things. This one, for instance, is a case in point. It can only be opened with the key—" she produced a key in her small hand, her diamond winking "—or with *plastic.* It's a waste of your time otherwise."

Was there a tinge of satisfaction in Myrna's voice? Willy wondered. Had she enjoyed making a fool of Willy? Had she done it on purpose? Willy sat down, tight lipped and humiliated, although no one else seemed to notice.

Later in the afternoon they were to begin training in Hwarang-do, a Korean martial art. The one the president's bodyguards were taught, Myrna had whispered to her. Willy couldn't imagine why Myrna was in the gymnasium, as the dark-haired agent was obviously not your typical new trainee, but there she was in her peach-colored suit, gold chains and all. Observing, probably—her face was calm, self-possessed and without a trace of nervousness. She was a cool customer, Willy registered, trying to ignore her own thumping heart as the male instructor flipped the first trainee flat onto his back with a terrible thud.

She watched intently as each new trainee approached the unsmiling instructor and in turn was tossed effortlessly to the mat. The women received no special treatment whatsoever. At least, Willy reflected, this instructor saw women as equals. It seemed to her, as she came nearer to the front line, that if a trainee could push a knee behind the instructor's to collapse it, pull his hair, or maybe jab him in the kidneys, it would block his ability to throw them. It was all a matter of leverage, the instructor himself had lectured. Anyone could do it.

Did she dare try?

Her turn came finally. She walked onto the mat and met the thin wiry instructor's eyes, which were on level with her own. He assumed what was now a familiar position; she assumed hers.

Then he moved in, reaching for Willy's wrist and upper arm. She let him spin her half around as he had the others and get her into the position behind his hip, but then she jammed her knee into his and felt it buckle. She yanked a handful of his hair back while jabbing a fist into his hard belly, and then elbowed his kidney area—anything to keep him occupied. At first he was stunned. Obviously he hadn't expected any resistance. Then he recovered and bent to flip her, but again Willy resisted, twisting away from him even though it was killing her arm to do so. Automatically, she reached around with her free arm and tried to scratch at his face—anything to keep from being flipped as easily as the others. In the end, of course, he did toss her onto the mat, but when they both rose he was grinning slightly.

"You will all do well to follow this girl's example," he called out in the echoing gymnasium. "She uses unorthodox moves, but what will that matter if her fast thinking saves her life or that of another? Remember, you must always improvise, no matter what you learn from me." And Willy did all she could to keep from gloating in front of the others.

She fell into bed that night, half-dead but still keyed up. So much for the first full day at The Farm. She lay there in the darkness, trying to relax her tired muscles, picturing Myrna in the officers' club, cocktail in hand, smiling at the other CIA instructors, perhaps in a floating chiffon creation. What was there about Myrna that grated so on Willy's nerves?

Willy rolled over, felt a twinge in her leg and wondered fleetingly how Gayle was managing. And Reeves—well, she'd better get *him* off her mind. He was probably this very second in the sack with Sue Lerner. Then, without any bridging thought, she was seeing Reeves and Sue locked in an embrace, naked, writhing in passion. She squeezed her eyes shut tighter in the darkness, feeling the sting of tears behind her eyelids. He deserved it, after all, didn't he? After being so patient with her for so long. And she deserved what *she'd* gotten, too. A woman who couldn't give herself to a man belonged out of the running. She had to admit the natural justice of it. Reeves....

She forced her thoughts away from that dead end. She felt herself drifting off to sleep. Strangely enough, just before she sank into the soft-shadowed down of slumber, another face appeared unexpectedly in her mind's eye—a lean, sardonic face, its features composed perfectly, a face from which all triumph was carefully extinguished—and she wondered, as sleep tugged at her, how he would have judged her abilities that day on The Farm.

The routine became second nature after only a few days. One of the college girls was gone on the third morning; the remaining one looked lost and sad, but determined. Willy took pity on her and found out her name was Ann Templeton, from someplace in Wisconsin. She'd majored in languages at Northwestern and had been recruited because, Willy guessed, she spoke Russian fluently and mandarin Chinese a little.

"My parents would die if they knew," she confided to Willy. "They think I'm at a language seminar. I thought this whole thing sounded so exciting." She sighed. "Maybe it will be." She turned hazel eyes to Willy. "But Larry—that was the guy who recruited me—said he'd visit me here. He was wonderful, and I haven't even heard from him."

Willy soothed the young girl. "You can't get any messages here, you know, except for something really important. No phone calls, either. He probably can't contact you until the training is over."

"Well, he could have told me that."

"He probably assumed you knew." Willy wondered about this Larry; wondered just how he'd convinced Ann to join the CIA. It sounded like a snow job. She felt sorry for Ann.

The Russian class, held Sunday morning, was interesting. Ann attended but it was really too basic for her; she'd already studied the language for several years and spent a summer as an exchange student in Moscow. Myrna was there, studying hard, taking notes, working over the strange Cyrillic letters. It was the first time Willy had seen Myrna work at anything; usually she slid through smoothly, without effort.

Willy picked up the language easily. She had a talent for languages, a quick ear. She'd picked up a smattering of French, German and Italian in her years on the circuit. Russian, of course, was more difficult, being Slavic rather than Latin based, but it began to make sense. Ann helped her.

Willy did some laundry Sunday afternoon and washed her hair. Then she pulled on her old jeans and a long-sleeved green T-shirt, which had seen better days, dragged a chair out into the October sun and sat down with her Russian notebook. It was still warm in Virginia, the trees were green and the woods around the compound echoed with bird calls and the rustle of tiny foraging animals.

She studied the Russian alphabet, copying the letters to fix them in her mind. When a shadow fell across the page she looked up, startled.

"How are you, Willy?" he asked in that cool dispassionate voice.

She jerked her neck up further, squinting in the sun; he seemed so tall, standing over her like that. "Agent Vandemeer." She stood up, her notebook almost sliding off her lap. She snatched at it. "I'm fine, thanks. Studying my Russian like a good girl." She gestured with her notebook. "What brings you to this neck of the woods?" she asked, hoping she sounded as casual as he seemed.

"Business. Thought I'd see how you were doing," he said noncommittally. "Got another chair?"

"Oh, sure. Sorry." She went into her room and pulled out a chair.

Hyde spun it around, straddled the seat, folded his arms on the back and eyed her carefully. "I hear you're doing quite well."

"Oh? Who told you that?" she asked, seating herself again.

"Myrna."

Willy couldn't help but remember her boast: "Hyde and I go back a long way."

"Myrna," she said. "Of course."

"Something wrong?"

"No, not at all. Myrna just rubs me the wrong way at times."

He was silent, studying her until she felt oddly self-conscious.

"I've got a letter for you," he said finally.

Her head snapped around. "What? I thought—"

"It came directly to me. It was cleared as personal so I brought it along."

"It came to *you*? But who knew—"

"A fellow named Reeves Baxter." His voice was toneless, but there was something in it Willy could not put her finger on.

"Reeves?" Her mind whirled in confusion. Reeves? Why would he...? How did he know Hyde's name? But of course, *she'd* told him. She shouldn't have. Oh, no. She'd blown it....

Hyde was casually taking a letter out of the pocket of his tweed sport coat. He handed it to her, his green eyes hooded and unreadable.

The letter had been opened. Of course, everything was censored. Quickly she unfolded it and scanned Reeves's familiar scrawling handwriting.

Dear Willy, I hope this reaches you. I want you to know I feel like a real heel for that last time I saw you. I need to apologize and I hope some sucker in the CIA doesn't keep this from you. It's important. I was a little mad at you I guess and I wanted to hurt you. And it was too damn easy to do it. Some big man it made me, huh, babe? Be good—wherever you are—and I'll see you soon. There's a foot of snow up on the mountain already.

Yours, Reeves

Wasn't that just like Reeves? Get a letter in to her. Use a top CIA agent's name. Buck the system. His apology, although no doubt sincere, was a message to Willy and to the whole damn Central Intelligence Agency that Reeves Baxter was a man to be reckoned with. He'd known it would be read, weighed, considered, delivered. He'd known all along. It sort of took the edge off his sentimentality.

Willy realized she'd been reading the letter too long. Quickly she looked up, feeling Hyde's gaze upon her. She smiled weakly.

"Fight with your boyfriend?" he asked.

"Not exactly." She flushed, praying he would never find out exactly what that little lovers' quarrel had been about.

He gestured to the letter she still held clutched in one hand. "That was privileged information, you know."

"I know." Defiantly. "Reeves had to know. He's in on the whole thing; the patrolman I told you about."

"And incidentally your lover?"

She felt more warmth rise to her cheeks and wanted desperately to turn her head away. But she forced herself to meet his eyes. They were ice green, hard, fathomless. "That's none of your business," she finally managed to say.

"That, little lady, is where you're wrong. The Company is quite tolerant of sexual dalliance among its employees as long as those relationships are heterosexual and not with enemy spies. He'll have to be cleared."

Stunned, Willy murmured, "Go ahead."

"You know that you could have gotten in real trouble over that little scrap of paper? Lucky I was there to run interference for you."

Embarrassment gave way to anger. "My goodness, I certainly am fortunate to have you for a protector," she shot back at him. "What would I do without you?"

"Probably get booted out of here." His voice was as hard and cold as steel.

Willy took a deep breath and tried to control her spinning emotions. "Look, I'm sorry I told Reeves. I *had* to. I trust him completely. There are some people, you know, who are so close they won't buy any kind of a cover story."

"They will if it's good enough."

"Well, I'm new at this." She rose to walk toward the building where her purse sat leaning against the wall. The act of putting the letter into the handbag gave her a minute to calm herself, to regroup. Hyde obviously was furious at her for giving Reeves his name. Maybe she had been wrong to do so. Still, it had been an innocent mistake, she tried to convince herself. And it was hardly fair of Hyde to try to get back at her by humiliating her that way. Her sex life was her business. It wasn't as if she was joining the CIA on a permanent basis. She was only doing this one job with them. He had no right....

She turned back around to face him. Well, she thought, he could say or do anything he damn well wanted to. She wouldn't let him get under her skin again.

She walked back to her chair, sat down and forced a smile to her lips. She'd simply change the subject, catch him off guard. "This is quite a place. Do you have to come up here every year to do your refresher course?"

He looked at her curiously, as if her words were hard to understand. "Refresher course?"

"Myrna's up here on one."

"Oh, sure. No, I do my working out in the city."

"I see." Had Myrna lied? She decided to get it all out in the open. "Is Myrna up here to be my guardian angel?"

He eyed her keenly. "No. What makes you say that?"

"Oh, I don't know. She seems to follow me around..." said Willy innocently. "I just wondered."

"What's the problem you've got with Myrna? I hope it's not serious, because she may be working with us on Snowbird. She's a good agent, a damn good one. I've worked with her before."

"So I understand," said Willy dryly and caught a sharp look Hyde threw at her.

The afternoon shadows were beginning to lengthen. Willy shivered a little. "Guess I'll go in. I want to study this Russian some more. Will you be at dinner?" She stood.

It seemed as if he almost hadn't heard, as if he was distracted. "Dinner? No. Myrna and I are going into town. We have a few things to talk over."

"About Snowbird?"

"No, about another job we were on. A few loose ends...."

"When do I see Andrea in Europe? Are there any definite plans yet?" She pressed on relentlessly.

"No, I'll keep you posted. It's being worked on, don't worry."

"Worry? Would I worry? Just knowing the good ol' CIA has everything under control..." she said sarcastically.

That got a rise from him. "Now listen, no more cracks like that. You came to us for help. The least you can do is accept it gracefully. Stop acting like a spoiled brat."

And it struck her suddenly that she *was* acting like a spoiled brat. She'd wanted to prick his thick skin. Well, she'd succeeded and if she didn't like the result it was only her own fault. "I'm sorry. Sometimes my mouth just runs away with me."

"Apology accepted. You do have a way...." He eyed her appraisingly, then looked at his watch. "Gotta go now."

"Myrna's expecting you."

"Yes. Take it easy, Willy. I'll keep in touch."

"Sure, okay."

He turned away from her. As he strode off down the path toward the officers' club Willy let out a long sigh, a breath it seemed she'd been holding since the moment his tall lean form had covered her in shadow.

TEN

Surprisingly, Willy was growing to enjoy The Farm. There wasn't a minute of the day that wasn't taken up; each thing she tried, each thing she learned, was new to her. A different and exciting world was opening up before her eyes—the world of intelligence gathering, of covert operations. She was just beginning to understand the role of the CIA abroad. It wasn't all spy stuff or stealing another country's secrets—although there was certainly enough of that. There were things like studying satellite infrared photographs and predicting drought or flood areas, and then taking that intelligence and trying to anticipate human disaster. She guessed that about half of the CIA's activities were actually necessary and helpful to Third World countries.

Myrna Carlson wasn't so much in evidence after Willy's first three weeks were completed. Presumably Willy was neither a threat to herself nor a security risk. Ann was doing well now and her recruiter did actually come to see her once. Amazing.

She had not seen Hyde since the day he'd brought the letter from Reeves. She wondered if he ever checked up on her progress without her knowledge. Probably he did.

She thought about her mother and father often at night and wondered if Rachel had spilled the beans to Edward about Willy's involvement with the CIA in her vow to help Andrea. Would her father approve or would he demand that she drop the whole thing? Of course she would never do that.

In just a few days she would be finished her crash training—it would be four weeks. The leaves were finally turning color in Virginia and she was remembering how lovely it could be back East in November. Often in between classes she'd stroll around the wooded acres staying, of course, clear of the high-security areas. Her life in Aspen seemed a terribly long way off. Was she really a painter, an art-gallery owner? It was, at times, unsettling not knowing precisely where she fit anymore.

She sketched a little when she had a few moments: the sprawl of buildings gathered around the mess hall, the faces of her fellow trainees, some of the rolling Virginia landscapes, a couple of studies of her instructors, especially the Hwarang-do expert, whose face was a fascinating blend of controlled violence and studied Oriental calm. Once she found herself idly drawing Hyde's face from memory: clean lines, hard precise shading, deep grooves in the cheeks, curved dark eyebrows, thin sensual mouth. She drew him with an ironic smile on his lips, an expression she'd seen him wear often, as if he'd found the world a bad joke but decided he'd best smile at it anyway. When she was done, she studied the handsome sardonic face. Then, very deliberately, she tore it up and threw it away.

Hyde found her walking late one afternoon in the woods, kicking the leaves ahead of her. "Hold up!" he called from down the path.

Willy turned to see him walking toward her. He almost looked like a college boy with his tweed sport coat and sweater underneath, and his khaki pants.

"Hello!" She waved, then abruptly her hand came back down to her side and she felt taut all over. She was pretty far from the buildings, the company of others.... The words of her instructor came back to her instinctively: "Always secure an alternate escape route." But she was being ridiculous. It was only the old infantile reaction to being in a lonely place....

"I always liked this spot myself," Hyde said when he'd caught up. "The autumn here is beautiful."

"It is." Willy pushed the sleeves of her lavender sweater up past her elbows and felt the late sun on her skin, warming her. The air was crisp for a change, considering how close they were to the Chesapeake Bay area. She tossed her honey-blond hair back over her shoulders, giving him a quick uneasy smile. "Autumn's my favorite time of year anyway," she said. Then, "Should we walk? I mean, do you have time?"

"A few hours. Then I've got to head back to Washington." He reached into his jacket pocket and produced an envelope. "I brought this along with me—" it was Andrea's letter "—but I'm afraid it's got to be destroyed. I thought it was only fair to let you do it."

She reached out and took it from him. "Thanks." Carefully, she folded it twice and stuffed it in her back jeans pocket.

"Will you burn it before you leave?" asked Hyde. "I'll have to check...."

"I'll destroy it. I promise." And she gave him a slight smile, patting her right back pocket to let him know the letter was secure.

She'd managed, almost, to put him out of her mind those last weeks. There'd been so much filling her thoughts. But now, with him walking alongside her, his hard green eyes reflecting the sunlight, his chestnut-brown hair thick and shining, the very color of the rich earth at their feet, and his easy, self-confident manner, it was hard not to imagine a man like that being on a woman's mind all the time.

"We've got a date in January set for your meeting with Andrea."

Willy stopped walking. "Where?"

"Switzerland. Wengen. A World Cup race."

She took a deep breath and let it out slowly. "It's really going to happen," she said pensively. "Before, it was like a fantasy."

Hyde was watching her closely. "You understand that this is just a tentative date. There's a lot of planning to do yet."

"And all for a few minutes with Andrea..." she mused aloud.

"That's exactly right. Months of planning and all for a few seconds. Can you understand now why it was necessary for you to come here and undergo a little training?" He paused, then explained slowly, as if Willy's understanding was of vital importance. "You might never use an ounce of what you've learned here. Then again, one tiny little word or gesture or bit of knowledge might mean the difference between success and failure of your whole mission."

"I know that now."

"I hope you do. Frequently someone who gets involved like this finds all the training a waste of time."

Willy smiled, averting her gaze from his. "I did at first."

"I know."

The path they were walking circled the northern perimeter of the huge compound that bordered on Interstate 64—Willy could hear the traffic occasionally from her bedroom window. She recalled her arrival in Camp Peary, the night drive, the way all road signs seemed to disappear when they had neared the highly sensitive area.

They walked on. As the sun slid lower in the afternoon sky, Willy shivered involuntarily.

"Cold?"

"A little."

"Want my coat?"

"Then you'll freeze." But he was already shrugging it off and draping it around her shoulders. "Thank you."

"You know," he said a few minutes later, "after you make contact in Wengen, you could bow out."

Willy stopped short. She even reached out and put her hand on his arm. "You can't be serious," she breathed, meeting his intense gaze.

"Oh, but I am."

Then she shook her head a little, laughing tightly. "I don't believe this, Hyde," she said. "After all I've gone through, how could you conceivably think I'd drop out?"

"I didn't say drop out." He watched her with unbiased interest then. "I simply meant that after you make contact with Andrea, almost anyone who skis could take her place on the mountain in Aspen."

"You *are* crazy!" Willy blurted out abruptly. "Do you know what it takes to even faintly resemble a downhiller?" She placed her hands on her hips. "Well, do you?"

He nodded. "I think so." Patiently.

"Then you can't possibly think some half-baked female agent could ski down that mountain?"

"I didn't say—" he began.

"Who did you have in mind?" Willy demanded, unable to contain her anger. "Myrna? Oh, she'd be cute skiing a downhill. She'd probably fall and get snow in her hair and have to leave the racecourse."

"Willy!" Hyde gripped her arms suddenly. "Will you calm down...."

Her chest was heaving and blue sparks flew from her eyes.

"I never said you *wouldn't* be switching in Aspen with Andrea. I only meant that no plan has been defined yet as fully workable." He relaxed his grip a little. "You really *do* get worked up, don't you?"

"Yes." She was suddenly acutely aware of his hold on her.

"I do know how important all this is to you, Willy." He dropped both hands from her arms. "But you've got to see it from my point of view. As what's known as 'Control' of this operation, the safety of everyone involved is my responsibility.

Willy finally let out a long sigh. "I know all that. I just don't want the CIA to leave me out in the cold. You've got to remember that Andrea trusts only me...."

"I know she does." Then, "Come on, it's getting really cold out here." He reached for her arm as if to lead her, but Willy inadvertently backed away from him. "Is something wrong?" A bemused look swept his stern features. "Did I hurt you a minute ago?"

Automatically Willy rubbed her arms, trying to smile. "No, I just...." She laughed then, too brightly. "Well, you know how it is.... We women nowadays like to do things on our own." She shrugged, feeling a complete fool.

Hyde was watching her closely, as if trying to fit her into a neat little box.

Sorry, she wanted to say, *but I don't fit into any little box and you'll never find out why.* She stared back at him for another long moment, then said simply, "Well, let's go. It is getting colder..." and she began walking ahead of him, leading the way back to her building.

In a few minutes they were at her door. "Home safe and sound," she smiled. "Well, thank you."

Hyde checked his watch. "I'll bet you're getting damn sick of the cafeteria food here," he said glancing up at her. "I've actually got a while yet before I have to take off. Would you like to leave the camp and grab a bite to eat in town?"

Willy never even took time to think. "Give me two minutes to change."

After exchanging her blue jeans for a plaid skirt and doing a hurry-up-one-minute makeup job, she grabbed her jacket and was ready.

"That was quick," commented Hyde as she came up to meet him in the parking lot.

"And I'll bet I could get the time down even more." Willy laughed. "Anything for a real meal!"

When they were through the security gate—where the BMW and occupants were given a full check—Willy asked, "Didn't you need permission to take me out of there? I mean. . . ."

"No." He turned his head for a moment in the growing darkness. "I'm your Control, Willy. You're fully my responsibility.

The town, which was near Williamsburg, had a population, or so its sign read, of four hundred and six people. And it had only one restaurant: a diner. And not a new fashionable one, either.

But the service and the food were both good and Willy savored every bite of the southern-style barbecued chicken and coleslaw. She even asked for more corn bread.

"I should be embarrassed to be stuffing myself in front of you—" she told Hyde as she licked the butter from the bread off her fingers "—but I'm starved for decent food."

Hyde smiled. She noticed it because it was the only smile she'd seen from him that whole evening. "It reminds me of college food service," he said as he took a drink of his coffee. "You know, Wednesday night mystery meat and all."

Strangely relaxed, Willy laughed. "Lord, I'd forgotten. Would I be breaching a national security act if I asked where you went to school?"

Smile number two tilted the thin hard line of his lips. "No. I went to Penn. State."

"You did?" For some unknown reason, she'd expected him to say Annapolis or West Point.

"Yeah. I was on a football scholarship."

"Football," mused Willy, remembering the C.U. football team in Boulder, the special nip in the air on those Saturday afternoons in the autumn, the thunderous roar of the crowd in the jam-packed stadium and the colorful hats and scarves. "And you were the star quarterback," she mused aloud.

Hyde raised a dark brow. "How'd you know?"

Willy grinned devilishly. "What else would my Control be?"

He told her—actually, Willy pried it out of him—about his parents and their nice, middle-class suburban Pittsburgh lifestyle. "My father's golf date on Sundays at the McKeesport Country Club is the highlight of his week," said Hyde.

"What do they think you do?" Willy sat back in the booth, idly flipping through the pages on the wall jukebox.

"They used to think I worked for the State Department."

"Is that true? I mean, your parents didn't even know?"

"They know now." He sipped again at his coffee. "Want dessert? They've got great hot apple pie."

"No thanks. I'm totally stuffed. But you go ahead." Hyde ordered for himself. "Well," said Willy, "how did they find out who you really worked for?"

He was quiet for a moment. If he'd just come right out and told her, Willy wouldn't have thought much of it. As it was....

"My ex-wife told them."

"Oh. How long have you been divorced?"

He frowned. "Awhile. It doesn't matter."

But it did matter, Willy thought—it meant everything to him. With men, when they talked about divorce, you just knew.

Willy did take a bite of his apple pie and thought that she'd never tasted anything so good in her life. There was one thing she could always say about the South, it produced great cooking.

When he paid the check, she was oddly reluctant to get up and leave. And even though she had only a few more days at The Farm, somehow, after such a relaxed evening, she hated to go back there.

"You've spoiled me," she told Hyde as he held the car door for her.

"Hate to go back?" He slid easily into the driver's seat.

"You got that right. It's so nice to feel free again."

"That's the way you feel when you get that first leave after boot camp in the military."

"I'll bet." She knew another thing about Hyde Vandemeer; he remembered his military training with great clarity.

She found that she liked driving with Hyde. Some men insisted on showing off the moment they got behind the wheel, but not him. He was a good safe driver and watched the speed limit. Amazing. Didn't all spies drive eight hundred miles an hour and shoot oil slicks out from the back of their million-dollar cars?

She told Hyde her thoughts. He laughed.

"You know," he confessed, "there are all kinds of gizmos they will put on our cars if we want them."

"I'm not surprised," quipped Willy as her glance strayed unintentionally to his profile, the dark shadow of his flat cheek, the strong nose, the imperious curl of his nostril.

He drove in silence for a time and she stared out the window into the inky-black night. They were on a back road—very much alone, it occurred to her—and she had to force herself to relax, to think about the pleasant easy evening she'd just had. It seemed unfair that the old tension threatened to creep up and destroy it all.

She took a calming breath, glancing toward Hyde. "Did you have to come to The Farm anyway or were you checking up on me specifically?" Now why had she gone and asked that?

He took his eyes from the road for a moment, looked at her, and then back to the road. "There was no special reason I had to come," he said offhandedly.

"Oh."

He stopped the car outside the compound, before they came to security. Willy was both confused and edgy as he turned off the motor and moved in his seat to face her.

She wished she could say something witty and clever; she should at least ask what he thought he was doing. She remained silent.

"You've done a good job here," he stated levelly. "My boss is quite impressed."

"Thank you," she managed. "Are you?"

He studied her face for an isolated moment. "Yes. I think you've done very well. You're an artist and a skier, not an agent."

"I could be an agent," she breathed.

"But it's not what you want. Right now it's an adventure. You'll go back to Aspen and back to painting." He paused as if weighing his next words carefully. "You live in a fantasy land, Willy. I know I've never been to Aspen and I shouldn't judge, but I get the feeling that it's all a sort of Disneyland in the Rockies where dreams can come true."

"Maybe. Maybe not." She stared straight ahead for a moment, reflecting. "I do know one thing, however: I feel as if nothing in my life will ever be quite the same after all this."

"Does that frighten you?" His deep voice touched her softly.

"No. I'm not frightened. I'm . . . confused is all. I'm not sure."

Then Hyde gave a short laugh. "In a year from now this will all seem like a fairy tale. You'll be painting, waiting for the ski season, seeing your boyfriend. It will all be the same."

Slowly, she turned her head to face him. In her heart she knew he was wrong. Still. . . . "I don't want it to be the same, Hyde," she said pensively. "I want to remember all this." Her voice was almost a whisper.

For a long tense moment she thought he was going to lean even closer, to perhaps press his lips to hers, but the moment passed and once again the night was a great dark ocean and they were two ships passing.

"I'll take you back," he said finally, turning in his seat. Then, after they'd cleared security, he was all business again. "On Tuesday I'll pick you up here at ten in the morning. Your flight leaves National at three. You're booked straight through to Aspen."

"All right."

"If for any reason I can't make it, Myrna will—"

"Give me a ride," she interrupted.

"Yes. Myrna will see you safely up to National."

They walked across the parking lot together toward her building. She felt somehow that the mention of Myrna had spoiled a pleasant event. Then, as if to underline her thoughts, Myrna appeared for a moment in the lighted walkway near Willy's room. Then she disappeared around the corner of the building.

Willy glanced over at Hyde, who was walking alongside her. No, he hadn't noticed Myrna or he'd have called out to her, no doubt. They had, after all, known one another for a long time.

They crossed the small patch of lawn and stood at Willy's door. "When will you contact me about Wengen? How will I know...?"

"Around the end of December, Willy. No sooner. We may have you write a short note to Andrea telling her you're going to be in Switzerland just so that there are no surprises. Surprises foul things up."

"Yes."

"Well... take care, Willy." The tilt of his lips fell short of a real smile.

"I will." Her smile wasn't much better.

"See you Tuesday if I can."

"Yes, Tuesday."

"By the way, don't forget to destroy that letter."

"Yes, the letter. I won't forget."

She watched as he retraced his steps across the lighted lawn. Then she let herself in without a key; there were no locks on most doors at The Farm. Too easy for everyone to pick anyway.

She sat on the side of the bed, her head in her hands, thinking. She might as well face it. If Hyde had tried to kiss her in his car she wouldn't have stopped him. There was something about Hyde Vandemeer other than extraordinary, macho-type good looks. He was, in spite of his hard impartial facade, a nice guy. He cared. He cared about his job, he spoke of his parents with warmth, he was obviously hurt by a divorce. He cared about his fellow workers. He seemed to care, she realized suddenly, about her.

When he mentioned that he didn't want her involved in the Snowbird operation he really did mean it for her own protection. When he held car doors for her or took her arm going down a set of steps, it was all sincere. Oh, she knew she wasn't the only one he treated respectfully, but still she appreciated it.

Funny, she thought, but until that very moment she hadn't realized what it was about Hyde Vandemeer that lured her despite that terrible old trepidation. And then it all seemed so simple, so utterly simple that a complete idiot could see it. My God, Willy thought, Hyde Vandemeer was simply an old-fashioned gentleman!

She lay awake a long time that night not because she was unable to fall asleep but because she wanted to think about Hyde, to remember each little glance, each seemingly meaningless gesture or word that he'd given her since that very first time they'd met in front of the Lincoln Memorial.

Somehow every small nuance seemed terribly important, and she longed to understand him. Was he capable of thinking about her when they were apart? Did she mean anything special to him or was she just a tool the CIA was using to get their hands on superstar Andrea Pavlevitch?

He was, she decided, an enigma. There really was no way of telling what went on behind those icy green eyes and the very polite gentlemanly gestures. Who and what was Hyde Vandemeer—agent, ex-soldier, divorcé, former football star?

She knew about secrets. Oh yes, she certainly knew about those. What secrets did he keep? Or perhaps he didn't keep any at all.

Somewhere around two in the morning, hours after she'd gone to bed, Willy finally forced the tension from her limbs and fell asleep. The last thing she would remember drifting through her mind's eye was Hyde's face, his handsome dangerous face.

* * *

It was the following morning that she noticed.

If she hadn't had to do laundry, she might never have seen it. She'd picked up her jeans from where she'd hastily tossed them on a chair the previous night.

The letter! she thought as she began to wad the jeans up for the laundry. Hyde would kill her if she forgot and lost it somehow.

She'd burn it right now.

It was odd that she just knew, but someone had handled that letter since she'd folded it up and jammed it into her back pocket. Now it was folded in half neatly, on an old crease, when she pulled it out of the jeans pocket—the back *left* pocket!

How peculiar.

She stood there in the middle of her room and got to thinking about it. She studied the neatly folded letter and then began puzzling about it all over again.

Either she was going crazy or someone had taken that letter out of her pocket and replaced it in the other pocket.

When she had slept? Good Lord....

No. Wait. She'd gone to dinner with Hyde....

Slowly, against her wishes, it all fell into place in her mind.

And she'd lay odds on it—she hadn't the least notion why—but she'd bet that while Hyde had her off the compound, good old Myrna had visited. Hadn't she seen Myrna coming from the direction of her room?

In a million years Willy couldn't explain how she knew, but she just did.

Purposefully, she stuck the envelope into her purse and walked out. She went straight to the cafeteria, certain of whom she would find there.

Yes. There she was. Sitting at a corner table with two men, a cup of coffee in hand. Of course.

It seemed to Willy that Myrna looked as guilty as hell, but that was probably her own imagination. Anyone as skilled as Myrna in locks and picks could surely manage to look innocent in a situation like this.

And yet there was something about her that was just not quite... right.

Maybe this spy stuff is getting to me, Willy thought, but she *knew*, she just knew.

Casually—too casually probably—approaching the table where Myrna sat, Willy smiled and said hi to the men and Myrna.

"Say," she began, trying to look dumb and innocent, hoping she wasn't coming on too strong, "I should ask you, Myrna, since you live in the same building...."

Myrna raised a graceful plucked eyebrow.

"Well, it's just that I think someone's taken something from my room. I wondered if you'd seen anyone strange around."

Was it her imagination or did Myrna's sallow skin turn just the tiniest bit ashy? Did her shoulders tense under the pale yellow silk blouse as she sat there realizing that she'd made an amateurish error? She'd put the letter back into the wrong pocket!

"What's missing?" asked one of the men.

"A gold bracelet. You know, there are no locks here or anything so I figured there was no problem. Have you had anything missing, Myrna?" She turned her gaze directly on the dark woman.

"No, not a thing. But surely you've only misplaced it. I mean—"

"Oh, I doubt that. I'm very careful with my things," she said pointedly. "I always put them in exactly the same place. And I had the strangest feeling someone had been in my room. You know, this training has made me terribly sensitive, I think. Well, I'll go back and look again."

She felt a small twinge of satisfaction as she left the cafeteria. Sides chosen, rules drawn up, plays made. Whose move would be next?

She was even more sure now, having needed proximity to Myrna's reactions to prove her suspicions. Well, not *prove* exactly, but it was enough for Willy.

Now to do something about it. She couldn't possibly tell anyone at The Farm. Operation Snowbird was top secret. She'd certainly been impressed with *that* fact often enough.

So whom did she tell?

One person came to mind. He was, after all, the only one to whom she could explain the whole thing, the only one *she* knew in the chain of command. You only went to your Control, you never skipped in the chain of command. Usually you never even knew anyone else in the chain but your direct Control.

Hyde.

But what would she tell him? That Myrna had searched her room and looked at the letter? Had Myrna seen it before? Probably not. Hyde had impressed upon her how sensitive it was. If the wrong person got hold of it....

Yes, she'd call him. And he'd just have to come down to The Farm again. She couldn't possibly say a word about it over the telephone.

It was four o'clock by the time Hyde had been sent for and arrived. Willy had waited for over an hour in front of her barracks, pacing the cement walkway, biting her nails. Where was he?

When he did drive up she all but pulled him out of his car.

"What took you so long?" she accused.

He seemed angry. In fact, he took her arm none too gently and began to lead her away from the compound area. Gone was his previous easy friendship. "This better be good," he said coldly. "I was just about to step onto a plane when I got this urgent message."

"Well, it is urgent!" Willy retorted indignantly.

They stopped by the edge of the trees. "All right now, let's have it."

"Myrna ransacked my room last night while we were at dinner." She folded her arms smugly.

"She what?"

"You heard. And what's more, she probably photographed Andrea's letter. Or maybe she copied it. I don't know."

Hyde was silent. His thin lips were drawn in a severe line. His nostrils flared slightly. Finally he spoke. "I suppose you have proof of this."

"No. I...."

"And of course you're positive that your room was gone through."

"Yes. I am."

"Would you mind explaining how you know that your room was searched?"

She told him. But it came out sounding awfully sketchy.

"I see," Hyde replied stiffly. "So let me get this clear. Because last night you saw Myrna near your room—not in it, or leaving it—but *near*, and then this morning you found Andrea's letter folded differently in what you believe to be the wrong pocket, you have come to the conclusion that Myrna rifled your room and photographed the letter."

"You make it sound, well, as if I'm the one who's crazy. They keep telling us we're supposed to be 'security conscious.'"

Silence. He merely studied her for a long moment, his clear green eyes hard and accusing. "Let me ask you this, Willy: Why do you think Myrna went into your room and copied the letter? Well," he urged relentlessly, "why?"

Willy took a deep breath. "Maybe she's got her own reasons. Maybe she's a Russian, for all you know."

"She's a double agent. Is that it?"

Willy looked around as if for help. "I don't know. All I know is that she did it. Don't ask me for exact reasons. Just say it's women's intuition, if you will."

"Perhaps I should have Myrna arrested," said Hyde in a dangerously low voice. "We'll just call it 'women's intuition, if you will.'"

He didn't believe her. Not a word of it. And yet as absurd as her accusations sounded out loud, she knew in her heart she was right. Forget that she hadn't liked Myrna from the first; forget that something about Myrna didn't quite fit the bill. It was more, much more. There had always been the plain and simple fact that Willy distrusted her and now she knew why. Yes, maybe that was exactly what Myrna Carlson was—a Russian agent.

"So you don't believe a word of what I've told you?" asked Willy finally.

"To be honest," he said slowly, "no. I think you've taken this spy stuff too much to heart. It happens. And I think you fail to realize that Myrna is a highly respected agent. She's got top security clearance."

"Tell me something," broke in Willy. "Has Myrna seen Andrea's letter before?"

He was quiet for a moment. "No."

"Then there you have it."

Hyde whistled through his teeth, exasperated. "What I have, Miss Wilhelmina Patterson, is a missed plane and two agents from MI6 who'll be damn good and mad when they get to Heathrow and I'm not there."

"I'm sorry. But don't you think this is rather important?"

"What I think," explained Hyde through clenched teeth, "is that this is a bunch of female nit-picking and jealousy. I knew we shouldn't use an amateur in an important operation.

She pulled the letter out of her pocket with a grand flourish. "Well then, if I'm so dumb I dare you to take this letter and have it checked for fingerprints. And I'll bet Myrna's are on it!"

Hyde stiffened. His dark brows drew together. "Do you mean that you haven't destroyed that yet?"

"No." Defiantly. "I kept it as evidence."

"Give it to me, Willy."

Slowly she handed it to him.

Then suddenly—she couldn't believe her eyes—he had his lighter out and the corner of the aerogram was already curling, blackening. She stared, spellbound, as tiny flakes drifted down from the paper and the flames devoured the letter greedily, right up to his fingers.

"Who the hell do you think you are? That was my property!"

"I'm sorry, Willy, but it had to be done. You should have followed instructions."

Her back went rigid. She felt as if he'd slapped her in the face. Fiercely she turned on him. "I knew, Hyde Vandemeer, that I never should have trusted the CIA in the first place. Andrea was right! Oh God, how right she was!" She spun around and began to half run back toward the compound when suddenly there was a viselike grip on her arm stopping her.

"Willy. . . ."

"Oh no you don't! Don't try to placate little old jealous me!" She stomped her foot and pulled against the firm grip on her arm. "Let go of me."

"What are you going to do? For God's sake, Willy. . . ."

She stopped struggling and looked him squarely in the eye. "I'm going to continue with this little farce and meet Andrea and help her get out and then, Agent Vandemeer, I never want to see any of you again."

ELEVEN

The aircraft designated Aspen Airways Flight 10 tilted precariously on its wing and began to make its approach to the Aspen airport. The flight was completely booked and the atmosphere in the cabin was tinged with a faint tension and excitement after the bumpy passage over the Continental Divide.

Hyde Vandemeer looked out the window. The sky was bright sapphire blue, the ground a sparkling glistening white, and the runway a broad black ribbon across the wide valley floor. Parallel to it ran the narrower black ribbon on a highway, and on the other side of that the winding glinting gorge of the river—the Roaring Fork River. Then the plane banked some more, and he caught a glimpse of the town nestled between the shoulders of two mountains. Suddenly it was gone and the plane bumped down to a perfect landing, its propellers reversing with a roar.

It was very obvious that Christmas was only a few days away; the small airport was crowded with masses of vacationers lugging skis and boot bags, dressed in everything from worn jeans to hot pink, diamonds and furs.

Aspen.

He waited in line for a phone and then leafed through the small tattered phone book and dialed the Aspen Alps. "Sorry, booked up. It's Christmas, you know." He tried the Aspen

Meadows, then Aspen Square, the Buckhorn Lodge and the Continental Inn. All booked up.

"Try Aspen Central Reservations," one of the desk clerks had suggested.

He tried. "If you leave a number I can get back to you in case of a no-show," said the disembodied voice.

He tried the Gant, the Holiday Inn, the St. Moritz Lodge and the Snow Queen. "Booked up."

Finally he relinquished the phone to an irate gray-haired man, picked up his bag and got himself a cup of coffee from a vending machine.

He guessed he'd been stupid to come out here during Christmas week without a reservation, but frankly it had never occurred to him. Of course, he wasn't used to a town this tiny with only a limited number of hotel rooms. He sipped at the tepid coffee and thought.

He'd been careless, perhaps, not to make plans before he booked a flight, but then he hadn't made up his mind to come until the last minute. And, to tell the truth, he preferred not to give Willy Patterson any warning. Willy was more easily dealt with when she was surprised, off-balance. It was a silly little ploy, but useful. It was better if he just showed up, provided information and remained aloof and businesslike. After all, this was not a vacation.

But now his plans were spoiled. He'd have to phone her. He looked at his watch: nearly 4:00 p.m. Would she be at home? At her gallery? Skiing? He detested miscalculating like that; it was the kind of error experienced Controls just didn't make. Well, no help for it now.

He had to wait for a phone again. He tried the Cooper Street Gallery number first.

"Willy? Let's see," said a pleasant female voice, "I think she went skiing but the lifts are closed so she's probably home by now. May I ask who's calling?"

He detected curiosity in the voice. "No, I'll be in touch later. Thanks."

At home. He tried to picture the place Willy would call home, but couldn't. Would she be different here in her hometown? Less prickly, or more? He wanted to see her in her chosen surroundings. "Disneyland in the Rockies," he'd called it. But he could tell already, without even stepping outside the airport, that this place was no Disneyland. No, Willy would never lie in a land of make-believe. She knew exactly what was real and what wasn't.

Except for her suspicions of Myrna, which were crazy and totally unlike her. He'd almost told Myrna one day what Willy had said, but then somehow it seemed too ridiculous to even joke about and he'd let it drop.

He dialed the number of her home. All the exchanges were the same here—925. Small town!

"Hello." Her voice was relaxed and huskily sweet. He recalled it with sudden poignancy.

"Willy? This is Hyde."

"Are you in Washington?" He could hear the abrupt tenseness in her voice and regretted the loss of her original easiness.

"No, Aspen. I'm at the airport."

"What?" Incredulity.

"I arrived a little while ago and can't find a place to stay."

"Just a minute. Let me get this straight. You just flew into Aspen?"

"Yes."

"During Christmas week, without a place to stay?"

"Naive of me, wasn't it?"

Silence, then, "Yes. This town is fuller than Miami Beach this week. Why didn't you let me know or something?"

"Frankly, in my vast ignorance, it never occurred to me there would be a finite number of hotel rooms," he said dryly.

"Look, stay where you are. I'll come and get you."

"I can get a cab."

"It's the least I can do. I'll think of something. Give me twenty minutes. I have to make a few phone calls."

"You really don't have to...."

"Oh, yes I do. Just sit tight."

So he waited, smoking one of his stale Winstons for lack of anything else to do, watching the remarkable mass of people in the airport, feeling slightly out of context in his city suit, tan trench coat and no skis. He'd just have to rent them.

He spotted Willy at least two minutes before she saw him. But that was good; it gave him time to study her, to remember the tall lithe figure, bundled now in a lavender-blue ski parka, the swinging blond hair and long lean legs. Her face was tanned; high color blushed her cheeks. She looked absolutely vibrant: healthy and cheerful and breathtakingly lovely.

When she saw him she hesitated for a split second, as if not sure it was him, then strode through the crowds to meet him.

"Hello, Hyde," she said, a minute smile curving her wide mouth. "Welcome to Aspen."

"Thank you."

"That yours?" She motioned to his small leather bag. "No skis?"

"No skis. I thought I'd rent them."

"Oh, it may be hard to find any decent ones, so you can use my dad's. They're in the Bahamas—mom and dad, that is."

She led him out to an old yellow Jeep parked right in front of the airport building where there were frequent official signs reading No Parking. There were no doors on the Jeep.

"It may be a bit chilly, but it goes," Willy said climbing in, and he withheld a chuckle, recalling what a tomboy she could be.

The Jeep rattled and banged so they didn't say much. She drove straight down Main Street, past brightly painted Victorian mansions and antique lampposts, then turned right onto a side street and pulled up in front of neat, cedar-sided, small Victorian house with a huge blue spruce in the yard.

"Home sweet home," she said a little too brightly.

"Wait a minute, Willy." Hyde put a hand on her arm.

"Look, I tried everyone I knew and there just aren't any rooms in this town. Maybe in a couple of days—"

"I'm sorry about this. Maybe I can fly out, stay in Denver."

She laughed. "You'll never get a flight out tonight. Maybe not even tomorrow."

He felt foolish, at a loss. "I hate to inconvenience you."

"I have an extra bedroom. You'll have to share the bath . . . and I'm gone all day anyway." She looked at him quizzically, her head to one side, her golden hair falling in a curtain onto one shoulder.

The sudden familiarity of her movement stabbed him; it could have been Sandy standing there for a heartbeat of time.

"What I'm really dying to know is what you're doing here. Lord, I thought I'd never recover from the shock."

"Business," he said levelly. "We have a letter for you to send to Andrea. And someone had to do a little reconnaissance on the mountain."

"You should have let me know."

He shrugged. "Someone had to come out here anyway."

"Why not Myrna?" she asked, her large blue-gray eyes meeting his steadily.

"She's on another job."

She didn't respond as he climbed down from her side of the Jeep. "Come on," she said. "Dinner's in the oven."

He followed her up the narrow walk between the banks of shoveled snow. The air was crisp, cold and invigoratingly dry; it had been nearly seventy in D.C. The afternoon sun was behind a craggy peak that shadowed the town but the brightness still lit the sky to a deep faultless blue.

She pushed on the door handle and gestured for him to enter.

"Don't you keep your house locked?" asked Hyde in amazement.

"No one does in Aspen. I guess that offends your sense of 'security consciousness'?"

"Brother!" he clucked, shaking his head balefully at her laughter.

She threw her parka onto a chair and kicked off her Sorel boots. "Just a minute, I have to check the oven."

He watched her bend over, push her hair back with a careless hand and poke at something in the oven. And again that vague disquiet stole over him, a fleeting unwelcome memory of another woman bending over another stove, her blond hair swaying forward. Another time, another place....

A potbelly stove crackled in a corner. Plants hung in the bay window. It was warm and homey and comfortable. She straightened and smiled. "I'll show you your room. Hope you have warm pajamas. The bedrooms get frosty at night."

"Actually—" he gave a slow grin "—I never wear pajamas."

She hesitated, eyeing him closely, then accepted his joke.

The stairs were narrow and lined with watercolors—Willy's—of local scenery, he supposed. They were very good. The spare room was tiny: an old brass bed, a dresser, an oak wardrobe.

"It's not much," she said, standing in the doorway, her arms crossed.

"It'll do just fine." He threw his bag on the bed. "I really appreciate this."

"No problem. After all, the Company put me up for a month, room and board. I owe you."

He couldn't decide if she was serious or being sarcastic.

"I've got to get back to the kitchen. Make yourself at home. The bathroom's right there." She pointed.

"I'll take you out to eat," he began.

She rolled her big eyes. "Too crowded. We'd never get in anywhere. There are *hordes* of people out there."

"It's that bad, is it?"

"Worse. Besides, I had this in the oven before you called."

"Is it eggplant Parmesan?" he asked lightly.

"No, it's a spinach-and-cheese casserole. Vegetarian. Very healthy." And she was gone.

Hyde changed into cords and a white turtleneck sweater. When he came back downstairs Willy was setting the table.

"Can I help?"

"No, you'll just make me nervous."

He paused. "Do you paint here?"

"Yes, in the studio." She gestured to a doorway off the kitchen.

"Mind if I take a look?"

"Go ahead, but don't criticize. I can't bear it." Then she laughed a little timidly.

He flipped on the light. The small studio was packed with canvases and sketches. A large unfinished watercolor stood on an easel. It was a symmetrical arrangement of pyramid-shaped mountains with a lake in the foreground. Autumn colors. It was excellent. He moved around, studying the stacks of works. Some sketches of an older woman—Gayle Martin, her gallery manager? The company computer had no picture of Gayle, only her life history and bank balance.

Some still-life studies. More sketches: a cat in several poses and a sketch of a muscular young man in repose. Baxter? The man had a splendid physique and she had sketched it in bold strokes, shadowing the sinews to show them off. Had she drawn it lovingly? Hyde found himself wondering.

"Oh, that old thing!" Her voice came from behind him. "That was quite a while ago."

"It's nice," he said.

"I did a better one but Reeves has it. I think he sent it to his mother or something."

Dinner was simple but tasty. A spinach casserole, rolls, salad, a half bottle of zinfandel. Willy did not eat much. She seemed nervous and a touch preoccupied. Was it his presence?

"I won't bother you," he said finally. "Just do what you normally do. I can take care of myself."

"I'll have to show you the place on the mountain."

"Of course. Whenever you want."

"What about the letter?"

"It's one we want you to recopy and mail from here to Andrea. It sets up a meeting."

"When?"

"January fourteenth at Wengen."

"Ah, yes, the Lauberhorn."

He looked at her questioningly.

"The downhill course. It's called the Lauberhorn."

"You've run it?"

She nodded. "About five times."

"Good. Then you'll be familiar with the setup."

"Where do I stay?"

"Everything will be arranged. Plane tickets, train schedules, everything."

"The Company takes good care of its own, doesn't it?"

"We try our best," he said coolly.

"So I see Andrea. What then? Will she know what this meeting is all about?"

"It's in the letter. She'll know, although nothing is stated outright. By the time you leave here in January you will have the plan so firmly in your mind you'll be able to give her every detail."

"I will? Well then, I'd better get started."

"That's why I'm here. To see the layout. To formulate a foolproof plan."

"I'll have to let Reeves know. He's absolutely essential to any plan."

"Of course. We'll cooperate fully with the ski patrol. But they won't know the precise details until the last minute. You must promise me that. The fewer who know the better."

"All right, but it won't be easy. Reeves is full of ideas...."

Hyde drained his wineglass. "You can think of something to put him off, I'm sure."

Her answer surprised him with its bitterness. "Oh yes, I'm very good at putting him off. I'll manage."

She seemed restless after the dishes were done. "Come on, I'll show you the fabled Aspen nightlife. It should be hopping downtown."

They walked the three blocks to the downtown mall area. People filled the streets. The antique lampposts were twined with evergreen boughs and the big spruce across from the Wheeler Opera House sparkled with tiny white lights. The snow crunched underfoot, voices chimed, intimate laughter and an occasional exuberant shout rose from the mass of people. The quaint storefronts were lit up, each with its own lovingly carved and painted sign hung in front.

"Very picturesque," mused Hyde.

"Isn't it?"

"Where's your gallery?"

"It's closed."

"Can I see it?"

"Okay, if you want."

Automatically, he took her arm. "Shall we try to blend into the crowd?"

She paused, looked at him oddly, then shrugged. "Sure, why not?"

Yet her body was tense as he held her arm. He wondered whether she feared running into Baxter. He pulled her deliberately closer and tucked her cold hand into his. She didn't actually resist, but her body was not pliant.

"Here it is." She pointed with her free hand to a dark shop front. Cooper Street Gallery read the wooden sign.

"Very nice. Good location," he commented.

"The rent's awful, but that's Aspen."

"You do all right?"

"Quite well, actually."

"You're a talented girl, Willy." He turned to look at her in the darkness. A streetlight struck her golden hair like sunlight on a bronzed helmet; her eyes were enormous shadowed hollows, her mouth a tender curve. "I can't wait to see you ski."

"Oh, half the people on Aspen Mountain ski as well as I do."

"Somehow I doubt that."

She seemed to retreat further into herself, like a small animal into its lair. What was bothering her? She'd never been quite this retiring before.

"Do you still want to go through with this whole thing?" he asked softly.

She stopped abruptly, pulling her hand from his. "Of course. What would make you think otherwise?"

"I thought maybe you'd reconsidered, being back in Aspen and all. We can get Andrea out by ourselves, you know. You needn't feel guilty."

"I've told you before and I'll tell you again—I'll be there. I'll do it. My mind hasn't changed one bit."

"Okay. I just wanted to make sure."

"Let's go back. I'm freezing. I skied hard today, too."

There was an edge to her voice he couldn't quite put his finger on. Was he putting her in an awkward position with Baxter?

She excused herself quickly back at her house, disappearing into her bedroom. He could hear the old floor creaking and her movements. Then all was quiet. He sat downstairs in front of the potbelly stove for a while, musing. Willy Patterson had a home, a place of her own. He envied that; he was a servant of a fickle power, unable—perhaps not wanting—to put down roots. At least, not after Sandy....

But a girl like Willy—she had refused even to *kiss* him that night because of her boyfriend. And she and Baxter weren't married. Such loyalty gladdened him yet made him wary, too. His training caused him always to look for ulterior motives, angles, reasons within reasons. Why, really had she not kissed him? A beautiful girl like Willy could not be sexually naive, not in this day and age. And yet she gave the impression of clean pristine purity, untouched by anyone. There was a part of her that held back. He wanted suddenly to know that part of her.

Did Reeves Baxter know her hidden side? he wondered.

"Wake up!" he heard her yelling from across the tiny hall. "It snowed last night!"

Hyde opened an eye, shivering under the quilt. It *was* frosty in the room. He sat up, pulled on his pants and padded out to the hall in his bare feet.

"Hurry up!" she called from downstairs. "It's a powder day!"

He looked out the many-paned window in the bathroom. It was snowing—big, downy flakes. A foot of new snow perched precariously on every branch of the big spruce.

"Willy, maybe you better go alone. I'm not up to your level," he began when he'd come downstairs.

"A big strong guy like you? What are you—a man or a mouse?" She laughed without restraint, busy frying eggs and toasting bread. "My father's stuff is in the shed. He likes me to keep it here for him. He's about your size." She eyed him measuringly. "I'll get it in a minute. Hope your feet are the same size."

"I can go into town and rent equipment...."

"Nope, no time. We've got to be in line at eight-thirty. Not a minute later. Everyone and his brother will be out today. Believe me."

He gave up trying to argue and dug into the eggs, toast and coffee, eyeing Willy pensively. Her mood was quicksilver this morning, excited, high he would have said, but not on drugs. Only on the anticipation of powder-snow skiing. She wore an odd outfit while cooking: pink flower-printed long johns, ski socks, a heavy deep-rose sweater.

"Excuse my union suit, but my ski pants are too hot." She ate an egg in three bites, nibbled a piece of toast, swallowed coffee. "You finish while I get my dad's stuff." She dumped her dishes into the sink and disappeared without giving him a chance to reply.

He shook his head, smiling to himself.

Luckily Edward Patterson's boots were only a little too big for him, Hyde thought as they waited in line at ski lift 1A. Everyone in the line was suntanned, young, lean and tense with excitement.

"Radio station said sixteen inches on top."

"Looks light, too."

"Best snow this year."

"Can't wait to try my new powder skis."

"Think we oughtta do North Star or Silver Queen first?"

"What a day," said Willy, grinning from ear to ear, her eyes reflecting the same blue of her parka.

It was good to see her so cheerful. He smiled back at her, noticing how the snowflakes touched her long golden eyelashes, rested there lingeringly, then finally melted. She was like a child on Christmas morning.

They rode up the lift, then up another. "See over there?" She pointed with a pole. "That's where the racecourse will be. That's the best place for the switch."

"Lord, Willy, I can't see a thing."

"It's the snow. Oh well, you'll have to come up here again, that's all."

He couldn't help but notice the minute details of Willy's face, so close were they sitting on the chair: her fine straight nose, the high cheekbones, the wide almost impish mouth, the straight blond hairs escaping from beneath her pale blue ski cap. She made a lovely winter picture sitting there—a child-woman breathlessly awaiting the morning's adventure. "Better quit swinging your skis," said Hyde. "They'll fall off, won't they?"

"Nope." Willy smiled. "At least, they haven't yet."

A figure in a red parka skied down below them, carving lazy, perfect turns in the untouched snow. Then another one followed and another.

"Patrol," said Willy. "They've been skiing what's known as the mine dumps, for avalanche control."

"Is it much of a problem here?" he asked.

"Sure, sometimes, but they keep at it. Dynamite, skiing the dangerous places."

"Has anyone ever been caught in a slide here?"

"Not in the patrolled area, but out-of-bounds there have been several over the years."

"Did they get them out?"

"Not all of them. One I remember they found the next June when the snow melted." He saw her shiver a little.

"Why would anyone ski out-of-bounds with this whole huge mountain right here?"

Willy looked at him, puzzled. "Do you know how fast the snow on this mountain gets skied off? I'll take you out-of-bounds this afternoon. You'll see how great it is. It's absolutely fantastic!"

She led him a merry chase all morning until his legs were aching. She did ski beautifully: fast and smooth, turning in an exquisite rhythm, her body reacting so easily, so naturally. Her muscles made instantaneous instinctive decisions without thought interfering in her fluid movements. Hyde was envious of her ability and talent in the snow.

Not that he was a beginner, but he wasn't in Willy Patterson's league.

The sun began to show through the clouds around eleven; it turned into a perfect day. She took him over to Ruthie's where the World Cup race would start. They skied the sunny course together, slowly.

"There," she said, pointing with a ski pole, "is the place we'll go into the trees." They looked over the edge of the course, down into the Castle Creek Valley. It was steep and brush covered.

"You sure they can make it?" Hyde asked.

"They'll have to do a little bushwhacking," she said, "but they can make it. I'll show you where they end up down on the road this afternoon. We'll have to drive out to it."

They had lunch at Sam's Knob. Hyde was all for a split of wine and the day's special, but Willy was too excited to eat much and she said wine made her knees wobbly.

"Isn't it wonderful?" she kept asking.

"Aren't you tired?" He could feel every muscle in his body begging for rest.

"Not yet. We have to go over and do Pandora's after lunch.

"What run is that?" Hyde pulled out his ski-area map.

"Put that away. Pandora's Box is out-of-bounds."

"Come on, Willy. You're crazy to take a risk like that."

"I ski there all the time. I know where it's safe. For Pete's sake, Hyde, I've been skiing this mountain for twenty years. Everyone goes back there when it's skied out in the area. And I mean *everybody!*"

"I'd rather not, Willy."

"Well, *I'm* going. You can ski down and wait for me."

Wilhelmina Dorothy Patterson was a total enigma. How could this brash childlike woman who was behaving like a tomboy be the same almost-timid female whom he'd cooked dinner for that night—the one who had frozen all over when he'd tried to kiss her?

What was it in this woman that eluded him, that compelled him to probe further?

At times Hyde felt he was close to the answer. It seemed to almost come to him when they were alone together, without a crowd around. She seemed almost . . . shy. Yes, that was it, he suddenly realized. When they were alone she was not the same open adventurous woman, but rather a timid little thing. But why . . . ?

"Hyde," she was saying, "are you or aren't you coming with me? Well?"

She was determined. There was no doubt about that. And she'd go ski her precious Pandora's Box no matter what Hyde did. He should just tell her to go ahead without him, but something perverse inside him wouldn't allow him to do it. What was there about this devilish young imp that made him feel so damn protective?

"All right," he gave in, "but it's against my better judgment. I want you to know that."

"Trust me!" Willy said gaily. "And you'll have the time of your life! Come on!"

He followed her behind the Sundeck restaurant at the very top of the mountain, through the trees over a bumpy narrow packed-down trail. Well, at least others had been this way. . . .

Then they came out at the top of a slope, a perfect pitch, open and inviting and utterly untouched.

"See?" said Willy. "You go first. One at a time. I'll wait here until you're down in case anything goes."

"Willy, this is suicide."

"But what a way to go!" She grinned, as high on the fluffy powder snow as any addict. "Go on."

He went, turning, feeling the powder boil up around him, almost choking as he inhaled it. It was a gorgeous run but he felt a vague unease even as he stopped at the bottom, safely over to one side.

Willy headed over to the steepest part of the slope next to the tree line and waved at him from far above. She started down, turning gracefully like a bird in flight. He watched from the bottom, enjoying the sight.

It all seemed to happen then in slow motion, each terrible incident an isolated frame of horror. He saw it and yelled but it was too late; the fracture line formed above Willy. Unaware, she carved a turn back toward the middle of the slope and then saw it. Her mouth opened slowly to scream and then the snow broke little by little above her, like a rift in the earth, a beautiful yet deadly wave sliding down the surface, taking her with it in a tangle of skis and foaming powder.

Abruptly someone speeded up the film and Hyde was tearing his skis off even as the avalanche ceased its fury and settled into frozen silence.

"Willy!" he bellowed, clawing his way up the slope.

No answer.

He struggled up the hill to where he'd last seen her. My God, was she under all that?

"Hey, what's goin' on?" yelled someone from far above him.

"Call the ski patrol! There's a girl buried under here," he yelled back. "Quick!"

"Good Lord!" he heard the person say. "Hang on. We'll get them!"

Hyde prayed as he never had before, even more than when he was in the that tight spot in the Mekong Delta. He scrambled up the hillside, panting. An ugly gash ran down the slope now, snow piled high on the uphill side of trees, a jumble of dirty rubble at the bottom.

How long could a person live under that? Was she even alive? Four minutes of oxygen starvation and the brain begins to die.... *My God, Willy.*

He dug with his gloved hands frantically, calling her name. The snow was packed like cement. Did she have an air pocket under there?

Where in hell was the patrol?

Finally they appeared—six figures at the top of the slope with shovels, probe poles, oxygen, a litter. Thank God!

"Where did you last see her?" called the leader of the group. He was very calm, very businesslike. A good-looking man—dark, worried.

"Here, right here."

"What in hell were you..." the patrolman began, then broke off and gave orders. They probed. Two more men arrived. They worked steadily spread an arm's length apart. Every second counted.

Hyde's mind kept screaming at them to hurry, hurry, but he knew they were doing their best. He dug himself, using a ski pole.

"Shovel!" the patrol leader suddenly shouted.

One of the men above him skied down fast with a shovel and began attacking the snow.

A blue patch appeared only six inches below the surface. Four men were digging now. Hyde stood behind them, drenched in sweat, panting.

And then, as more of the figure was uncovered, he closed his eyes and prayed again.

At last they had her out, lying flat on the snow. Her blue hat was gone, her hair was wet and tangled, and her eyelids were white with tiny blue veins in them. Her face was as pallid as the snow, her lips slightly blue.

"My God," whispered the patrol leader. "It's Willy...." Then he raised his gaze to Hyde's.

"Is she...?"

"She's alive," breathed the patrolman, and his eyes never left Hyde's.

She was given oxygen and bundled onto the toboggan. Hyde kneeled and held her cold hand, rubbing it, but she was unconscious. Pale, beautiful, oblivious. He clung to her hand irrationally, rubbing it, willing the slim fingers to move.

"Lucky we got her so fast. A few more minutes..." said the patrol leader grimly.

"Will she be all right?" asked Hyde, exhausted now that relief was flooding him. He was afraid to take his eyes from her face. He could only kneel there, holding her limp hand.

"Don't know. We'll get her to the hospital. Who're you, pal?"

"A friend of hers. Hyde Vandemeer." He finally looked up again and saw worry and anger and jealousy mingled on the patrolman's handsome face.

"So you're Vandemeer. Look, pal, you almost got her killed!"

"She wanted to come here. I was against it. Damn it, this is no time for an argument. Get her out of here."

It was only when Hyde was riding to the hospital in the back of the ambulance with Willy that he realized just exactly who the angry patrolman had been. Baxter. Reeves Baxter, of course.

It was later that afternoon when Willy finally woke up and he saw those blue eyes open, all dark and cloudy, blink, then finally focus.

"Willy?" he breathed.

"Hyde?" Her voice was very weak.

"Yes, I'm here. You're okay now, Willy."

"What...what happened?" she asked, frowning, trying to remember, slipping momentarily back into the frozen dark world.

"You were caught in a slide. We got you out. Your friend Baxter has been calling all afternoon to find out how you are."

"Reeves?"

She was still terribly confused. He stroked the hair off her forehead as if she was a child. "You're going to be fine."

"It hurts..." she began.

"You've got some broken ribs."

"Oh." But he knew she didn't really understand.

The young tanned doctor told Hyde that she would be fine, that she was only suffering from shock and exposure and two broken ribs.

"Damn lucky," he commented.

"Yes," replied Hyde tightly.

He phoned the patrol shack on the mountain and left a message for Baxter that Willy would be all right, then waited around the hospital for a while, smoking two more crushed Winstons.

"You may as well go on home," said a pretty young nurse. "She's just going to rest. She'll be fine."

He went in to see her once more but she was half-asleep.

"Bye, Willy. I'll call later."

But she didn't really hear him.

He caught a taxi, but had to share the back seat with the driver's German shepherd. Only in Aspen. He was dropped at Willy's place. He thought about her Jeep; they'd left it in a friend's driveway that morning. It would still be fine. A big old yellow tomcat was carrying on at the back door. He fed it from a can in the refrigerator.

Should he water her plants? Call anyone? Her parents? God, no, she'd never forgive him.

He rummaged around in her kitchen, found an old bottle of tequila and mixed a shot with some orange juice. He sat in front of her cold potbelly stove, sipping the sweet mixture and wondering how Willy was.

And suddenly he felt very much alone.

TWELVE

The Tippler Bar generated excitement and noise at 6:00 p.m. Everyone was comparing stories about his own incomparable powder day, laughing, boasting, quickly swallowing his beer to order another and go on talking about the high it gave him to ski Red's or Aztec or Ruthie's.

Hyde didn't mind the noise; it kept him company and relaxed him because of its easy familiarity. He stood alone at one end of the bar, idly watching the crowd, sipping on his beer. But the wall of noise could not entirely blot out his tension. It had been a nerve-racking day. It certainly wasn't the first emergency he'd been close to, but it was sure as hell the first time he'd seen an avalanche bury someone.

Poor Willy. He couldn't forget the way her face had looked when they took her away on the toboggan. She was too impetuous sometimes; a young kid, really. He'd known lots of thrill seekers—had been one himself not so long ago. She'd needed to push herself, to find her limits, and she had. Brother, had she ever.

He nursed his beer, too tired to drink much, not wanting to talk to anyone, but not really ready to go back to Willy's lonely house, either. Somehow it wouldn't be right to go back there with her in the hospital and all.

The crowd ebbed and flowed: the red-cheeked tourists in flashy fur parkas, the old-timers, seamed and weathered in grungy faded jackets, the gorgeous young girls with tight-assed ski suits, the handsome men. He had the feeling that the focus could change but the crowd would always be the same. He admired people like the ones that filled the Tippler. They had that certain aura that goes with the competent use of their bodies: good body lines, glowing health, a physical fitness that verges on beauty. The Aspen look.

"Excuse me," he heard a soft voice saying, and the man standing next to him moved aside to let someone through.

And then she stood in front of him, her face still pale, a bruise on her forehead, her wintry blue eyes begging him for . . . something. Forgiveness?

"Willy!" he gasped in surprise. "I thought you were still at the hospital."

"Well, I left," she replied softly. "I just couldn't stay there another second."

"Why the hell not?" he asked, abruptly angry. "What are you doing traipsing around by yourself? You almost got yourself killed today!"

"I know." She didn't meet his hard eyes. "That's why I had to find you. I tried my house first, then a couple of bars, then here." She laughed weakly. "And it's a good thing you were here—I might not have made it to too many more places."

"You crazy kid." Then he grew worried. "You okay for sure? You want to sit down?"

"Yeah, I wouldn't mind," she said, forcing a smile.

He led her over to a small table, noticing that she sat down with great care, trying to subdue a grimace of pain.

"Your ribs hurt?" he asked gently.

"Yes, some." She was very quiet, as if not knowing what to say next. Shy. Yet this time they were surrounded by people.

"Want a drink?" he said to break the silence.

"No, thanks. They gave me some pain pills at the hospital and told me no alcohol."

"A soft drink then?"

"Yes, thanks." She looked at him as if she was grateful for small favors.

This certainly wasn't the Willy he knew! Subdued, quiet, unsure of herself. Where was her spirit, her fire? He missed it, much to his surprise.

"Willy . . ." he began.

"Hyde . . ." she started to say.

They looked at each other, not sure whether to laugh.

"Let me say it before I lose my nerve," she said then.

"Look Willy, you don't have to. . . ."

"Yes, I do." She paused to draw a breath. "I want to apologize to you for taking you in there. I'm sorry. I was wrong." Her eyes held his, searching, waiting for his verdict.

"Willy, it's okay. You didn't have to leave the hospital just to say that. It doesn't matter. It's over. You're safe. Don't torture yourself."

"But I was so . . . so—" she searched for a word "—*wrong*. I didn't know."

Unconsciously he put his hand over one of hers, which lay on the table like an averted glance.

"It was all my fault. My God, I almost got us both killed. And I caused everyone all sorts of trouble. I can't forgive myself."

She watched him so intently that he felt strangely uncomfortable and looked down at his drink. When he looked up again her sea-blue eyes were brimming over with tears, and one big glistening drop rolled slowly down her cheek.

"Willy . . . don't."

"I'm sorry. I can't help it." She sniffed and wiped a hand across her eyes. "It's that codeine they gave me, I guess."

She seemed so helpless, sitting there, crying silently in the midst of the loud gaiety of the après-ski crowd.

He squeezed her hand reassuringly. "Come on, let's get out of here."

She looked up at him gratefully, smiling tremulously through her tears.

He drove her Jeep slowly, not needing to ask her the way and pulled up in front of her little Victorian in the west end. They walked up the path to the front door without saying a word. He pushed the door open for her and snapped on a light.

Silently he handed her a Kleenex box from her kitchen. "Sit down, Willy. Take it easy. Do you want me to get something for you?"

"Maybe a cup of tea if you wouldn't mind."

"Sure."

Competently he went about fixing it, leaving her alone to regain control and wipe her eyes.

He brought her the tea, fragrant and steaming. She sipped at it, relaxing a little as if the fear and horror and confusion were finally fading a little.

"Oh, Hyde, I was so dumb! I'm so ashamed. You must think I go off half-cocked like that all the time."

"Don't be silly. I know you better than that. And to be honest, I have to respect your guts."

"My guts! It was pure ignorance!"

"No, I mean dragging yourself from the hospital, coming to apologize to me."

"Oh."

He sat down on the couch next to her. "Any idiot can get caught in an avalanche," he said somberly, "but it takes real courage to apologize."

"I had to." She was looking down at her hands.

"Okay, apology accepted. Let's forget it."

She nodded and took a deep breath, but he could see her fighting tears again. It was partially the drug, he knew. She put her face in her hands then, embarrassed.

"Willy." He put his arm around her shoulder, at a loss, not knowing how to comfort her. If Sandy had ever cried, she did it on her own time; he'd never seen it. "Come on," he said, feeling singularly helpless.

Then her face was turned up to his, wet with tears, and his lips were brushing her forehead, her salty wet cheeks, her pink inviting mouth.

And then suddenly she sat up, her hands balled into white fists in her lap. "I can't...."

A frown crossed Hyde's brow. "Your ribs hurt."

"No, no." Her voice was husky with emotion. "It's not that...."

"Then what? Is it Baxter?" He tried to turn her face toward his but Willy pulled away with a grimace. He ran a hand through the thickness of his hair, defeated. "Look, I've put you in a bad position with Baxter...."

"No. You don't understand, do you?" She turned those wet sea-blue eyes onto him, imploring. He thought, at first, that her near-hysterical condition was from a combination of injury, exhaustion and drugs. But there it was again, that elusive something, as if she wanted to tell him something but couldn't. Once again he couldn't quite grasp it.

"Willy," he said carefully, "let me take you up to bed and tuck you in. You're exhausted."

"But you know I can't sleep with you," she protested with a short bitter laugh. "Oh no, I can't...."

He helped her to her feet. "I understand." They proceeded to the narrow stairs leading above.

In her room, Hyde carefully forced her to sit on the edge of the bed as he searched for her nightgown. Then he pulled her turtleneck off, purposefully not touching the bandaged ribs or the satin smoothness of the peachy flesh above the white tape. And all the while he felt uncomfortable in the avuncular role; this was not the way he would have envisioned this scene between them.

As he unhooked her bra, he felt even more uneasy. Perhaps if she would react somehow.... But her body was flaccid, silent tears oozing out from under closed eyelids.

"Come on, Willy," he urged as he tried to get her arms into the nightgown. But she remained unresponsive. Once his fingers brushed the side of her hip as he struggled with her jeans and he felt ridiculous then. He should have just let her sleep on the couch.

Once she mumbled, "You don't really understand," but that was all. Then her head lolled back a little more.

He had tried to be all business as he'd undressed her and tucked the heavy quilt up around her chin. Yet as he stood in her doorway before snapping off the light he couldn't forget that his hands had brushed along her silky thighs, had touched the soft flesh of her high breasts.

Hyde switched off the light, closed her door and swore softly into the cool darkness.

The red lights on her clock read 3:05 when Willy opened her eyes.

She was in bed—her bed. Alone.

Automatically, her hands felt her arms and her brain registered that she was dressed in her nightgown. Recollection slowly flooded back, the images in her mind hazy at the edges. The avalanche. Hyde. The hospital. Hyde. Then she was at a bar somewhere and Hyde was slipping her nightgown over her head, his warm hands touching her.

And even as the memory of his gentle touch filled her thoughts a warmth, a tingling, crossed her belly and her breath snagged curiously in her lungs.

She sat up slowly. He would be across the hall. Her heart beat more rapidly. She knew beyond a shadow of a doubt what she wanted to do, had wanted ever since he'd practically shown up on her doorstep in Aspen. She'd told herself that as far as she was concerned he was merely doing a job, and that neither of them had been looking for an emotional entanglement. But that had been a lie. She'd convinced herself of a commitment to Reeves. But then, what commitment had there ever really been with Reeves?

And now she knew. She'd been running away from Hyde the whole time. Afraid. Just as she was always afraid when it came to sex.

But she wanted him.

It was not the codeine. It was not the fact that she'd nearly been killed that day and needed the comfort of another human being. Strangely, Willy could not even say that she'd fallen head over heels for him. She hadn't thought that far yet. No. She'd been running away too quickly.

She stood in the hall staring through the darkness at his door. Beyond that threshold, she sensed, was her salvation as a woman; yet she was terrified to find out. What if she couldn't? What if she didn't have the nerve to finish this travesty? What if she really was abnormal, frigid, and just using an incident from her youth as an excuse?

Excited and terrified, reluctant yet eager, she put her hand on his doorknob and turned it.

She knew, once she took that final step, that there could be no turning back. If she lay there unresponsive, afraid, frigid, she'd have to live with it forever. But not knowing—that was worse.

And then she was inside, closing the door behind her—that point of no return.

What if he didn't want her? Good Lord, she thought suddenly, panic-stricken. What if Hyde told her to leave?

"Willy?"

Her heart hammered painfully in her breast. "It's me," she breathed.

Silence. Horrible awkward silence.

Oh God. What was he thinking? Did he know the agony she was suffering? *Oh Hyde, please,* she prayed, *please love me tonight...*

And then she could hear the old bed creaking and he was there, a tall shadow standing over her in the inky-black room, and his arms were coming around her and he was naked and his mouth was covering hers as they stood locked in an embrace in the cold silent night.

Hyde could not have been more careful as he helped her out of her nightgown, and Willy thanked God for his consideration. If he'd just taken her to his bed and mounted her, it would have been intolerable.

"Hyde, be gentle," she whispered against his lightly furred chest as he steered her toward the bed.

"Do your ribs hurt?" He eased her down onto her back and sat next to her on the bed.

"No...."

"But just be gentle," he mimicked softly into the night. "Is that it?"

"Yes," she breathed as she realized that she was waiting for him, longing to be touched by those long-fingered, capable hands, to be kissed over and over by his thin cruel mouth....

Hyde knew, she discovered, exactly what she longed for. As if her mind was directing his hands where to roam, Willy received her wish.

Reeves had always been patient but never like this. Hyde's touch burned a smoldering trail on her skin. She hadn't known....

His mouth took hers and her lips parted beneath the searing pressure as his hands searched the soft hollows of her flesh. He kissed her neck, along her collarbone, lower to her breasts, across the tape to her belly, then back up until their lips touched, searching hungrily once more.

Deep in her stomach she could feel a warm core and it began to grow, spreading outward. It glowed warmer, then hot until she longed for the fire to be put out, yet at the same time she felt that she'd die if it was.

"Oh Hyde," she sighed and his corded arms pressed her to him as if his need was as great as hers.

"I don't want to hurt you," he said quietly in her ear.

"You won't," she breathed, longing for the first time in her life for release.

"Are you protected?"

She couldn't think—she only knew that she wanted Hyde Vandemeer in a way that she'd never wanted any man....

"Are you?" he urged.

"Yes, I'll be all right," she whispered, remembering wryly her optimistic trip to the doctor when she'd begun dating Reeves. But her attention quickly returned to Hyde. Suddenly she felt a great emotional tenderness toward him.

He was lying next to her, his mouth tracing a gloriously burning path across her breasts, his hands caressing the leanness of her thighs, the soft down between her legs. If he didn't enter her soon...

"You get on top, Willy," murmured his gentle voice. "I don't want to hurt you."

She moved as his hands directed her, but a sudden spurt of fear burst through—what if she still couldn't find fulfillment? What if the sensations dissolved as soon as they were together?

He guided her hips with his hands. Then he was deep within and her back arched and a cry of unspent passion, held within for so long, escaped her lips.

It was torment, but a lovely torment as she felt hot waves of desire sweep her over and over and over. It seemed as if she were riding one of those burning waves, heading toward a sun-kissed shore. Then she was crashing on that shore and Willy knew she had never felt anything so wonderful.

She fell against his damp chest, gripping him fiercely, tears wetting his flesh. She could hear the slowing rhythm of his heart and she knew that he, too, had ridden that wave.

They lay together on that shore, spent, slicked with sweat in the cool night, completely joyously sated.

Willy awoke in the morning cuddled next to his warm long body. With a finger she traced the outline of his unshaven cheek, his strong straight nose, a dark eyebrow. He'd given her everything. No matter what happened when they finally rose from that bed, she could never put into words the deep gratitude she felt for this hard, yet tender man.

Hyde rolled his head to the side, opened his clear eyes and yawned. "Are you smiling or am I just a conceited male?" he asked lazily.

"I'm smiling," Willy whispered.

"Good. It's great for my ego." Teasing, yet still careful, he pressed her to his side. "You know," he said finally, "neither of us has eaten since lunch yesterday."

"Who's thinking of food?" Willy nuzzled her face into his sinewed neck, biting him playfully, naturally. He even tasted good—all male, salty sweet.

"I am." As he sat up and ran a hand through his sleep-tossed hair, a terrible fear gripped her. It was over. He'd made love to her last night, but that was all.

He was done with her.

A frown crossed his features. "Willy? What's wrong?"

She tried to smile. "Nothing. I'll fix breakfast." She began to push herself into a sitting position but abruptly Hyde's arms were around her, reassuring her with their strength.

Finally, he turned her around to face him. "Don't you know when a man's kidding?"

Willy looked perplexed. "But you...well, you never did...you're always so serious...." And then he was pulling her down under the quilt again and his hands began to play that exquisite tune on her flesh, and she forgot where she was or that they'd even talked about food....

She was to think later that if they hadn't stayed in bed for that extra hour, Reeves never would have found her standing in the door of the guest room, her hair tangled and flying around her face, her nightgown undone.

It was however, she would also think later, probably for the best.

"I'm sorry," Reeves said with some degree of uncertainty as he stood at the bottom of the steps. "I should have knocked."

But his apparent confusion was short-lived as Hyde came out of the door behind her.

Willy felt sick. She could feel the tension in the air crackling between the two men and there wasn't a damn thing she could do or say. The scene spoke only too eloquently for itself.

"I just thought I'd stop by and see how you were." Reeves's dark eyes sparked dangerously.

Willy's lips moved. Nothing came out. She tried again. "I'm . . . fine," she managed, still feeling the terrible vibrations surging between the two men.

"I called the hospital early this morning and they said you were gone. I couldn't believe it! What in hell's the matter with you, babe?" he blurted out angrily.

"I felt better and they let me go," she tried to explain.

"Well, I can see why. You had your own personal guy waiting to play doctor with you."

"Reeves. . . ."

"Oh, for cryin' out loud, never mind. Willy. I've gotta go." And he turned and stalked out of the house, slamming the door behind him.

She fixed breakfast but Hyde was suddenly obscure, remote, careful. He hardly ate a thing. She dressed in jeans and a heavy Irish knit, which covered the tape. Then she stood in his doorway, her arms folded stiffly across her chest.

"We never made a commitment to each other," she managed to say with difficulty.

Hyde was buttoning his shirt. He did not turn in her direction. "You better explain that to him." Cold, hard, toneless.

Willy's heart sank. She was losing him. "He knows that, Hyde. He's the one who wanted his freedom."

Slowly Hyde came around to face her. His eyes were a clear frosty green. "You know, Willy," he said smoothly, "you should just take things as they come. Don't try to excuse them. Accept it. We both feel like hell for what happened here. . . ."

Willy froze. He was wrong! So very wrong! "Is *that* what you think?" she lashed out. "That I...I hop from bed to bed, then don't even give a damn?"

For an endless moment he studied her with that dispassionate interest she detested. "What I think," he finally stated, "doesn't matter. The point is that I let professionalism go by the wayside last night." He turned away and began placing his belongings into the small leather bag. "No harm's been done," he said then, "unless Mr. Baxter refuses to work with us in March."

Willy's eyes narrowed as burning anger flared within her. "You cold, calculating, son of a bitch!" she threw at him. "And I actually gave a damn about you!"

She wouldn't even offer to give him a lift to the airport. Hyde said nothing as he dialed for a taxi.

In fact, neither spoke until Willy saw the Mellow Yellow cab pull up in front of her house.

She dropped the curtain and turned to face him. "Your cab is here."

"I'll be in touch before the fourteenth." He picked up his bag and headed for the door. *Leave,* her mind screamed, *just leave!* "Don't forget to copy the letter to Andrea in your own handwriting and have it mailed by the first of the year." He was almost out the door.

As Willy watched his unyielding back, tears sprang hotly to her eyes. "Oh, by the way," she breathed, "Merry Christmas." For a moment she thought he was going to turn around and say something. But the moment passed and he was gone.

THIRTEEN

The plain manila envelope came to Willy's post-office box on January tenth, after she had despaired of ever hearing from the Company again. It came routinely, unheralded, without a return address. It was postmarked Denver, Colorado.

Inside were plane tickets: Aspen to Denver to Geneva return with a stopover in D.C.: train tickets: Geneva, Interlaken, Wengen return; a typed slip with the name of a hotel, the Carousel. She remembered it as a place much too ritzy for young ski racers.

In the envelope, too, was a new passport with a recent picture. There was even five hundred dollars' worth of Swiss francs, a Swiss train schedule and a schedule of the World Cup races at Wengen, including practice runs. They had thought of everything.

A slip of paper fell out of the folded-up train schedule. Willy picked it up and scanned the bold handwriting. It was from Hyde and was quite short.

> Be very careful in Wengen not to act suspicious. You're a tourist on a holiday. Try to use other tourists as cover. Do not lie—the truth is always your best bet. Good luck and don't ski out of bounds over there. I'll be at your debriefing back in Washington.
>
> Hyde

She read the letter again, trying to decipher any emotion in it, but could only find a vague protectiveness, the same thing any Control would feel for his first-time operative.

She'd have to tell Reeves. Her relationship with Reeves Baxter had undergone a curious metamorphosis since that morning before Christmas. He'd called her up to apologize that same afternoon. She remembered his words very well.

"I was an ass this morning," he's said. "It was just plain old male jealousy."

"It was as much my fault, Reeves."

"Hell, you've got every right. No commitments, we've said all along."

"No commitments," she'd repeated dully.

"Are we still friends?"

"Of course, and I never thanked you for my rescue. I'm really grateful. . . ."

"Goes with the territory, babe. Just don't make a habit of it. You all recovered now?"

"Pretty much. I have sore ribs."

"Okay, babe, I'm at work. Gotta go now. Next time when Uncle Reeves asks you about some guy, tell him the truth."

"It *was* the truth, *then,*" she'd said.

"Sure, babe."

Reeves had been a friend since then; he'd taken her to a party and out to dinner once, but she knew he was dating Sue Lerner, even skiing with her on his days off.

She still depended on him for Snowbird's success and she knew she could trust him. It was just that she still felt raw about that period in her life—those two days when she'd nearly been killed, found sensual fulfillment—love, if she dared call it that—and lost it all just as quickly. It wasn't in Willy to be bitter, but she had quiet pensive moods more often than previously and found herself questioning many aspects of her life. She didn't know anymore whether she hated Hyde Vandemeer or whether she continued to feel something special for him. She merely tried her damnedest to forget him.

She wasn't successful.

Willy arranged for Gayle to manage the gallery while she was gone, took care of a dozen little details, packed a small bag—she'd only be there a couple of days—and had Gayle drive her to the airport.

"What a crazy thing to do—just taking off for Europe like this," said Gayle.

"I want to get away for a while and see some races in Switzerland, maybe run into some old friends."

"What about that new friend, the one that called just before Christmas? He sounded very sexy. And after going through that awful ordeal with the avalanche and all, I'd think you two would be like this." Gayle held up two twined fingers.

"It didn't work out. You know how that is...."

"Sure, Willy, I know. But he sounded like quite a man."

The two CIA agents who secretly followed Willy Patterson from Denver to Geneva left her as she got out of her cab in front of the Geneva train station. One of the men, dressed as unobtrusively and conservatively as a Swiss banker, nodded almost imperceptibly to Hyde Vandemeer, who stood at a kiosk, his face hidden in a newspaper. Hyde, who acknowledged that responsibility had been given over to him, meant to stay very much in the background, using Agent Weston—Ted Weston—as a front. Even though Hyde was dressed as a European businessman, complete with hat, mustache, umbrella and glasses, Willy had sharp eyes and might recognize him, even from a distance. After all, she'd been trained to do just that.

It promised to be perfectly routine, a short coincidental meeting between two old friends, and that was all. But Hyde knew how many things could go wrong in this sort of "simple" operation. A million variables existed and most of them meant bad luck: poor timing, a nervous field operative, one glass of wine too many at lunch, anything—including the most serious but most remote possibility—a tip-off by a mole, a double agent.

Switzerland was beautiful, especially as they neared Interlaken. The Rhone Valley was winter-gray and somber but the white-capped peaks visible everywhere on the horizon, glistening in the winter sun, were jagged and spectacular.

Hyde sat in a car behind the one Willy had chosen. Ted sat in the compartment with her, reading his *Paris Soir*. He was to speak only French if she struck up a conversation. Hyde hoped Ted's accent would pass.

He asked himself again if he had done the right thing in not telling Willy she would be tailed from the moment she got to Denver. It was routine, but knowing Willy she'd be sure to object strenuously. And then, too, she'd react more naturally in Wengen if she didn't know she had an audience. He was confident that Willy would never find out she was under close surveillance every second.

At Interlaken Willy had to wait an hour or so for the next cog railway train up to Wengen. Hyde had a chance to watch from inside the train station as Willy stalked from one end of the platform to the other. Excited, he guessed, and a little nervous, too. She wore gray flannel slacks, a white silk blouse and a short sheepskin jacket. She looked very young, very American, very chic. He watched her through his clear glass lenses and remembered the feel of her long lithe body under his hands, the sound of her breathing, her small cries of passion.

Quickly he turned the thought off. It was poison, one of those dangerous variables. The events of that night had been due to her proximity and her terrible need. It had been nothing else—merely an interlude.

Two young men loaded down with ski bags and boot bags, dressed in ski sweaters, were watching Willy, he noted. One of them gestured toward her, trying to persuade his friend of something. They were handsome young men, slim and dark and thrilled with themselves. Ski racers on their way to Wengen, he guessed. French or Italian.

The more aggressive one stepped onto the platform into Willy's path and spoke to her. Damn, he wished he could hear. Ted would report to him later. Hyde could see Willy glance a little nervously around her and his first impulsive reaction was to rush to her aid. But that was utter madness. Then he saw her blond head bend perhaps a little reluctantly toward the young man's dark one. The man pointed to his bulging ski bag. Willy smiled finally and said something, her hands gesticulating as if she was trying to make him understand her language. She looked at her watch, nodding, and the young racer led her over to his friend. Introductions were obviously made. Then the three of them went into the crowded café-bar that opened onto the platform and were lost to Hyde's sight.

Well, Hyde thought, she'd been told in his note to use people as cover—strangers, acquaintances, anyone if necessary. Perhaps Willy was simply remembering her lesson. Perhaps....

Half an hour later they came out. The aggressive young man had his arm linked through Willy's; they had evidently had a shot of schnapps or something, for their faces were flushed and even Willy laughed without constraint. The young racer couldn't keep his hands off Willy and Hyde was ready to rush out and strangle the fellow again, but she accepted it with grace and good cheer, or she was at least making a damn good show of it. Anyway, she seemed to be having fun, turning into a carefree young ski racer in front of Hyde's eyes. It was good for the operation that she be relaxed and natural, he reminded himself. An Italian ski-racer boyfriend would be good cover while she was in Wengen. He wondered again whether she was doing this deliberately.

The miniature toylike train finally came, disgorging skiers and more skiers. Willy and her two new friends climbed aboard, the young men very solicitous and helpful. Ted got on the car behind them. Hyde would follow on the next train; he couldn't take any chances that she'd see him.

There were no cars allowed in Wengen; it was one of those picture-perfect Swiss towns perched on the side of a mountain with the famed Eiger looming above it like a juggernaut. People walked and pulled sleds; horse-drawn sleighs jingled gaily on narrow streets. By the time Hyde checked into his hotel it was late and Ted Weston was waiting for him in the tidy wood-paneled room.

"She's meeting Romeo for a late supper in an hour," Ted announced. "No problem. She's as well protected by the Italian stallion as if we had a brigade around her."

Hyde ripped off his little mustache, rubbed at the itchy spot and loosened his starched shirt collar with an impatient finger. "I want someone on her every second."

"Too bad Myrna couldn't make it. She's a natural."

"Uncle sent her to Grenada for some damn thing.... Who's on her now?"

"Barry."

"All right. I'll relieve him at ten."

"She's not going anywhere, Hyde," protested Ted. "Let's all get a good night's sleep for a change."

Hyde turned on him coldly. "I said I want someone on her every second and I meant it."

Ted shot him a long look that plainly said: "Who're you protecting her from, Hyde old boy? The KGB or Romeo?"

Willy was living it up in the Carousel Hotel bar with Romeo and two other grinning young men. They sat around a bubbling cheese fondue and ordered another carafe of wine from time to time. She had changed her blouse to a pale blue crocheted sweater, which flattered her long graceful throat and strong shoulders.

When Hyde slipped into a dark booth in the corner of the bar she was laughing and talking animatedly with Romeo, her white teeth sparkling in the low-ceilinged, candlelit room.

It was one in the morning before the party broke up. Hyde felt a vast chagrined relief when Romeo left the hotel with his friends—without Willy.

It was a gray morning with a dull grainy sky pressing down on the small town. The last downhill practice was scheduled for that day on the Lauberhorn at ten in the morning; women first, then the men. Andrea Pavlevitch was listed as number twenty-five.

Hyde dressed in his ski gear, stuck his mustache back on and added a navy blue wool ski hat and goggles. He and Ted would be posted on the slopes with all the other spectators, for in Europe even the practice runs drew hundreds of fans. Barry and his partner would be nearby in case of trouble. Another team would watch Willy's hotel until she left it. Hyde felt a tightness in his chest, a familiar tension, but not for himself this time. No, this time it was for his field operative.

He checked his Walther and stuck it in his parka pocket. Ted was doing the same thing. They were like damn robots, it registered in his mind. Automatically he went over the contingency plans, the plans they'd readied in case of a slip-up, but he hoped none would be necessary. There was even one ultimate plan to snatch Andrea right off the course today—Myrna had formulated that one—but it was much too dangerous and unlikely to succeed. Uncle had accepted it only in case of a major foul-up, and Hyde had secretly decided he'd never put it into effect.

What he really hoped was that none of these plans would be needed, that it'd all go as smooth as silk, that Willy would never know she had six private bodyguards.

"Lousy day," remarked Ted, hunching his shoulders as they walked to the téléférique. "Flat light." Ted, Barry and his partner Steve, were the only other agents Uncle could dig up who skied, although none of them was great. They'd had to send to California for Barry, to Berlin for Ted, and Rio de Janeiro for Steve.

"This girl of yours better know what she's doing," Uncle had growled. "We're fouling up schedules in three stations. I've got three chiefs on my back."

"She's good. She'll do it," reassured Hyde.

"Do you know how much of the taxpayers' dollar this operation is using up?"

It was Uncle's constant refrain, but then he had budget troubles like everyone else.

"The taxpayers will think it's worth it when we unveil Andrea Pavlevitch, sir," he had reminded his boss impassively.

"Yeah, you're right. It better come off okay," he had grumbled, subsiding.

Willy was easy to spot. She stood near the bottom of the course on the Lauberhorn wearing a bright red one-piece ski suit and a white hat, her goggles pushed up on her head casually. Perhaps too easy to spot, thought Hyde. He stayed behind her in the crowd while Ted worked his way closer. It didn't matter if she saw Ted. He looked entirely different today than he had yesterday.

The Canadian women were beginning their runs, streaking like yellow arrows past the finish line in the aerodynamic tuck. Then came the French women. The Americans had already run. Suddenly there was a roar up higher on the course; someone had fallen. A girl skied down slowly alongside the fence a couple of minutes later, her head hanging, dejected.

That's how Willy will look in Aspen, Hyde realized. *That's the part she'll play.*

Then the Russians. Andrea, seeded first, had the first run. Hyde could hear the muted roar from the top of the course; it grew in intensity as the favorite streaked down toward him. He strained to see Willy over the crowd. She was tense, her head turned toward the last curve that hid Andrea from her view. Her hands were clenched around her ski poles.

There was Andrea, flashing down in a tuck, skiing powerfully, taking the last curve strongly, her legs vibrating with the speed and force of her turn, her powerful thigh muscles bunched under the white downhill suit. She swept through the finish line to a resonant cheer from the crowd, straightened and checked her speed, throwing out a huge plume of snow, which covered the closest spectators. A grin lit up her Slavic-looking face as she waved to the crowd and stepped out of her bindings.

Andrea Pavlevitch.

He'd never seen her ski before; he had had no reason to. He was impressed despite himself. Her time flashed up on the electronic board, and the crowd bellowed its approval as a teammate hugged her. And this was only a practice run....

Then he saw Ted gesturing to him, trying to catch his eye. Willy's tall red figure was skiing nearer to the barrier fence, obviously trying to get Andrea's attention. Hyde moved a little closer, saw Andrea's head snap around and a broad smile light up her face. She was good—utterly unselfconscious, as if this was a chance meeting with an old friend. Andrea went to the gate and opened it to let Willy in. They hugged each other, Andrea giving Willy big Russian kisses on each cheek. Ted was right on the other side of the fence. Everything was going like clockwork.

The two girls went over to one side of the area inside the fence set aside for the racers. In the middle an Italian girl was being filmed by various foreign television stations, ABC among them. Good, Hyde thought, no one could try anything with TV coverage so close. But then why should anyone try anything? No reason at all.

Willy and Andrea were talking quickly, intensely, quietly. He wondered if Ted could hear anything. Willy's white hat bobbed up and down as she nodded to Andrea, her mouth moving all the time. They both were oblivious to their surroundings, their faces intent, somber. Damn! Willy should remember to smile, look cheerful. But perhaps no one but him would notice; perhaps he was sensitive to her expression only because he knew Willy's face so well, had seen it in his mind's eye for so many weeks now. . . .

It was going fine, he assured himself. They'd been talking two or three minutes, plenty of time to get the rough plan across. Details could be gone over later in Aspen, where Hyde would have more control over security.

Then suddenly it all began to fall apart. Two men dressed in dark Windbreakers rushed up on foot to the girls. He saw Andrea's head jerk up, her eyes widen. Willy's face seemed to freeze into a weak smile.

KGB.

One man was saying something to Andrea, his face dark, scowling. The other took Willy's arm and led her away, practically dragging her, trying to shove her under the fence. She was turning to see Andrea over her shoulder, obviously afraid to say anything. Hyde's heart was hammering in his chest—stay cool, Willy, stay cool. Still he had to fight an overpowering urge to go to her aid. *She'll do fine,* he told himself and anyway, Ted was closer than he was to her—Ted was the logical one to go in first. . . .

But where was Ted? There, behind Willy and the KGB man. *Don't do anything yet,* he thought. *Too soon. Wait. This may be nothing.* What in hell had alerted the KGB? Was it merely routine, part of security? Was Andrea suspect? Did they know something? They couldn't. Willy's cover was too good.

He felt his body tense again, ever ready to move if they tried to take Willy.

But no, Andrea was pulling at the arm of an older man in a Russian warm-up suit—her coach, Hyde guessed—talking vehemently to him. The coach called to the KGB man holding Willy and said something. Andrea's face relaxed. Willy smiled weakly and replied to the coach.

There was a short argument. The coach tried to persuade the KGB man. It didn't work, but he did let go of Willy's arm. She said something to Andrea, ducked under the rope, waved once to the Russian girl, retrieved her skis and went over to the nearest lift line where she quickly and astutely lost herself in the crowd.

Good girl. She hadn't panicked. It had been close there for a second. Hyde drew in a deep breath and felt cold sweat on his palms inside his gloves.

The defector had been contacted. Operation Snowbird had been initiated. Phase one was complete.

FOURTEEN

Willy's hands were still trembling as she got into the téléférique line. She felt slightly faint and dizzy—in reaction, she supposed.

What had happened?

Why had those two men—KGB, Andrea had whispered—been so angry? Had they known something? But they couldn't.... Her letter to Andrea? It had been utterly innocent even if they had seen it, and she had to assume they censored all of Andrea's mail. General tightening of security?

Wow, she had been scared there for a minute. And so had Andrea. No wonder she wanted out—that kind of life *was* intolerable.

But Andrea had been fantastic. So had her old coach—thank goodness he'd remembered Willy from years before when she'd raced. She remembered him, too—but what was his name? Yuri something. Sure, they had all known each other on the circuit. It was a small select world, after all. At least he'd made them let her go.

"Pardonnez-moi," said a Frenchwoman icily, stepping on Willy's ski boots in the crowded line. Willy uncharacteristically let the woman shove ahead. Her mind still whirled with apprehension and uneasiness. Had Andrea understood well enough in that short time? Lord, she hoped so. She didn't dare try to see her again. It had been such a short time, not even five minutes. She tried to remember everything they'd said

but her mind seemed fuzzy, returning over and over again to the look on the KGB man's face, the unrelenting grip of his hand on her arm. She shivered, remembering.

She hoped she'd done all right....

It was when the téléférique cabin swung up into the air that Willy saw him standing below.

Hyde.

Her heart gave a great leap in shock. Her mind could not work quickly enough to account for his presence there; a million questions flew at her like shards of glass.

He had a funny mustache and goggles and hat, but she knew it was he instantly, unquestionably. No one else in the world had that air of cool self-sufficiency, that mysterious alertness that seemed to wink from his body even when he was still, that special pitch and carriage of his handsome head.

The téléférique was carrying her higher; she strained to see him.

What was he doing there?

Following her was the obvious answer.

Slow anger began to burn within Willy. He didn't trust her. He'd lied to her. "I'll be at your debriefing in Washington," he'd written. He'd conveniently left out the information that he'd be tailing her in Wengen! Is that what a Control did? Deceived his operative, misled the poor unsuspecting chump? Was *anyone* to be trusted?

Suddenly two men burst out of the crowd far below, skiing toward Hyde. As the lift carried her farther and farther away, the figures receded from her vision. They converged on Hyde, flanking him—dark sinister figures, complete strangers. Were they Andrea's two KGB men? She couldn't tell; it was too far away. The two men wore dark outfits—they could be.

Oh, my Lord.

Had she somehow blown Hyde's cover? Did the Russians know all about him?

Hyde was skiing off, slowly, with the two men. Not toward the lift, but down to the town of Wengen.

Why didn't he try to escape?

He couldn't. They had guns on him. There were hundreds of innocent people around. What could he do?

Her heart thundered in her chest and her gloved hands clenched into fists. Where were they taking him? Should she let someone know? Who? She'd been taught never to contact anyone except her Control. They never told her what to do when her Control was compromised.

"Vous cherchez quelqu'un?" asked a voice next to her. "Do you look for someone?"

"Non, merci," she answered automatically, her lips stiff, her smile forced.

"Voudriez-vous skier avec moi, peut-être?" asked the same voice. "Would you like to ski with me?"

She turned to look at the man for the first time. He was approaching middle age, graying, lean and fit. His French accent was odd. Perhaps he was German or Scandinavian. He looked vaguely familiar; perhaps he'd been on the train the day before.

"Non, merci, Je vais chez moi."

She started back to the Carousel, unable to get her thoughts in order, much less ski. It began to snow as she walked back to the hotel; small damp flakes that scurried in the raw wind. She had a moment's thought that snow would ruin the downhill race the next day. Andrea....

Had those men really been KGB? They must have been. But then, what would they do to Hyde?

Fear for Hyde's safety nagged at her the entire afternoon. She tried to put him from her mind, told herself a hundred times that he was all right, that those men—whoever they had been—had talked to him for a few minutes and then they'd all gone their separate ways.

She tried reading a Swiss magazine in the hotel lobby and then went window shopping. It was while she was shopping that she once again saw the pleasant prematurely graying man who'd spoken to her on the lift that afternoon. She smiled absently at him but he was busy looking through postcards in a shop and didn't seem to recognize her without her ski outfit.

She even took a long sauna in the hotel's spa. It only made her feel drained.

She'd leave tomorrow. Her ticket was for the day after but she couldn't do anything else there. She'd better leave as soon as possible. Perhaps they were after *her*, too. Maybe they had given Hyde a drug—she dredged up the names from one of the courses at The Farm: scopolamine or triple Amytal—and he was telling them about her right now. Maybe. . . .

Was it her fault? Or was the KGB so informed about CIA agents that its men would pick one up anywhere, anytime? They couldn't do that, could they?

She ate dinner early, alone. Strangely, she even wished she'd bump into Antonio, the nice Italian—anyone. She was lonely and afraid, terribly on edge. It was silly, but Antonio would take her mind off her troubles. Tonight, of course, he was eating with the team, getting a massage, resting up for the big race tomorrow.

One hell of an agent she made, Willy thought bitterly. Scared to death of her own shadow!

She went back to her room, locked the door carefully, checked the window latches and even wedged a chair against the door handle. She recalled, while she got in to her nightgown that at The Farm she'd been taught not to panic, not to call for help and compromise the operation until she was sure there was a real problem. She didn't like it, but she knew she'd have to wait until she returned to Washington to do anything. Either Hyde would be at her debriefing or he wouldn't. If he wasn't, well, then she'd sound the alarm. She could phone a certain number when she landed in Washington. They would come and get her. Then she'd tell them all about what she'd seen.

As she lay in bed she wondered about Andrea. Had they taken her too? Or was Hyde's possible capture unrelated to Operation Snowbird? What had he been doing in Wengen, anyway? Was he really here just to watch her?

When the soft knock sounded on her door she gasped, bolted upright in bed, reached to snap the bedside light on, but then pulled her hand back as if it had been stung. "You're better off in the dark on home ground," she remembered the instructor saying.

Noiselessly, adrenaline coursing through her, she got up, crept toward the door in the dark and stood to the side as she'd been taught: bullets can penetrate most doors easily.

"Who is it?" she called softly.

"A friend. Let me in, Willy."

Her heart leaped like a wild thing, pounding drumbeats in her ears.

"Hyde?" she gasped, shot through with hope and fear and shameless longing.

"Yes. Let me in, please."

She dragged the chair away from the door, fumbled—it seemed like forever—with the lock, and pulled the door open.

He stepped inside, closing the door behind him and flipping on the light switch.

Willy stood trembling in her nightgown, staring at him, her eyes brimming with relieved tears. Then she couldn't hold back; she had to touch him, assure herself that he was really there in front of her, unhurt, free.

She took a step toward him and her hand went out as if to touch him, and then she was in his arms and he was stroking her hair, silently, soothingly.

"I thought," she breathed against his chest, "I thought they had captured you."

"Willy. . ." He stopped in the middle of whatever he was going to say and pulled back, looking at her quizzically, his green eyes boring into hers. "Captured? What are you talking about?"

"I saw it from the téléférique. Two men—they came at you and took you with them."

"Two men? You mean after you talked to Andrea?"

"Yes, they took you. I thought—"

"Willy," he said quietly, patiently, holding her arms in his strong hands, "those were CIA agents, men with me."

Comprehension dawned in her eyes. "You mean. . . ." She paused and drew in her breath. "You mean you were never in any danger? They weren't the KGB?"

"No. They were with me."

She turned her back to him, trying desperately to rearrange these new pieces in the puzzle. Then abruptly she turned on him again. "You were all here because of me?"

An uncomfortable pause, then, "Yes."

"Why didn't you tell me?"

"I thought it better not to."

"I see." Anger burned in her suddenly. All that wasted worry.... "You should have told me." She looked at him narrowly. "If you and your men were such a big secret then why did you come knocking at my door? Tell me *that!* You sure blew your cover this time, Agent Vandemeer!"

"I know," he said simply, "but I was worried. Ted told me you were acting so strangely this afternoon."

"Ted?"

"One of my operatives. He kept an eye on you."

"The gray-haired man," said Willy tightly. "I should have known. Tell him for me, will you, his French accent is lousy."

"He knows," said Hyde dryly. "Look, I'm sorry if you were worried. I had no way of knowing you'd seen me. It was sloppy." He stepped closer to her; the mingled aromas of fresh mountain air and masculinity reached her nostrils.

"Hyde, don't..." she said as he reached a hand toward her. She was angry with him. He'd no right not to tell her that the CIA would be there all along. No right whatsoever.

Yet her anger was tinged with relief, too. Relief that he was there in her room unharmed. How she'd worried all afternoon!

She lifted her smoky eyes up to meet his gaze. And then she wished he wasn't so devilishly handsome. How was she supposed to stay angry?

"I wanted to tell you that you did well today," he said then.

"Thank you," she whispered. "But I was scared. Those men.... You saw?"

"Most of it. They were KGB."

"I know."

He frowned. "It doesn't make sense. Did they know who you were?"

"I don't think so. Thank heavens for old Yuri, Andrea's coach. He remembered me."

"Good thing. But did you have time to tell Andrea enough?"

"Yes, but barely." He was so close, so terribly close. He loomed over her, blotting out the rest of the room, suffocating her with his presence. She wanted to retreat but didn't know how. "Hyde, why did you come here tonight? Isn't it . . . well, sloppy?"

He glanced sideways. "I told you, I was worried. Ted reported—"

She allowed herself a tiny smile. "You were worried about your operative. Thought I'd blow it or something?"

"Something."

"You need to trust me more," she saia gently.

A gravid silence fell between them, then he spoke. "Willy, I've thought a lot about the last time I saw you."

She felt herself flush. "I've put it out of my mind."

"That was a nasty crack I made about you explaining to Baxter. . . ." He seemed to have difficulty getting it out.

"Yes, it was."

"I apologize."

She bowed her head, remembering the pain of their last leave-taking. And then, inevitably, she felt his hand cup her chin, turning her face upward to his.

"You're quite a woman, Willy Patterson," he said gently.

There was no longer any holding back. He recognized it as well as she did; she knew from the intensity of his green gaze, from the feel of his hand on her face. Suddenly she longed for him desperately. She longed for his strength and surety, his long lean limbs and knowing hands, his comfort and his tenderness.

She closed her eyes and melted against him, giving in, giving up. His lips touched hers, burning; his hands pulled her close to the hard wall of his chest. "Willy," he murmured against her mouth.

Her arms went around him, locking her body closer to his. They stood in the middle of the room, thigh to thigh, hip to hip, mouth to mouth, swaying together like a lone tree in a high wind, tossed around by the storm of passion. And then he was taking off his jacket, undoing her nightgown, drinking in the sight of her body, all lean lines and spareness.

"You're lovely," he breathed, reaching out to touch her hip, smoothing his hand down her flank as if he was a sculptor and she his virgin marble.

"Let me help you," she said, feeling shy but wanting to see him, see every part of him. She unbuttoned his shirt slowly, then ran her hand down his lightly furred chest, feeling the hard smoothness of it. Her head bent to kiss his chest—little, tickling kisses that made him tense with wanting her. His chest rose and fell quickly; he pulled her to him and kissed her.

"You're torturing me," he said lightly.

"Good. You deserve it." Then she unbuckled his belt, slipped her hands around his waist and felt the hard thrust of his hipbones and curve of lean flanks. "I've never done this before," she confessed.

"What?"

"Undressed a man."

He slipped off his pants and stood before her while she studied him silently. "Is it the artist looking at me like that? Or the woman?" he asked, laughing quietly.

"I don't know," she breathed.

"Come here." He held out his arms to her.

She went to him and was enfolded in his strength, held against the warm-cold satin of his skin. Then they were kissing, their tongues meeting, the sweet syrup of their mouths mingling.

He led her to the bed and pulled her down beside him. His hands began to stroke her, touching her everywhere and burning a smoldering path on her skin. A now-familiar ache developed deep in her belly and began to assert itself.

This time there was no surprise, only pure, white-hot desire mounting higher and higher. Willy could hear her own love murmurs and Hyde's breathing. She thought their hearts must be beating together, just as their bodies rose and fell together in primeval rhythm. And then she rose on a tide of sensation, rose and cried out in the throes of her release, felt him thrust against her in his own fulfillment, and she fell slowly, throbbing and sated, back to earth.

They lay together in complete peace. One of his arms was flung across her breast, a welcome fetter; one leg was tangled with hers. His chest rose and fell in a measured cadence; sweat beaded his brow.

"Was that good for you?" Willy finally had to ask. She hated herself for being so inexperienced. She wished she could tell him, but shied away from the thought. It would be too humiliating.

He turned on his elbow and traced her lips with a finger. "Aren't I supposed to ask you that?" He smiled.

"Are you?"

"I don't have to. You made your feelings quite evident."

She turned her head away, embarrassed. Had she been disgraceful? She felt his warm lips touch her throat.

"It was perfect for me. Perfect," he said softly against her skin.

"Was I too . . . well . . . too forward?"

He grinned suddenly, a rare boyish grin. It changed his whole expression. "I adored it. Don't turn into one of those women who hides her passion, Willy."

She dozed, content, held in his arms, her cheek against his shoulder, her skin touching his, warm and reassuring. She awoke to his kisses, returned them and felt him grow hard against her.

They made love tenderly this time, lingeringly, without the desperate passion of the previous time. Her last thought before she fell asleep was wonderment at the fact that she'd once held back from this kind of release. Had she just been cured of her problem or was Hyde Vandemeer the agent of her deliverance?

When she awoke it was light out and unaccountably Hyde was standing by the door to her room, completely dressed. She sat up, feeling his distance from her even as he turned to face her.

"I have to go now," he said.

No word of love or closeness, not even a smile. His eyes were hooded, his feelings hidden beneath the familiar aloofness.

"Hyde. . . ."

"I'll see you in Washington." He cut her off as he put his hand on the door handle.

It was like a physical blow, the pain deadened into numbness by its speed and unexpectedness. "Look, Willy, you did a good job here. Better than I did, to tell the truth," he said wryly. "You have to be hard in this business. It makes you hard."

It occurred to Willy to wonder at his cryptic remarks, but shock overrode her wonderment.

"You can't get involved," he was saying, his voice the essence of practicality. "It's a bad habit."

"Do you mean that last night was nothing but a *bad habit?*" she asked incredulously.

"I'm not a man who trusts women, Willy. I've been burned before."

"So you retreat into your damn job?"

"Yes. It's a helluva lot better than sticking my neck out. I've got to go now. Have a good trip back."

"Hyde, please...." She was begging and she hated herself for it.

He turned toward her, his green eyes meeting hers with great and deadly courtesy.

She couldn't bear it and turned away. "Nothing," she muttered.

"So long, then."

She heard the door open and close and felt the sudden absence of him in the room as a tangible thing, with shape and form. An unspoken cry reverberated endlessly on her lips.

FIFTEEN

He was good-natured and he wanted to talk and that would have been okay except that Willy was totally preoccupied.

She needed time to think, time to settle her thoughts about Hyde—that was in the background of her mind always and, she suspected, would be for a long time. But there was something else on her mind, something of immediate and desperate importance, and she needed time to sort things out so that they made some kind of sense.

It was a thought that had occurred to her on the return train ride to Geneva. She'd been going over in her mind the contact with Andrea once more, reliving those awful moments when the two KGB men had come upon them and the stark terror she'd felt.

Why had those men interrupted two old friends in a seemingly innocent meeting?

Why indeed, unless the Russian authorities had been warned that Andrea was thinking of defecting? In that case, *any* foreign contact would be suspect. The authorities in Russia had actually only to be alerted to the vague fact that one of their star athletes was turning soft.

That would explain the bizarre happening in Wengen, all right. Willy formulated the next logical question in her mind: Was Operation Snowbird being compromised by someone?

Willy thought hard. Who knew about Snowbird? Her mother—but that was ridiculous—she herself, Reeves, Uncle, probably several other agents about whom she knew nothing. The five other men in Wengen with Hyde. Who else?

Myrna Carlson.

Willy's initial dislike of Myrna came back to her forcefully. And then there was that episode with Andrea's letter. And yet Hyde trusted Myrna totally; he had worked with her. But wasn't that what a mole did best—secured his fellow workers' trust?

Willy needed time to think, to piece together all the little bits of knowledge she had in her possession concerning Agent Myrna Carlson and Operation Snowbird.

"So how hard is it to get a room in Aspen in, say, February?" the nice man sitting next to her on the plane was asking.

"Easier than Christmas," Willy remarked offhandedly, "but harder than January, which is generally a low season."

Two more hours and they would land in Washington and supposedly she would be debriefed. She contemplated how it would be to face Hyde again and wondered if the guy next to her would doze off so that she could think without constant interruption.

"Well, I think that's just great," said the businessman from Richmond, "being able to ski all winter like that. Aspen in December, Switzerland in January. I'd cut off my right arm to manage that."

"What exactly do you do?" asked Willy politely as she crossed a stockinged leg, fidgeting in her seat.

"Oh, software, that sort of thing." He smiled and again Willy was struck by his attractiveness. Generally she liked to talk to strangers as long as there were other people around. She'd always had a knack for it, especially in her gallery where a friendly word went a long way toward a sale. But today....

The stewardess came by to inquire: "Would anyone care for an afternoon cocktail?"

Willy shook her head but Tom nodded. Good, she thought. Maybe it would relax him; he'd doze off then.

She waited until he'd finished his drink and they'd exhausted the subject of Aspen. Then she excused herself, heading down the narrow aisle toward the lavatory. If she took her sweet time surely he'd close his eyes for a minute.

Willy wore a calf-length brown wool skirt and matching jacket with a soft mauve silk blouse underneath. She straightened her blouse, combed her hair and fooled with her makeup longer than necessary. Then she combed her hair once more. By the time she opened the door there were three people waiting in line and they looked rather displeased with her as she sidled past them down the narrow aisle.

Wouldn't they be surprised to know that she normally dressed in jeans and spent maybe thirty seconds a day on her makeup?

Thank goodness the friendly man's eyes were closed.

She sat down gingerly and quietly took out and opened the airline magazine. If he awakened, he wouldn't disturb her reading. Then it struck her: at The Farm they'd taught her to always look occupied when in a tight spot.

If she hadn't been so distracted, she'd have smiled to herself for remembering automatically.

It was difficult sitting there trying to put Hyde out of her thoughts and concentrate on Myrna. And yet Willy had promised herself not to think about him. She hated to admit it, but she'd fallen for him. Hard. And now there remained the heartbreaking task of getting over Mr. Hyde Vandemeer. It wouldn't be easy.

Concentrate, she told herself. Sift through the pieces of the puzzle. So what, really, were the facts? One, Myrna had at lest handled Andrea's letter at The Farm, if not copied it or something. Or was that a fact? Couldn't it have been someone else?

No. Sometimes when you just know you're right you've got to stick with it. Also, Willy had practically seen Myrna leaving her room.

So Myrna had handled the letter.

Two, the Russians were suspicious of Willy, or at least of Andrea talking to an American. Oh, sure, the Russians were always jumpy whenever an athlete or scientist made "outside" contact, but that dreadful scene on the Lauberhorn had been above and beyond the normal Russian paranoia.

Somebody had said something to someone. In short, Willy felt certain, the Russians thought they had reason to be suspicious.

Myrna.

But why her? Willy asked herself. Why not someone else? Why not Hyde or Ted or Hyde's boss or even a secretary at the CIA?

Willy's mind circled but refused to come to rest. There was something about Myrna that had never quite rung true. Like the little chip off a saucer that wouldn't quite fit when you tried to glue it back on. It belonged but it just wouldn't fit anymore.

Myrna's clothes were wrong for her. But did that make her suspect?

She wore too much makeup, her hair was too perfect. So what?

And that accent of hers. That tinge of hillbilly beneath the facade of correct speech. And that huge winking diamond! How tasteless.

How expensive for a . . . a girl from West Virginia.

Was that it? Did the obvious amount of money Myrna spent on herself not jibe with her income or probable background?

Maybe, just maybe.

And if that was true, how would she get that extra income? A leak here, a photographed document there?

The landing gear was grinding down beneath Willy's feet. She looked up quickly from the magazine.

"You know," said her fellow passenger, "you must find that Chevrolet ad mighty interesting."

Willy looked down. How absurd! Whom had she thought she was fooling anyway? "Well—" she smiled weakly at him "—I have been thinking of getting a new car. . . ."

It did not escape her thoughts, as she was approaching the U.S. customs agent, that perhaps her whole wild theory about Myrna might be pure and simple jealousy. Hyde thought so . . . but then, Agent Vandemeer had a lot of things fixed in his mind that weren't true.

"Miss Patterson?" There was a tap on her shoulder.

Startled, she turned around quickly. "Yes?"

"There's a message for you, ma'am. Would you mind coming this way?"

"Who . . . ?"

He took her arm before she could finish, whisking her through an aisle next to customs.

He was CIA. She knew that immediately by the cool impersonal way he gazed at her, by his fluid movements, by the plain gray wool suit that left him indistinguishable in a crowd. Still, her heart hammered in her breast as they moved steadily through the terminal area.

She'd thought that she'd be met by a familiar face. Hyde, actually. In a way, she was relieved; in another way she was very much disappointed and a little afraid, too.

He led her through a door marked Private, then down a long inconspicuous hallway and through another door. He never said a word or smiled; he only held doors open for her and led the way continuously.

For a moment Willy felt like turning and running away. Why couldn't they leave her alone? Just let her go back to Aspen?

Down another corridor. At the end of the long narrow hall was an elevator. It seemed to Willy as if she was looking down a tunnel to a small dark hole at the end.

They rode the elevator down. One floor. Two. She wasn't exactly certain.

"You know my suitcase will be gone for sure by the time I get back to baggage," Willy commented as the elevator dropped.

He smiled, if anyone in his right mind could call it that. "That's all been taken care of." Clasping his hands in front of him, he rocked back on his heels.

He led her down a brightly lit corridor to a door marked Official Use. Inside was a plain white room with a long table and eight chairs. That was all. Above the table were two long fluorescent tubes lighting the room almost too much. It smelled freshly painted, and the carpet was barely worn. It was as sterile as an isolation ward.

Willy felt sweat bead her brow. She turned to face the agent who still stood in the doorway. "Did they set this room up just for me?" She tried to smile smartly.

"If you'll just be seated," the agent said easily. Then he closed the door behind him.

She was alone. She walked to a chair at the end of the table and sat down, placing her purse in front of her. The temperature in the room was probably seventy-two—perfect—but a chill seized her nevertheless.

It was, she decided, like waiting in a doctor's office. Soon the nurse would come in and tell Willy in a dispassionate voice to take her clothes off.

She sat wondering if they'd allowed enough time for her to catch her flight. But of course they had. So where were they? And if that man hadn't been CIA? But who else could he have been? she asked herself as she discovered that she was chewing a fingernail.

Debriefing, she knew, could take five minutes or five years. What would they do? Pick her brain, hypnotize her, merely ask questions? She hadn't learned much about debriefing at The Farm. It seemed to be a taboo subject. Perhaps the mystique surrounding it was nurtured by the Company and that was why it worked.

There was no wall clock. She glanced at her watch. It was night in Switzerland, early afternoon in Aspen.

Then suddenly Willy had a thought. Were they watching her? No one-way mirrors. How silly and melodramatic she was being.

Five more minutes passed before the knob on the door turned and a man carrying a portable tape deck entered. Behind him—and Willy's heart gave an anxious lurch—was Myrna.

The door swung shut.

"Willy," said Myrna in a sweet voice, "it's good to see you."

Willy tried to smile. Was *Myrna* to debrief her? Good Lord, if she was, then Willy could never tell her what had been said between herself and Andrea.

"Hyde was supposed to be here," said Myrna as she pulled out a chair across from Willy, "but he phoned. Car trouble. I'm afraid I was the only one available who knew you personally." Again she smiled, her teeth brilliantly white capped, alongside smashing red lipstick that matched the red crepe dress beneath her trench coat. "We always try to debrief with a familiar face around." She paused, opening a briefcase she'd set on the tabletop. "Don't you think it lends a more comfortable air if we're old acquaintances?"

"Of course." Willy swallowed hard.

"This is Simon and he's going to tape our little session." Myrna smiled at the man who'd entered with her.

I've got to think, to plan something, Willy thought frantically. What if I tell them a pack of lies? Won't they know? Give the tape a voice stress test or something?

Willy felt hot and then cold all over as she watched Myrna leaf through some papers. The other agent rewound his machine and checked it.

Hyde's car had broken down....

Suddenly Willy sucked in a breath. It hadn't broken down. That was too convenient. Someone had tampered with it.

Willy's eyes met Myrna's across the table.

"Are you really, Willy?"

For a moment Willy just stared at her. Finally she nodded.

"Simon? Would you start the tape please?" Myrna turned toward Willy. "You understand this session is being taped?"

It was all for the machine now; Willy could see the tiny reel going around and around. "Yes," she replied.

"Please state your full name, the date today and our location."

Willy did so.

"Now, Miss Patterson," said Myrna, clasping her hands together in front of her, "you met with Andrea Pavlevitch, the Russian hopeful for a gold medal in the downhill, just yesterday?"

"Yes."

"In Wengen, Switzerland. Is this correct?"

"Yes," answered Willy, but she was already thinking that that fact was the last Myrna would get out of her.

"And during this meeting, what, to the best of your recollection, transpired?"

Willy looked down at her hands, took a deep breath and met Myrna's dark eyes. "The meeting was broken up by the KGB."

The door swung open then and Willy's breath snagged in her throat to see Hyde standing there, a look of unconcealed impatience on his handsome face. "Shut off the recorder," Myrna requested. Then, "Hyde, I'm surprised you made it."

He looked slowly from Myrna to Willy and back. "Car trouble," he said.

"Yes," Myrna smiled, "I know. When you called in they sent me over. Willy's flight leaves in—" she checked her Rolex "—thirty-five minutes."

A little of the tension seemed to flow out of him then. "We'd better get on with it, I'd say." He pulled up a chair and sat down. "Take up where you left off, Myrna," he said.

All eyes turned toward Willy.

She hated them all at that moment, especially Hyde. He'd hurt her so terribly, and now this. Sitting there with Myrna when he knew how she felt about that woman.

How dare he!

Well, she'd give them all an earful. She'd be damned if she was going to jeopardize Andrea's freedom just because the CIA was too blind to see when something had gone foul.

"Start the tape, Simon." Myrna began again, "So Willy, you were saying how your meeting with the Pavlevitch girl was broken up by the KGB?"

"That's right." Coolly. Yet she could feel Hyde's eyes on her and she twisted her hands in the folds of her skirt beneath the table.

"Surely something was said before...?" Myrna was watching her intently.

"All that was said," asserted Willy levelly, "was that Andrea was not certain anymore about wanting to defect. For a split second Willy's gaze met Hyde's. Then it was once again fixed raptly on Myrna.

"Can you explain that more fully?" urged Myrna, her easygoing voice tinged with what seemed to be anxiety.

"It's quite simple, really," Willy said as impassively as possible. "Andrea, it would seem, has changed her mind."

There was a moment's silence. "Now, Willy," began Myrna again, "surely you don't mean that Andrea would put you to all that trouble and then—"

"That's what happened." Willy crossed her legs tautly beneath the table, feeling the weight of the uncomfortable situation bear down on her.

Myrna's cold stare pinned Willy,. "I don't know what game this is," she said in a barely controlled voice, "but in case you don't realize it, Willy, we *are* on the same side here."

Willy answered her with frigid silence.

"Well . . . ?" urged Myrna.

Again silence. Willy was all too aware of the three pairs of eyes locked on her, fixing her to the chair like so many daggers. She tore her gaze from Myrna finally, glanced uneasily in the direction of the agent with the tape deck, and then past him—anywhere but the direction of the one pair of eyes she could not conceivably meet.

Time became strangely disjointed in the sterile little room. Seconds went by like minutes, minutes like eternities.

Willy swallowed, hard.

"Shut off the recorder," came Hyde's dangerously low tone finally, his green eyes flashing, scathing. "All right now, Willy. What the hell do you think you're doing?"

In answer, she compressed her lips more tightly and folded her arms across her chest. Outwardly she wore an expression of silent defiance; inwardly, her lunch was chasing its tail around her stomach.

"Answer me, Willy."

She took a deep breath. She was uncertain of everything at that moment, but the one thing she did now was that she had to get out of there and quickly.

"Nothing else happened." She stood up. Her knees were wobbly. "Now, if you don't mind," she finished tersely, "I have a plane to catch." She forced her feet toward the door, slowly, with false confidence—exactly the way she'd learned to at The Farm.

"Aren't you going to stop her?" came Myrna's incredulous voice. "Hyde?"

Then Willy's hand was on the doorknob. They'd never let her go. *Never!*

Yet why would they stop her? To what avail?

The cooler air in the hallway struck her in the face, fanning her hot cheeks as she forced her feet forward, moving down the long corridor toward the elevator.

Oh God, she pleaded silently, *don't let them come after me. Please, let me just get out of here!*

It took an eternity for the elevator to arrive. When she turned around inside its protective wall, however, he was there, coming down the corridor, his countenance as cold and rigid as stone.

Quickly, with her heart beating wildly, she reached for the Close Door button. She pushed it. Pushed it again.

Oh God!

The automatic doors began to close but then his hand was there, checking one of them. The doors moved back again to the open position making dull metallic thumps.

Involuntary tears sprang to Willy's eyes as she backed up in the small space. "Don't!" she breathed, her voice rasping.

"Willy." He was standing in front of her, his hands by his sides, the obdurate veneer of his face replaced by confusion. "Why? Why did you lie in there?"

"I didn't," she managed, looking from side to side as if for escape.

"You know you did. And I know it. I'm asking you why."

"Because of Myrna!" she spluttered. "Because you and everyone else are as blind as bats when it comes to that woman!"

Hyde let out an exasperated sigh. "You still really believe that, don't you." It was not a question. "And all because you think, *think*, mind you, that Andrea's letter was disturbed one night."

"I know it was!"

The elevator reached the main floor and opened. Hyde pushed the Close Door button and waited while Willy made a useless effort to slip around him.

"I don't want to have to keep you in here by force," he said, blocking her path. "Please Willy. We've got to sort this whole thing out. If it takes all night...."

Finally the doors closed again. Willy sagged against the back of the elevator, defeated.

"That's better," said Hyde. "Now why did you lie in there?"

"I detest you," she blurted out as she felt a wave of claustrophobia sweep her.

"Fine," he replied coldly. "Now why did you lie?"

Willy shot him a hard look. "Someone tipped the KGB off about my meeting with Andrea."

"And what makes you think that? They're always quick to react with suspicion in situations like that."

"You saw them! And you forget," she said in a weary voice, "I've been around them before. On the race circuit with Andrea. I'm telling you, they reacted abnormally!"

He was silent for a long moment, his green eyes pinioning her, judging, evaluating. "Is that all?" he asked finally, the complete machine.

"No. What about your car today?" Willy took a few shallow breaths—she *had* to get out of there.

"I had a little fuel line trouble." He shrugged.

"And Myrna conveniently showed up on the scene to debrief me. That way, Hyde, no matter what happens or where she might be assigned, she'll know as much as possible about the plot...."

"You really think that Myrna Carlson is a plant? A Russian?"

"No." Willy played her only trump. "I think a woman who comes from her background, wears the very best makeup and clothes, along with Rolex watches and big fat diamonds, needs a lot more money than the CIA pays her." She held her breath.

At last, Hyde was not so quick to defend her. *Good,* thought Willy. *Maybe he's catching on after all.*

Finally he said, "What if you're wrong? Everything you've said is pure conjecture on your part, Willy. There's no proof, no evidence."

"Do you believe me?" she asked slowly, fixing his eyes with hers.

For a moment frozen in time he returned her gaze steadily. Then he said, "I'm sorry, Willy, but no."

"Then that's that," she whispered, tears springing hot and scratchy to her eyes. "I want to catch my plane."

"I won't let you miss it, Willy." His voice was softer now, less mechanical. "And I do understand why you felt you had to lie in there just now. But listen." He took her chin gently in his hand, tipping her face up to his. "You've got to put all this aside if we're to help free Andrea."

Willy answered him with silence. What did she owe him, the man who had so cruelly, deliberately, hurt her? She owed him nothing, big fat zero.

"Look," he tried anew, "if you're really paranoid. . . ." He caught her indignant look. "Let me rephrase that. If you're really uptight about Myrna, I'll make damn good and sure she's totally wrapped up with another case until this one is closed."

Willy's eyes snapped up to meet his. "You will?"

"Yes. She doesn't have to know anything. I'll have it all cleared through Uncle. All right?"

Hesitantly Willy said, "Well . . . maybe." Then, "But she might still find out about the details. I don't know. . . ."

"Willy." His voice was patient, empathetic, the perfect Control. "You know that no one will know all the details of Snowbird except me, don't you? Not even you. Each member of the team knows only his own particular job; no one knows any more than he absolutely has to. That's procedure. Myrna couldn't possible find out until the thing's practically in progress."

"You're sure there is no way she'll hurry up with this other case and arrive in Aspen? You're sure?"

"I'll make it impossible." He smiled tentatively.

"All right."

He released the button by the door and suddenly the cool air was hitting them and a long white corridor stretched before Willy.

"I'll walk you to your plane."

She didn't really want him to but it seemed, as he kept pace with her easily, that she had no choice. Soon . . . soon, she'd be rid of him and all his messed-up divorce problems and that would be that. No more Hyde Vandemeer: cool, so seemingly undeviating, yet, she knew, so vulnerable.

"You're sure you can handle Myrna?" Willy asked as the Delta Airlines agent verified her ticket at the gate. She was informed her luggage had already been checked through. "I mean . . ."

Hyde's look was impassive. "I can handle her, Willy. You forget, I do have seniority."

"I'm sorry, but I don't know who to trust." She wished she hadn't spoken aloud. After that night in Wengen, she trusted him the least. "Well," Willy said turning to leave, "good-bye."

Hyde studied her a moment. "Just one more thing."

Willy looked at him, expectant. "What is it?"

He bent his head toward her ear as the ticket agent watched them impatiently. "I promised to get Myrna out of the way. Now you understand that this is a pretty lousy thing I'm going to do...."

"Yes." Of course it was, she thought. Myrna was his "once in a while" girlfriend.

"All right," Hyde said. "Then I think it's only fair that you consider doing me a favor."

Willy's back went rigid. "What?" she breathed suspiciously.

"Consider waiting on the sidelines now that you've made contact and Andrea knows her defection is being worked on." He noted without surprise Willy's outraged glare. "We can get her out any number of ways once she's in Aspen."

Willy was about to speak when the ticket agent approached. "I'm sorry," he said with disdain, "but you'll have to board now."

"In a minute," responded Hyde coolly.

"No, sir. Now." The agent stood his ground.

Hyde reached into his pocket, pulled out his laminated ID card and snapped it in front of the agent's eyes. "Now back off till I'm through here," barked Hyde, a cold unspoken threat in his voice. Then he turned back to Willy, his eyes still that crystal-clear green they became when he was angry. "Will you just consider it?"

She looked at him for a long moment. "No. And I'll tell you why. I'm sick of you using people and pushing them around and I wish to God I'd never gone to the CIA nor met you, *Agent* Vandemeer! This is one kid," she fired at him hotly, "that you're not going to shove around anymore!"

She spun around, walked down the silent boarding tunnel and closed the Hyde Vandemeer chapter of her life forever.

SIXTEEN

Just before Valentine's Day Willy got a lacy, red-flocked valentine in the mail. When she saw the Washington postmark her heart flip-flopped humiliatingly out of control.

But if was only from her father's office in Washington. Her parents were coming to Aspen in a few days. Would Willy please see that their condo was clean and stocked? Love, Dad. Of course, they always came out in February when the weather began to get warmer, the days longer.

She hated even to be reminded of Washington and that awful, demoralizing scene. Hyde, Myrna, the KGB. It was like some sort of cheap spy thriller. She still writhed painfully inside when she thought of Hyde, but then she made herself remember that he had been good for her, had taught her something invaluable: she was a normal woman with normal desires. That *was* important. Unfortunately the desires were all for the wrong man.

She revved up the old jeep as she left the post office and drove up Mill Street toward the ski lift. She was to meet Reeves at noon and they planned to go over the course, trying to dodge into the trees and heading down the Midnight Mine side of Aspen Mountain to Castle Creek Road. A trial run.

She parked the Jeep so that one wheel was perched precariously upon a snowbank—for lack of any other parking place—and walked to the chair lift. It was warm and sunny—

no-hat weather. Willy rode up to the top and skied down the ramp. Reeves was waiting for her, his usual grin in place, a walkie-talkie strapped on his hip.

"Hi ya, babe. Nice day, huh?"

"Sure is." She squinted into the sun, then put her sunglasses on.

"I told the guys I had to check something out on Midnight. Tom and Benny wanted to come along but I sent them off to put up some fences. So I have the radio—" he slapped the black box on his hip "—in case of any trouble."

"All set, then?"

They skied off down Dipsy Doodle, up a lift and down to where the start of the racecourse would be in less than a month. Scattered crews of volunteers were already working at setting up fences, foot packing the snow and running cables for the television cameras and electronic timing equipment.

"Okay," said Reeves, "the women's course starts here, a little lower than the men's. Andrea will be starting right there." He pointed with a ski pole. "You get in place and pretend you're her. I'll follow."

Willy knew the course, had even skied it once in her career as a racer. She started down Ruthie's, to the left, alongside the evergreens that marked the edge of the ski-area boundary. She was in a tuck, hair flying out behind her; it wasn't very steep yet. Then came the flat road—the aerodynamic tuck was crucial here to lower wind resistance—then the left hand curve onto the road to Aztec, which was easy except for the big rolling bumps that could throw you.

The rows of trees narrowed toward the road. There was a turn and then the top of the wall of Aztec appeared. There! Willy leaned on an edge of her ski, skidded to the left, throwing up a big wave of snow and darted off into the trees.

"Good!" she heard Reeves yelling behind her. "I could hardly see you with all the snow!" He skied up to her through the trees by the side of the trail.

"I'll be waiting here," Willy said, "in the same suit as Andrea. Can you see me from the trail?"

He backed up out of the trees. "Get in a little deeper. There. Can't see a thing." He frowned. "How are you going to get a downhill suit like hers?" he called out.

"It's all arranged. That's *their* problem." They both knew who *they* were.

"Okay, so you come out of the trees and ski down the rest of the course looking sad and frustrated as if you were Andrea. Then what happens at the finish line?"

"There'll be a Company team there waiting for me. Just in case. And they'll put me in a car and drive me away to the safe house where Andrea will also be taken as soon as she reaches Castle Creek Road."

"Where's the safe house?"

"I don't know. They only tell you as much as you need to know." Willy shrugged.

"Secretive SOBs, aren't they?" Reeves grinned.

"You said it."

"Now we switch identities. You're Andrea. And I'm here on duty with a couple of other guys...."

"Don't tell them anything," Willy warned.

"Naw. They won't know anything till Andrea skis into the trees."

"Okay, so now we take you—Andrea—boy, is this confusing—down to Castle Creek Road to meet another team of CIA men, right?"

"We may as well try it," said Willy. "No avalanches today, okay?" She grinned weakly.

"I promise. No avalanches, babe. But if there's a big storm before the race, I can't promise miracles...."

"We'll just have to hope."

They took off over the side into the rough scrub oak and brush, making a long traverse across the face, then zigzagging back and forth among rocks, stunted pines, prickly bushes.

"This is warm work," said Reeves, taking off his Windbreaker with the white cross on the back, tying it around his waist and wiping his forehead with a muscular forearm. "You timing this thing?"

"Got it. We started at 12:42."

Another long traverse and they were definitely lower. "I've never done this particular descent before," said Reeves, "and now I know why!" After rolling up the sleeves of his wool shirt he pushed off across the steep face.

"Don't get below the bridge over Castle Creek," Willy reminded him, "or we'll have to wade across."

"It might feel good after this!" He laughed. "It's a good thing Andrea's a strong skier. I'd hate to take a snow bunny in here."

"She's tough. Don't worry."

Finally they got down to a dirt road that led out to Castle Creek Road.

"Okay," said Reeves, "we know it can be done. How long?"

Willy checked her watch. "Just under an hour, but we didn't push it. It could be done faster."

"Spare me," Reeves moaned. "What I do in the name of patriotism!"

He'd parked his Datsun pickup on Castle Creek Road that morning, but they had to walk with skis over their shoulders a little ways to reach it. "Did you mark exactly where we came out?"

"Yes, just above that house—" she pointed "—near that stunted pine next to the big one. I'll have to point it out to Hyde before race day."

"It better not be snowing hard that day. We could get lost up there."

"You'll have a radio?"

"Sure. Tell your team what our frequency is so we can get in touch if anything goes wrong."

They threw their skis in the bed of the truck and Reeves drove around to the front of Aspen Mountain and the lift.

"Ride up with me, babe," he said. "I'll treat you to lunch."

"Thanks. Then I'll take a couple of runs. It's too nice to stay inside. You know," Willy began as they sat down together on the moving chair lift, "I never told you about Myrna, did I?"

"Myrna?" Reeves hung his ski poles through the bars of the chair.

"Sure you want to hear this? It's a long story."

"It's also a ten-minute lift ride. Shoot."

"Well, she's an agent like Hyde in Clandestine Services. . . ."

"Wait a minute." He laughed. "*What* services?"

Willy colored a little. "Clandestine. I know it's crazy, Reeves, but you haven't any idea how very crazy the whole CIA really is. Anyway," she went on, "Myrna got into my room on The Farm and read Andrea's letter. She may have photographed it, I don't really know. . . ."

"I don't get it."

"I know, but listen to the whole thing . . ." and she went on to explain to Reeves her unproven fears about Myrna.

"Wow, that's quite an accusation," said Reeves. "I mean, that would make her a traitor and all."

Willy's head tilted as if to say "I know."

"But if that's true, well, shouldn't someone look into her background? Brother, you'd think they'd do something." He thought a moment, his thick dark brows drawn together. "Do you have any proof?"

"No. That's the trouble. And everyone in Washington thinks she's wonderful."

"*Everyone?*" asked Reeves pointedly. "That sounds like female jealousy, Willy. Is *everyone* that big macho agent of yours?"

Her lips tightened. "He's not *mine.* And yes, he trusts her completely. He sounded just like you, in fact!"

"If you really think this Myrna is jeopardizing Snowbird, something's got to be done. We could all be caught in a pretty pickle."

"Hyde Vandemeer promised me that he'd put her on another assignment. He promised."

"Will that prevent her from lousing things up?"

"If she doesn't know the plan, she can't reveal it, can she? It's obvious she doesn't know it yet or we'd have already been sold out and you can bet Andrea would be back in Russia under house arrest or something."

"Where is Andrea now?"

"She's racing this Saturday at Grenoble. It's going to be on TV. Would you like to come over and watch it with me? I'll get plenty of beer in."

"Well, actually—" Reeves's eyes slid over Willy's shoulder "—I was going to take Sue skiing...."

"Oh, well then, another time," said Willy lightly.

"Look, Willy, I'm sorry but—"

"Hey, I understand. Don't worry about it."

"Willy." Reeves turned to face her, his dark eyes serious for once. "I'll break that date if you want me to." His simple words were filled with a crowd of unspoken thoughts, all of which Willy understood clearly. He wanted to know where their relationship stood, where she stood; he wanted her to choose, to take him or let him go. It was her choice, her burden.

She liked Reeves, she really liked him: his cheerfulness, his easygoing ways, his frank open nature. He was so full of fun, so pleasant to have around; they got along so well. And yet, there was something missing. Now Willy knew what it was and she could never erase that knowledge.

"No, Reeves," she said quietly but firmly, "don't break that date." Her shimmering wintry eyes met his dark ones; understanding flowed between them like an electric current.

"Okay, Willy," he said slowly.

"Another time. After all, we're still—pardon the awful cliché—friends, aren't we?" she asked softly.

"Sure, babe. Friends. You know I'd do anything for you."

"I feel the same about you."

It wasn't so bad not being Reeves Baxter's "girl" anymore. It was easier between them, really, and Reeves was happy with Sue Lerner.

It hurt a little, though, and Willy was lonely. At least she had time to paint—she actually completed four canvases—saw some old friends around town and made dates to ski with them. She even took over full-time in the Cooper Street Gallery for a few days so Gayle could visit her oldest son at the University of Colorado in Boulder.

Her life was back on track as much as it could be that crazy winter. February was a breathing spell, the eye of the hurricane. She had to laugh; even her fingernails had a chance to grow back in. Hyde and Myrna and Operation Snowbird seemed to recede into the background, a half-forgotten dream from a child's fairy tale.

And yet they did exist. Willy knew she would have to see Hyde again and deal with Andrea's defection. She tried to put it out of her mind for the time being. It was something she didn't need to think about yet.

And then Representative Patterson and his wife arrived, flown in on a private Lear jet by an old friend.

"Well, Jim was just on his way so we scooted up to New York and grabbed a ride," explained Rachel, kissing her daughter. "You know your dad. He hates commercial flights."

It was all bustle and laughter and plans for skiing and cocktail parties.

"Did you get the mice out of our condo?" asked Rachel, shivering. "Last time. . . ." They were waiting for Edward in front of the airport.

"The manager promised he set traps. Mother, don't you want to relax a little? Don't you have enough of this stuff in D.C.?"

"You know your dad. It seems there are a few men here he needs to see. Some state representatives and someone big in the shale-oil business." Rachel looked at her daughter disapprovingly. "*Jeans.* Can't you ever wear anything else? All those nice clothes you have."

"Mother, everyone wears jeans in Aspen. *You* did when you lived here year-round."

"I was younger then and nothing was going on in Aspen in those days."

"Well, I'm young now and nothing's going on in my life now."

"Oh? What about Andrea?"

"I can't really say much about it right now."

"And Reeves?"

"That's off."

"Willy, what are we going to do with you? Twenty-seven years old and not married? In my day you'd have been called an old maid. Now, I realize that we were pressured far too much to settle down in the fifties, but dear, sooner or later—"

"Later," asserted Willy, ending her mother's often repeated lecture. "Oh, here comes dad."

"Sorry, but I had to thank Jim for the ride. How are you, Willy? You're looking great. Love that Aspen style!" He hugged her, sending out an aroma of expensive after-shave and cigars. "Don't tell me you still have that old Jeep? Good Lord, child, it's going to blow up one of these days!"

"I kind of like the old wreck." Willy smiled, leading them over to it.

"If it's the money, I'll lend you a few thou to get a new one."

"No, dad, I can afford a new car. I don't want one!" She laughed.

"Maybe for your birthday."

"Edward, leave her alone," interrupted Rachel.

She drove them to their four-bedroom condo with Jacuzzi, sauna, indoor pool and free bartender service for parties, and helped them with their bags. Edward immediately went off to meet someone; Rachel shut the door behind her and stared at Willy curiously. "Well, what is it?" she asked finally.

"What do you mean?"

"Come on, Willy. I'm your *mother*."

"Nothing's wrong. I'm fine," she said evasively.

"You look like you've lost your best friend."

"Don't be silly, mother."

"Is it Reeves?"

"Sort of. That's part of it."

"Willy—" her mother put out a hand, touching her arm lightly "—does it have anything to do with...well, with that old trouble?" Her voice was soft, anxious.

Willy stood up and began to walk across the miles of expensive gray carpet. "No, not really."

"No one's . . . hurt you?"

A starkly clear image of Hyde's face alight with passion, hovering over her, flashed through her mind. "No, no one's done anything to hurt me." The absurdity of her words almost made her laugh.

"I'm glad to hear *that*. It is Andrea then?"

"Partly."

"What's the other part?"

"Nothing."

Rachel threw her hands up in mock-despair. "All right, be a secretive brat. But you can't fool me. It's man trouble."

"Oh, mother."

"And what about Andrea? That poor child. All alone and doing such a brave thing. . . ."

"It's pretty well planned. I can't really tell you. . . ."

"Oh, don't I know about keeping secrets! You just be careful, my girl, and if you get in any kind of trouble, your dad can always pull a few strings."

Willy had to laugh at her mother's simplistic reasoning. She could just see Edward Patterson trying to pull strings in the Kremlin. "Thanks, mother. I'll remember that. You haven't said anything to him, though, have you?"

"Mum's the word, kiddo."

Rachel examined herself in the huge hall mirror and tucked a wisp of blond hair into place. "I'm planning a party for dad's sixtieth birthday, dear. In two weeks. We'd so like you to be there."

"Fly back to Washington? But it seems as if I just got back."

"This will be quite a do, Willy. Everyone will be there. Unfortunately the president will be out of town, but the first lady may stop by."

"Sounds too rich for my blood."

"Not at all. Why, there will be all sorts of young men there—aides, lawyers, you know."

"You're trying to marry me off."

"Of course, dear, but it'll be a good party in addition. Louis is catering it. One reason we left this week is because the whole house is being repainted from top to bottom."

"All for dad's birthday?"

"Sure. Why not! And I bought him a brand-new Porsche. A lovely dark red one. But it's a secret till the night of the party. February twenty-seventh."

"I'll see."

"Your father will buy your ticket, Willy, if it's a matter of finances."

"Good Lord, no. Will you lay off the poor starving daughter routine? I'm doing fine."

"That's nice, dear." Rachel cocked her head, looking at her daughter. "You'll come then. Good."

That night Edward and Rachel invited Willy out to dinner with Jim of the Lear jet and Vic of the shale oil. "Bring a friend," suggested her father, so Willy asked Gayle and they walked from Willy's house to the Parlor Car Restaurant at seven-thirty to meet everyone.

The Parlor Car was, as everyone in Aspen knew, a private Victorian railroad car, used by presidents in the past, now retired into elegant leisure as a gourmet restaurant serving only a select few each night.

The Patterson party practically filled the narrow car.

"Darling," gushed Rachel, at her Washington-hostess best, "this is Jim Shore from New York and Vic Hampstead from Denver. This is my daughter, Willy, and her friend Gayle Martin."

Introductions over, they ordered cocktails. "I'm so glad you wore a skirt," whispered Rachel into Willy's ear. "I was afraid you'd show up in jeans."

Vic immediately snatched up Gayle, and Willy heard them discussing the shale-oil collapse on the western slope of the state. Jim Shore was obviously her job tonight.

"He loves to ski, honey," Edward was saying. "Will you show him around? My old legs can't keep up with you young folks."

Jim wasn't so young, perhaps forty or a little older, but he looked as if he was in good condition. Maybe he *could* ski.

"I understand you used to race," began Jim. He had bright blue eyes, curling light brown hair and smooth fair skin; he looked rich and very well cared for, as if he had a facial and massage at least once a week. He wore a blue cashmere sweater that matched his eyes.

"Yes, I was on the U.S. Ski Team for several years while I was at C.U."

"You must be an excellent skier."

"I do all right." She shrugged, always embarrassed by praise. Then, to change the subject, she inquired, "How do you know dad?"

"My law firm did some work for him last year. We got to comparing notes about Aspen. I've been visiting here for years."

"Jim is quite an art collector, Willy," Rachel put in then, turning to Jim. "Did you know our Willy is an artist? Very good, too. That watercolor in my front hall in Alexandria is hers."

"You mean the one of Pikes Peak?" Jim looked at Willy with new respect. "I've always admired it."

"Thank you."

"I'd like to see your work, Willy, and perhaps buy something."

"Stop by my gallery—on Cooper Street."

"I will."

And so the dinner progressed, marked by polite conversation, exquisitely prepared food, and the company of interesting, well-bred people.

Jim liked Willy; she could tell. His interest showed in his deep-set blue eyes, in the tilt of his head, in the masculine pitch of his body. She could tell.

And he was a perfect catch: good-looking, fit, wealthy, a skier, an art collector. Perfect.

Why, then, couldn't she throw herself wholeheartedly into the game? What was missing?

Was it ice-green eyes and tousled chestnut hair? Or Hyde's look of being the chosen one to the detriment of all others? Was it the uncompromisingly lean jawline, the hard straight mouth, the slight ironic smile that merely lifted the corners of his mouth, a mouth she knew could soften to utter sensuality?

"Can we drop you ladies off?" asked Edward as they were putting on their coats.

"We're so close, I can walk," replied Willy.

"My car's at Willy's. I'd like to walk, anyway, after all that food!" Gayle said with a laugh.

"May I walk you home?" asked Jim. "I could do with some fresh air myself."

They strolled the few blocks to Willy's house. It was cold and clear with a million diamonds scattered in the black velvet of the night sky. Their breath made puffs of white, like plumes, in the darkness.

"I've always loved Aspen. I plan on retiring here," Jim Shore was saying.

Was he trying to tell her something? Willy felt too sensitive all over, as if she had a fever. It was his close attention, she realized.

"Bye, you guys," said Gayle, getting into her car. "Nice meeting you, Jim."

"My pleasure." He had a light congenial voice, which skimmed over the significance of things.

Then they were alone.

"I'd like to see you again," he said with greater intensity than she had credited him with.

"Sure, we can go skiing...."

"That's not exactly what I meant."

"You can call me. I'm in the phone book." She tried to sound polite. Why was she so on edge? Was it her old fear come back to haunt her? She'd thought that was gone for good. Or was it merely disinterest pressed too closely by this stranger's desire?

"I will." His hand reached out. "I'm so glad we met tonight."

She shook his warm hand but let it go as soon as she could. Why this distaste? He was a nice man, an attractive man. She was perfectly safe....

"Good night, Willy. I'll be in touch."

"Good night."

And then she was safe within the familiar boundaries of her little house, her back leaning against the locked front door.

She expelled a long breath and a sigh as she tossed her gloves onto the couch and shed her sheepskin coat. If Jim did call her, she decided, she'd go out with him. He was a nice man, a decent man who was very obviously interested in her.

She threw two split logs into the potbelly and sat down on the couch. It wasn't really all that late; she could paint a little, but she really didn't feel like it. Idly she glanced around the cozy, dimly lit room.

And that was when her mind conjured him up; he was standing negligently in the doorway to the kitchen, his green eyes fixed on her. Then he was stooped, casually putting a match to the kindling in the potbelly, his strong, lightly furred forearm stretched out below the rolled up shirt-sleeve.

He kept moving around her house, unwanted, an intruder. She couldn't call the police on this one though, and for the life of her she couldn't fathom why he'd appeared that particular night. She'd been doing just fine without him.

Irritated, feeling the injustice of the situation, she turned off the lights and went up to her bedroom.

But he was there, too. It was that night again after the avalanche and she couldn't shake the hazy yet strangely living memory of his gentle strong hands removing her clothes, directing her naked arms into her nightgown, pulling the heavy quilt up around her chin. Then he was in the doorway and before he snapped off the light he paused for a long moment, his green eyes resting on her.

It was natural, although she fought it desperately, that Willy would recall the dramatic conclusion to that endless beautiful night.

Why was it still so painful? She could neither escape nor forget the memory.

Then the telephone next to the bed rang. Willy nearly jumped out of her skin. It couldn't be . . . *him*. . . .

She picked up the receiver on the second ring. "Hello?" Tentatively.

"Willy, did I wake you? I'm sorry."

"Oh, no, I was just . . . reading. . . ."

"Good. Look, it's silly to bug you at this hour, but in case you're an early riser, I thought I'd see if you'd like to go skiing in the morning."

"Well . . . sure. Yes. I'd like that very much. Lift 1A then. At, say, nine?"

"Nine it is. Sorry again if I woke you."

"Oh no, that's all right. And thanks, I mean, really, I appreciate the call, Jim." More than he would ever know. . . .

SEVENTEEN

"I swear," Willy vowed, "when I get back to Aspen, I'm staying there for the next twelve months and going absolutely nowhere!" She kicked her feet idly behind her from her prone position on her mother's bed. "I don't care if I win a trip around the world."

Rachel finished tracing the fine pale line of her brow with a dark cosmetic pencil. "You have been away from home a lot," she remarked casually. "First that extended art show...."

"It was mostly classes, mother."

"Oh...yes, and then there was that sudden trip to Europe."

"I told you about it. And it wasn't sudden."

Rachel frowned. "It's all got to do with Andrea, hasn't it?"

Willy rolled over onto her back, put her hands behind her head and stared at the ceiling. "I wish I could tell you everything...."

"But you aren't supposed to."

"Well...no, I really can't yet."

"Is it dangerous, Willy?" Rachel came to stand over her. "I've tried not to think of that."

"No. It really isn't. At least, nothing at all like you're thinking." Then she moved to a sitting position, wrapped her arms around her mother's waist and gave her a tight squeeze. "Who would worry about me if you didn't?"

"Your father, silly." Rachel smiled, gently kissing her daughter on her honey hair.

They took a walk around the grounds. Although it was not yet spring there was a hint of it in the air, and the buds on the cherry trees, maples and willows were swelling.

There was a smell indigenous to the soft damp winter earth in the south, an odor of bark and dead leaves and brown dry grass. It was an unusual scent, but warm and promising new life just around the corner. Willy drew the air deep into her lungs.

"I sometimes think I could live here," she mused aloud.

"I wish you did, sweetie," said Rachel. Then, pointing back toward the large white frame house, she remarked, "Look . . . the first crocuses."

"My goodness," Willy exclaimed as her eyes followed the path of Rachel's hand. "We won't have sprouts for two months yet in the mountains."

Linda came loping up, her tail beating the air madly. Willy picked up a pinecone and tossed it for her.

"Your father would murder you for that," scolded Rachel mock-sternly.

"Why?"

"Linda is trained to chase birds and only on hand signal. Never tennis balls or sticks or pinecones, dear."

"Sorry." Willy frowned, then laughed and went chasing after the playful dog until she tackled Linda in a pile of leaves. The dog barked and protested while Willy laughed uncontrollably, her turtleneck and jeans dirt and leaf covered.

It must have been the barking of the dog, not to mention Willy's giggling, that concealed the noise of the intruder. All Willy knew was that suddenly Linda's ears perked up and she was growling, her fine golden head totally motionless, turned toward the front of the house.

Willy rolled onto her side, craning her neck to see as the dog suddenly leaped toward the figure now crunching through the leaves.

"Linda! Come back here," Rachel was calling.

"It's all right, Mrs. Patterson," came that hauntingly familiar voice. "I'm sorry if I startled you. I did ring the bell."

But how had he found out she was in Virginia so quickly? It was weird, as if she was being shadowed every second. But of course, he'd merely phoned Gayle. Her heart swelled and then sank. She hadn't expected to see him, she wasn't prepared....

"Mr. Vandemeer, is it?" Rachel had no difficulty recalling as she walked toward Hyde, patting her leg for Linda to heel.

"Yes. You've a good memory," said Hyde easily as they shook hands.

Lord, he was slick, Willy thought as she came to her knees, brushing the leaves off her jeans. Slick and smooth with that cool masculinity of his. And look at how her mother was responding, as if she was his oldest friend!

It made Willy suddenly angry that he would dare intrude into her home life. Was there nothing left she could call her own?

"Hello, Willy," he was saying as they both walked up to her. "I heard you were in the Washington area and I thought I'd look you up."

Willy stood, avoiding his outstretched hand. How very polite of him. Then she had a sudden childish notion—a way of lashing out at him. A false smile curved her wide mouth. "You needn't act as if we're old friends," she said sweetly. "My mother knows exactly who you are, Hyde."

He met her sparkling blue eyes with his contained steely gaze. "Am I supposed to be angry, Willy, that you confided in your parents?"

Rachel rolled her blue eyes heavenward as she caught Willy's glance. "Ah, Mr. Vandemeer," she began, "I'm afraid that I'm the only parent, as you put it, who knows what's going on. Willy's father would be, shall we say, furious?"

Hyde gave a sympathetic shrug. "I can fully understand that, Mrs. Patterson."

"Rachel."

"Yes, Rachel." He smiled a clean white smile. "And if I might suggest trying to keep as many people in the dark as possible until after our friend is safe?"

"Of course." She returned his winning smile.

Willy sighed, shoving her hands in her pockets. "I assume," she said bleakly, "that you haven't come out here to chitchat with my mother."

"Willy, really...."

"It's all right, mother."

"I think," said Hyde, "it would be a good idea if I took Willy out for a while. Maybe to dinner. We could talk—"

"I really would rather not," she interjected with obvious haste.

"It's all right, dear," said Rachel. "Go off with Mr. Vandemeer...Hyde...and have a good time."

Willy could have throttled her mother for leaving her no out whatsoever.

"Now go on up and change," Rachel was suggesting, "and I'll fix Hyde a drink while he waits."

"We could just have a drink here," Willy said, angry at Hyde, angry at her mother and at the whole awful situation.

"Dinner, Willy," Hyde insisted coolly.

Dripping wet, with only a towel around her, Willy stood contemplating the contents of her closet. She hadn't the least idea what to wear. Hyde was dressed casually: blue shirt, brown sweater, tan sport coat. Perhaps she should dress to the tee. Then he'd have to take her somewhere très chic and he'd be uncomfortably underdressed. But knowing him, he'd stop by his place and change.

She chose a softly pleated wool skirt in gray flannel and a pale rose crepe blouse. She had very few pairs of shoes with her so she wore her old standbys: black leather pumps. At least she'd be almost on eye level with him. Any advantage she could get....

Rachel, as always, had been the perfect hostess. Hyde, by the time they were driving away in his car, admitted to being thoroughly charmed.

"Your mother," he told Willy, "is a gem. I thought for sure she was going to give me the third degree." Then Willy discerned again that easy smile he'd worn earlier on his lips, the way his nose seemed to be straight as an arrow when he smiled, and the sensual curl of his nostrils. His hair was longer than it had been in Switzerland. As the BMW took the curving hills of Virginia with ease, she recalled the feel of his rich chestnut-colored hair under her fingers; its smooth thick texture, the way it felt crisper at the back of his neck. And in spite of all her efforts to quell it, she felt that forbidden warmth in her belly, that tingling sensation only Hyde inspired.

Damn him, she swore silently. How easily he was manipulating her. Why did he have to come back into her life now? She'd prepared herself for World Cup week but this was too soon. She wasn't ready.

Hyde did, after all, stop by his Georgetown apartment to throw on a coat and tie. "I thought we'd go to Harry's Place out near American University," he said as they were greeted in that funky vestibule by the spry Mrs. Rohrstad.

Willy had wanted to stay in the car, protesting ridiculously that she didn't feel like climbing his stairs. Then, before humiliating herself further, she'd agreed to come in with him.

"It's not the best of neighborhoods," he'd explained, "and I'd feel better if you weren't out in the car alone."

So she'd followed him, wondering how in the name of heaven she was going to make it through the whole evening with him.

It simply wasn't fair to ask her to do this yet. She needed more time....

His apartment was exactly as she remembered: cozy, crowded, a little untidy. It smelled faintly of after-shave and smoke. At the glass door to the rooftop the old cat was scratching. While Hyde changed, Willy gave Tomcat a saucer of milk and a piece of questionable salami. She guessed that if Hyde could eat it, then certainly the cat could.

She wandered back into his living room, wishing she was at home in Alexandria, or better yet, Aspen. It was too hard, too soon.

Bent over, she leafed through his magazines on the coffee table, moving aside a white piece of notepaper with handwriting, scribbled on it so that she could sit down on the couch.

"Your mother invited me to your father's party tomorrow night," Hyde called from the bedroom.

Willy's stomach flip-flopped. "I hope you told her you couldn't make it." She couldn't help but notice the signature on the note. Myrna.

"I didn't say that, not exactly," he called again. "I told her I'd try to make it."

Willy didn't reply. She hadn't been able to stop herself from turning the note on the cushion toward her eyes, scanning it even though she knew it was wrong to do so.

Myrna was sorry that she'd missed Hyde. "Another time, my love," it read.

"All ready," Hyde was saying from where he stood in the bedroom doorway. Then he noticed Willy's head bent, studying the note. "What's that?" he asked casually, approaching as he was tightening the knot in his tie.

"I...I didn't mean...." Willy's voice faded away; her cheeks flamed scarlet.

He picked up the note, half bending over her to reach it. His after-shave wafted around them, making her feel dizzy.

After he'd read it, he crumpled it up and made a perfect nonchalant toss into a wastepaper basket. Willy had no idea what to say or do or think. She knew now that her suspicions about Hyde and Myrna were true. She knew that she never should have read his personal message and that because of her nosiness, her heart was breaking all over again.

"Are you ready?" Hyde asked.

She forced herself to meet his gaze. He was looking at her intently yet with no shame or malice. He might never have caught her reading his note.

"Sure," she fumbled in reply, rising from the couch, feeling as though her limbs had turned to jelly.

She should have told him to drive her home, but she didn't. Somehow it would have been like admitting defeat. If Myrna, and heaven knew how many others, could accept what little tidbits he threw at them, then that was fine. To each his own. But not Willy. She would not share him, she would not cry and weep and wail because he'd treated her love so casually. No. She would neither run from him nor would she chase after him. He could live his life however he chose. She would live hers with her head held up. Whatever he wanted to say to her at dinner she'd listen to, but that was all. He'd take her home afterward and she could let out the breath she already felt she'd been holding all evening.

The maître d' seated them in the posh, softly lit restaurant off Wisconsin Avenue. They were in northwest Washington, at the very outskirts of the capital, and Willy was unfamiliar with this particular area.

"It's a bit overdone in here," said Hyde from across the candlelit table, "but they've got the best lemon veal in D.C."

Willy nodded, smiled faintly and buried her head in the menu. When she didn't come up for air after five minutes, Hyde said easily, "Want me to order for you?"

No one had ever done that before. Still, she barely had an appetite so what did it matter anyway? "All right."

The veal was, she had to admit, excellent, although Hyde did have to finish hers. He had ordered a nice chardonnay in which Willy took a greater interest than the food. She wondered, as she sipped from her long-stemmed crystal glass, if Hyde was ever going to get down to business. What sort of game was he playing this time?

He'd been terribly nice to her all during dinner—a characteristic usually alien to Mr. Vandemeer. She wondered exactly why he was going to all the trouble.

The spacious paneled room adjoining the dining room was a piano bar. An elderly black man was skillfully playing mood-setting jazz from the thirties, his piano surrounded by a crowd of fans. The music and occasional laughter wafted into the dining room pleasantly, relaxing the diners, often enticing them to order another cocktail, more wine.

"Do you like jazz?" Hyde asked as he pushed his cleaned dinner plate aside.

"It's not my favorite," Willy commented, "but I like some of it." She looked toward the bar. "He's quite good."

"He is." Hyde leaned back in his chair, stretching his legs out a little. "I come here sometimes just to hear him. His name is Freddy."

"Do you come alone?" The words had escaped before she could stop them.

"Willy...."

"I'm sorry," she added quickly. "That's none of my business." She looked around uneasily.

There was a long awkward silence. Then, "I come here once in a while with Ted," Hyde said finally, his voice noncommittal.

"Ted?"

"A friend from the Company. Actually, you know him. You spoke to him when you first contacted the Company and, would you believe, he's the one with the lousy French accent?"

"Oh." Her gaze slid down and away to a spot on the tablecloth.

Hyde reached into his coat pocket and pulled out a crumpled pack of cigarettes. "Do you mind?" he asked.

Willy shook her head. "I didn't know you smoked."

"About three a month." He shook one out, had to straighten it a little, then put his silver lighter to it. "Tastes good." The blue smoke streamed toward the ceiling. He squinted an eye a touch.

"You ought to quit altogether."

"And you should never ski in avalanche areas."

Willy smiled inadvertently. "Touché!"

For a time he sat shamelessly studying her in the dim candlelight, as if he had all the leisure in the world to do so. She was horribly aware of the flickering light as it danced in his green eyes, of the unfathomable expression on his thin straight lips. She tried to participate in his game, to meet his gaze head-on and let him know that she no longer cared; she'd put Hyde Vandemeer in cement boots and dumped him in the Potomac. Still, she couldn't keep up the easy facade as well as he; she supposed he was far more adept at this sort of thing.

"Look," she breathed finally, "you brought me to dinner and it's getting late. I haven't all night...."

"And you'd like to get down to business."

"Yes, I would." She sipped from her coffee cup, holding it in both hands.

"Fine. I just thought it would be terribly rude of me to pop in on you with strictly business."

"I wouldn't have minded." She watched him stub out his cigarette, seemingly collecting his thoughts.

He clasped his hands in front of him on the table and leaned a little closer to her. "I'd like you to consider sliding into the background of Operation Snowbird."

She took a deep breath. So that was it. The same well-trodden subject. "No," she declared firmly. "I'm in. All the way."

Hyde sighed deeply. "Of course I know that has been your attitude, but I hoped that with the actual operation only days away now, you might have reconsidered." He reached into his pocket to take out another cigarette.

So, Willy thought, beneath the cool exterior he was not so relaxed after all....

The smoke curled up between them. "I want you to know," he said, "that we have located a female operative in Peru who skis rather well."

"No!" Sudden panic filled her. "Why are you doing this to me? Why, Hyde? You know I can handle it. You know, for God's sake, that Andrea will have a nervous breakdown if anyone but me is in those woods ready to switch places."

"You could wait down on Castle Creek Road for her. It would be a thousand times safer."

"Nothing is going to go wrong," Willy whispered ardently. "Nothing."

Hyde sat back in his chair. "Spoken like a real pro, Willy," he scoffed, folding his arms stiffly.

Willy let out a quavering breath, exasperated. "You'd have me believe that you really care, Hyde," she bit out acidly.

"Come on, Willy," he said in a very low voice. "You know I do."

"Oh, sure!" Her eyes glistened wetly now in the candlelight. "Like you cared in Switzerland? Come on, Hyde, I'm not a stupid drooling little female like Myrna!" She couldn't stop herself; in spite of the intimidating scowl cloaking his face she went on in an ardent whisper. "You really think you can take a woman to bed a couple of times and she'll be eating out of your hand! Really Hyde, you should know better. Correct me if I'm wrong, but it didn't work with your wife, did it?" She went on relentlessly lashing out at him, praying she would hurt him as much as he'd hurt her. "No, it didn't work with the ex-Mrs. Vandemeer and it's not going to work with this woman, either."

He met her tirade with icy masterful silence.

"Haven't you anything to say?" she taunted fearlessly.

Slowly, slowly, he leaned toward her. "Only that I think you'll jeopardize this whole operation because I didn't fall at your feet and beg for your love."

Willy's head snapped back as if she'd been slapped. Tears of anger and burning humiliation stung her eyes; her chest rose and fell heavily as if she was panting.

He ignored her. "The truth hurts, doesn't it, Willy? You don't like to think of yourself as one of those nasty vindictive females who'll do anything to spite someone who refuses to set you up on that pedestal."

Her lips were trembling so terribly that the words came out garbled but the message was clear nonetheless. "Go to hell." Then she was on her feet, her napkin falling unheeded to the plush carpet, her hand clasped over her mouth as she snatched up her purse. She began to run, pushing her way through the throng in the piano bar, bursting through the door and fleeing down the sidewalk.

A taxi! She had to find a taxi! She stopped, her chest heaving, her arm over her head waving back and forth frantically. Where was a cab? There had to be one!

And then she saw him walking steadily toward her.

Fear constricted her throat. She gasped and began to run again, but he was too quick for her and almost instantly his hands were on her arms and he was spinning her around roughly.

"No!" she panted. "Leave me alone! Oh God, just leave me be!"

Calculating he shook her, his face a mask of dark concerned shadows. "Calm down, Willy. I'm sorry. I didn't mean...."

She fixed a gaze on him, her eyes flashing hatred. "Of course you didn't...you bastard! And I'll tell you something else—" she gasped, tears streaming down her cheeks hotly "—I never asked you to put me up on any pedestal! I just didn't want to be hurt...not again! You were my first love, Mr. Hyde Vandemeer! Do you hear me? I had to force myself to get into bed with a man before you."

Again he shook her. "What the hell are you talking about? What about Baxter?"

Willy struggled against his relentless hold. "I never felt anything with him. But he cared. Something you wouldn't understand!"

Confusion slid across his face. "I don't get it...why? Why me?"

"I don't know." Willy sobbed then, her struggles lessening as exhaustion began to overcome her. "I just don't know why, after all these years, *you* had to be the one to ride up on a white horse!"

"What years?" Stern lines scored his face. "Tell me what you're talking about."

Willy sobbed. "Two boys . . . when I was just a kid. . . ."

Slowly comprehension spread across his stony features. "My God," he whispered. Then, as time hung suspended like high-tension lines between them he whispered, "No wonder. No wonder it was so . . . fresh with you. Oh God, Willy. . . ." He pulled her toward him slowly, gently, forcing her into the protective arc of his arms even though she remained still and unyielding. "Can you ever forgive me?"

Slowly, inevitably, the tension drained from her body and she let herself sob against his coat. Waves of crying swept over her and then receded, spent. She'd never let it out before—she'd been so afraid to cry, to let anyone know. She'd been afraid to face the humiliation, the shame.

Afraid until now.

Finally she brought her head up, sniffled and tipped her chin back to see his face more clearly. The car lights played on his features oddly in the cool eastern night, and she hadn't the least idea what she saw in those hard yet familiar hollows of his face.

Strangely, as the strong grip of his hands pressed into her arms, she knew his thoughts didn't matter. Unwittingly, Hyde Vandemeer, despite his seemingly impenetrable surface, had breathed warmth and security back into her soul.

EIGHTEEN

They had talked for a long time after that, walking together through the cool night, alone in their preoccupation with each other. Willy could hardly remember the things she'd told him, the things he'd said in return. They hadn't been earth-shaking things, just small warm comfortable words two people who care about each other might say.

She accepted his difficulties with relationships, forgave him the pain he'd caused her. He could be so solemnly kind and caring; there was still so much hidden under his brittle exterior, so much to discover about him.

He held her hand as they walked, a simple loverlike gesture. He had taken her back to his car, driven her out to Alexandria. Thank the Lord he hadn't pressured her into anything physical. It was as if he knew her innermost feelings better even than she herself. He had kissed her forehead, opened the car door for her and said good-night soberly—a knight-errant returning his lady fair to her father's castle.

It was like being sixteen again and having a terrible crush on someone, thought Willy, the next evening as she finished dressing before the party. She'd chosen a black crepe cocktail dress with a halter neck to show off her fine shoulders and a swirling flare to the bottom of the skirt. She'd also decided on her highest heels—she was proud of her height—and her hair was pinned up in a French knot. Some eye shadow, mascara, a touch of blush and red lipstick.

She wondered if Hyde would even recognize her tonight.

Her father's birthday party was just starting. She could already hear the voices downstairs, the opening and closing of the front door. She felt like Cinderella on her way to the ball to meet Prince Charming.

Hyde had promised to come to the party and Willy knew he would be there because he wanted to see her as much as she wanted to see him. She was, she could finally admit to herself, crazy-mad in love with Hyde Vandemeer, and she didn't care who knew it anymore.

It had taken that ugly scene the night before to break through his damned reserve, his fear of being vulnerable, his years of cool detachment from emotion. His cruel words had hurt Willy badly but the pain had been worth it a hundred times over. She'd finally gotten through a tiny chink in his armor and found the man underneath.

She was as excited and nervous as a teenager to be seeing him again. She remembered his face as she'd last seen it the night before: soft, loving, *feeling*. It had been a beautiful face, far more attractive than his usual cold chiseled mask.

Finally she was ready. The house was filling up; she could practically feel the throb of the crowd below as she left her room and descended the white painted colonial staircase.

Rachel Patterson was resplendent in a deep purple creation covered with fringe and beads, which Willy would never have had the nerve to wear. But she did look radiant and young and lovely standing next to her husband, Edward, in his very expensive dinner jacket.

A dinner jacket! She'd never told Hyde how formal the party was. Did he even own a dinner jacket? But there were men there in dark suits, too, she noticed, breathing a sigh of relief.

There was a huge buffet table set up in the formal dining room, and a bar in the corner of the living room. The house overflowed with festivity and flickering candelabra and champagne punch. Every woman appeared beautiful in the soft light, every man seemed a Don Juan. The talk was quiet still, the typical Washington gossip of who slept with whom and how much money so and so made. Endlessly fascinating to the Washington crowd.

Willy didn't even mind it tonight; it didn't matter. She was merely smiling, sipping a glass of punch, biding time until Hyde arrived.

"Happy birthday, dad," she said, kissing him. "Mother, you look absolutely stunning!"

"So do you, dear. No jeans, I see," whispered Rachel, winking.

"Thought I'd put them in the wash." Willy grinned back.

Then Rachel took Willy aside. "I'm going to wait until everyone is here, and then you go and get his birthday present from the Sterlings' next door and drive it up right in front. What a surprise! I can't tell you how complicated it was to get the damn thing here without his knowing!"

"Just give me the high sign."

"You look like a dream, Willy. I'm so glad you and that nice young man hit it off last night. You weren't so keen at first...."

"Things change," said Willy, blushing in spite of herself.

"He's *very* attractive, your Hyde, but I must say, he's quite intimidating with those cold green eyes! I like a jollier sort, but then, *chacun à son goût*, as they stay. Each to his own."

Rachel was the perfect hostess, flitting through the large rooms like an exotic deep purple butterfly, saying exactly the right thing to this ambassador, whispering a *soupçon* of gossip to that senator, diverting the conversation of two Capitol Hill adversaries at precisely the crucial moment.

At eight o'clock Hyde still hadn't arrived. He had had to work late, she supposed, but disappointment began to tarnish the edges of her gaiety.

At eight-thirty Rachel nodded to Willy. It was with a certain sense of relief that she left the brilliantly lit house by the kitchen door and walked across the winter-brown lawn to the next-door neighbors' garage.

Susie and Chicky Sterling were, of course, at the party so Willy just raised the garage door herself, found the keys under the floor mat of the new dark red Porsche and started it up. It certainly was different from her old Jeep, she acknowledged as it roared softly to life. It *smelled* so new! The drive next door to her parents' house was fun, if a little short. *Wow!*

Won't dad be shocked! she thought, grinning and wishing, totally out of context, that Hyde was beside her in the darkness in the flashy red car. Maybe he'd arrive while she was gone....

She was driving up to the front of the house, honking the horn, and Rachel was dragging her husband out to see the car with crowds of people behind them.

"Happy birthday, Eddy!" cried Rachel, beaming.

"I don't believe my eyes!" boomed Edward, thunderstruck.

Everyone howled with laughter. Edward Patterson was usually the least excitable politician on the hill, smooth and unflappable.

Willy laughed too as she swung her long shapely legs out of the car and handed the keys to her father. "Happy birthday, dad!"

Her father took the keys, staring at them as if mystified.

"Go on!" the crowd shouted. "Go on!"

Willy melted back into the throng, giggling at her father's expression. No one had ever seen him so bewildered before.

And then she felt a soft touch on her bare arm and turned. Her heart bounded with immense pleasure and she felt her face go soft with welcome. "Hyde."

"I got here just in time for the surprise," he said into her ear. "Your mother's idea?"

"Of course."

"Not a bad idea as presents go," he said wryly. "I'll give her the date of my birthday...."

"When is it, by the way? There are so many things I don't know about you."

The throng was oohing and aahing around them as Edward started up the new car. Hyde's face was shadowed. Struck on the temple by the light from a window, it looked like burnished bronze.

"March fifteenth," he replied. "Beware the ides of March."

"Why beware?" she asked, teasing.

"Look what happened to Julius Caesar," he answered lightly.

Everyone was streaming back inside the warm house, laughing, talking, a party crowd, ready for more surprises, more excitement.

"Hungry?" asked Willy. "There's tons of food...."

He wore a dark suit with a faint pinstripe—very up and coming young Washingtonian—a white shirt, a striped tie in crimson and gray and silver. And he was looking at her with a kind of mixed amusement and wonder. "I couldn't see you very well out there. You're a knockout." His green eyes scanned her slowly, deliberately, as if to impress every detail on his mind forever.

"Better than jeans?" she quipped, a little embarrassed but loving it at the same time.

"Not better, just different," he said.

"Well feast your eyes. This is my once a year costume. I'm disguised as a society girl."

He grinned. "I *was* hungry but I forgot there for a minute."

"Come on." She pulled his arm, leading him to the buffet table where she started piling a plate with food for him. "Louis catered it," she announced loftily, pulling her face into a smirk.

"Oh, Louis," Hyde said, playing along with her. "I never have anyone else do mine. I do adore his whipped cream salmon croquettes."

"*Croquettes?*" Willy laughed. "That's a *game!*"

"Oh no, it's Louis's most famous dish."

Hyde had a droll yet boyish sense of humor. She'd never heard him tease before or laugh unrestrainedly more than an isolated time; she'd never traded jokes with him or felt that he was relaxed. She enjoyed his company at the party; she hoped he enjoyed himself as much. It was delightful to have such a handsome man by her side. The women all flicked catlike glances at him: curious, tentative, interested.

"The ladies can't keep their eyes off you," Willy whispered into his ear. "I may have to fight them off."

"That's funny. I thought the men here tonight exceedingly rude, eyeing you so blatantly. I was just rolling my sleeves up." Hyde grinned.

Rachel welcomed Hyde warmly. "I'm so glad you could make it. We have every branch of the government represented here," she quipped.

"So glad to be of service." Hyde bowed slightly. "By the way, Mrs. Patterson, my birthday is March fifteenth, but I lean toward blue."

Rachel laughed, always ready with a repartee. "I'll get you a model to put together. Edward," she called, waving him over, "come say hello to Willy's friend, Hyde."

"Welcome, young fellow. Did you get a load of my toy? I tell you, I never was so damned surprised in all my life." Edward held out his big hand to Hyde.

"Happy birthday, Representative Patterson. Lovely party. And your two women are the belles of the ball."

"Aren't they, though?" boomed Edward.

They ate cold shrimp, pâte on crackers, marinated artichoke hearts and mushrooms, petits fours. Willy licked the frosting off her fingers like a child while Hyde laughed at her, wiping a crumb from the corner of her mouth.

"When can we leave gracefully?" Hyde finally asked.

"We?" Willy quirked a golden brow at him.

"You're coming to my place to have a nightcap, aren't you?" he asked mock-innocently.

She leaned close to him, feeling desire pulse in her belly. "Of course. We can go anytime. No one will notice. I'll just tell mother." She hated to leave him even for those few moments, jealous of the time spent away from him. It was wasted time, empty.

"Let's go," she said a moment later, breathless, coat over her shoulders.

Then they escaped the smoky, noisy, swirling crowd and slipped into the cold dampness of the February night.

He took her in his arms right there, even before they'd reached his car, and kissed her until she was half sobbing and bursting with desire.

"Will your parents mind?" he asked, his lips moving on hers.

"I don't know. I don't care. I don't think so. Oh, Hyde...."

Then they ran hand in hand like children toward his car

"Wait!" Willy exclaimed, pulling on his hand to stop him. She bent to slide off her high heels. "I can't run in these damn things," she explained.

"You'll freeze," Hyde laughed.

"I'm used to bare feet. Never could stand shoes." And they ran again together to his car.

She kept her hand on his thigh during the drive into Washington. She loved the feel of his muscles flexing when he pressed on the gas or brake. The lights of the cars coming toward them in the night flashed in her eyes like a mad kaleidoscope: exciting, promising, beckoning. She felt as if the world were transformed, or as if she herself were a different person. Everything opened up for her and yet she was not vulnerable. She was powerful, filled with passion.

His apartment was beginning to look familiar to her with its homey clutter. And yet they could have been anywhere—it would not have mattered.

They clung together in the entry hall with its insane Victoriana, they laughed at Mrs. Rohrstad's taste and loved it together, they kissed in Hyde's doorway, then in the living room, hands clinging, feeling, touching, nerve ends tingling under the onslaught of an overload of sensation.

He unzipped her dress to stroke the warm satiny skin of her back and waist. She unbuttoned his shirt, reaching her hands under it and around his chest.

Small whispered endearments echoed in the darkness: sighs, groans, quick intakes of breath. They never bothered turning the lights on.

Somehow they made it to his bedroom. Clothes fell in a sighing heap on the floor. Moonlight through the window touched a gentle hollow, a flank, an arm, a chest, a leg, in whorls of pearly opalescence.

She tumbled into a maelstrom of quivering sensations. Flesh pressed hard against her breasts—closer, always closer until the distance between them was nothing, less than nothing, negative distance.

"Oh God!" Willy heard herself cry once, but he muffled her cry with his lips—hard and soft, satin and steel. She knew she was clawing at his back, thrusting against him violently. But she was lost in responses and it didn't matter. Nothing mattered. They rose and fell together, his sweat-slicked skin sliding over hers. So good. So beautiful.

And then the peak: a great hot bright flower blooming in the night. Its petals falling, falling, lightly fluttering to the ground in quiet radiance.

"Oh," Willy breathed finally. "Oh."

Hyde still lay on her, his long lean body collapsed over hers. "Am I too heavy?" he asked at last.

"No, stay." She pulled him closer, kissing his damp neck and pressing her sated loins into his. "Don't move."

"You can't breathe."

"I don't need to . . ."

"For a girl who had an unfortunate experience in her youth, who insists she was afraid of sex, you certainly have compensated well," Hyde breathed into her ear.

"It was you, all you."

"I'd like to believe that, my girl, but really—"

"Hyde, I tell you, it's only you. I. . . ." She was going to say "I love you," but something stopped her. It was too soon, too fast. "I only want you."

"You're something," he said, marvel filling his voice. He bent his head, kissing along her collarbone in tiny butterfly kisses up to her neck.

Finally they slept, so close that when one stirred in the night the other stirred too. Once she woke up feeling sudden panic, and reached out a hand. He was there. She wakened him, shaking his shoulder. "Will you leave me in the morning again?" she asked, terribly anxious, half dreaming.

"No, my sweet. I'll be here. Go to sleep." His warm hand stroked her naked shoulder, soothing, calming.

She slept.

"It's nine o'clock," Hyde was saying softly in her ear. "I have to go to work soon."

She snuggled close to him, slid her arms around the warm bulk of his body. "I won't let you."

"And you have a plane to catch."

"This afternoon."

"Want some coffee?"

"Sure."

He got up, lean hips and muscled back, hard-sinewed arms and legs a glorious rhapsody to her eyes. Willy dozed, completely at peace, completely happy, completely in love. Then the aroma of coffee woke her and he was there, gazing down at her with a kind of regretful awe in his green eyes, a coffee mug in each hand.

"Hyde?" she asked. "What is it?"

"Nothing." But there was something withheld from her....

"Do you want to talk?" Abruptly the glorious illusory mist was dispelled. She sat up, pulling the covers up to her armpits.

"I'm freezing," he answered illogically, putting the mugs down and sliding in under the covers. She noticed instantly, painfully, that he did not allow himself to touch her.

"Hyde?" Her eyes were huge and blue gray like the fathomless ocean on a wintry day, pleading, guessing in spite of her desire not to.

He sipped his coffee pensively, silently. She sat stiffly, feeling awkward and vulnerable in Hyde's bed, naked—so close yet so far from him despite what they'd shared.

"Look, Willy," he finally began. "I'm not an easy person to get along with."

"Is that an excuse or a justification?" she asked carefully.

"Neither. I'm trying to explain...." He ran a hand through his tousled hair; a line ran down between his dark curving brows. "I had a bad time with Sandy...." He looked up cautiously. "My ex-wife. She...well, I guess she really hurt me." He gave a short harsh laugh. "Oh, wouldn't she just love to see her handiwork now? She did more than she ever suspected."

"Hyde." Softly, caressingly. She wanted desperately to put a hand out, to touch him. She didn't dare.

He met her eyes with his. Bitterness filled his gaze like venom. "I should never have touched you in the first place, never have started anything. It was stupid of me—stupid and unforgivable."

"I forgive you," she whispered.

His ice-green eyes softened. He reached a hand out to touch her face lightly. "Don't. I'm not a whole person. Something's frozen inside of me. I guess it's fear, fear of being hurt like that again." He averted his gaze, staring out the window as if trying to find the words with which to explain. "I can take what you have to give, Willy, but I can't reciprocate. I can't make a commitment. I can't, and I won't. It would be too cruel."

"What happens to me then?" she asked, feeling tears well up in her eyes. "I thought...." She willed the tears not to fall, swallowing hard.

"It would only get worse later on. Don't you see? It's better to cut it off now, before things get too . . . involved."

"What if I refuse to just let things drop? I can be pretty persistent, Hyde."

He turned a faint sad smile to her. "And I can be crueler than you'd ever imagine."

"Isn't it worth a try? I think we could have something good between us. We could try together."

"Willy." He took a deep breath, looked upward to the ceiling and started again. "You're a wonderful woman: smart, strong, loving, talented. What do you want with an old scarred war-horse like me? I have nothing to offer you. No fortune, no talents, a hell of a nasty job, an awful temper. Our lives are a million miles apart. We have nothing in common. You can't base a relationship on that. It's too hard, even with a normal person."

Then, finally, she did reach out and put a hand on his arm. "You *are* normal. Isn't it normal to react when someone hurts you? You can heal the wounds. With help. You can try...."

"And fail." He gave a quick ugly laugh, shaking his head. "No, it isn't worth it. I can't handle that sort of thing. I'm too old, too used up. I haven't got the energy to start all over again."

Willy sat silently, drained and numb. Was joy ever without its twin, pain? Hyde had given her womanhood; now he took from her the reason for possessing it.

"Operation Snowbird cannot be put in jeopardy by this . . . thing between us, Willy. Can you handle that?"

"Yes. Can you?" Stiffly.

"I'll have to, won't I? We won't see each other much. I'll be in Aspen a couple of days and even then we'll have to stay apart. I'll make it as easy as possible for you...."

"Thanks," she threw in, noting a line of pain crease his brow for a split second. Then she sighed. "All right, Hyde. I can be just as mature and civilized as you. Don't worry, I won't throw any female hysterics in front of the Russians."

He was staring at her with contained and painful approval, carefully devoid of ambition. "Good. Then we'll be...well, I won't say *friends,* but co-workers, acquaintances."

"Sure, Hyde." She looked down at her hands clutching at the folds of the blanket. Anguish crawled sideways, crablike, across them.

He got out of bed and went into the bathroom. She heard the shower turn on as she sat there in his bed, still warm and sated with lovemaking. His scent still clung to her, faint and musky and beloved, while he soaped and scrubbed himself in the shower, carefully washing every trace of her person away.

Quietly, unthinkingly, blindly, Willy got up, retrieved her black dress and heels and dressed, wrapping her coat around herself tightly as if to hold herself together. She'd forgotten her purse last night, she suddenly realized. She hadn't a penny. Oh God, she couldn't face him again.... She looked around desperately. His suit pants lay on the floor in a heap. She went over to them, kneeled down and felt feverishly through the pockets. A twenty-dollar bill, a few tens, some ones. She took the twenty, dropping his pants as if they were red hot, and crushed the bill in her hand.

She found a pencil in the kitchen and used the back of a laundry bill to write: "Borrowed twenty for a cab. Pay you back in Aspen."

That was all.

Then she fled down the stairs and left the building, stumbling along the sidewalk like a drunk, blinded by tears, her arm waving disjointedly like a broken marionette for a taxi.

When a cab pulled up at the curb and the driver rolled down his window, she laughed a little, slightly hysterical and hiccuped. "Alexandria, please," she managed.

The cabby's world-weary eyes met hers in the rearview mirror. "Late party, lady?"

"Yes, a party," she repeated automatically.

The cabby shook his head to himself, turned on the meter, shifted gears. "It takes all kinds," he muttered.

NINETEEN

World Cup week in Aspen was to Willy and to so many other participating locals a week of incredibly good times, international glamour and high tension. It was a week of TV cameras following everyone who was anyone everywhere, of network vans blocking the streets and movie celebrities strolling, smiling and vibrant, through the snow-packed malls. And it was a week of money. There was so much money in Aspen it could be scented in the pristine air. Each shop proprietor and lodge keeper and restaurateur watched his cash register fill to overflowing.

And the races hadn't even begun yet.

It snowed heavily the first three days of World Cup week—so heavily that very few flights made it into Aspen. Whenever that happened the car-rental agencies in Denver rented out every last unit they had. No one wanted to wait, stuck at Denver's Stapleton International, while the white gold drifted from the skies over the majestic Rockies.

And so in spite of the heavy March snows the tourists arrived, packing the tiny western slope town to capacity, cheerfully spending their money for a week in Aspen where one was assured of casually rubbing elbows with oil sheikhs, visiting dignitaries, top-billed movie and television personalities and world-renowned athletes. They were all there in Aspen, filing into the shops, driving through the streets, skiing the spiraling slopes as if they truly belonged.

By Wednesday, while the trial runs of the World Cup were going on, the tension in the atmosphere of the town had begun to mount. Everyone watched the weather reports. Eyes were turned heavenward; it *had* to stop snowing, and soon, or the races would be canceled. The Denver weathermen called for clearing on Thursday and Friday with the possibility of snow again late Saturday and maybe Sunday, the day of the finals—the day Andrea Pavlevitch's name would resound worldwide—but not for winning the downhill. Andrea Pavlevitch would never finish the race....

Lord, Willy thought as she finished writing up a sales slip in her shop, it *had* to quit snowing. The more the heavy spring snow piled up, the greater the danger of an avalanche when Andrea skied down the back side of the mountain to safety. Willy worried incessantly about it.

And then again, if it snowed too much, if the racecourse couldn't be cleared of new powder, if the visibility was too bad, they wouldn't hold the races at all.

It *had* to stop soon....

"Hi, Will!" came a man's friendly voice from the door of the gallery. "What's going on?"

She looked up and smiled. "Hi to you, Will," she said. "Where've you been keeping yourself?"

William Keinast—Will—was sheriff of Pitkin County. He'd known Willy since she was born, and had been a good friend of the Pattersons for many years before that.

She watched him browse through the shop as she made his way toward the counter. At fifty-nine, a year younger than her dad, Will was still a fine figure of a man. Thick silver hair showed under the sheriff department's Stetson, his seamed face was healthily tanned and the muscled stomach beneath the blue denim shirt and silver-buckled belt was unquestionably flat. Tall, polished western-cut boots completed the picture. Not surprisingly, Will had once posed for a Marlboro ad.

"It had better stop snowing," he said as he leaned his arms negligently against Willy's glass countertop.

"I'll say." She shook her head.

"How come that gal Gayle's been runnin' the show so much? You fixin' to sell out?" he asked in that western drawl of his—people tended to forget that Aspen was still, in many ways, an old western silver-mining town. Will Keinast might have lived in the 1880s....

"I am *not* selling out, Will." She stiffened her back, playfully severe. "I've just been busy."

"Jet-setter." He scowled as he pulled a fat cigar from his blue denim shirt pocket.

"Oh sure." She grinned. "Don't I just wish." Then, "you aren't going to light that *thing* in here...."

White teeth flashed beneath a neatly trimmed gray mustache. "Maybe I am, maybe I'm not...."

He was up to something. Willy knew him too well. But what? "Okay, Will. Let's have it."

He laughed, a deep masculine chortle. "Aren't so dumb, are you? Well, I'll tell you what, little gal. Your dad asked me to check in on you from time to time...."

"But why?" She raised a blond brow.

"Says he knows you too well and that you and your mother are up to something. 'Fraid you got him concerned."

So that was it. Edward Patterson hadn't been too preoccupied to notice that his daughter, had been to Washington a lot. And then, too, his wife could never keep a secret from him.

"Tell dad for me, Will—" she tried to sound flippant "—that he can just mind his own business. He's been on that House committee too long and he's starting to think like Robert Ludlum, for Lord's sake."

"So you think that's it, do you?" asked Will, smiling as he watched her with a practiced eye.

"Yes. He's getting senile... like you," she put in impishly.

"Should put you over my knee," growled Will, "but guess I'll let that pass, young gal. Just do me one favor...."

Willy nodded, relenting. After all, if Will wanted to look out for her then she sure as heck wasn't going to tell him not to. You never knew when having the men in blue on your side might come in handy.

"You just call on me anytime if you need anything. Anything at all, Will, you hear me?"

She stood at attention. "Yes, sir!"

"All right, gal." He straightened back up to his six feet one. "Be seein' ya."

Willy smiled. "Okay. And pray that it quits snowing. You can do that for me right now." Then he was gone. Well, she thought, she couldn't fault Will Keinast and her dad for caring. She just hadn't realized how inner tension could communicate itself so subtly to those who were close to a person.

She walked to the plate-glass window overlooking the Cooper Street Mall. Above the bare crab apple treetops and Victorian lampposts of the mall the sky was deep gunmetal gray, and white flakes still drifted down lazily. The tourists thronged the malls and streets, oblivious to the fact that if it didn't stop snowing soon there would be no World Cup.

Willy squeezed her eyes shut tightly, whispering a silent prayer: *Let it stop snowing, please let it stop....*

Hyde swore a blue streak when he landed at Stapleton on Friday morning and found out there were no flights going to Aspen.

"You wouldn't want to fly in the blizzard anyway," said the smiling ticket agent at Rocky Mountain Airways. "Can you imagine trying to land, sir? I'm afraid you don't realize the danger."

Hyde's green eyes bored into the agent's coldly. He detested officious, patronizing employees no matter where he ran across them. "So you suggest," Hyde said sharply, "that if I'm going to get to Aspen I'd better rent a car?"

Again, the agent smiled. "That would be the logical solution, sir...but...I'm afraid that due to the length of the storm, all rental vehicles will be taken by now. Of course, you shouldn't take my word for it."

"Why do I get the feeling," snapped Hyde, "that you're enjoying this?" He turned on his heel and went toward the steps leading below to the car rental.

Of course, there were no cars whatsoever to be had. Nor were there any buses leaving to get him there by eight that evening. He tried a couple of taxi-cab drivers but too many taxis had already filled up and left for the mountains—some of them had to service the airport. Requesting help from the local FBI office was out as was the Denver police. A CIA agent desperate to get to Aspen? And what was the CIA doing on an operation within the continental U.S. anyway?

There *was* someone he could call, someone who was familiar enough with a situation like getting stuck in Denver that she would have a ready solution.

Still, he didn't like calling on her, having to depend on her at this point. Their relationship was way too tenuous, and he'd prefer to see as little of her as possible, not only for her anonymity and safety but for his own peace of mind.

It hadn't been easy cooling their relationship. It was certainly for the best, but it had been hard nevertheless. Willy Patterson was a special person, a very special woman. He really did hate to call on her, particularly when he was so darn irritated by this unexpected disastrous delay in Denver.

Reluctantly, he dialed the number in Aspen. "Hello?" came that husky-sweet voice.

"Willy."

Utter silence but for the buzzing static on the line, then, "Hyde?"

"I never thought I'd catch you at home. Listen, I'm stuck in Denver...."

"Well, of course you are," she said carefully.

He cursed, unable to contain his irritability. "Does everyone within a thousand-mile radius know that but me?"

"Yes. It's winter in the Rockies, Hyde. It snows."

"Really. I hadn't noticed."

"You realize," she said as if walking on eggshells, "that the racers' press reception is tonight at eight?"

"Of course I know that!" he couldn't help but growl. Then he glanced around. Several people in the crowded airport were staring at him. No wonder....

"Let me think," said Willy carefully. "I assume you've tried the car rentals and taxis...."

"Brother. Of course I have."

"All right. The buses?"

"Yes. Full and their schedules are ridiculous anyway."

"Give me a sec." A long pause over the line. "Be at the Ship Tavern in the Brown Palace Hotel in downtown Denver at three. Just wait there at the bar and I'll have a ride to Aspen for you."

"When will that put me in Aspen?"

"Seven or seven-thirty, unless there's a problem getting over Vail Pass." Then, "Don't forget—the Ship—"

"Lord, Willy!" he complained, "how dumb do you think I am?" and the moment he hung up the receiver, he realized that Willy had been too impersonal on the other end of the line. Well, he couldn't blame her.

The two Irish coffees he had at the Ship Tavern, along with a hearty lunch of delicious Colorado prime rib, finally relaxed him. And, he had to admit, he was curious to see the famous center of western elegance and hospitality: the Brown Palace Hotel.

The time there passed quickly. He did, however, realize that if Willy screwed up and couldn't get him a ride, he wouldn't be able to give her instructions in time and they'd have to contact Andrea somehow at another time and place before the race. Where and when? The Eastern-bloc racers were watched so closely and that press reception was still ideal....

It took him several seconds to realize from his position on the bar stool that it was Willy approaching him, dressed like a real westerner in boots, jeans and jean jacket, a blue-and-white plaid shirt and turtleneck beneath it. She could have been doing an ad for Levi's against the elegant hotel decor. She looked fabulous; many a lunching Denver businessman's eye followed her easy movements.

Then she was standing there in front of him, her honey hair falling over one eye in that tauntingly familiar yet achingly new way, her wide sensual mouth serious, controlled. "Well?" she breathed. "Let's go."

He paid his tab and followed her out, unable to keep his gaze from straying to the back of her snug-fitting jeans. He was thoroughly surprised to see her there, he realized, as they strode down the long tiled corridor toward the lobby. He certainly hadn't expected anything like this. The doorman held the door for her, tipping his hat. She smiled brightly and Hyde had the sudden urge to pull her to him and taste those warm pink lips right there in front of God and everyone.

But he wouldn't. He knew that. It was simply that he hadn't been prepared to see her in Denver. Willy Patterson, he was discovering, was not the kind of woman a man could dismiss when she was in his presence.

He held the driver's door for her, catching a faint whiff of her perfume. "Whose car?" he asked off-handedly as he climbed into the passenger seat.

"Gayle's. You remember. My manager." Expertly Willy pulled out into the downtown Denver traffic. Thank heavens, by rush hour they'd be in the foothills of the Rockies on Interstate 70, way ahead of the weekend stream of humanity that would head for the ski areas.

Willy looked awfully serene, Hyde registered, as if being back in Aspen for the past week had done her a world of good. She seemed happy and relaxed, young and carefree. He should have been glad for her, but somehow he felt strangely envious of her apparent happiness.

And yet he wondered if it was all a facade. Was Willy really so lighthearted? He would have bet she'd taken his last little speech, his sadistic curtain call, hard. She was that kind of woman—warmhearted, too impetuous for her own good. And the way she'd left him that morning still rankled. Not that she hadn't had every right....

He wondered suddenly, watching her fine profile as she drove, if he wasn't just the littlest bit resentful because she wasn't tearing her hair out and wailing over him. He buried the thought instantly.

Just then she looked over at him for a second, an appraising gleam in her somber blue eyes. "I owe you a twenty," she finally said, turning her gaze back to the wet road.

"No, don't be silly," he hastened to say, embarrassed.

"I pay my debts," she insisted coolly. "Hand me my purse, please." She fumbled around in it, driving one-handed.

"You're going to kill us both over a lousy twenty dollars," he grumbled. "Forget it."

"Forget it? No way. Here." She stared straight ahead through the windshield, holding her hand out to him. In it was a crumpled twenty-dollar bill. "Take it."

He took it.

She drove in utter silence for a time. The atmosphere in the car was tense, a little awkward. Damn! It would have been so much easier to have flown into Aspen. To have to ask Willy for help, for Pete's sake, was rotten.

"Sorry about snapping at you on the phone," he offered as he automatically looked to the left then right, back-seat driving, watching the heavy traffic on Denver's Larimer Street.

"Relax," Willy said, glancing over at him. "I *do* know how to drive, Hyde."

"Umm."

The sun streamed down on Denver through parted boiling gray clouds. It was actually warm and the streets were quite slushy.

Hyde slipped out of his winter coat and turned toward Willy. "At least the storm's breaking."

She shook her blond head ruefully. "Don't I wish. Look, this is Denver, not the mountains. I can guarantee it's still coming down hard up there."

Hyde looked due west toward the foothills, which sloped steeply up from the high prairie on which Denver was built. Some big country up there; it was mostly hidden now by a solid storm-gray curtain suspended in the winter sky, but the presence was there, the tall, craggy Rocky Mountains, the Continental Divide. Willy had told him on his last visit to Aspen that if a raindrop hit the exact line of the divide, half of it would flow to the Pacific, the other half to the Atlantic.

As the Audi climbed steadily higher into the foothills on I-70, Willy said, "Here we go. The road will be murder in a minute. The good old Rocky Mountains!"

Hyde looked over at her, her proud strong chin, the determined set of her wide mouth. "You really love it here, don't you?"

"Yes." She glanced over at him as she steered the car past several eighteen wheelers crawling up the inside lane. "But I love it back East, too."

For a long moment, he simply gazed quietly over at her.

They climbed ever higher up toward the Eisenhower Tunnel, which bored through the divide for almost three miles. The country was nothing short of spectacular and if they'd had time, Willy told Hyde she would have taken him up over the old U.S. 6 route that used to be the only way. "The Loveland Pass route," she explained, "can take your breath away in more ways than one. Not only is it hairy and steep, but it's at twelve thousand feet."

"I'll take the tunnel."

He sensed it again—her unnatural constraint—and knew she was holding back. She was doing a good job of it, pretending she felt nothing, as if they were old acquaintances. He had to give her credit. She talked easily, but only about completely neutral subjects. Smart girl. He hated to be the one to have done this to her. She deserved better....

The road ran down a steep icy grade all the way into Dillon where Willy stopped at a fast-food joint for a cup of coffee. When they returned to the car, she tossed the keys to Hyde. "I've gotten us this far," she said coolly, "now it's up to you. Can you handle the icy roads?"

"Of course." Hyde looked up into the leaden snowy sky as he wiped off the white stuff from the car's back window. "It snows in Pittsburgh, you know."

He found I-70 not too difficult as the highway department snowplows and cinder trucks did a better than average job of road maintenance. Still, he hadn't quite the nerve of Willy when it came to flooring it in icy conditions.

"You better step on it a little," she suggested when they'd made it over Vail Pass, "or we'll be late."

"You want me to get us killed?"

"It's front-wheel drive. We won't have any problems."

She was right. And by the time they reached Glenwood Springs, Willy reassured him that they'd make Aspen by seven-fifteen. "You'll have time to change," she suggested, "before the reception."

"Don't you think my dark suit and tie are appropriate?"

"Jeans and a sweater would be dressy, Hyde."

"Umm."

The little Audi began to climb again from the Colorado River Valley floor up beside the Roaring Fork River whose source was twenty miles beyond Aspen at the top of Independence Pass.

"It's fabulous," Willy told him, "but you've got to see it in the summer 'cause it's only open then."

"So there's only one road into Aspen in the winter?"

"That's right."

"There's got to be another way in and out."

"Only if you're willing to walk for days over high passes on skis or snowshoes. Otherwise, this is it."

To the left and right of them, climbing inevitably up from the river bottom, as they neared Aspen, were the taller peaks. In many ways the valley resembled Switzerland and Hyde could picture it in the summer, the high meadows spangled with wild flowers, the aspen trees and evergreens dotting the steep hillsides and the forbidden barren cliffs looming beyond.

"The snow doesn't always melt in the summer way up high," she told him. "It depends on the snowpack...you know, the depth."

"And if you have lots of snow," Hyde recalled, "they get to water their lawns in Phoenix and Los Angeles...."

"And Denver."

"Amazing."

They didn't speak of Andrea then or of precisely how Willy was going to contact her that night at the party for those few vital seconds of final instruction. They didn't talk about Sunday or the World Cup finals or how it would all fall together. Hyde refused to speak of the danger to both Andrea and Willy. He had managed, for a few hours, to put it all aside. And Willy—she was simply too confident that it would all work out. Hyde wished, often, that he had that same measure of beginner's confidence. He prayed, too, that Willy's was justified.

As the Audi made its way down Main Street in Aspen, Willy said, "You know I generally hate the drive in and out of Denver in the winter, but it didn't seem so bad today."

Hyde glanced over at her silently, nodding his head. The drive hadn't been bad at all. "I'm at the Gant," he said. "You'll have to tell me how to get there."

"Take a right then."

They pulled up in front of his luxurious hotel complex. Hyde glanced at his watch. "We've only got thirty minutes to change and get there. Where is the reception, anyway?"

"About four or five blocks from here," said Willy as she slid across into the driver's seat. "I'll run home and change while you check in. I'll wait for you right here in twenty minutes."

Her window was rolled down, and Hyde bent over to speak to her. "Thanks again for the ride, I know it was a lot of trouble for you."

Willy smiled, putting the Audi in gear. "No trouble at all, Hyde." Then she drove off and he was left staring after her, wondering just how much pain she felt, just how much she hurt beneath her blithe easy exterior. He thought fleetingly about their times in bed, that first sweetly innocent time, and the others, when Willy had been able to give and receive without her old apprehensions surfacing. In most ways it had been good between them and now it seemed that they were able to be friends. An unusual relationship. Still, he had to ask himself, would a plain old "friend" want to beat the daylights out of two boys—men now—who'd harmed Willy so long ago? Would "just a friend" be so worried about Willy's possible danger in Snowbird?

He turned and walked into the Gant's lobby. And too, friends were not supposed to hurt so damn bad when they met.

He checked in, found his room near the heated pool and quickly changed into slacks, green turtleneck and dark parka. He looked at his watch—Willy would be out front waiting—and put the room key in his pocket, closing the door behind him.

He crossed through the crunching snow toward the parking lot. It was, of course, Sandy's fault that he wasn't about to get himself in a position to be burned again. He'd be really crazy to do so. He looked up to see the Audi standing near the check-in area and Willy, her window down, craning her neck anxiously for a sight of him.

"Oh there you are!" she called, waving. "I was getting worried...."

How ironic, he thought. Willy was worried about him when, for the past nights all he'd done was worry about her incessantly until he'd had to take a stiff brandy to bed just to get to sleep.

"We'll be just on time," he reassured her as he folded his lean frame into the passenger seat. Quickly, he confirmed the information she was to relay to Andrea. "And don't worry, Willy, it's all going to go like clockwork. Okay?"

"Okay, Control—" she smiled thinly "—I trust you." And in spite of all the self-discipline he'd mustered, his heart gave one huge thud before he could settle it back down.

When the tall, well-muscled woman with the Slavic features and thick dark hair walked into the private reception room at the Continental Lodge, there was an automatic expectant hush, then a standing ovation, whistles and cheers.

That she was worlds apart from the crowd in so many ways, that she was anything but pretty and was muscled to the point of intimidating many a man, that she was a Russian, mattered not at all.

This was the seasoned star of the most dangerous and breathtaking of all skiing events, the downhill. This was the twenty-five-year-old winner of the gold medal and numerous other medals and cups and ribbons.

Andre Pavlevitch—almost a household name in numerous parts of the world. When the great Russian skier approached a starting gate all spectators drew a collective deep breath.

She smiled, waving her long powerful arm. "Thank you! Thank you very much, my friends!"

Willy felt her heart hammer in her breast as she looked in Hyde's direction and then back to the Russian woman. There were several men in dark parkas entering behind Andrea. They were certainly not coaches. And Willy knew that when she did get a chance to be alone with her, it would only be for a very few seconds at best. She prayed that the ugly scene in Wengen would not be repeated here; she prayed that even if they were suspicious of Andrea, there would be a moment....

Andrea was making her way toward a group of racers—Americans, East Germans, Canadians, French—and the press were all over her, light bulbs flashing, pencils scratching away, questions and more questions. Willy despaired that she would ever find a moment alone with her.

The room was moderately lit and crowded. Several tables of food stood at opposite ends; there were two bars set up for the nonathletes. Willy and Hyde had decided not to be seen together in public at all before the day of the race. Still, Willy worried that the KGB would recognize him somehow. Hyde had assured her, several times, that the KGB men covering the racers wouldn't know him from Adam.

She tried to quell her nervousness as the minutes ticked by. Everyone knew the racers would only spend a short time at the reception. Then they were to be off to dinner and early to bed. They were not in Aspen to socialize, after all.

Willy glanced at her watch as she stood chatting with her old coach on the U.S. Ski Team. The team members would probably only stay a very few more minutes. She'd have to make a move toward Andrea, and soon.

Surreptitiously, she looked for Hyde in the long crowded room. Yes, there he was, near the bar at the opposite end of the room from where Andrea stood. He appeared so self-possessed, so negligent, that Willy could hardly believe it. She herself was as tense as a fully wound spring.

Willy's chance came finally due to a quick and clever move on Andrea's part only a couple of minutes before the Russian team was to be ushered out. Andrea had been standing near one of the bars, surrounded by press and racers and those who felt terribly self-important just being near her. Abruptly she had looked around the room, standing on her tiptoes. She smiled and cried, "Veelee! Veelee Patterson!" as her slanted eyes met and locked with Willy's.

The throng parted reluctantly as Andrea made her way over. "Veelee!" Hot on her heels were two of the dark-clothed men. Andrea waved again. "Veelee!"

Willy took a deep breath, and holding it, began to work her way toward her friend.

They met, embraced, and Willy knew it was now or never. Into Andrea's ear she whispered, "Sunday. A ski patrolman wearing an orange-striped scarf. Look for him. The road before Aztec. The trees are just below him to the left."

"Orange-striped scarf," Andrea whispered back, squeezing Willy. "Just below."

Willy smiled stiffly, feeling as if her knees were buckling. It was, she would think later, a good thing Andrea was holding her up or she might have collapsed from sheer nerves.

They were apart then, still holding hands however, and chatting. "So very good to see you," Andrea was saying.

"Yes, and I wish you good luck on Sunday, Andrea. Good luck to your whole team. Let's hope it stops snowing."

"Thank you, Veelee." Andrea winked, giving Willy's hands a firm squeeze.

"We must go now," came the stalwart Russian coach's voice. "Very nice to see you again, Veelee Patterson."

"Yes." Willy forced herself to smile. "Good luck." And then they left, the whole team and the East Germans right behind them. It wouldn't do to let them fraternize too long with the decadent westerners....

Willy expelled her breath with a quaver, turning to give Hyde a triumphant sign. And that was when she saw her—Myrna—standing next to Hyde.

No! Willy's mind screamed, *it couldn't be*...

But it was Myrna, as petite and smiling and expensively dressed as ever. How? Why was she there?

The long room seemed to pulse and the walls to move ever closer. Then Hyde's eyes caught hers and she couldn't breathe or speak or think. It seemed, somewhere in her panic-stricken mind, that her whole life was flashing past and at its focal point was Hyde, tall and strong and masterful. His green eyes, across the room, held her rooted, spellbound, totally in his power. He'd lied to her so smoothly, and he'd betrayed her trust. He'd known that Myrna would show up; they'd probably had the whole weekend planned for months.

Suddenly it was as if all the air had gone out of the room and she couldn't catch her breath. Frantic, she tore her eyes from his and searched the room for an avenue of escape. Her gaze returned to him. He was saying something to Myrna and his face appeared cruel and demonic. And then he was coming toward Willy slowly but steadily through the crowd and she knew she couldn't bear to be near him ever again.

She half ran, pushing her way through the throng. She was approaching the exit when Hyde finally caught up.

"Hold it, Willy!" He grabbed her arm, pulling her around to face him. "Hold it! You've got to listen...."

Willy's face contorted in rage and pain. "Listen to what? More lies! Let go of me! We can't be seen together. Remember?" she managed to pull free because Hyde didn't dare create a scene in the crowded lobby. And then she was alone outside in the cold winter night, running through the parking lot toward Gayle's car.

When she had finally climbed inside the Audi and the doors were locked, she leaned her head against the cold steering wheel and let out a long desperate sob. He'd betrayed her, utterly.

She really should not have been so completely shocked to see him there in her house. He'd had plenty of time to get there ahead of her since she'd driven the car back to Gayle's and then walked the six blocks home.

Nevertheless her heart leaped and adrenaline pounded through her veins when she saw him standing in her kitchen door, leaning a casual shoulder on the doorframe, his shadowed features devoid of expression. Had she really, once, trusted him, given herself to him?

"Get out!" she breathed.

"Not until we talk." Hyde took a couple of steps in her direction.

"Talk?" Willy backed up. "I'd say we've done all the talking we'll ever do. Now get the hell out of my house! I need time to think."

"Willy...."

"No, Hyde, no." She turned around and pressed a fist to her mouth to stem the cry that tore at her throat. He'd betrayed her... he'd betrayed Andrea!

There was a long gravid moment of silence and Willy could feel the blood pound in her veins. Finally, he spoke. "She just showed up, Willy. I don't know exactly why. She's on a three-week break and said she wanted to see the World Cup."

"Oh sure!" Willy cried, spinning around. "It's not enough to lie to me and betray me but now you've got to start lying all over again! Well . . . don't bother!"

"Willy. . . ."

"Don't!"

"Willy," he said firmly, "listen to me, for God's sake. I had no idea she was coming here. None whatsoever. Think, will you? Give me a little credit, Willy. I've never betrayed you and I'm telling you the truth now. Until an hour ago, I had no idea Myrna was around. I thought she was still tied up in the Philippines."

Willy knew, deep in her heart, that he was telling her the truth. Hyde had never been and was not now a liar. He was a lot of things; he could be cold and calculating, he could intimidate the best of them with those ruthless green eyes of his and the cruel mouth. But he didn't need to lie.

Suddenly Willy felt a wave of exhaustion sweep her. If only she had a way of explaining to Hyde, of making him see the obvious. . . . "You know," she said, "you're blind. And you'll probably tell her the whole operation just so she can relay every last detail to the KGB. We wouldn't want old Myrna to miss a thing.

"She doesn't know what's going on." He raked a frustrated hand through his hair. "She never did know. Not even the Company men working directly on the operation know everything. They won't until the very last minute."

She took a long shaky breath. "But Hyde," she whispered in a husky voice, "don't you see? It's enough time for Myrna to find out and ruin the whole thing!"

Carefully, slowly, Hyde came to face her and took hold of her shoulders. "She is *not* a traitor, Willy. I promise. Do you understand?"

Anger welled within her as her eyes flashed up at his. "Then why is she here? Tell me that! Think about it for Pete's sake, Hyde, *think!* Why else would she be in Aspen at this particular time? Why?"

He dropped her shoulders as if he was too weary to hold on. Then he turned and began to pace the floor slowly. Finally, he spoke. "I never meant you to find this out," he began, "but after Switzerland and the bizarre behavior of the KGB, I did have Myrna checked out."

"Hyde . . ."

"Let me finish. I had a security clearance done on her that went from her birth right up to her latest job in the Philippines. She's clean, Willy. As pure as the snow in your front yard."

But she wasn't. And Willy knew it, had known it ever since Andrea's letter had been disturbed back at The Farm. Convincing Hyde, however, was an exercise in futility.

Willy sighed as she stepped out of her boots and shrugged off her parka. "Just do me one favor, Hyde," she asked quietly. "I believe that you really do trust Myrna and I guess there are...several reasons why you would...." She hadn't meant to imply that sleeping with Myrna was one reason, but the inflection in her voice had certainly told him that. Too unnerved, however, to stop, Willy went on, "I only ask you—no—beg you, Hyde, to get Myrna out of town." She waited, breathless, watching him intently, his broad back to her as he leaned a shoulder again on the doorframe.

"I can't," he finally told her. "There is a certain bond, a trust if you will, that goes with our calling. I can't ask her to leave."

"I see." Willy's voice was ragged. And then she didn't care anymore, and she had to know, she *had* to. "Is Myrna staying with you? Was she at the Gant when I dropped you off?"

Slowly Hyde turned toward her, his green eyes searching her face with great solemnity. "I only saw Myrna at the reception a few minutes after Andrea showed up. I was as surprised as you. . . ."

A sob locked in Willy's breast. "I . . . I believe you. But is she...did she ask to stay with you?" She waited, her thoughts paralyzed.

"Yes. She asked." Hyde's face was a mask, his thoughts veiled by the rigidity of his features.

He left a few minutes later after trying to convince Willy that everything would be fine on Sunday. Of course, Willy had argued differently but to no avail. Myrna's very presence in Aspen was proof enough for Willy, and no matter how little the woman knew, she would somehow find out about the switch before gate time. And Hyde wouldn't change the plan. There was absolutely no way of convincing him.

So it was ruined. All of it.

Willy stalked her house like a wraith late into the night. They'd come so far. She'd made it through The Farm, through Switzerland, through the planning and trial runs. Everyone knew his role. It was ready—had been ready, she corrected her thinking miserably. How she hated to give in! And that, she sensed suddenly, was exactly what her hardheaded Control expected her to do! Well, she wouldn't.

Good Lord, Willy thought, she'd been pacing the floor all night, defeated, miserable. How could she? Since when did Wilhelmina Dorothy Patterson throw in the old towel?

She walked to the window overlooking Hopkins Street and pulled back the curtain. There was still a little better than a day to come up with something. It wasn't at all hopeless. It was never hopeless until you'd lost, they'd taught her at The Farm. You had to be clever, double-think, outthink the enemy. You always needed more intelligence, a keener brain, a more ingenious plan, an alternate escape route.

An alternate escape route....

And then slowly, slowly, a humorless smile touched her lips and Willy knew exactly what she had to do.

Yes, she mused as her heart began a heavy pounding in her breast, *it just might work....*

TWENTY

"Hello, Willy." The voice on the phone was vaguely familiar, smooth, eastern. "It's Jim Shore."

"Oh." She hoped she hadn't hesitated too long. "How are you, Jim?"

"Fine. Look, I'm calling from my office in New York. It's about 10:00 a.m. here and I'm just finishing up some work."

"On Saturday?"

"Sure, I'm taking a few days off. The World Cup beckons."

"Oh, so you'll be in Aspen...." Willy knew what was coming next.

"At about four this afternoon. I'm flying the Lear. How's the weather?"

"Okay. No new snow forecast till tomorrow. After the races, I hope."

"Good. I was wondering whether you'd have dinner with me?"

Willy thought furiously. She'd be a nervous wreck by tonight. Should she give an excuse? But no, maybe some decent male company would be nice for a change. "I'd love to."

"Great! I'll pick you up at six sharp. We'll get in early to beat the crowds, okay?"

"Sure. See you then, Jim."

Reeves took the morning off on Saturday and picked Willy up at ten-thirty in his old Datsun truck.

"How you doing, babe?" he asked, but his old endearment only made Willy smile. There were a lot of memories between them—mostly good ones. Reeves truly was a friend now. Their inconclusive romance had died a long overdue death and become conclusive friendship.

"Fine, but nervous about tomorrow. You?"

"I figure it's going to be a ball." Reeves grinned.

He drove to the Gant where they were to meet Hyde for a final briefing.

"Do we really have to go through this?" Reeves asked. "I mean, we really could do it ourselves."

"Just grin and bear it," said Willy. "These guys have to put in their hours, you know. Meetings, meetings. Hyde is good, though, and we do need them for afterward."

There were seven men all crowded into Hyde's suite. From the entranceway Willy recognized Ted—the prematurely graying agent from Wengen—and nodded to him, but he did not acknowledge her. And, too, she was rather taken aback by the group. She'd expected only Hyde to be there.

"Come in. Baxter, good to see you again. Willy." Hyde nodded coolly, as if there had never been a thing between them—neither lovemaking nor the quarrel of the night before. She knew that look of his only too well: removed yet in control.

"I wanted these men to see you two. It's vital in case they need to identify you quickly in an emergency situation. Willy, could I ask you to change into this suit as you'll be wearing it tomorrow. The bathroom's in there. Thank you." Uninflected voice, expressionless features.

She took the white downhill suit from him wordlessly, meeting his eyes with her own challenge as if to say, "Sure, Hyde, we all know this game you're playing." She had the satisfaction of seeing his green eyes flicker infinitesimally.

She went into the bathroom and began pulling off her clothes to put on the white skintight stretch suit. It had a tiny red hammer and sickle on the thigh. She noted that it was made by the same Swiss company as the U.S. Ski Team's suits. She checked herself in the mirror; it fit skintight for less wind resistance, stretchable for movement. She had no long underwear on, of course, so the line of her panties showed and no bra, so she kept her turtleneck on. Well, so what. Those men weren't really looking at *her*.

When Willy reappeared, Reeves was checking out a portable radio with Hyde, the one he would use on the mountain. This one was tiny, the newest state-of-the-art device. Hyde guaranteed perfect reception regardless of weather or distance or intervening mountainside. "You're with Snowbird Two," Hyde was saying. "That man will be One—at the starting gate. He'll tell us all when she starts. Then there are Three and Four." He pointed to two men. "Four is at the finish. Three will ski down to the finish as soon as she passes him."

He carefully refrained from mentioning the men's names, Willy noticed.

Hyde was pointing to a map. "I'll be waiting here with the rest of the men on Castle Creek Road. I've been out there to scout the place out. It's workable. We can see them skiing down for quite a distance. And there's a thick stand of aspens so we'll be hidden from the road. It should be simple, but we're prepared for any problems."

Problems, Willy thought dryly, *oh, you'll have problems all right, with Myrna around!*

"Oh, there you are," Hyde said, noticing her finally. "Take a look, men. Andrea has the identical suit with a white helmet. She'll give Willy her helmet at the switch point. You've all seen Andrea. She's heavier than Willy, but as far as features—hair and so on—they'll all be hidden by goggles and helmet."

Willy felt like an artist's model taking up a post. She knew every bump and hollow in her body showed. Reeves was grinning unabashedly at her. The other men were studying her as if she were an algebra problem. Hyde stared at her with no expression at all on his handsome severe face.

"Okay, Willy," he dismissed her. "You can change back now," and he turned his back on her to continue speaking. "Reeves, I want you to accompany Willy down to the finish line...."

"But I thought I was going to take Andrea down the back."

"I want you with Willy. Just in case. She's terribly vulnerable there for a few seconds. I don't want any problems at the finish line. Put another man on Andrea. A good one."

"Sure." Reeves shrugged, mollified. "I can do that."

Willy heard them through the bathroom door. *Boy, can he manipulate people,* she thought. *He's done it to me, to Reeves, to my own mother for Pete's sake! To Myrna? No,* answered Willy silently, pulling back on her jeans and tugging on leather boots. *Not Myrna.* Myrna had him hornswoggled and hog-tied, as Will Keinast would say. She'd just have to take care of Myrna on her own....

Willy and Reeves were finally excused like schoolchildren after lessons. The CIA men had left earlier, seven identically nondescript, fluidly moving, slightly ominous, silent men. When they were gone from the room Willy couldn't for the life of her recall their faces or what they were wearing. She wondered if their mothers could.

She and Reeves stood at the door. "Then that's it," she said to Hyde, who was still standing in the middle of the room. "Everything is set."

"Yes," Hyde agreed, "and if everyone does his job the schedule should move like clockwork. Your friend Andrea will be a free woman."

"Free?" said Reeves abruptly. "Maybe after you get done with her she'll be free."

Hyde was shaking his head as if Reeves's statement was so absurd that it ought to be dismissed without comment. Willy could feel the tension in Reeves as he stood close to her, pulling open the door. She herself could hardly wait to get out of there, to breathe in the cold mountain air, to be away from Hyde's discerning cold eye.

"Well," she said, "goodbye, Hyde." Then, "See you tomorrow...." Reeves was pulling on her arm, his gaze locked with Hyde's for the moment.

"Yes... after Andrea is free," Hyde was saying.

A tiny secret smile touched Willy's lips. "Maybe sooner," she said archly, letting Reeves lead her into the fresh air.

She took a deep breath as she closed the door behind her. "Whew! That's one down! I sometimes wonder who's the enemy—them or *us!*"

"I know what you mean. But I'll tell you, as much as that guy bugs the hell out of me with all his cool macho air, I gotta admit that this little item is nifty." Reeves took the tiny radio out of his pocket and held it up. "I wish they'd let me keep it."

"Fat chance." They walked to his beat-up Datsun. "You going out tonight with Sue?"

"Yes, why?" Reeves eyed her cautiously as he opened his door. It creaked protestingly.

"Oh, I didn't mean...." Willy rushed to explain. "What I did mean was, maybe you'd like to meet my date and me for dinner." She got into the pickup on her own side.

"Who is it? Vandemeer? The guy really does tick me off, Willy."

"No," she responded hastily. "Not him. And besides, we can't be seen together before tomorrow. It's someone from New York—a lawyer, Jim Shore. He's flying in today."

"Is this your new man, Willy?"

"No, just an...acquaintance. That's why I'd like a little comic relief, if you know what I mean."

"A tough customer?"

"Not really. I hardly know him. I just can't deal with anything heavy tonight of all nights, you know?"

"So now I'm good old Uncle Reeves?" He laughed.

"Come on."

"You won't claw Sue's eyes out?" he demanded facetiously.

"No, I promise." She grinned. "I'll hold myself back, I swear."

"Okay then. What time?"

"Early. He's picking me up at six. I'll call and tell you where to meet us."

"The sooner the better, babe!"

It hadn't taken much persuading to convince Jim that four was more fun than two; if he was put out by the change in plans he had the good grace to hide it.

"How about the Chart House?" he'd asked.

"Fine. Let me phone my friends." She omitted any mention of her past relationship with Reeves. After all, it had nothing to do with Jim Shore at all. They were all going to be "just friends" for the night.

By six-thirty the bar of the Chart House was packed, skiers standing three deep all along the polished wood, ordering strawberry or banana daiquiris made with fresh fruit.

Willy had worn black velvet slacks for the occasion, and a shell-pink silk blouse with a mandarin collar. Jim, knowing Aspen, wore gray flannels and a sweater.

When Reeves saw them come in, he stood up and waved them over.

"Hi, Willy." That was Sue Lerner, tall and slim, smooth dark hair, perfect classic features.

"Hi, Sue." *So we're to be friends,* thought Willy, relieved.

Introductions were made all the way around. Jim was a pleasant man, fitting himself to any company. It seemed that he'd always wanted to be on the ski patrol. "My childhood dream," he said with a smile. And how coincidental that Sue's father belonged to the same country club as Jim back in Long Island....

Reeves winked at Willy, enjoying the who-do-you-know game that strangers in Aspen played with consummate skill and endless variations.

Willy piled her plate with goodies at the salad bar.

"You're going to eat all that?" asked Jim.

"It's practically all I eat here. I love salad."

It was a pleasant meal. The conversation ebbed and flowed easily. Reeves cracked his inevitable jokes; Sue laughed at everything he said, pressed close to him and put her hand on his leg under the table. She was obviously crazy about Reeves Baxter. Willy wondered how crazy Reeves was about her. But it was none of Willy's business anymore. She wasn't jealous of Sue Lerner, she was only envious of their relationship—sunny, seemingly without insurmountable problems. And Reeves *showed* a girl how he felt. He wasn't all closed up inside like a nasty old clam.

She knew Jim wanted more from her than she was giving him, more than she was able to give him. She was sorry; he deserved better.

"Going to watch the downhill tomorrow?" Jim was asking her.

Willy's heart gave a squeeze. Tomorrow. The downhill. It was so close, after all these months and months of planning. Tomorrow. "Actually, I've got to work. With all these people in town, the gallery should be open, and I promised Gayle she could watch the races." She felt Reeves's amused gaze on her and willed him to wipe the smile off his face.

"Too bad. I enjoyed skiing with you that last time. But then I guess you've seen one or two races. . . ."

"That I have!" Willy said brightly.

Jim turned to Reeves. "Any tips on the best place to watch it?"

"The bottom of Aztec's my favorite," said Reeves, his dark eyes flashing mischievously. "And make sure to watch the women's race. That Pavlevitch girl from Russia is supposed to burn up the course."

"I wouldn't miss it for the world," agreed Jim Shore.

"Neither would I," replied Reeves feelingly.

They finally finished the coffee, the Grand Marnier, and the conversation.

"We'd better get going now, I think," Reeves said. "I'm a working boy. Gotta get up early tomorrow. Big day."

He and Sue walked ahead of Willy, working their way around the now-crowded tables of the dining room. His hand rested possessively on the small of Sue's back, just as it had once rested on Willy's. She couldn't help feeling a little sad, a little lost, a little relieved.

And then, before she could recover from her small sadness, she thought she saw a familiar profile across the dimly lit dining room: the graceful line of a cheekbone, a jawline, a strong neck. She strained her eyes to see. It would be. Of course *he'd* be there tonight, his darkly burnished hair gleaming in the candlelight. It hurt to see him there, so far away across the room, the distance between them light-years of pain and misunderstanding and passion. It hurt even more because she was with a truly nice man who liked her and she didn't want *him* at all. No, she wanted, always and forever, uselessly, the dark-haired devil across the room.

As Willy moved around another table heading toward the exit she saw the other person with him, the other dark head, only this one was perfectly coiffed and Willy could almost see the big diamond on her finger wink smugly from across the room.

Damn him! Willy thought. How *could* he be so taken in by that traitorous woman? Another thought struck her simultaneously: After their dinner, wouldn't they naturally go back to his place? Or hers?

How very convenient for him that she had taken her vacation in Aspen. How dumb could a man be, anyway?

"Willy," Jim was saying, "I asked you if you wanted to stop by that table and say hello. I can wait in the lobby if you'd like...."

She hadn't realized that she'd stopped in her tracks and had been gaping—how mortifying! "No thanks, Jim," she said quickly, blushing. "It was just someone I thought I knew. Guess I was wrong..."

Waiting in line Sunday morning to get up the lift was one of the hardest things Willy had ever done. It was at least a half hour wait because everyone else wanted to get up on the mountain to watch the downhill, too. Her stomach kept jumping with impatience and, in addition, she was too warmly dressed—the downhill suit was under warm-ups and a parka. She felt claustrophobic. Reeves had offered to take her up on a snowmobile or allow her to cut the long lift line but they both decided that would be too obvious. Hyde had said, "First and foremost, do *nothing* to draw attention to yourselves."

So she waited, her heart pounding, the back of her neck prickling, the adrenaline rushing uselessly through her body. *Easy,* she told herself, *easy. Not yet. Relax.*

But it didn't do much good.

The women were racing after the lunch break so there was no hurry. God, she wished it was over—Andrea safe, Reeves safe, she herself safe and Hyde Vandemeer and Myrna out of her life. It was even worse than she'd imagined; her doubly private secret. She couldn't tell anyone—not a soul. It sat on her shoulders like an oppressive burden.

The weather was partly cloudy with on again-off again flat light that made it difficult to see the variations in terrain. And warm. The course would be soft, the racers' times slow. Willy wondered if it was hard for Andrea to blow her chance, her *last* chance, at the World Cup. She'd done well all season but she needed a win in Aspen to clinch it. Did that bother her? Or was it secondary to her defection? Well, Andrea Pavlevitch would go out with a bang, one way or the other.

Would it be hard for the Russian girl to adapt to America? Was it awful for her to think of never seeing her own country again? Willy wondered how *she* would feel in the same situation—lonely, afraid, full of trepidation. My Lord, Andrea was brave, doing this all on her own. Such a terrible decision. Willy wondered too what Andrea would do in America. Coach? Hyde had once mentioned that the CIA gave defectors translating jobs occasionally, but Andrea would hate that.

What *would* her life be after today? Was she excited at this point, or just plain terrified? Willy hoped Andrea was better off than she herself. Willy was a bundle of nerves, reverberating like a tuning fork, ready to burst at any moment.

Finally she reached the top, stepped out of her skis and ducked in to the patrol shack.

Reeves was there, looking as nervous as Willy had ever seen him, which was about a hundred times less nervous than she felt.

"Everything okay?" he asked quietly. "You look scared to death."

"Everything's all set. It's just me. I've got stage fright."

"Hope the weather holds. Damn it." Reeves pulled aside the ragged curtain—the patrolmen's idea of interior decoration—and peered up at the sky.

"It'll hold," Willy said fiercely. "But the avalanche danger?"

"We threw some charges in there this morning to make sure. It slid, all right," replied Reeves offhandedly.

"So it's safe?"

He shrugged. "As safe as we can make it. Nothing's one hundred percent. They'll carry rescue beacons anyway."

Willy nodded, thinking, tied up in knots inside.

"It's a little early. We can't go yet. You want lunch?" asked Reeves.

"Heavens, no!"

"A glass of wine?"

"Reeves, I'd gag."

He changed the subject. "Nice fellow, that Jim Shore. We had a good time last night."

"Me too," she lied, remembering Hyde and Myrna, her burst of illogical anger and jealousy and her sense of betrayal.

"I thought you were a little quiet."

"Just nerves."

"He likes you, that Jim."

"Reeves, for God's sake, leave me alone!"

"Sorry, sorry. I just thought old Uncle Reeves's advice might make a difference."

"*I'm* sorry. It's just that romance is the farthest thing from my mind right now."

"That Vandemeer's really got you going, hasn't he?"

Her head snapped up. Was it that obvious? It couldn't be. It was only that Reeves knew her so well. "Don't be ridiculous!" she said angrily.

"Okay, I won't be," said Reeves mildly.

At one o'clock she exchanged her parka for one of the patrol ladies' official red parkas—the only way she'd be able to cross the racecourse to her spot in the woods. She and Reeves and two other patrolmen skied the old Midway Road trail to Ruthie's. The women were just getting ready to start. The timing was crucial: too late and they'd be noticeable crossing the course, too early and they'd be just as noticeable. *Do nothing to draw attention to yourselves.*

But their timing was impeccable. All eyes were on the starting gate where the women milled around in their tight colorful suits, checking their ski edges, stretching, adjusting boot buckles, helmets, goggles, in an endlessly jittery, heart-pounding prerace routine.

"You go ahead," Reeves told her. "We'll follow closely and keep an eye on things. Todd will go into the woods with you." He kissed her cheek. "Good luck, babe."

Willy smiled nervously and pushed off across the racecourse heading toward the trees. It was normal for a patrolman to be on the course. They could go anywhere, in fact there were regular stations all along the racecourses where patrolmen waited with toboggans and first aid in case of a bad fall.

A patrolman with a garish orange-white striped scarf was stationed just above one of the CIA men, Snowbird Two. The patrolman grinned at Reeves's group. He'd been told only that he had to wear that scarf and stand in that particular spot until the women had raced.

"Hey, Baxter, my feet are freezin'. When can I go?" he called.

"Soon, buddy! I'll let you know."

Willy skied down a little ahead of them on the western edge of the course, careful not to intrude upon the narrow strip the racers used. Getting into the trees with the patrolman Todd would be chancy, but it was a spot nobody could reach to watch the race so Reeves had figured they would be pretty safe. And patrolmen had to go into odd spots to look for lost skis, poles, gloves, even lost people. If the KGB were around, they'd—hopefully—accept a patrolman disappearing into the trees as part of his duties.

In the trees at last. No one had seen them. Willy heaved a sigh of relief. Snowbird Two was stationed just at the edge of the trees, looking very inconspicuous as a boundary judge. "Snowbird Two here," he'd spoken softly into his radio as they'd passed. "Eggs in the nest. Over."

Willy unzipped her parka and warm-ups, leaned against a tree trunk and took several deep calming breaths. She smiled at Todd, who stood several feet away from her.

Then they heard the roar of the crowd from Ruthie's. Willy's heart jumped under her ribs.

The downhill had started!

She and Todd looked at their watches automatically. Andrea was seeded third in this race, behind a French girl and an Austrian. They knew the racers were started one minute apart; they knew it would take Andrea about fifteen seconds to reach them.

Countdown began.

Todd's eyes were glued to his watch, but Willy's were straining through the snow-covered spruce trees toward the course, toward the spot where Andrea would fake her fall and slide into the trees.

The CIA man outside the stand of trees was droning "Twenty seconds, nineteen, eighteen..." until Andrea would start. Willy was as jumpy as a racehorse at the gate. She only wanted to start her long-planned role, her well-rehearsed, agonized-over part. Soon, soon. The seconds ticked by endlessly. "Thirteen, twelve, eleven...."

Would Todd go along with her plan? He had to. There was no other way. *He had to.* The others didn't matter. Snowbird Two would find out soon enough but he couldn't follow where she was going and the patrolmen didn't know enough about the operation to figure out what had happened.

Soon, soon. "Eight, seven, six, five...."

Willy imagined Andrea's start, and inadvertently her knees flexed in the tight white suit. Her hands clenched the poles and she bit her lip. On edge, ready, she waited along with Andrea for the timer. "Three, two, one, go!"

They could hear the crowd on Ruthie's give a great resounding roar when Andrea broke the starting beam. The noise rolled down toward them, filling the area with huge waves of sound. Then the announcer's amplified voice could be heard in English, French and German: "Andrea Pavlevitch, number three. A good start for the Russian hopeful! She's hit at least forty on Ruthie's. She's hot, ladies and gentlemen!" The sound reverberated off rocks and trees and packed snow, echoing along with the crowd's unified voice.

Soon, soon. Andrea was in a tuck right now, legs quivering, heart pounding, mouth open to suck in every precious bit of oxygen.

"Right about now," said Todd.

How did Andrea feel? Was she scared? Would she hit the right spot?

Willy tensed, straining her eyes, waiting. It was almost over now. *Please don't mess up,* she prayed. *Let it work!*

And then, a disappointed roar, a prolonged "aah" from the crowd, a scratching swishing sound, a plume of snow sprayed on the air like a fan.

Andrea appeared between the trees, on her side, in a controlled slide.

Good Lord, Willy thought, *it was going to work!*

TWENTY-ONE

Hyde's head pounded mercilessly as he stood, shoulders hunched against the cold, peering through the binoculars up at the crest that formed the back side of Aspen Mountain.

He hadn't had a hangover in a long time and this one, combined with the lack of oxygen in the high altitude, was a whopper. He'd just have to hope that it faded before Andrea made her escape and appeared up there on that razor-edged ridge.

Along with three other Company men who stood near the rented Eagle on Castle Creek Road, he scanned the area far above them again. Still no sign of skiers, but then it was too early to expect them anyway. When Andrea made her fake fall into the trees, he'd be contacted by radio from the front side of the mountain. He let the binoculars hang around his neck, blew into his hands and hunched his shoulders, swearing through the white plumes of his breath.

Lord, he was chilled to the bone!

He thought about the previous night, wishing he was still relaxing by that roaring fire in Myrna's place. But then that's how he'd gotten smashed and in this woozy state in the first place. Myrna, who'd gone up that morning to watch the races, would be laughing herself sick if she could see him right then.

He let his thoughts drift as they would, trying not to think about Willy up there, waiting in the trees, ready to take Andrea's place on the racecourse. Willy would ski slowly, dejected of course, down the west side of the slope until she was near the bottom where the CIA would give her cover, surrounding her as they quickly got her to a waiting car and safely away.

Those, Hyde knew, were the critical seconds—when Willy removed her helmet and the Russians realized that they'd been duped. No, there should be no reason for them to go after Willy, especially with armed CIA men surrounding her, and Hyde guessed that they'd begin to search the course frantically for Andrea. It would take them forever to figure out what had happened, and by then Andrea would be safely with him in the rented car on her way to the safe house.

It was a cinch to work. And, he had to admit, it had been Willy's plan from the first. Willy's and her friend, Reeves's. Baxter, it seemed, had turned out to be an okay guy after all. In a way, as insane as it seemed, Hyde hoped that Willy and Baxter might work things out, although he kind of doubted they would; Baxter—somewhat like himself—was not the type to make a commitment. Had Reeves Baxter been the marriage route himself? Probably.

Hyde squinted, looking up toward the mountain beneath a shielding hand. The sun was peeking in and out but it promised to cloud over entirely pretty soon.

"Heard anything on the radio?" he called to John, who was waiting by the Eagle.

"Nothing yet."

"Let me know. . . ."

Myrna had been pretty smashed herself last night and more aggressive than he'd ever seen her. Had she come to Aspen, as Willy had suggested, with the intent of sleeping with him the whole weekend? Perhaps. . . .

They'd run into each other shortly after Willy and Baxter had left the Gant. Hyde had gone for a few runs on the mountain and then stopped at Little Nell's bar for a beer because it was easy to ski right up to the bar. He let the events of the previous afternoon drift in his mind; it was easier than thinking about Willy and those few dangerous minutes she'd soon face.

"Why, Hyde," exclaimed Myrna with mock surprise as she came strolling up to him at Little Nell's. "Been skiing?"

"Yes." He sipped his beer, studying her over a rim of the glass. She was wearing a tight fuchsia Bogner suit. He remembered, without a bridging thought, something Willy had said at The Farm: If Myrna got snow in her hair, she'd probably want to leave the course.

"Great day. Say, you wouldn't buy an old friend a drink, would you?"

He bought her the drink. Why not? Just because Willy was down on Myrna certainly didn't mean that he had to be. He and Myrna were, after all, old friends.

They talked, mostly about the races that morning, the excitement of the G.S.—Giant Slalom—the terrible fall the Italian racer had taken, and his broken pelvis.

"I got a room at a tiny little place called the Snow Flake," Myrna told him. "It was really a pain finding anything."

He felt he owed her an explanation; the night before he'd merely said there wasn't room at his place. "I've got to keep my mind on the operation," he'd said over their drinks, "and I didn't think I could do that so well with you in the room."

"Should I be flattered," Myrna asked with a smile, "or insulted?"

He looked at her intently for a moment. "Flattered."

Dinner seemed like a good idea, especially after several more drinks. They went to their respective lodgings and then met at the Chart House at eight. There was, of course, an hour wait, so naturally they had another drink at the bar and by the time they were seated, Hyde was well on his way to being loaded. He wasn't too concerned, though, for everything connected with Operation Snowbird was in readiness; there remained only the actual execution on Sunday. And besides, wasn't drinking an agent's most familiar release? There were dozens of well-documented drunks in the CIA. It was an occupational hazard.

It did cross Hyde's mind that Myrna never asked him a thing about the operation, and if Willy was right about her, surely Myrna would be at least gently trying to prod details out of him. She never did.

After the excellent dinner they walked through the mall looking up at the brilliant night stars that typified the Colorado sky. A clear sky and no snow.

"They'll hold the finals tomorrow for sure," Myrna commented. "That probably relieves you a great deal."

"You bet," he stated simply. Of course Myrna knew the defection would occur during the races—it was obvious. Still, he was careful to say no more. For Willy's sake, not his own.

They danced at the plush Victorian-style Paragon. There were two mellow slow dances and some Everly Brothers tunes he recalled from the late '50s. They had an after-dinner drink before leaving. It was Myrna's idea to stop by the liquor store for a bottle of Grand Marnier.

"I'm on vacation—" she laughed, taking Hyde's arm possessively "—and at last *I* can live it up!"

Dutifully, he walked her back to her room at the Snow Flake and didn't see why not when she asked him in for a nightcap, although he'd already had more than enough.

He built a fire while she got two glasses. Then they lounged on the soft carpet, leaning against the couch in front of the fire, silently enjoying it. A man could get used to life in Aspen awfully quickly.

Myrna was easy to be with, but then, she always had been. Other than a few pouts here and there she never complained or demanded. She was a free spirit, a woman of the '80s.

It was Myrna who first kissed him, her dark red lips tracing a line across his jaw and up to his mouth. "You need a shave," she murmured against him, pressing her full breasts into the hardness of his chest.

He kissed her back leisurely, feeling heady from all the booze and the lack of oxygen at eight thousand feet. She was warm and pliant in his hands and knew all the right places to touch him. He was glad he was there, glad he could relax and enjoy Myrna without tension, without the kind of tension he'd felt lately with Willy.

Soon Myrna was out of her clothes, stretched out in front of the fireplace with the amber light flickering over her skin sensually. She was still a lovely woman at thirty-five, her breasts still well-rounded and firm, her thighs tight although on the stocky side, her skin soft, silky. Hyde drank her in for several long minutes, and then eased his fully-dressed weight down on top of her as his lips parted hers and his tongue entered her mouth playfully. She pressed herself up against him and moved her body sensually beneath his as her long polished fingernails dug at the back of his shirt.

"Take off your clothes, darling," she whispered. "It's been so long...."

It had been a long time, so long that he couldn't exactly remember when they'd last slept together. There had been, he recalled fleetingly, that time in Washington—in September—when he'd dozed off with Myrna right beside him. Nice manly act.... And since then? Well, there had been only one woman. Curiously, he'd only wanted that one person.

He hadn't meant to conjure up her image. Yet it had happened. Myrna, who lay beneath him, took on the fair rosy features of another and her dark hair in his fingers became silky blond and the full breasts pressed against his chest were suddenly smaller and firmer. He wanted that other woman desperately, yet in his muddled intoxicated brain he knew that this was not she but another. This was Myrna.

Abruptly he pushed himself off her and sat next to the fire with a bemused look on his face as his eyes roamed her.

"What is it, Hyde?" she breathed as she rolled onto her side. "Something's very wrong."

He couldn't tell her. "Nothing is wrong. I guess I'm just drunk, Myrna." He ran a hand through his tousled hair, trying to clear his brain.

Myrna watched him closely. "It's that girl." It was not a question. She pulled on her sweater and panties, casting him a dark look. "I should kick you the hell out of here," she said quietly.

"Why don't you?" he asked sincerely. "That was a damn rotten thing I just pulled."

"That's for sure, and not the first time, either...." She came to her feet and walked toward the tiny kitchenette with their glasses in her hand. When she came back, they were full again. "Do you want to talk about it, Hyde?"

He shook his head. About the last thing he wanted to do was think or talk about Willy Patterson, especially with another woman and one that Willy distrusted to boot.

"All right then, let's just sit here and have a drink, for old times' sake."

"It's really late. I should go," he said. But hadn't he already been enough of a jerk to Myrna? If she wanted to share a last drink with him then he really ought to....

How many hangovers in his life could he attribute to guilt? Not a whole lot, but enough. Those times when he'd already been a jerk for one reason or another and hadn't the heart to say no. This was one of those few times. He couldn't just say, *Sorry, Myrna, but I can't sleep with you because my mind's on another woman and no, I really don't have time for that last drink....*

They talked about this and that until almost dawn and the fire had long since died down to softly glowing embers. Even though he sipped on his drink and in reality was a whole lot more sober than he'd been when he walked in, the combination of skiing and too much to drink and no sleep left him with a splitting fuzzy head, which no cold shower on earth was going to cure.

He had breakfast with his CIA team in his Gant suite and went over the minute details of Operation Snowbird. It was Sunday morning, time they all were told about the switch and Willy and the Aspen Ski Patrol leader's part in it all. It occurred to him to tell them all the importance of keeping this to themselves, but then that was so basic, and too, he'd have to mention Myrna's name in particular and he hadn't the heart to do that. Not after his marvelous performance with her the previous night.

He would have liked to be on the face of the mountain when Willy skied down to the finish line, but as he very well knew, the senior officer on the operation must stick with the "main objective" if at all possible.

He stressed some details of the operation more than others. "When Willy skis up to you she'll still have on her helmet so that the Russians' confusion will increase. They should react like parents whose child has suddenly disappeared. They'll begin to search for the real child and the mistaken one will go unnoticed."

The team of seven men nodded. It was all very basic.

"You'll take Willy to the safe house. It is, by the way, right here."

Several of the agents looked surprised.

Hyde smiled in spite of his headache. "Uncle's idea. The Russians will never figure it if it comes to that. Which it won't." He grew serious once again. "Remember, Willy is in the greatest danger for those few seconds at the finish line after she removes that helmet and before the Russians realize what's happened. Then they'll begin the frantic search for Andrea and you should be able to drive off unhindered."

It was all set. And now he stood half-frozen, his head pounding, waiting, his binoculars sweeping the ridge every so often even though he knew that they would receive a call on the radio long before they saw anyone.

When the call finally did come, Hyde felt his heart lurch nervously in his chest.

"Control, Snowbird One here. She's flown the coop. Over."

Then, a few moments later, "Control, this is Snowbird Two. Over."

"She's flown into the trees. We're standing by. Over."

"Good. Let me know when she starts down."

Twenty seconds passed. Nothing. Lord, Hyde thought, suppose Andrea had really hurt herself in that fake fall? Then things would get sticky. The ski patrol would have to bring her down the back side of the mountain on a toboggan and then it might really be touch and go, timewise.

Why hadn't they called? How long did it take to switch a hat for a helmet?

Forty seconds.

In spite of the cool temperature, Hyde felt sweat pop on his forehead.

A minute.

"Control? Over."

"Yes. Over."

"This is Bird Two. White suit is coming out of trees. Good cover by ski patrol leader. Thank God. Over."

"And? Over."

"Head is hung. Perfect show from up here. Patrol is still moving along with the subject. Cover looks excellent. Over."

"Good." Then, "Birds Two and Three move down to join One and Four."

It didn't take more than three or four minutes until the radio scratched on again. "Snowbird Control. Come in."

"Go ahead," said Hyde.

"Our bird is coming in for a safe landing. It'll all be over in a minute now. We'll report as soon as we're away."

The whole team held its breath; these were the crucial moments. In seconds Willy would remove that helmet and the Russians would be momentarily stunned. But then, by the time they realized what had happened, the Company would have Willy safely away in the car.

She had practically done it. In a matter of seconds, she would be out of his life forever. Operation Snowbird was nearly over.

And then Hyde heard it—the slow grinding of a four-wheel-drive engine. Who was it? Just some passerby, a local?

He spun around, trying to see through the trees to the road. A big Land-Rover trundled toward them down the dirt road. He was aware of the rest of the team standing behind him, tense, worried. Was this one of those damn variables?

And then he knew who it was but it was too late. By the time he'd reached into his parka pocket for his Walther, three men in dark ski outfits had jumped for the car and had the drop on all of them.

KGB.

"Control?" the radio barked. "Can you read? Over?"

The biggest of the Russians quickly snatched the radio from Hyde's hand, depressed the red button several times, waited and depressed it again so that anyone on that frequency would think Hyde's radio was malfunctioning or that the storm that was now moving in was interfering with transmission.

"Damn smart, aren't you?" Hyde muttered through clenched teeth.

The big Russian grinned through his wide Slavic lips. "We are not so stupid, CIA." Then, "Please to drop all weapon here." He indicated a spot by his feet. The three team members and Hyde did as they were told, were frisked carefully and expertly and then they backed off at the KGB's insistence.

How did they know? The question slammed against Hyde's mind again and again. *How did they know?* The obvious answer he avoided. It couldn't be . . . it was someone else . . . another operative on his team . . . someone who had all the details, who knew about the switch. It couldn't be Myrna. She knew nothing.

"You CIA make no move and we leave you in good health," the big Russian was saying.

Hyde nodded, shooting the KGB leader a cold look as he did so. There was no defeat in Hyde's eyes; it wasn't over yet.

They waited in a group like angelic choirboys, not because the big Russian had told them to but because one of the two others held an automatic pistol trained on them.

The snow finally began to fall, lightly at first and then more heavily. All eyes remained fixed on the ridge above save for those of the KGB agent who still had the gun on them.

Hyde knew that sooner or later Andrea and her escort would appear. It took around forty-five minutes to ski from the trees where Andrea had faked her fall to where he and the others waited on Castle Creek, Willy had told him.

It had been almost twenty-five minutes already.

They could do nothing but wait. The minutes dragged by on leaden feet, endless and agonizing. There was nothing Hyde could do; no radio, no gun, no way to get a message to the Russian woman who was skiing down that steep mountainside in the snow hoping for a new life at the bottom. All she would get would be a one-way ticket to Siberia—forever. He couldn't bear the irony of it, the waste, the disappointment.

They waited.

The snow drifted down in tickling crystals, chilling them, making the visibility terrible. The Russians spoke quietly together, watching the mountainside intently.

Who had told them?

Suddenly one of the KGB agents barked something in Russian and the big one raised his binoculars. "Ah," he said, "our Andrea." Then he lowered his glasses and looked over at Hyde, glowering. "Please stay calm, CIA, and soon we are all gone. No trouble, yes?"

The last thing the Russians wanted was trouble, especially on American soil where they'd be hunted and trapped like rabid rats. Still, the one holding the gun on them looked young and a bit nervous. Obviously the KGB agents sent on these races were not top drawer—those Hyde had met before would not have left four CIA men standing without at least tying up their hands. No. In fact, Hyde suspected that that single mistake on their part might well mean victory yet for him and his team. He had one trump card and only one, but it was good, and after having frisked him, they'd be doubly surprised.

Quietly they waited. The big confident Russian even let Hyde use his binoculars for a moment to watch as Andrea and her escort traversed the crest of the steep pitch.

Time moved incredibly slowly; it was as if every one of them held his breath. The snow drifted relentlessly down. At times the Russian woman was visible skiing along with the patrolman whose bright red parka wasn't too hard to spot. But then heavy sheets of snow would move across the steep slope and they would disappear in the gauzelike veil.

Still, each time they became visible again they were a little closer.

Hyde began to think hard. There would be a moment as Andrea skied up when all attention would be on her. He might have five or six seconds at best to move if he had any time at all. But five seconds would do it.

Then it would be up to the Russians. Would they risk shooting if that's what it came down to? Or would he be lucky and be close enough to disarm the Russian holding the gun on them?

"Soon," the big man said, "all will be done here." He smiled. "You should not try to kidnap famous Andrea. No?"

Hyde felt like laughing. The KGB were not *that* stupid. They knew as well as he that Andrea was defecting. It was all a game, though—just the usual propaganda.

Hyde grinned back through thin cruel lips. "Sure."

Now the skiers had disappeared into a stand of bare aspens at the base of the mountain. In less than a minute they would be crossing that footbridge and entering the meadow.

He just prayed that the patrolman and Andrea would keep their cool. If they didn't....

He glanced over for a moment at his most experienced agent, Ted, his face remaining expressionless. Yes. Ted knew what he was planning. Ted knew the trump card Hyde would play.

They were on the footbridge. Hyde watched all the players intently, each in turn. The two young KGB men seemed nervous and triumphant all at once. This was, Hyde sensed, their first time in action. The big burly one—typical KGB thug—wouldn't hesitate to kill if he thought he'd live through it. In the U.S. he couldn't be sure though, and Hyde would be very interested to know exactly why he had been assigned to baby-sitting the racing team: either he had zero brains or he'd fallen out of favor with a superior. Hyde guessed the latter. The big one didn't look or move like any dummy.

Then there were his own men: Ted, Frank and Doug. They were all experienced, all chosen for this particular assignment because they were skiers of varying degrees. Ted, of course, he'd worked with before—thus Ted knew about the trump. The other two, well, he'd have to trust their judgment and hope for that nebulous edge all agents and gamblers hope for—luck.

The ski patrolman. Hyde looked at him as he crossed the bridge ahead of Andrea. The patrolman would simply have to stay out of the way.

And Andrea Pavlevitch. She worked every day under pressure, so hopefully she'd react quickly and get into the Eagle with no fanfare. Then they could get the hell out of there when the time came.

Hyde watched her closely as she trailed the patrolman. He hadn't noticed at the reception but she'd lost weight in her legs and shoulders—odd for a racer in her condition.

They were in the meadow and it was obvious that the patrolman was just realizing what had happened. But one would have thought he'd be more shaken to see the KGB. Maybe he didn't recognize them . . . ?

Hyde glanced at the young KGB man with the gun; he was still watching the group of CIA men, ignoring the patrolman and Andrea's arrival. Surely he would look around, take that one glance at Andrea. . . .

Suddenly something told Hyde—instinct, years of intelligence work—that the players in this little drama were not behaving quite as they should. No. There was that little something...cues were being missed as in a movie where the sound is out of sync just that fraction of a second.

Slowly, inevitably the plot unfolded before him as if he'd become merely a spectator. All eyes seemed to be on Andrea as the big one spoke.

He gestured for her to get in the car. Then he said something in Russian, the inflection of his voice hard and dangerous.

Andrea reached up, her white stretch suit pulling taut under the arms and across the breasts as she removed her goggles and hat simultaneously. Hyde knew those high firm breasts as surely as he knew that face. . . .

Willy.

My God!

TWENTY-TWO

How long Hyde stood there like an idiot, his mouth hanging open, he never did know. But since the moment Andrea—Willy, that was—pulled off the white, snug-fitting hat and shook out her honey-blond hair, he had been dumbfounded.

And then Willy's eyes found his and he saw in their frosty blue-gray depths a blaze of triumph. His blank mind behaved like a dead motor, trying to turn over, grinding, dying, then grinding again. Finally his thoughts sputtered to life slowly. If Willy was here, then it was Andrea at the finish line. No. By now, she'd be at the safe house if the Company agents had caught on soon enough and maneuvered her away. Good Lord....

His thoughts began to take hold, no longer sputtering. Of course Andrea was safe? The Russians had believed the skier in the white suit to be Willy from the moment she came out of the trees. They believed it because the CIA traitor had told them and because it made perfect sense. Of course they ignored Andrea at the finish line because they were convinced the girl in white was Willy.

What had seemed to Hyde to take long minutes to put together in his mind had actually taken only a few seconds. His green eyes continued to search Willy's face with a combination of disbelief and admiration. My God, the nerve, the guts....

She'd done it! She'd known all along there would be a tip-off and she'd single-mindedly, doggedly, fooled them all. For crying out loud!

A slow smile began to uptilt the corners of Hyde's lips as he stood locked into a world with Willy that had room only for two.

It was merely a few moments after he realized what had actually become of Andrea that the KGB leader came to the same unbelievable conclusion.

They'd all been standing there, frozen in those few moments of time, staring at Willy in awe.

Then suddenly, as if an invisible director from above had yelled "action," the players came to life.

"She's safe," Willy breathed, oblivious of the KGB. "She's safe, Hyde. We heard it over Todd's radio...."

Hyde shot her a congratulatory smile and then looked at the KGB agent holding the gun on them.

Yes. The inexperienced young Russian had indeed taken his eyes off the CIA men and was, for the instant, gaping awe-struck at the American girl in the white racer's suit with the tiny red hammer and sickle on the thigh.

Hyde had a split second to make his decision: either he would lunge for the KGB man's gun, or he would stoop and pull out his own slim Walther PPK that was tucked, safely concealed, in the top of his heavy boot.

He made up his mind. Simultaneously, he gave Ted the high sign to go for the KGB man with the gun, and stooped to feel quickly for the cold deadly steel of the Walther.

The big Russian saw it all happening and moved with surprising agility toward Willy, pulling out his gun and grabbing her at the same instant Ted toppled the younger KGB man and Hyde's own hidden gun was flicking into view.

Willy gasped as the burly Russian locked his gun arm around her neck, the other hand gripping her hair, forcing her head back.

Hyde's stomach leaped into his throat. The son of a bitch could snap her neck like a matchstick in an instant.

"Hold it, Ted!" Hyde yelled sharply as his agent was rising from the ground off the KGB man's body, the Russian's gun now in Ted's hand. "Everybody just take it easy...."

The big Russian grinned, yanking on Willy's hair harder until Hyde could see her gritting her teeth in pain.

He knew then, if he got the chance, he'd kill the Russian.

"You give us Andrea," the Russian said, "and we give you her." His eyes rolled downward toward Willy's head.

Hyde determined immediately exactly what he had to do but for the Russians' benefit, he appeared to be in deep consideration, unable to come to a decision. He let the seconds stretch out, wishing he didn't have to for Willy's sake yet knowing that the Russians had to believe they had the CIA over a barrel.

"Get Andrea now—" the big Russian grunted, squeezing his forearm against Willy's neck with more force "—or her neck will break!"

Hyde let his Walther PPK drop to the snow-packed earth, and indicated to Ted to do the same. Then he looked at his men as if to say "we're beaten, guys," but in reality they had all gone through a hostage handling course very much like this one at The Farm and all Hyde had to do now was wait for the right moment and give the signal. He didn't even need his own gun to pull it off.

He tried to put Willy from his thoughts—the danger she was in—and the danger she'd be in when they all made their move.

He knew the percentage rate of success in this particular situation was damn good, and that the hostage had a better than seventy-five percent survival rate if everything was executed properly.

Still, this was no stranger, nor was it a rehearsal. This was for real and this was Willy. And there was always that other twenty-five percent. . . .

Hyde met the big man's eyes. "I'll get Andrea." That was the first step in the plan—offer to go yourself.

"No," replied the Russian as if he'd read the CIA manual and knew the lines.

Good, thought Hyde, relieved. The Russian didn't know this game. "How then do I get Andrea?" he asked, allowing the Russian to feel comfortably in control.

"I go with girl here and you. We go together. Others wait."

Perfect. The Russian was reacting exactly as predicted. And now the pendulum would swing in the CIA's direction, for with his last two predicted responses, the CIA agents couldn't fail to see the plot unfolding. At that very minute they would be reviewing in their minds their roles, checking their respective distances between themselves, the KGB men and the Russians' Land-Rover.

Just like in the manual....

If only the son of a bitch wasn't half choking Willy to death.

Forget it, Hyde told himself. *Forget it's Willy, for Pete's sake.*

Hyde tried to look desperate and dejected, like the loser in the game, when he replied. "All right. I'll go with you and the girl." He shrugged then, putting the ball back in the Russian's court.

"My car." The Russian nodded toward the Land-Rover.

Hyde felt like kicking his heels in the air. The big stupid thug. He'd gone all the way now! Hyde could smell victory, almost taste it...so near, so near. In a minute Willy would be safe, in his arms, and as God was his witness, he'd never let that crazy brilliant girl out of his sight again!

Now, for just a little luck....

"We go." The Russian nodded. Slowly he began to drag Willy toward his vehicle while giving directions to his agents. Presumably he was telling them to scatter as soon as the vehicle moved away. There would be no reason for the CIA or the KGB to do battle once the principal players were removed from the scene. It would be touchy, but the Russian fully expected that they'd all scatter and get clear. It would never get that far anyway, Hyde smiled to himself.

They were nearly at the Land-Rover, Hyde following slowly, carefully behind by about five long paces. No point getting the Russian on edge.

Yes, Hyde thought, *it would all be over in a few seconds now....*

Suddenly everything changed. The pendulum swung in the Russian's direction as Willy began to struggle and cry out.

"No! Hyde no! We can't let him get Andrea." Her voice was choked off by the huge forearm and she struggled more frantically, flailing her arms, kicking wildly as he easily lifted her off the ground.

"Willy...don't," Hyde tried to tell her, but he doubted she could hear or was even listening.

Dear God, he thought helplessly, she'd come this far, so very far, and in another minute she'd ruin it all....

Abruptly he knew. It struck him like a brick on the head and he went hot then cold as the knowledge slammed into his brain: he didn't give a damn about the CIA or whether or not the Russians got Andrea back; he didn't care if a hundred people in the process were injured. All he gave a damn about at that precise moment was Willy.

The Russian's hold on her neck was so strong that she could see dots swim before her eyes from the lack of oxygen.

But Willy didn't care. Not anymore. She kicked with her ski boots backward again and tried to reach around her with her fingers to scratch the brute's face.

He merely choked her harder with his forearm.

Somewhere she could hear a voice—Hyde's voice. He was saying "don't" over and over but she couldn't stop because she'd rather die than see the Russians get hold of Andrea again.

Why was Hyde doing this? Why? Anger boiled within her, making her impervious to pain. She kicked out again backward and thought she caught the Russian on the shin.

From the corner of her eye she could see Hyde's form and it looked like he was backing off, retreating. On the other side of her was a Land-Rover, the Russians' car. In a minute the brute would be stuffing her into it. She couldn't let that happen! Uselessly she fought against her captor with every ounce of strength she possessed, cursing Hyde under her breath for going along with the Russian.

Didn't Hyde know she'd rather die than give Andrea back?

"Stop struggling." She heard Hyde's voice clearly then, and discerned the desperate edge in it. "Stop it, Willy."

In pain and in rage she dug the heels of her boots into the snow, pushing with all her might against her captor, trying desperately to remember the self-defense techniques she'd learned at The Farm: leverage, balance, unexpectedness. She doubled over violently, pulling the big Russian along with her. She tried to jab his solar plexus area. She bucked and she kicked. Her breath was coming in short harsh gasps while his arm pressed against her neck. Next he tried to spin her around, presumably to strike her or knock her out cold. Then all hell seemed to break loose and she was free, lying sprawled on the snow and Hyde was above her, struggling with the Russian over the gun.

Holding on to her neck with a hand, she pushed herself away from the two struggling men, her back coming to rest finally against a rear tire of the vehicle. She could see a flurry of movement near the CIA men. One of them—Ted—had a gun and the two KGB men were backing up, their arms raised over their heads.

Still, in spite of the seeming victory on the part of the CIA, Hyde was busily losing his battle and there wasn't a thing anyone could do about it. The huge Russian had him pinned against the passenger door, that strong forearm beneath Hyde's chin, pushing upward. In a moment the immense man would break Hyde's neck....

Willy never thought about it. She just did it, mindlessly. She moved, almost having to drag herself, toward the legs of the two struggling men and then she sunk her teeth into the bigger one just below the knee as hard as she could. The next thing she knew she was lying on her back, stunned, the taste of blood in her mouth from the force of his kicking her off. But then Hyde was there, hunched over her, calling her name. His face looked deathly white against the snow and was lined with...worry. Yes, he was worried. About her.

"My God, Willy? Can you hear me? Please Willy...." And she was being scooped up into those strong arms while cold snow was being pressed to her lip by another man.

"Hyde?" She tried desperately to shake off the haze in her brain.

"Willy," came his voice, "thank God." Then, while he cradled her in his arms and made another snowball that he pressed to her lip himself, he became all business. "Ted, toss their guns into the river and get them all into the Land-Rover." He looked off to his side and Willy followed the direction of his gaze. The big Russian was struggling to his feet, his Slavic features contorted in rage. "Get the hell out of here before I keep a promise to myself and kill you," Hyde said in a dangerous low voice. Willy never doubted for a moment that he'd do it. Nor, apparently, did the Russian.

He spoke to his fellow KGB officers and in moments they had piled into the Land-Rover under gunpoint and were gone.

Willy's head was still fuzzy; she couldn't understand. "You can't let them go . . ." she whispered.

Hyde tipped her chin up toward him with great care. His eyes roamed her face while he pushed her snow-packed hair from her eyes. "They'll be flying out of here within the hour."

"But Andrea?"

"They've lost. They know it. Thanks to you and with no help from me whatsoever. Lord, Willy," he said in a low voice, "you knew all along there was a mole. I never listened, Willy. I thought I knew it all."

"Myrna," Willy suddenly remembered.

"Lie still."

But she was already struggling groggily to her feet. "Someone told her. I knew they would, I knew it. . . ."

"Told her what?" came a sheepish voice near them.

Both Hyde and Willy looked over at Ted curiously. Instantly, Willy knew.

She shrugged Hyde's helping hands from her arms and half staggered over to Ted. "Someone told Myrna about the switch," she breathed, fixing him with determined stormy eyes.

Ted was silent for a long moment and Willy was beginning to wonder if she could stand there unassisted when she felt Hyde's presence behind her, his hands pulling her gently against him, his warm breath in her hair.

"You told Myrna about the switch," Hyde said in a tight voice.

Ted nodded affirmatively, bowing his head a little. "This morning. We just sort of bumped into one another after breakfast. I...well—" he coughed into his fist "—Myrna and I were sort of close for a while. You know how that can be when you're involved that way, Hyde."

Willy felt the tension emanating from Hyde's body; his hold on her arms tightened. She longed to turn in his arms and hold him to give him comfort. Of course, he felt it was all his fault, all his fault that he had trusted Myrna, that he had placed his faith in her and expected her to live up to it.

Willy hated Myrna at that moment, hated her for hurting Hyde so terribly, for taking his trust and betraying it. Fierce protection toward him surged within her suddenly, but she knew that he was like a wounded animal: she dared not try to touch him then or even get too near.

"Who's the sheriff around here?" he was asking Willy. "Do you know him? Can we call on him?"

Willy smiled weakly. "Yes. He'll do anything he can to help us."

"Okay." He turned Willy around in his arms. "I hope someday you can forgive me," he said quietly, and Willy felt tears press against her eyelids, hot and scratchy.

"Hyde . . . I . . ." she began, but he silenced her with a gentle finger to her lips.

"Later, Willy." Then he looked over her head. "Ted, I want you to get Willy up to the hospital and have this cut checked out while I contact the sheriff. We're going to need a roadblock if I know Myrna—"

"No," Willy whispered, "I'm not going to any hospital for a silly cut lip. I'm going with you."

Hyde's dark brows drew together in a frown. "Over my dead body you are!"

Willy thought quickly. "Fine. Then just try to get some cooperation out of Sheriff Keinast—"

"Willy—" Hyde's dark brows drew together dangerously "—are you trying to blackmail me at a time like this?"

She kept her face as impassive as possible. "No," she said, "I *am* blackmailing you, Hyde."

TWENTY-THREE

She could see Hyde pulling the tattered shreds of his training around himself, turning once more into the impassive-faced Company man who could snap out orders, outthink anyone, respond to any emergency.

"Ted, Willy and I are going to the—" he thought for a second "—the Snow Flake Lodge. Myrna may still be there. Call the sheriff." He turned to Willy questioningly.

"Will Keinast, but maybe I'd better—"

"Okay, in a minute."

"We'll see if she's still there. Otherwise she's either at the airport or on the road. Right."

Willy turned her face up toward the increasingly heavy snow. "You can bet she's not flying."

"We'll stop at the airport to check. I want roadblocks set up on Highway 82. No one leaves Aspen without being cleared. Ted, you and John go to the—where, Willy? The sheriff's office."

"The old country courthouse on Main Street, downstairs."

"Right. And stay with the roadblock. You can identify her."

"She could be long gone," said Ted, his head no longer hung in embarrassment.

"She could be. It's a chance we'll have to take. Come on, Willy." He strode to the CIA's rented Eagle and opened the door for her. "You sure you're okay?"

"For *this*, I'm okay, believe me."

He started the car and pulled out of the dirt road, spraying gravel and snow behind him. It was beginning to snow harder; he flicked the windshield wipers on. Everything was shrouded in white, silent and muffled.

Hyde pounded the steering wheel furiously. "I should have known! Damn it, Uncle should fire me for this stunt! Myrna. I can't believe it." He pulled to a shuddering halt at the corner of Castle Creek Road and wrenched the car around to the right, toward town.

"She needed the money. I don't think it's politics with her. It's just money."

"She even told me once that her grandmother left her that diamond and I believed her," he said acidly.

They sped through town, turning and twisting on the slippery roads, and slid to a halt in front of the Snow Flake Lodge.

Hyde raced up to the desk. "Is Myrna Carlson still here?" he asked the lady behind the desk. She was obviously the owner in residence; it was a small place.

"There's no Myrna Carlson registered," she began doubtfully.

Hyde pulled out his wallet and flipped it open. Willy, coming up behind him, heard him snap, "CIA," and saw the lady's eyes widen. "Room 14, I think," he said impatiently.

"Oh, you mean Mary Carter," said the lady, relieved. "Why, she just checked out about half an hour ago. I remember 'cause I asked her wasn't she going to stay for the rest of the races."

"Her car," pressed Hyde.

"Car?"

"What was she driving? Or did a taxi pick her up or what?" He prodded patiently, slowly, as if to a child.

"She had a car. Let me see, it was blue."

"Do you have a record of the license number?"

"Of course. On the registration card she filled in."

"Get it."

The woman rummaged through a stack of cards; it seemed to take forever. Willy thought Hyde was going to burst. She put a hand on his arm as if to hold him down.

"Here it is. A Buick Riviera, blue. License RR-1382."

"Can we use your phone?"

"Go right ahead."

Hyde turned to Willy. "Call this Keinast of yours. Tell him. A roadblock just out of town in case she's still here somewhere. The airport covered—she could have driven here—the car and license number."

Willy was already dialing. The phone rang three times. It was three lifetimes. "Sheriff's Department."

"Can I speak to Sheriff Keinast? Please, it's an emergency. Tell him it's Willy."

When he finally came on the line, Willy was pacing as far as the telephone cord would allow.

"Hey there, Willy! What's up?"

"Will, I'm with a CIA man. Listen. There's a woman named Myrna Carlson who—"

"Listen yourself, Willy. Did you know I've got four Russian coaches in my office and that Pavlevitch girl has disappeared?"

"Will, please. It's about that. I can't explain now. Here, listen to Agent Vandemeer. He'll explain what he needs. Please, Will, I'm calling on you for that help, now. This is deadly serious."

She handed Hyde the phone. He gave his orders clearly, quickly, crisply. Description, car, roadblock. He hung up and looked at Willy for a second, his green eyes softening. "Come on, then. We're going to the airport."

He had to wipe snow off the windshield. It was piling up quickly. He drove as fast as he dared but the conditions were hazardous, the visibility poor. Cars had their lights on.

The airport was crowded with people sitting glumly on their boot bags, waiting for flights that would not take off—not that day. Passengers milled around trying to rent cars, waiting in line for a sandwich, a telephone, a taxi. Outside the snow piled up on the black runway.

Willy checked the luggage department and the ladies' room. She even surprised a little girl perched on the toilet in one stall.

No Myrna.

Hyde checked the restaurant, the car rentals and the men's room. They met back at the front door.

"She didn't turn in her car," he said.

"She's driving then. In this."

"Let's go."

When they reached the Eagle, Willy suddenly stopped. "Hyde, let me drive."

"You're crazy."

"No, I'm not. I'm used to these conditions, remember? I can get us there faster. I know this road like my own backyard. Hyde, please."

He was silent a minute, thinking, weighing. "Okay. You're on. Make it fast, Willy." He tossed her the keys.

She pulled out of the airport as if a demon was after her.

Hyde whistled. "Holy Moses, don't kill us!"

"She has at least half an hour on us."

"Myrna's no Mario Andretti," Hyde said dryly.

Willy concentrated on the road. Shale Bluffs was curvy and tricky but the Eagle handled well—a nice heavy car for snowy roads. "Do you think she'll turn west on I-70 instead of east!" she suddenly asked, horrified.

"You mean toward Grand Junction? I doubt it. Where can you go from there?"

"Utah, Salt Lake City, L.A. and points west."

"No way. Myrna's an eastern girl. She'll run true to form. She'll go where she knows the territory and some people."

"Hyde, we have no proof. What if we catch her and your boss lets her go?" Willy leaned forward, trying to see if that car up ahead of her was slowing down.

"*When* we catch her, she'll go through a complete debriefing, a psychiatrist's report, the works. They'll use drugs on her if she won't cooperate. There's no way out for Myrna."

She maneuvered past the Snowmass turnoff; the road was fairly straight there. Killer 82, as it was affectionately called, was the most-traveled highway in Colorado except for the interstates. It was a winding, two-lane country road.

"What will happen to her?"

He shrugged, his dark brows drawn together. "A trial. Prison."

Willy pressed her lips tightly together. She had almost said, "Poor Myrna." But no, that woman deserved all she got.

The snow fell steadily. The windshield wipers swept back and forth untiringly, hypnotically. "Hyde? Did you...I mean...how much did you like Myrna?" She stared straight ahead but felt his steady gaze on her.

"I liked her. She was comfortable, convenient. Nothing more."

"Does it bother you that she and Ted...? I mean..."

"No, not really. I knew about Myrna's life-style."

"I saw you in the Chart House last night...."

"With her.... Yeah, well, we got pretty smashed last night." He watched Willy again measuringly. "I think maybe she was trying to get me drunk." Then he gave a short harsh laugh.

"Did you get drunk?"

"You might say so."

"But it wasn't *you* who spilled the beans to her."

Willy glanced over at him quickly. "Were you drunk enough to...." Her voice trailed away.

"To what?" he prompted quietly.

There was a long awkward silence. Then, "You know... to..."

"No. I wasn't drunk enough for that, either."

Her pulse began to beat a little faster. "You didn't have to tell me that," she began.

"You asked."

"I know, but you didn't have to tell me." And she gave him a quick embarrassed look before training her eyes back onto the highway.

They were passing Woody Creek, Aspen Village. The Phillip's curves came along soon. Willy pulled out to pass a slow-moving Pinto, jammed her foot on the gas, sped by and pulled back into her lane.

"Take it easy," breathed Hyde.

"No, damn it!" Her voice softened. "Why didn't she succeed in seducing you, Hyde?"

"Because of you," he said simply, and Willy's heart surged with tenderness.

Old Snowmass. The gas station whipped by the window, a blur of color in the storm. Slushy ruts were building up on the road, pulling the wheels askew.

"Darn snow," said Willy.

"It's slowing Myrna down more than it is us," Hyde said, pulling that old crushed pack of Winstons out of his pocket. "I think I'll smoke."

"Nervous?" Willy grinned.

"Who me?"

El Jebel. A few bent-over trees were visible out of the car window, bowing their branches to the wind and whipping snow. Willy passed two cars and a truck where the road widened for the turnoff.

"For Pete's sake, don't *pass* her," said Hyde.

"Don't worry. I'm watching who I pass. My Lord, would she stop somewhere and let us go by?"

"Sure, she might, but my guess is that she thinks no one's after her."

"How did she do it, Hyde?"

"She had obviously contacted them last winter, angling for more money. That explains Wengen. But at that time she had no plan to give, no idea when or where or how. They were on a general alert. She must have been frantic to get the final plan last night."

"Do you think she knows exactly what happened?"

"Yes," he said tightly, "she would have waited around long enough to find out. If Andrea hadn't made it she would have had to disappear anyway, but with a fortune. This way, the Russians will be after her as well. They always think double-cross. As soon as she heard Andrea was taken away by us, she knew someone would put two and two together sooner or later. She'd want to be back in D.C., get Uncle's ear, perhaps. Or maybe just disappear." He shook his head in wonder, blowing out a stream of smoke. "If it hadn't been for you, it might have been years before we found out about her."

A car skidded in front of them, drifting sideways across the road. Willy turned the wheel, stepped on the gas and slipped deftly past on the inside, barely missing a slow-moving truck in the other lane.

"Nice," managed Hyde.

"Yeah—" Willy laughed tightly "—but I'm chewing my nails like mad."

Hyde chuckled. "I hate long nails on women anyway."

The two lane finally ended at Carbondale, where it turned into a four-lane highway. The snow seemed heavier, if anything, leaving only a narrow, one-car-width track on the inside lane.

"Snowplows aren't out yet," said Willy.

But they did come upon one just before they got into Glenwood Springs, passing it so quickly it might as well not have been there at all.

"Nice car," said Willy, referring to Hyde's rented Eagle. "Maybe I'll trade in the old Jeep for one. Dad's been nagging me to for ages."

"That old Jeep is an antique. Put it out on your lawn for display. You could charge admission."

"Is that a blue Buick?" asked Willy suddenly. "It's hard to see."

"I can't tell."

She pressed on the accelerator, pushing past the point of safety to catch up to the blue car.

"No, it's a Chevy," said Hyde. His hand had gone automatically to his pocket. A gun? Willy wondered. Would he shoot Myrna?

"When do I get to see Andrea?" she asked suddenly. "She'll be so alone. She doesn't know a single person. I'm her only American friend."

"Soon. She's in a safe house now. She needs papers, a case worker, money, a place to live. It all has to be arranged."

"How long does that take?"

"A week or so, maybe more."

"Can she stay here, with me?"

"No, Willy, she'll have to be debriefed at Langley."

"But Hyde . . ."

"Rules are rules."

"Please, at least can I see her before she leaves Aspen? Come on."

He sighed. "I'll see to it."

"Thanks Control," she muttered sarcastically.

She was forced to slow down in the city of Glenwood Springs, chafing at the delay. Had they missed Myrna completely? Was she going to turn off at the Eagle County airport and fly from there? But the weather was no better in that direction, it appeared.

Finally Willy was through Glenwood, turning east on I-70. The interstate was a nightmare: flashing blue snowplow lights, cars off the road, an accident, police cars, traffic crawling along the snow-clogged highway, slipping, sliding, stuck on hills. Willy steered a course around the slower cars, drifting over onto the shoulder a few times in a controlled skid.

"What if they close the highway?" Willy asked suddenly. "It'll be dark soon. Then we'll lose her for sure."

No answer.

"Glenwood Canyon is coming up. The road turns very narrow, very curving; it's dangerous."

"I remember . . . where it follows the Colorado River bed. You want me to drive?" asked Hyde.

"No, I'm okay."

Then they were in the canyon, its towering walls blotted out by the snowstorm. All Willy could see was the narrow winding road ahead of her, the monotonous swish of the wipers, the red brake lights of the car in front of her—the blue car in front of her.

Blue! "Hyde, is that a Buick?"

He strained to see. "I think so. Yes, a Riviera! License RR-1382!"

Willy pulled up as close as she dared and saw the dark head inside the Buick snatch a quick look over her shoulder before hunching back over her wheel. The Buick pulled slowly away from them, wavering all over the road and skidding a little on a curve.

"She knows," said Willy.

"Don't lose her." Hyde's hand reached into his pocket.

The snow slashed down. One of the windshield wipers was iced up, not clearing a strip of the windshield. The road was glaring white ice. Darkness began to fall particularly early in the high-walled canyon. Grimly Willy drove, her eyes burning in her head, her shoulders aching with tension.

"Keep on her tail. She'll give up if you push her. She can't keep this up."

"Neither can I," snapped Willy, pulling the car out of a skid.

"You're doing great, kid. I'll put you up for the congressional Medal of Honor. Watch it. She's trying to cut you off!"

Myrna drove erratically, equally as terrified of the icy road as of the car chasing her.

"Come on," Hyde was muttering, "come on."

The white-crested, boiling Colorado River was barely visible on the right down below the road; a dark entity, set aside from the frozen white of the rest of the canyon. Many a car had gone off the road into that river over the years. It beckoned, as close as the lane of oncoming cars, their headlights reflecting painfully off the slanting snow into Willy's eyes.

Swerving, Willy pulled up on Myrna's car until they were practically bumper to bumper. Trying to force her off the road, Willy felt her tires sliding on the ice but fought for control.

"Hyde, I'm scared," she whispered once, and she felt him place his hand on her arm.

They roared on into the gathering dusk, two cars going far too fast for the conditions, passing other vehicles recklessly, barely avoiding innumerable accidents.

"She can't keep it up," muttered Hyde, pounding a fist into his hand.

Willy tried humor to lighten the situation. "Will you bail me out if I get arrested for speeding?" She knew she couldn't keep it up much longer, either.

Finally it happened. On a long curve to the right, with the ice lit up like glass by the headlights, Myrna's car was skidding. It turned as if in stop-motion, lazily, sliding broadside off the road, going through the barrier, turning over slowly and stopping half in the cold dark river, wheels spinning futilely in the snowy darkness.

As Willy braked too quickly, she felt her car skid. She let up and braked more slowly. Her heart was leaping like a wild thing; she felt herself gasping as if she had run a long-distance race. Then she was skidding to a stop off the road in snow and frozen mud and Hyde was leaping out of the car before it had even stopped, racing toward Myrna's car.

Willy watched in a daze, her headlights illuminating the whole scene: Hyde pulling on a door, trying to get it open. Then he had to climb up onto the car to get at it. He was tugging at something—someone—the wind plucking at his dark hair, his jacket, the snow plastering against him.

"Hey, lady." Someone was banging on Willy's window. She jumped, startled, tore her eyes from the horrible scene in front of her and rolled down the window.

"Is that person dead?" asked a man in a cowboy hat. "What a humdinger of a crash that was!"

"How would I know?" whispered Willy. "Can you please help him?"

A dozen cars stopped. People asked questions, chattering, hunching over in the storm. Willy still sat, half-collapsed over the wheel, numb and aching. She barely noticed when the police cars drove up, when the ambulance wailed to a stop in front of her, loaded a stretcher and took off into the storm.

Hyde was talking to a policeman, his head close, snow dusting his hair and his shoulders. He pointed to her, talking some more. Still she sat numbly in the car.

And then the police cars were leaving, their red taillights disappearing into the blizzard, and Hyde was coming toward her, tall and strong in the headlights, his face stern and worn looking.

"Willy, are you okay?" he asked softly, touching her face through the open window.

"I don't know...." She turned her eyes up to his. "Myrna?"

"A little beat up. She'll live. She was lucky."

"Lucky?" Willy felt a hiccup of hysterical laughter well up in her chest. "Lucky?"

"Relatively speaking...." He opened the car door and pushed her over gently. "*I'll* drive now."

She moved like an automaton, exhausted, her mind blank.

"I have to go to the hospital in Glenwood Springs where they're taking Myrna," he said apologetically. "I'm sorry. It shouldn't take long. I have to arrange for her to be transported as soon as possible to a security hospital. Do you mind?"

"No." Her voice was flat.

"Willy. . . ." He paused as if searching for words. "You did well today."

"Thanks, Control," she said apathetically.

"I mean it." He turned on the car, shifted and pulled slowly onto the roadway in the pitch blackness. The snow still fell heavily, ceaselessly, reflecting millions of shining crystals in the twin tunnels of the car's headlights. The wipers kept up their external swishing, again and again, brushing away a swath of white stuff only to brush more away on their return trip. The narrow road back through Glenwood Canyon was dark, seemingly deserted; they could have been the only two people alive in the world, encased in their own fragile shell of warmth and security in the storm.

Tiredly, Willy let her head fall onto the back of the seat. "It's over, isn't it?" she murmured.

"Operation Snowbird?"

"Everything."

The car moved slowly through the blizzard, a beacon in the darkness, alone and isolated.

"Everything," she repeated.

"Aren't you glad?"

"Yes and no. It's like graduating from school. There's so much you leave behind. Memories. . . ." Her voice trailed off.

"Yes. Memories," came Hyde's deep voice, a curious edge to it.

The lights of Glenwood Springs appeared ahead as a diffused glow. The world was coming back.

"Willy?"

"Yes." She hadn't the energy to raise her head from the back of the seat. It was all over.

"Do you think . . . ?" She could hear him swallow. There was a strange tentativeness to his voice. "Could you ever leave Aspen?"

What kind of an odd question was *that?* "I leave it all the time. I just always come back. What . . . ?"

"I mean more permanently."

"Hyde, what on earth—"

"I mean—to live somewhere else." He hesitated an eternal moment. "Like Washington."

She raised her head from the headrest to look at him carefully, warily. He was staring straight ahead at the snowy road, his profile strong, a furrow on his brow.

"What do you mean?" she asked cautiously, afraid to let herself think or feel.

"Willy, don't make this harder for me than it is." There was a desperate urgency in his voice. "I want to know if you could live in Washington—with me."

"Hyde?"

"This is a proposal, damn it!" he blurted out.

TWENTY-FOUR

It couldn't be Hyde sitting next to her saying those words. She refused to believe it. "But you said...it was no good. You said..." The words were hard to form; a stunned and sudden surge of happiness began to glow in Willy's heart.

"I've said a lot of things in my time. Damn fool things, too. I was wrong about a lot of things. I want to try again. With you, Willy." He turned toward her; the headlights of a passing car gilded his features for a moment. Then it was gone.

"Are you sure?" was all Willy could find in her mind to say.

"Sure enough. Nothing's ever one hundred percent in this world, Willy. It's worth a try, isn't it?"

"But Hyde, do you... I mean... do you *love* me?"

He laughed a low chuckle. "I love you so much I'm willing to give up my most cherished promise—never to make a commitment again."

"Oh, Hyde." A smile pulled at Willy's lips and tears glistened in her eyes. "Really, truly?"

"Really, truly," he repeated soberly.

She leaned over to rest her head on his shoulder and put her arms around his neck. "Do you know how long I've loved you?"

"No, how long?"

"Forever, but I was too dumb to know it. Oh, Hyde...." She sighed with pleasure.

"You haven't answered my question," he said gently.

"What question?" she murmured absentmindedly, smiling to herself in the darkness. Nothing was important but the knowledge that Hyde loved her. Her mind sang the words over and over.

"Could you ever leave Aspen?"

"Oh," she said in a small voice, brought back suddenly to reality.

"There are a few things to settle, you know," he said quietly. "I can't ask you to give up your whole life: skiing, painting, your business, your house. I'm not *that* macho."

She thought for a moment, staring straight ahead at the dark ribbon of highway, knowing this was a vital moment, savoring it, but knowing with certainty what her choice would be. Then, slowly she affirmed, "I can paint anywhere, Hyde."

"But you love the mountains so." His voice was torn between hope and uncertainty.

"We can come back, can't we? Hyde, we can have the best of both worlds. We'll keep my house—"

"Willy, my sweet, it sounds so easy when you say it like that."

She turned toward him, nuzzling her face into his neck. "It *is* easy. We'll *make* it easy. Haven't you ever heard that love conquers all?"

"Even the muggy Washington summers?" Hyde laughed ruefully.

"We'll need a place with a swimming pool," Willy said firmly.

He laughed quietly. "Sure. Why not?"

"And I'll sell the gallery to Gayle. She'll jump at the chance. It'll give me an outlet for my work. Maybe I'll even open a gallery in the big city," she mused.

"You're sure?" Now it was his turn to ask.

"Hyde, I'm absolutely positive. As much as I love Aspen, I love you more."

"I don't want you ever to regret it. Sometimes you seem so young and impulsive."

"And sometimes you can be an old fuddy-duddy." But her voice was full of love and laughter; it caressed him.

"You'll cure me of that, I'm sure," he said dryly.

"In short order, my love."

"Your parents?"

"You've got my mother intrigued and my dad snowed. They'll love you. And just think, you'll be responsible for bringing their errant, old-maid daughter back into the fold. Not to mention doing them the favor of *marrying* her."

"We'll have to go to Pittsburg," Hyde ventured.

"Of course. I can't wait to meet your folks."

"Will it work, Willy?" Hyde asked, suddenly full of trepidation.

"It *will* work, Hyde."

The car was filled with silence and hope and love. It washed over them both, soothing and full of joy.

Finally Hyde bent his head and kissed her hair. "You know, I think the snow's letting up."

Willy looked out the car window. "It is, Hyde." The storm was slackening, the heavy curtain of snow giving way to a finer gauze veil.

He pulled off the interstate and drove down the nearly deserted main street of Glenwood Springs, following the policeman's directions to the hospital.

"This should take only a minute, Willy."

She got out of her side of the car, standing up for the first time since they'd left the Aspen airport hours before. Her muscles were so stiff and cramped that her knees almost collapsed under her. Hyde was at her side in a second, holding her in his strong arms.

"I must be getting old." She laughed, clinging to him.

He kissed her on the lips but drew back to smile at her. "Never. You'll never grow old."

She looked up at the night sky, feeling as free and happy as a bird. "Oh look, Hyde! The snow's stopped and there's a star!" She pointed to a lone diamond in the night sky.

"The storm's over," he said softly, looking up with her.

And then another star appeared as the clouds drew apart like the opening of a curtain, and another.

"Is that a good omen?" breathed Willy.

"Of course it is," replied Hyde, holding her closer.

FRIENDS
AND
LOVERS